Praise for *The Eagle's Conquest*

"Scarrow manages to summon u... glory and the gore that characte... Outstanding military history fro... ... ... genre."

—*Booklist*

"Has all the hallmarks of Bernard Cornwell at his best."

—*Oxford Times* (UK)

"This book quickly becomes a page-turner . . . a cracking good read."

—*Historical Novels Review* (UK)

Praise for *Under the Eagle*

"Readers will devour this spectacular tale of intrigue, adventure, and glory in the Roman legions . . . distinguished by its meticulously detailed portrayal of life in the mighty Roman army."

—*Booklist*

"A thoroughly enjoyable read. The characters are so lifelike they almost spring off the page. An engrossing storyline, full of teeth-clenching battles, political machinations, treachery, honor, love, and death."

—Elizabeth Chadwick, award-winning author of *The Marsh King's Daughter*

WHEN THE EAGLE HUNTS

Also by Simon Scarrow

Under the Eagle
The Eagle's Conquest

WHEN THE
EAGLE HUNTS

Simon Scarrow

Thomas Dunne Books
St. Martin's Griffin ⚑ New York

THOMAS DUNNE BOOKS.
An imprint of St. Martin's Press.

www.stmartins.com

Library of Congress Cataloging-in-Publication Data

Scarrow, Simon.
    When the eagle hunts / Simon Scarrow.
        p. cm.
    ISBN 0-312-30535-4 (hc)
    ISBN 0-312-30536-2 (pbk)
    EAN 978-0-312-30536-9
    1. Macro, Lucius Cornelius (Fictitious character)—Fiction.
2. Cato, Quintus Licinius (Fictitious character)—Fiction. 3. Great
Britain—History—Roman period, 55 B.C. – A.D. 449—Fiction.
4. Romans—Great Britain—Fiction. 5. Druids and Druidism—
Fiction. 6. Abduction—Fiction. I. Title.

PR6119.C37W48 2004
823'.92—dc22   2003058778

First published in Great Britain by Headline Book Publishing,
a division of Hodder Headline

10 9 8 7 6 5 4

For Joseph and Nicholas –
thanks for the inspiring swordplay

THE ROMAN ARMY CHAIN OF COMMAND IN BRITAIN IN 44AD

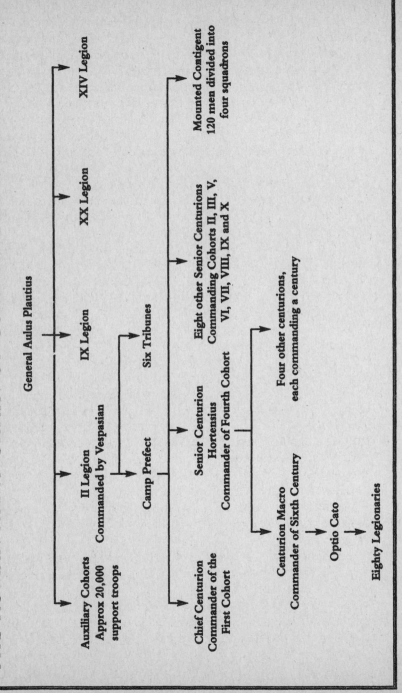

The Organisation of a Roman Legion

The Second Legion, like all legions, comprised some five and a half thousand men. The basic unit was the century of eighty men commanded by a centurion with an optio acting as second in command. The century was divided into eight-man sections which shared a room together in barracks and a tent when on campaign. Six centuries made up a cohort, and ten cohorts made up a legion, with the first cohort being double-size. Each legion was accompanied by a cavalry unit of one hundred and twenty men, divided into four squadrons, who served as scouts and messengers. In descending order the main ranks were:

The *legate* was a man from an aristocratic background. Typically in his mid-thirties, the legate would command the legion for up to five years and hope to make something of a name for himself in order to enhance his subsequent political career.

The *camp prefect* would be a grizzled veteran who would previously have been the chief centurion of the legion and was at the summit of a professional soldier's career. He was armed with vast experience and integrity, and to him would fall the command of the legion should the legate be absent or *hors de combat*.

Six *tribunes* served as staff officers. These would be men in their early twenties serving in the army for the first time to gain administrative experience before taking up junior posts in civil administration. The senior tribune was different. He was destined for high political office and eventual command of a legion.

Sixty *centurions* provided the disciplinary and training backbone of the legion. They were hand-picked for their command qualities and a willingness to fight to the death. Accordingly their casualty rate far exceeded other ranks. The most senior centurion commanded the First Century of the First Cohort and was a highly decorated and respected individual.

The four *decurions* of the legion commanded the cavalry squadrons and hoped for promotion to the command of auxiliary cavalry units.

Each *centurion* was assisted by an *optio* who would act as an orderly, with minor command duties. Optios would be waiting for a vacancy in the centurionate.

Below the optios were the *legionaries*, men who had signed on for twenty-five years. In theory, a man had to be a Roman citizen to qualify for enlistment, but recruits were increasingly drawn from local populations and given Roman citizenship on joining the legions.

Lower in status than the legionaries were the men of the *auxiliary cohorts*. They were recruited from the provinces and provided the Roman Empire with its cavalry, light infantry and other specialist skills. Roman citizenship was awarded on completion of twenty-five years of service.

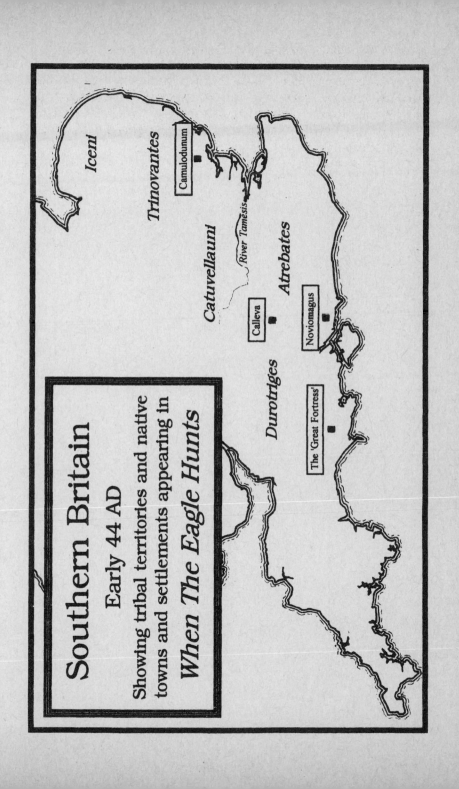

Southern Britain

Early 44 AD

Showing tribal territories and native towns and settlements appearing in

When The Eagle Hunts

Iceni

Trinovantes

Catuvellauni

Camulodunum

River Tamesis

Atrebates

Calleva

Noviomagus

Durotriges

The 'Great Fortress'

Chapter One

The heaving tumult around the ship was frozen for an instant by sheet lightning. All around, the foaming sweep of the sea stilled as the stark shadows of the sailors and the rigging scored the brilliantly lit deck of the trireme. Then the light was ripped away and darkness gripped the vessel once more. Black clouds hung low in the sky and billowed across the grey waves rolling down from the north. Nightfall was not yet upon them, yet it seemed to the terrified crew and passengers that the sun must have long since quit the world. Only the faintest smudge of lighter grey away to the west indicated its passage. The convoy was hopelessly scattered, and the prefect commanding the newly commissioned squadron of triremes swore angrily. With one hand firmly gripping a stay, the prefect used his spare hand to shield his eyes from the icy spray as he scanned the foaming wave tops around them.

Only two ships of his squadron remained in sight, dark silhouettes heaving into view as his flagship was raised on the crest of a great wave. The two ships were far off to the east, and beyond them would be the rest of the convoy, spread across the wild sea. They might still make the entrance of the channel that led inland to Rutupiae. But for the flagship there was no hope of reaching the great supply base that equipped and fed the Roman army. Further inland the legions were safely nestled in their winter quarters at Camulodunum, in readiness for the renewal of the campaign to conquer Britain. Despite the best efforts of the men at the oars, the vessel was being swept away from Rutupiae.

Looking across the waves to the dark line of the British coast, the prefect bitterly acknowledged that the storm had bested him, and passed the order for oars to be shipped. As he considered his options, the crew hurriedly raised a small triangular sail from the bows to help steady the vessel. Since the invasion had been launched the previous summer, the prefect had crossed this stretch of sea scores of times, but not in such dreadful conditions. Indeed, he had never before seen the weather turn so rapidly. That morning, which seemed so very long ago now, the sky had been clear and a brisk southerly promised a quick crossing from Gesoriacum. Normally no ships would put to sea in winter, but the army of General Plautius was short of supplies. The scorched-earth tactics of the British commander, Caratacus, meant that the legions depended on a steady supply of grain from the continent to get them through the winter without depleting the stockpiles necessary for continuing the campaign in the spring. So the convoys had continued to cross the channel whenever the weather permitted. This morning the prefect had been fooled by perfidious nature into ordering his laden vessels to set out for Rutupiae, never dreaming that they would be caught in this tempest.

Just as the coastline of Britain had come into view above the choppy surface, a dark band of cloud had thickened along the northern horizon. The breeze quickly strengthened, and abruptly veered round, and the men of the squadron watched with growing dread as the dark clouds bounded down on them like foaming ravenous beasts. The squall had struck the prefect's trireme at the head of the convoy with appalling suddenness. The shrieking wind snatched the vessel by the beam and tilted it over so far that the crew had been forced to abandon their duties and grab the nearest handhold to save themselves from being thrown over the side. As the trireme ponderously righted itself, the prefect cast an eye around the rest of the convoy. Some of the flat-bottomed transports had been rolled over completely and close by the dark humps of their hulls tiny figures bobbed in the foaming sea. Some waved pathetically, as if they truly believed that the other vessels might yet be able to rescue them. Already the convoy's formation had been blown to pieces and each ship struggled for survival, heedless of the plight of all others.

With the wind came rain. Great icy drops slashing diagonally down on the trireme and stinging the skin with their impact. Very quickly the bone-numbing cold made the sailors slow and clumsy in their work. Huddled in his water-proofed cloak, the prefect could see that unless the storm eased soon, the captain and his men would surely lose control of their ship. And all about them the sea raged, scattering the ships in every direction. By some quirk of nature the three triremes at the head of the convoy were subjected to the worst violence of the storm and were quickly blown far from the rest – the prefect's trireme furthest of all. Since then the storm had raged for the whole afternoon and showed no signs of slacking as night drew on.

2

The prefect reviewed his knowledge of the British coastline and mentally scanned the coast. He calculated that they had already been swept well down the coast from the channel leading to Rutupiae. The sheer chalk cliffs around the settlement at Dubris were just in sight of the starboard beam and they would have to battle the storm for some hours yet before they could attempt to approach a safe stretch of the shore.

The ship's captain staggered along the heaving deck towards him and saluted as he approached, keeping one hand clasped firmly to the taffrail.

'What is it?' shouted the prefect.

'The bilges!' the captain called out, voice hoarse from the effort of shouting his orders above the shrieking wind for the last few hours. He jabbed his finger at the deck to make his meaning clear. 'We're taking on too much water!'

'Can we bail it out?'

The captain tilted his ear towards the prefect.

Taking a deep breath, the prefect cupped a hand to his mouth and shouted, 'Can we bail it out?'

The captain shook his head.

'So what now?'

'We have to run before the storm! It's our only hope of staying afloat. Then find somewhere safe to land!'

The prefect gave an exaggerated nod to show he had understood. Very well then. They would have to find somewhere to beach the ship. Some thirty or forty miles down the coast the cliffs gave way to shingled beaches. Providing the surf was not too wild, beaching could be attempted. That might cause serious damage to the trireme but better that than the certainty of losing the ship and all the crew and passengers. With that thought, the prefect's mind went to the woman and her young children sheltering below his feet. They had been trusted to his care and he must do everything in his power to save them.

'Give the order, Captain! I'm going below.'

'Aye, sir!' The captain saluted and turned back towards the waist of the trireme, where the sailors huddled by the base of the mast. The prefect watched for a moment as the captain bellowed his orders and pointed to the furled sail on the spar at the top of the mast. No one moved. The captain shouted the order again, then viciously kicked the nearest sailor. The man cowered back, only to be kicked again. He leaped for the rigging and began to make his way aloft. The others followed, clinging to the stays as they struggled up the swaying ratlines and transferred themselves to the spar. Bare frozen feet pushed down onto the toe-line as they inched out above the deck. Only when every man was in position could they undo the ties and release the sail as far as the first reefing point. That much sail would be all that was necessary to give the vessel steerage way as it ran before the storm. Each burst of lightning briefly silhouetted the mast, spar and men in harsh black against a dazzling white sky. The prefect noticed that lightning made the rain seem to stop in mid-air for an instant. Despite the terror that gripped his heart, he felt a thrill of excitement at this awesome display of Neptune's powers.

At last all the men were in position. Bracing his solid legs on the deck, the captain cupped both hands and tipped his face up towards the mast.

'Unfurl!'

Numbed fingers worked frantically at the leather ties. Some were less clumsy than others and the sail loosened unevenly from the spar. A sudden shrilling through the rigging heralded the renewal of the storm's wildest efforts and the trireme recoiled from its wrath. One sailor, in a more weakened condition than his comrades, lost his grip and was hurled into the darkness so quickly that none who saw it happen marked where he fell into the sea. But there was no pause in the sailors' efforts. The wind tore at the exposed parts of the sail and nearly succeeded in prising it free of their grip before the sailors managed to tie down the reefing lines. As soon as the sail was set, the men climbed back along the spar and painstakingly made their way down to the deck, their haggard faces testimony to the cold and exhaustion they were suffering.

The prefect made his way to the hatch coaming at the stern and carefully lowered himself down into the pitch-black interior. The small cabin seemed unnaturally quiet after the shrieking, buffeting wind and rain on deck. The sound of whimpering drew him aft, where the timbers curved together, and a flash of lightning through the hatch revealed the woman wedged into the stern, her arms tightly held round the shoulders of two young children. They shivered, clutching their mother, and the youngest, a boy of five, cried inconsolably, face drenched with spray, tears and snot. His sister, three years older, just sat, silent but wide-eyed with terror. The trireme's bows suddenly lifted to a huge wave and the prefect pitched towards his passengers. He thrust an arm out against the hull and fell sprawling against the opposite side. He took a moment to recover his breath, and the woman's voice spoke calmly from the darkness.

'We will come through this, won't we?'

Another flash of lightning revealed the panic etched onto the pale faces of the children.

The prefect decided there was no point in mentioning that he had decided to try and beach the trireme. Best save his passengers any further anxiety.

'Of course, my lady. We're running before the storm and as soon as it's passed we'll make our way back up the coast to Rutupiae.'

'I see,' the woman replied flatly, and the prefect realised she had seen through his answer. Clearly a perceptive woman then, a credit to her noble family and to her husband. She gave her children a reassuring squeeze.

'Did you hear that, my dears? We'll be warm and dry soon enough.'

The prefect recalled their shivering and cursed his thoughtlessness.

'Just a moment, my lady.' His numbed fingers fiddled with the clasp fastening the water-proofed cloak at his throat. He swore at his clumsiness, and then the pin came free. He drew it from around his shoulders and held it towards her in the darkness.

'Here, for you and your children, my lady.'

He felt the cloak drawn from him.

'Thank you, Prefect, it's most kind of you. Let's cuddle under this cloak, you two.'

As the prefect drew his knees up and hugged his arms round them, trying to create some centre of warmth to draw comfort from, a hand gently tapped him on the shoulder.

'My lady?'

'It's Valerius Maxentius, isn't it?'

'Yes, my lady.'

'Well then, Valerius. Shelter under this cloak with us. Before the cold kills you.'

The casual use of his informal name momentarily shocked the prefect. Then he mumbled his thanks and shifted over, joining the woman under the cloak. The boy sat huddled between them, shivering violently, and every so often his body was wracked by sobbing.

'Easy there,' the prefect said softly. 'We'll be all right. You'll see.'

A series of lightning flashes illuminated the cabin, and the prefect and the woman glanced at each other. Her look was questioning, and he shook his head. A fresh deluge of silvery water splashed through the hatch into the cabin. The great timbers of the trireme groaned all around them as the fabric of the vessel was subjected to forces its builders had never dreamed of. The prefect knew that her seams would not stand much more of this violence and eventually the sea would swamp her. And all the slaves chained at the oars, the crewmen and these passengers would drown with him. He cursed softly before he could stop himself. The woman guessed his feelings.

'Valerius, it's not your fault. You could never have foreseen this.'

'I know, my lady. I know.'

'We might yet be saved.'

'Yes, my lady. If you say so.'

Throughout the night the storm swept the trireme down the coast. Halfway up the rigging, the captain braved the biting cold to search for a suitable place to try to beach the trireme. All the time he was conscious that the ship beneath him was ever more sluggish in its response to the waves. Below decks a number of galley slaves had been unshackled to help with the bailing. They sat in a line and passed buckets from hand to hand, to be emptied over the side. But it was not enough to save the ship; it merely delayed the inevitable moment when a massive wave would burst over the trireme and sink her.

A desperate wailing reached the captain from the slaves still chained to their benches. The water was already slopping about their knees and for them there would be no hope of salvation once the ship foundered. Others might survive a while, clinging to the debris before the cold finished them, but for the slaves, drowning was certain and the captain could well understand their hysteria.

The rain turned to sleet and then to snow. Thick white flakes swirled in on the wind and layered themselves on the captain's tunic. His hands were losing all sensation and he realised he must return to the deck before the cold weakened his grip on the rigging. But just as he took the first step down, he glimpsed the dark loom of a headland over the bow. White spray burst over jagged rocks at the base of the cliff, barely half a mile ahead.

The captain rapidly swung himself to the deck and hurried aft towards the steersman.

'Rocks ahead! Hard over!'

The captain threw himself onto the timber handle and strained with the steersman against the pressure of the sea surging past the broad steering paddle overside. Slowly the trireme responded, and the bowsprit began to turn away from the headland. In the glare of the lightning, they could see the glistening dark teeth of the rocks rising from the crashing waves. The roar of their pounding carried even above the howling of the wind. For a moment the bowsprit refused to swing any further towards the open sea and the captain's heart was seized by dark, cold despair. Then a fluke in the wind carried the bowsprit round, clear of the rocks, barely a hundred feet off the bow.

'That's it! Keep her there!' he screamed at the steersman.

With the small spread of mainsail straining under the pressure of the wind, the trireme surged forward, up and over the wild sea. Past the headland the cliff opened out onto a pebbled shore, behind which the land rose with a scattering of stunted trees. Waves pounded up the beach in great sweeps of white foam.

'There!' The captain pointed. 'We'll beach her there.'

'In that surf?' shouted the steersman. 'That's madness!'

'It's our only chance! Now, on the tiller, with me!'

With the paddle biting in the opposite direction, the trireme swung in towards the shore. For the first time that night the captain allowed himself to believe they might yet emerge from this tempest alive. He even laughed with exultation at having defied the worst of the wrath that great Neptune could hurl at those who ventured into his domain. But with the safety of the shore almost within their reach, the sea finally had its way with them. A great swell rolled in from the dark depths of the ocean and lifted the trireme up and up, until the captain found that he was looking down on the shore. Then the crest passed beneath them and the ship dropped like a stone. With a jarring crash that knocked all the crew off their feet, the bows were impaled on a jagged sliver of rock some distance from the base of the headland. The captain quickly regained his footing, and the firm deck under his boots told him that the ship was no longer afloat.

The next wave forced the trireme to pivot round, so that the stern was nearest the beach. A rending crash from forward told of the damage being wreaked. From below came the cries and screams of the slaves as the water cascaded down the length of the trireme. Within moments she would settle, and succeeding waves would dash her and all aboard onto the rocks.

'What's happened?'

The captain turned and saw Prefect Maxentius emerging from the hatch. The dark mass of land close by and the glistening black of spray-soaked rock were explanation enough. The prefect shouted down through the hatch for the passenger to bring her children up on deck. Then he turned back to the captain.

'We must get them off! They must get to the shore!'

While the woman and her children huddled down by the stern rail, Valerius Maxentius and the captain struggled to lash several inflated

7

wineskins together. About them the crew made ready with whatever they could find that might float. The screaming below deck intensified into spine-chilling shrieks of abject terror as the trireme settled further into the dark sea. Abruptly the screams were cut off. One of the crew on deck shouted and pointed to the maindeck hatchway. Not far beneath the grating, seawater glinted. The only thing preventing the ship from slipping beneath the water was the rock on which the bows were pinned. One large wave would finish them now.

'Over here!' Maxentius shouted to the woman and her children. 'Quick!'

As the first waves began to break over the deck, the prefect and the captain lashed their passengers to the wineskins. At first the boy protested and wriggled in panic as Maxentius tried to pass the rope round his waist.

'Stop it!' His mother slapped him. 'Be still.'

The prefect nodded his thanks, and finished tying the boy to the makeshift floats.

'What now?' she asked.

'Wait by the stern. When I tell you, jump. Then kick as hard as you can for the shore.'

The woman paused to look at the two men. 'And you?'

'We'll follow you as soon as we can.' The prefect smiled. 'Now, my lady. If you will?'

She allowed herself to be led to the aft rail, and carefully climbed over, clasping her children to her sides, braving herself to jump.

'Mummy! No!' the boy cried out as he stared wide-eyed at the wild sea beneath his feet. 'Please, Mummy!'

'Aelius, we'll be all right. I swear it!'

'Sir!' the captain yelled. 'There! Look there!'

The prefect turned and through the snow-flecked storm he saw a monstrous wave rushing down on them, white spray whipped off its crest by the terrible wind. He just had time to turn back to the woman and scream out an order to jump. Then the wave crashed over the trireme and rolled it onto the rocks. The crewmen on the maindeck were swept away. As Maxentius threw himself backwards over the stern post, he caught one last glance of the captain gripping the main hatch grating, eyes staring at the doom about to engulf him. Icy darkness closed over the prefect, and before he could shut his mouth salt water filled his nose and throat. He felt himself turned over and over as his lungs burned for want of air. Just when he thought he must surely die, his ears momentarily filled with the din of the storm. Then it was gone for an instant, before his head broke the surface again. The prefect gasped for air, kicking out to stay on the surface. The heaving sea lifted him up, and he saw the beach not far off. There was no sign of the trireme. Nor a single soul of her crew. Not even the woman and her children. The swell swept him a little closer to the rocks, and the prospect of being smashed to pieces caused the prefect to renew his efforts to swim for the shore.

Several times he felt certain that the rocks would claim him. But as he struggled towards the beach with all his failing strength, the headland began to protect him from the wildest waves. At length, exhausted and despairing, he felt his feet brush the shingle bottom. Then the riptide drew him back from the shore and he cried out his rage to the gods that he should be denied salvation at this last moment. Determined that he would not die, not yet, he gritted his teeth and made one last supreme effort to make the shore. Amid the pounding foam of another wave, he swept painfully over the pebbles and braced himself to resist the undertow as the wave receded. Before the next wave could crash down on the shore, Maxentius scrambled up the steeply sloped shingle and then threw himself down, utterly spent and gasping for breath.

Around him the storm raged and fresh flurries of snow swirled through the air. Now that he was safely ashore, the prefect realised just how cold his body had become. He shivered violently as he tried to summon the energy to move. Before he could do so, there was a sudden scattering of stones nearby and someone sat down beside him.

'Valerius Maxentius! Are you all right?'

He was surprised at the strength of the woman as she lifted him up and rolled him over onto his side. He nodded.

'Come on then!' she ordered. 'Before you freeze.'

She drew one of his arms across her shoulder and half supported him up the beach towards a shallow ravine lined with the black forms of stunted trees. There, in the shelter of a fallen trunk, the two children crouched in the sodden mass of the prefect's cloak.

'Underneath. All of you.'

She joined them, and all four huddled as tightly together as they could within the wet folds, shivering violently as the storm raged on and snow settled about them. Looking out towards the headland, Maxentius could see no sign of the trireme. It was as if his flagship had never been, so completely had it been obliterated. No one else seemed to have survived. No one.

A sudden scrabbling of shingle caught his ear above the howling wind. For a moment he thought he must have imagined it. Then the sound came again, and this time he swore he could hear voices as well.

'There's other survivors!' He smiled at the woman, easing himself to his knees. 'Over here! Over here!' he called.

A dark figure appeared round the corner of the ravine opening. Then another.

'Here!' The prefect waved. 'Over here!'

The figures were still for a moment, then one of them called out, but the sense of his words was lost on the wind. He raised a spear and signalled to unseen others.

'Valerius, be quiet!' ordered the woman.

But it was too late. They had been seen, and more men joined the first two. Cautiously they approached the shivering Romans. By the loom of the snow on the ground, their features slowly became visible as they came nearer.

'Mummy,' the girl whispered. 'Who are they?'

'Hush, Julia!'

When the men were only a few paces away, a distant burst of lightning lit up the sky. In its pale glow the men were briefly revealed. Above their crudely cut fur cloaks, wildly spiked hair billowed in the wind. Beneath, fierce eyes blazed out of heavily tattooed faces. For a moment neither they nor the Romans moved or said a word. Then the little boy could take no more and a thin scream of blind terror split the air.

Chapter Two

'I'm sure it was around here,' muttered Centurion Macro, glancing down a dark alley leading up from the Camulodunum quayside. 'Any ideas?'

The other three exchanged a glance as they stamped their feet in the snow. Beside Cato – Macro's young optio – stood two young women, natives from the Iceni tribe, wrapped warmly in splendid winter cloaks with fur trims. They had been raised by fathers who had long anticipated the day when the Caesars would extend the limits of their empire into Britain. The girls had been taught Latin from an early age, by an educated slave imported from Gaul. As a consequence their Latin had a lilting accent, an effect Cato found quite pleasing to the ear.

'Look here,' the oldest girl protested. 'You said you'd take us to a snug little alehouse. I'm not going to spend the night walking up and down freezing streets until you find exactly the one you're looking for. We go in the next one we come across, agreed?' She looked round at her friend and Cato, fierce eyes demanding their assent. Both nodded at once.

'It must be down this one,' Macro responded quickly. 'Yes, I remember now. This is the place.'

'It had better be. Or you're taking us home.'

'Fair enough.' Macro raised a hand to placate her. 'Let's go.'

With the centurion leading the way, the small band softly crunched up the narrow alley, hemmed in on both sides by the dark huts and houses of the Trinovantes townspeople. Snow had been falling all day and had only stopped shortly after dusk. Camulodunum and the surrounding landscape lay under a thick blanket of gleaming white and most people were indoors huddled around smoky fires. Only the more hardy of the town's youngsters joined the Roman soldiers looking for dives where they might enjoy a night's drinking, raucous singing and, with a little luck, a bit of fighting. The soldiers, armed with purses bulging with coins, wandered into town from the vast encampment stretching out just beyond the main gate of Camulodunum. Four legions – over twenty thousand men – were sitting the winter out in crude timber and turf huts, impatiently waiting for spring to arrive so that the campaign to conquer the island could be renewed.

It had been an especially harsh winter and the legionaries, shut up in their camp and made to live on an unrelieved diet of barley and winter vegetable stew, were restless. Particularly since the general had advanced them a portion of the donative paid to the army by Emperor Claudius. This bonus was given to celebrate the defeat of the British commander, Caratacus, and the fall of his capital at Camulodunum. The townspeople, mostly engaged in some form of trade or other, had quickly recovered from the shock of defeat and taken advantage of the opportunity to fleece the legionaries camping on their doorstep. A number of alehouses had opened up to provide the legionaries with a range of local brews, as well as wine shipped in from the continent by those merchants prepared to risk their ships in the winter seas in return for premium prices.

The townsfolk who were not making money out of their new masters looked on in distaste as the drunken foreigners staggered home from the alehouses, singing at the tops of their voices, and spewing noisily in the streets. Eventually, the town's elders had had enough and sent a deputation to General Plautius. They politely requested that, in the interests of the new bonds of alliance that had been forged between the Romans and the Trinovantes, it might be a good thing if the legionaries were no longer allowed into the town. Sympathetic as he was to the need to preserve good relations with the locals, the general also knew that he would be risking a mutiny if he denied his soldiers an outlet for the tensions that always accompanied the long months spent in winter quarters. Accordingly, a compromise was reached, and the numbers of passes issued to soldiers rationed. As a result, the soldiers were even more determined to go on a wild bender each time they were allowed into the town.

'Here we are!' said Macro triumphantly. 'I told you it was here.'

They were standing outside the small studded door of a stone-built store shed. A shuttered window pierced the wall a few paces further up the alley. A warm red glow lined the rim of the shutters and they could hear the cheerful hubbub of loud conversation within.

'At least it should be warm,' the younger girl said quietly. 'What do you think, Boudica?'

'I think it had better be,' her cousin replied, and reached for the door latch. 'Come on then.'

Horrified at the prospect of being preceded into a drinking place by a woman, Macro clumsily thrust himself between the woman and the door.

'Er, please allow me.' He smiled, attempting to affect some manners. He opened the door and ducked under the frame. His small party followed. The warm smoky fug wrapped itself around the new arrivals and the glow from a fire and several tallow lamps seemed quite brilliant after the darkness of the alley. A few heads turned to inspect the new arrivals and Cato saw that many of the customers were off-duty legionaries, dressed in thick red military tunics and cloaks.

'Put the wood in the hole!' someone shouted. 'Before we all fucking freeze.'

'Watch it!' Macro shouted back angrily. 'There are ladies present!'

A chorus of hoots sounded from the other customers.

'We already know!' A legionary nearby laughed as he goosed a passing bar woman carrying an armful of empty pitchers. She yelped, and spun round to deliver a stinging blow before skipping off to the counter at the far end of the alehouse. The legionary rubbed his glowing cheek and laughed again.

'And you recommend this place?' Boudica muttered.

'Give it a chance. I had a great time here the other night. It has atmosphere, wouldn't you say?'

'It certainly has an atmosphere,' said Cato. 'Wonder how long it'll take before a fight breaks out.'

His centurion shot him a dark look before turning to the two women. 'What'll you have, ladies?'

'A seat,' Boudica responded tartly. 'A seat will do nicely, for now.'

Macro shrugged. 'See to it, Cato. Find somewhere quiet. I'll get the drinks in.'

While Macro steered a way through the throng to the bar, Cato looked round and saw that the only place left was a rickety trestle table flanked by two benches, right by the door they had just entered. He pulled back the end of one bench and bowed his head. 'There you are, ladies.'

Boudica curled her lip at the roughly hewn furniture presented to her, and might have refused to sit had her cousin not quickly nudged her forward. The younger woman was called Nessa, a brown-haired Icenian with blue eyes and round cheeks. Cato was well aware that his centurion and Boudica had arranged for her to come along to keep him distracted while the older couple continued their peculiar relationship.

13

Macro and Boudica had met shortly after the fall of Camulodunum. Since the Iceni were nominally neutral in the war between Rome and the confederation of tribes resisting the invaders, Boudica was more curious than hostile towards the men from the great empire across the sea. The town elders had rushed to ingratiate themselves with their new rulers and invitations to feasts had flooded into the Roman camp. Even junior centurions like Macro had found themselves asked to attend. On the first such night he had met Boudica. Her forthright nature had appalled him at first; the Celts appeared to have a distastefully egalitarian attitude towards the gentler sex. Finding herself standing next to a centurion, who in turn stood next to a barrel of the most powerful beer he had ever encountered, Boudica wasted no time in grilling him for information about Rome. At first her open approach inclined Macro to regard her as just another of the horse-faced women that made up the majority of the higher class of Briton. But as he endured her questioning, he slowly became less and less interested in the beer. Grudgingly at first, then more willingly as she artfully drew him into a more expansive discussion, Macro talked to her in a way he had never before with a woman.

By the end of the evening he knew he wanted to see more of this lively Icenian, and stammered out a request to meet again. She gladly assented, and extended an invitation to a feast being held by her kinsman the following night. Macro had been the first guest to arrive and stood in embarrassed silence by the spread of cold meats and warm beer until Boudica arrived. Then he watched in horror as she matched him drink for drink. Before he knew it, she had slapped an arm round his shoulder and was hugging him tightly to her. Looking round, Macro observed the same forwardness in the other Celtic women and was trying to reconcile himself to the strange ways of this new culture when Boudica planted a boozy kiss on his lips.

Momentarily startled, Macro tried to break away from her powerful embrace, but the girl had mistakenly taken his writhing as a sign of his ardour and merely tightened her grip. So Macro gave in and kissed her back, and on the alcohol-saturated wings of passion they had collapsed under a table in a dark corner and fumbled the evening away. Only the limp side effects of the beer prevented the consummation of their mutual attraction. Boudica had been decent enough not to make an issue of it.

They continued to meet almost daily from that point on, and sometimes Macro invited Cato to join them, mainly from a sense of pity for the lad, who had only recently seen his first love murdered at the hands of a treacherous Roman aristocrat. Quiet and shy at first, Cato had been slowly drawn out by Boudica's infectious sociability and now the two could hold a conversation for hours. Macro felt himself being slowly frozen out. Despite Boudica's claim that she only had relationships with grown-ups, Macro was not reassured. Hence the presence of Nessa – at Macro's suggestion. A girl Cato could get stuck into while he continued wooing Boudica.

'Does your centurion often frequent places like this?' asked Boudica.

'Not always as nice as this.' Cato smiled. 'You should feel honoured.'

Nessa missed the ironic tone and sniffed in disgust at the suggestion that any right-thinking person should deem it a privilege to be led to such a dive. The other two rolled their eyes.

'How did you manage to get permission to be out?' Cato asked Boudica. 'I thought your uncle was going to burst a blood vessel that night we had to carry you back home.'

'He nearly did. Poor chap's not been quite the same since and only agreed to letting us out to stay the night with some distant cousins provided we were escorted.'

Cato frowned. 'So where's the escort?'

'Don't know. We got separated in the crowd near the town gate.'

'On purpose?'

'Of course. What do you take me for?'

'I wouldn't presume.'

'Very wise.'

'Prasutagus is probably peeing himself with worry!' Nessa giggled. 'You can bet he'll be searching every drinking hall he can think of.'

'Which makes us quite safe, since my dear kinsman – another cousin incidentally – would never think of this place. I doubt he's ever even ventured into the alleys behind the quay. We'll be all right.'

'If he does find us,' Nessa's eyes widened, 'he'll go mental! You remember what he did to that Atrebate lad who tried to chat us up. I thought Prasutagus was going to kill him!'

'Probably would have if I hadn't hauled him off.'

Cato shifted nervously. 'Big lad, this kinsman of yours?'

'Huge!' Nessa laughed. '*Sa!* Huge is the word all right.'

'With a brain in inverse proportion to his physique,' Boudica added. 'So don't even think of trying to reason with him if he comes in here. Just run.'

'I see.'

Macro returned from the bar, arms raised to keep cups and jug above the throng. He set them down on the rough surface of the bench and politely filled each of the pottery mugs to the brim with red wine.

'Wine!' Boudica exclaimed. 'You do know how to spoil a lady, Centurion.'

'Beer's off,' explained Macro. 'This is all they have left, and it's not cheap either. So drink up and enjoy.'

'While we can, sir.'

'Eh? What's the matter, lad?'

'These ladies are only here because they slipped away from a rather large male relative who is probably looking for them right now, and not in the best of moods.'

'Not surprising on a night like this.' Macro shrugged. 'Still, we're well out of it now. We've got a fire, drink and good company. What more could you ask for?'

'A seat nearer the fire,' replied Boudica.

'Now then, let's have a toast.' The centurion raised his mug. 'To us!' Macro raised his mug to his lips and downed the wine in one go then slammed the mug back down. 'Ahhhh! That hit the spot! Who's for more?'

'Just a moment.' Boudica followed his lead and drained her cup.

Cato knew his limitations with respect to wine, and just shook his head.

'Suit yourself, lad, but wine's as good as a knock on the head for helping you forget your troubles.'

'If you say so, sir.'

'I do say so. Particularly if you have some bad news to break.' Macro looked across the table at Boudica.

'What news?' she asked sharply.

'The legion's being sent south.'

'When?'

'Three days' time.'

'First I've heard of it,' said Cato. 'What's up?'

'I'd guess the general wants to use the Second Legion to cut Caratacus off from any escape route south of the Tamesis. The other three legions can clear up on the north side of the river.'

'The Tamesis?' Boudica frowned. 'That's a long way off. When is your legion coming back here?'

Macro was about to give some glib and reassuring answer when he saw the pained expression on Boudica's face. He realised that honesty was the right course of action in this situation. Far better

16

for Boudica to know the truth now than for her to resent him later.

'I don't know. Maybe a few more campaign seasons, maybe never. All depends on how long Caratacus continues to fight on. If we can crush him quickly then the province can be settled straightaway. As it is, the wily bastard keeps raiding through our supply lines, and all the while he's trying to negotiate with other tribes to get them to join him in resisting us.'

'You can hardly blame the man for fighting well.'

'I can blame him for it if it keeps us apart.' Macro reached for her hand and gave it an affectionate squeeze. 'So let's just hope he's bright enough to realise he can never win. Then, once the province is settled, I'll get some leave and come and find you.'

'You expect the province to be settled that quickly?' Boudica flared up. 'Lud! When will you Romans learn? Caratacus leads only those tribes under the sway of the Catuvellauni. There are many other tribes, mostly too proud to let themselves be led into battle by another chief, and certainly too proud to meekly submit to Roman rule. Take our own tribe.' Boudica gestured to herself and Nessa. 'The Iceni. I know of no warrior who would dream of becoming a subject of your Emperor Claudius. Sure you've tried to woo our chiefs with promises of alliance and a share in the spoils of those tribes Rome defeats on the battlefield. But I warn you, the moment you try and become our master, Rome will pay a high price in the blood of its legions . . .'

Her voice had become quite shrill, and for a moment her eyes blazed defiantly across the table. Drinkers at neighbouring benches had turned to look, and conversation was briefly stilled. Then heads turned back and the volume slowly rose again. Boudica poured herself another mug of wine and drained it before continuing, more quietly. 'That's true of most of the other tribes as well. Believe me.'

Macro stared at her and nodded slowly as he took her hand again and held it gently in his own. 'I'm sorry. I meant no slight on your people. Honestly. I'm not very good with words.'

Boudica's lips lifted in a smile. 'Never mind, you make up for it in other ways.'

Macro glanced round at Cato. 'Do you think you could take this lass over to the bar for a while? My lady and I need to talk.'

'Yes, sir.' Cato, sensitive to the needs of the situation, quickly rose from the bench and held his arm out to Nessa. The young woman looked to her cousin and was given a faint nod.

'All right then.' Nessa grinned. 'You be careful, Boudica, you know what these soldiers are like.'

17

'*Sa!* I can look after myself!'

Cato did not doubt it. He had come to know Boudica quite well over the winter months and his sympathies were with his centurion. He led Nessa through the crowd of drinkers to the counter. The barman, an old Gaul judging by his accent, had eschewed the Roman fashions of the continent and wore a heavily patterned tunic, upon the shoulders of which rested his pigtails. He was rinsing mugs in a tub of dirty water and looked up when Cato rapped the counter with a coin. Wiping his hands on his apron, he shuffled over and raised his eyebrows.

'Two mugs of heated wine,' ordered Cato, before he considered Nessa. 'That do?'

She nodded, and the barman picked up two mugs, and made for a battered bronze cauldron resting on a blackened grate over faintly glowing embers. Steam curled up from inside and, even where he stood, Cato could smell the scent of spices above the beer and the underlying sour smells of humanity. Cato, tall and thin, looked down on his Iceni companion as she eagerly watched the Gaul dip a ladle into the cauldron to stir the mixture. Cato frowned. He knew he should make some attempt at small talk, but he had never been good at it, always fearing that whatever he said sounded either insincere or merely stupid. Besides, his heart was not in it. Not that Nessa was unattractive in looks – her personality he could only guess at – it was just that he still grieved for Lavinia.

The passion he had felt for Lavinia ran through his veins like fire, even after she had betrayed him and run to the bed of that bastard Vitellius. Before Cato could teach himself to despise her, Vitellius had drawn Lavinia into a plot to kill the Emperor and cold-bloodedly murdered her to cover his tracks. An image of the dark tresses of Lavinia's hair settling into the blood spreading from her cut throat filled Cato's mind and he felt sick. He longed for her more than ever.

All his spare passion was devoted to cultivating a burning hatred for Tribune Vitellius so great that no revenge could be too terrible to contemplate. But Vitellius had returned to Rome with the Emperor, having emerged a hero from his botched assassination attempt. As soon as it was clear that the Emperor's bodyguards would save their master, Vitellius had fallen upon the assassin and killed him. Now the Emperor regarded the tribune as his saviour for whom no reward or honour could be sufficient expression of his gratitude. Staring into the middle distance, Cato's expression hardened into a thin-lipped bitterness that startled his companion.

'What on earth's the matter with you?'

18

'Eh? Sorry. I was thinking.'

'I don't think I want to know.'

'It was nothing to do with you.'

'I should hope not. Look, here comes the wine.'

The Gaul returned to the counter with two steaming mugs, whose rich aroma excited even Cato's taste buds. The Gaul took the coin Cato handed him and turned back towards his rinsing tub.

'Hey!' Cato called out. 'What about my change?'

'No change,' muttered the Gaul over his shoulder. 'That's the price. Wine's in short supply, thanks to the storms.'

'Even so . . .'

'You don't like my prices? Then fuck off and find somewhere else to drink.'

Cato felt the blood drain from his face and his fists clenched in anger. He opened his voice to shout, and only just managed to pull himself back from the brink of a terrible rage and a desire to tear the old man apart. With the return of self-control, he felt horrified at such a lapse in the rationality he prided himself in. He felt ashamed, and glanced round to see if anyone had noticed how close he had come to making a fool of himself. Only one man was looking his way, a thickset Gaul leaning on the far end of the counter. He was watching Cato closely and one hand had moved towards the handle of a dagger in a metalled scabbard hanging from his belt. Clearly the old Gaul's hired muscle. He met the optio's gaze and raised his hand to wag a finger at him, faintly smiling with contempt as he warned the young man to behave himself.

'Cato, there's a space by the fire. Let's go.' Nessa gently pushed him away from the counter towards the brick hearth where fresh logs hissed and crackled. Cato resisted her touch for an instant but then yielded. They picked their way between the customers, taking care not to spill the heated wine, and sat down on two low stools alongside a handful of others who craved the fire's warmth.

'What was all that about?' asked Nessa. 'You looked so scary back there at the counter.'

'I did?' Cato shrugged, and then carefully sipped from his steaming mug.

'You did. I thought you were going to go for him.'

'I was.'

'Why? Boudica told me you were the quiet type.'

'I am.'

'Then why?'

19

'It's personal!' Cato replied sharply. Then quickly relented. 'Sorry, I didn't mean it to sound like that. I just don't want to talk about it.'

'I see. Then let's talk about something else.'

'Like what?'

'I don't know. You think of something. Do you good.'

'All right then, that cousin of Boudica, Prasutagus, is he really as dangerous as he sounds?'

'Worse. He's more than just a warrior.' Cato saw the frightened expression on her face. 'He has other powers.'

'What kind of powers?'

'I-I can't say.'

'Will you and Boudica be in any danger when he finds you again?'

Nessa shook her head as she sipped from her mug and spilt a few drops of wine down the front of her cloak where they glistened with reflected firelight for a moment, before soaking in. 'Oh, he'll go bright red in the face and shout for a bit, but that'll be all. Once Boudica makes eyes at him he'll just roll over and wait for her to tickle his tummy.'

'Fancies her then?'

'You said it. Fancies her something rotten.' Nessa craned her neck to look across the room at her friend who was leaning over the table and cradling Macro's cheek in the palm of one hand. She turned back to Cato and whispered confidentially, as if Boudica might somehow hear her, 'Between us, I've heard that Prasutagus has quite fallen in love with her. He's going to escort us home to our village once spring comes. I shouldn't be surprised if he takes the opportunity to ask Boudica's father for permission to wed her.'

'How does she feel about him?'

'Oh, she'll accept, of course.'

'Really? Why?'

'It's not every day that a girl gets offered the hand of the next ruler of the Iceni.'

Cato nodded slowly. Boudica would not be the first woman he had met who placed social advancement before emotional fulfilment. Cato decided he would not tell his centurion about this. If Boudica was going to ditch Macro and marry someone else, then she could tell Macro herself. 'A shame. She deserves better.'

'Of course she does. That's why she's messing around with your centurion. Might as well have as much fun as she can, while she can. I doubt Prasutagus will give her much of a free rein once they're married.'

A sudden crash sounded from behind them. Cato and Nessa turned and saw that the door to the alehouse had been kicked open. Squeezing through it was one of the largest men Cato had ever seen. As the man straightened up, rather awkwardly, his head met the thatch. Swearing angrily in his native tongue, he ducked and moved forward to where he could stand erect and have a good look round at the customers. He was well over six feet tall, and broad to match. The bulging muscles under the hairy skin of his forearms made Cato gulp as with a sick sense of inevitability he guessed who the new arrival was.

Chapter Three

'Oh dear!' Nessa winced. 'Now we're for it.'

As Prasutagus glared round at the drinkers, they fell silent, and tried not to meet his eyes while carefully keeping him in clear view. Cato looked beyond the Iceni giant. In the nook by the door, Boudica and Macro were out of the new arrival's line of sight, and Boudica quickly indicated to Macro that he should get under the bench. He shook his head. She jabbed her finger down insistently, but there was no swaying the centurion. He swung his leg over the bench, ready to confront the new arrival. Boudica quickly drained her mug and dived under the bench herself, pressing into the wall furthest from Prasutagus. In doing so she jolted the table and her mug tipped off the edge and shattered on the stone floor.

Prasutagus whipped out a dagger from beneath his cloak and spun round, ready to pounce on any foe sneaking up behind him. He weighed up Macro's stocky physique as the centurion rose to his feet, and then the Iceni warrior roared with laughter.

'What you laughing at?' Macro snarled.

Nessa squeezed Cato's arm and gasped. 'Your friend's a fool!'

'No,' Cato whispered. 'It's your kinsman who's in danger. He's had a skinful and he's pissed Macro off. He'd better watch it.'

Prasutagus patted the centurion heavily on the shoulder and said something conciliatory in his native tongue. The knife disappeared back into his cloak.

'Hands off!' growled Macro. 'You may be a big bastard, but I've taken down harder men than you.'

The warrior ignored him and turned towards the other customers, resuming his search for his wayward female relatives. Nessa had risen to her feet to better view the confrontation and was too slow ducking down out of sight again.

'Ahhh!' roared the giant and he ploughed forward, roughly pushing aside anyone in his path. 'Nessa!'

Before he could consider the wisdom of his action, Cato moved to place himself between them, hand raised to stop the approaching warrior.

'Leave her alone!' His voice quavered as the stupidity of his action sank in.

Prasutagus swatted him to one side, grabbed Nessa by the shoulders and, true to her description of the man, began to bellow at her. Cato picked himself up from the floor and threw himself at the Briton. Prasutagus barely shifted. A moment later a heavy hand slapped the side of Cato's head and his world flashed white before he dropped like a stone, out cold.

By the door, Macro roused himself. 'That was way out of order, sunshine!' He thrust his way through the crowd towards the fireplace. Behind him, Boudica struggled out from under the bench.

'Macro! Stop! He'll kill you.'

'Let the bastard try.'

'Stop! I beg you!' She flew after him, making a grab for his shoulders.

'Let go of me, woman!'

'Macro, please!'

Prasutagus became aware of the commotion behind him and paused in his rough handling of Nessa to spare a glance over his shoulder. At once, he thrust Nessa to one side and swivelled his great frame round, bellowing out a torrent of words in a mixture of relief and rage. Macro stopped a little short of the giant, looking around for anything he could use as a weapon to even up the odds. He seized a crutch lying on the ground beside an unconscious tribesman and held it like a cross-staff. But before he could make a move on Prasutagus, a crashing blow to the back of his head laid him out – Boudica had felled him with a pottery jug. Stunned and dizzy, Macro struggled to his hands and knees.

'Stay down!' hissed Boudica. 'Stay down and keep quiet if you know what's good for you.'

She advanced on her cousin, eyes blazing and mouth clenched in outrage. Prasutagus continued shouting and waving his great arms about. Boudica drew up in front of him and slapped him across the face, again and again, until his tongue stilled and his arms hung limp.

'Na, Boudica!' he protested. '*Na!*'

She slapped him once more, and pointed a finger in his face, daring him to say another word. His eyes burned and he clenched his teeth, but he uttered not a sound. The other drinkers watched in fascinated silence for the next development in the confrontation between the hulking great warrior and the tall haughty woman who defied him so openly. At length Boudica lowered her finger. Prasutagus nodded, and spoke quietly to her, with the barest nod towards the doorway. Boudica called to Nessa and then led the way out into the street. Pausing a moment, Prasutagus glowered round at the customers, daring anyone to laugh at him. Then, kicking the prostrate optio to one side, he stormed out of the alehouse, hurrying after his charges before they could run off again.

Every drinker in the establishment watched the open doorway for any sign of the warrior's return. As conversation quietly resumed, the old Gaul nodded to his hired muscle and the man wandered over to the door and closed it. Then he casually worked his way over to Macro.

'You all right, mate?'

'Been better.' Macro rubbed his head and winced. 'Shit! That hurts.'

'Not surprised. That's quite a woman.'

'Oh yes!'

'Saved your bacon though. You and the lad there.'

'Cato!' Macro hurried over to his optio, who was propped on an elbow and shaking his head. 'You still with us?'

'I'm not sure, sir. Feels like a house fell on me.'

'Not far off!' chuckled the hired muscle. 'That Prasutagus can get pretty heavy-handed.'

Cato looked up. 'Oh really?'

The Gaul dragged Cato to his feet and brushed the straw from his tunic. 'Now if you two gentlemen wouldn't mind, I'd like you both to leave the premises right away.'

'Why?' asked Macro.

'Because I fucking say so,' replied the hired muscle, with a smile. Then he relented a little. 'You just don't mess with a high-ranking Iceni warrior. Especially a drunk one. I'd hate to think what will happen to my master's business if Prasutagus comes back with a few friends and finds you two still here.'

'Do you think he will?' asked Cato, eyeing the door nervously.

'Just as soon as he works out some kind of connection between his lady friends and you two. So best be off, eh?'

'Fair enough. Come on, Cato. Let's find somewhere else to drink.'

Tugging their cloaks tightly about their shoulders, Macro and Cato ducked under the lintel into the street. The shaft of orange light slanting across the snow in the alley was abruptly cut off as the door was firmly closed behind them. There was no sign of Prasutagus and the two women, save for the disturbed tracks in the snow leading up the alley.

'What now?' asked Cato.

24

'There's another place I know. Not quite as nice as this. But it'll do.'

'Not quite as nice . . .'

'Do you want a drink or not?'

'Yes, sir.'

'Then shut up and follow me.'

Hot on the trail of the Roman army had come traders in luxuries and vices to satisfy every taste. Phoenician pimps had arrived and set up their travelling brothels in the grimmest quarter of Camulodunum. Ramshackle barns and warehouses were bought cheaply and gaudily painted with graphic depictions of what was on offer inside, together with the prices. The more ambitious of the pimps also sold alcohol at inflated prices to the men waiting their turn. This led to a growth in the number of small drinking houses, all of them vying to attract custom. And then there were the usual quacks and magicians who guaranteed to cure every ailment from syphilis to impotence, and pedlars who offered an unlimited range of goods – swords that never blunted, charms to ward off arrows, pairs of dice that 'magically' always landed on VI, protective sheaths made of the finest kid goat stomach linings. Cato was all too familiar with this kind of tack and tat; the less salubrious districts of Rome were packed with such traders who offered an even wider range of carnal pleasures and miracle remedies.

Macro led Cato to a low wooden building in a dimly lit street where a trickle of human waste ran down the middle of the narrow way; an unpleasant dark streak in the churned-up snow. Inside, the air was heavy with the stench of cheap scent designed to take the minds of the customers off the even less pleasant odours that curled into their nostrils. The two legionaries pushed through the doorway into a dim room with a slatted wooden floor. Several tables and benches were arranged haphazardly around the place and a bar counter rested on two barrels. The proprietor and two of his tarts sat with bored seen-it-all expressions that did not quite square with the wall decor which displayed garish cartoons of laughing men and women engaged in anatomical experiments of mind-bending complexity.

Only two of the tables were occupied by a handful of legionaries who had come for a drink immediately after returning from patrol. They were wearing some of the new segmented armour as they huddled over a large jug of wine. In the far corner sat a group of junior officers from the Second Legion. One of them looked up at the new arrivals, a wide smile instantly spreading across his face.

'Macro, my lad!' he bellowed, rather too loudly, and the trio at the bar looked up in irritation. 'Come over here and share a brew.'

As the others squeezed up, Macro made the introductions.

'Lads, this is my optio. Cato, this lot of wine-sodden louts are the cream of the legion's officer corps. In a kinder light you might just recognise one or two faces. Please make the acquaintance of Quintus, Balbus, Scipio, Fabius and Parnesius.'

The men looked up blearily and nodded a greeting. Clearly a great deal had already been drunk.

'A good bunch of lads,' Macro said heartily. 'I served with them before they were all made up to centurions. First time we've had a chance for a get-together since I was promoted. One day, if you live long enough, I'm sure you're going to join us in the centurionate, eh lads?'

As the others roared out their agreement, Cato did his best not to look too appalled at the prospect, and helped himself to a drink. It proved to be another variety of the rough wine imported from Gaul and Cato winced as the sour liquid burned its way down his throat.

'Heady stuff, eh?' Balbus grinned. 'Just the sort of thing to set you up for some hand-to-hand with the tarts.'

Cato had no intention of coming that close, if the women at the counter were anything to judge the profession by. Besides, the only woman on his mind was Lavinia, and the best way to rid his mind of her for the moment was to drink.

Several cups of wine later his eyes felt as if they were perpetually swinging round and round, and it was worse when he shut them. Some kind of focus was needed and his gaze wobbled over to the group of legionaries at the other table, and the segmented armour they were wearing.

He jabbed a finger at Macro. 'Is that stuff any good, sir?'

'Stuff? What stuff?'

'That kit they're wearing. Instead of chain mail.'

'That, my lad, is the new issue of armour the legions are being equipped with.'

Parnesius stirred his head from where it rested on his folded arms and shouted out in a parade-ground way, 'Body armour, segmented, legionaries for the use of! Get it fucking right, son!'

'Ignore him,' Macro whispered to Cato. 'He works in the quarter-master's office.'

'I guessed.'

'Oi! You lot!' Macro called out to the other table. 'Let's be having you. The optio here wants to see your new armour.'

The legionaries exchanged looks. Finally, one of them replied. 'You can't tell us what to do. We're off duty.'

'Don't give a shit. Get your arse over here,' Macro shouted. 'I mean NOW!'

First one, then the others, meekly rose from the table and came over. They stood at the side of the table while the officers examined their equipment with some curiosity.

'How's it wear?' Macro asked, rising from the bench for a closer examination.

'Well enough, sir,' the first one to rise from his seat responded. 'Lighter than chain mail. And it's tougher. It's made up of these solid strips.'

'It looks like shit. How can you move in that?'

'It's articulated, sir. It adjusts to your movements.'

'You don't say?' Macro tugged at the armour, and then lifted the cloak at the back. 'Fastened by these buckles, I take it.'

'Yes, sir.'

'Easy to get on?'

'Yes, sir.'

'Expensive?'

'Cheaper than the mail.'

'How come you lot in the Twentieth are the only legions to get this issue? It's not as if you do much fighting.'

The officers laughed as the legionary fumed at this slight. He barely managed to recover his temper enough to reply, 'Dunno, sir. I'm just a squaddie.'

'Stop calling him sir,' one of the other legionaries hissed. 'We don't have to now.'

'I can't help it.'

'Don't do it!' the legionary said firmly. 'Otherwise what's the point in being off duty?'

'You!' Macro thrust a finger into the man's chest. 'Just shut it! You talk when you're fucking told to and not before. Understand me?'

'I understand,' the man replied firmly. 'But I'm not obeying orders.'

'Yes you fucking are!' Macro swung a fist into the man's midriff, and swore violently as it connected with the new armour. With his other hand he smacked the man in the face, sending him reeling into his comrades. Macro's follow-through swung him round and he collapsed onto the man he had hit with a howl of laughter.

'OK, lads, rank doesn't apply. Let's ruck!'

Every officer, except Cato, lurched to his feet and piled into the legionaries who, like Cato, just stared dumbfounded – until the first few blows had landed. Then, drunken wits recovered, the legionaries fought back and the bar was filled with the sound of crashing tables and benches. The barman hurried his women out of the room.

'Come on, Cato!' Macro called out from beneath a legionary. 'Get stuck in!'

Wobbling to his feet, Cato took aim at the nearest legionary and swung his fist as hard as he could. He missed completely and struck the wall instead, badly grazing his knuckles. He tried again, and this time the blow landed on the side of a man's head with a painful jarring sensation. Cato became aware of a fist flying in towards his face, and for the second time that night the world went white. With a grunt he sagged to his knees and tried to shake his head clear. When his vision returned, Cato saw a legionary standing over him with a stool raised above his head. Instinctively he thrust his head forwards and smashed it into the man's crotch. The legionary folded under the impact and crumpled to one side with a howl of pain, both hands clutched between his legs.

'Nice move, son!' Macro bellowed.

The blow to his head and the excess of wine he had consumed made Cato's head swim horribly. He tried to get to his feet, and failed, but through the shouts and crashes of furniture he became aware of the distant pounding of footsteps.

'Provosts!' someone shouted. 'Get out of here!'

Abruptly the fighting stopped and there was a mad scramble for the back of the bar. The main door opened and a squad of soldiers with black cloaks appeared. Cato was dragged to his feet by Macro and thrown bodily in the direction of the small rear door that the other brawlers were spilling out through. In a whirl of images Cato found himself out in the street, running clumsily after Macro. The centurion broke away from the main group and went weaving down an alleyway. The sounds of pursuit had faded when Cato became aware that he had lost track of Macro. He stopped and leaned against a wooden wall as he fought to catch his breath. The world around him was spinning sickeningly and he desperately wanted to throw up, but there was nothing apart from bile rising in his throat.

'Macro!' he called out. 'Macro!'

In the near distance a voice shouted, and the sound of jostling armour grew louder.

'Shit! What have I done?'

A hand grabbed hold of his arm and yanked him to one side, through a door and into the darkness of a building. Something hit him hard in the stomach and Cato dropped to his knees, gasping for breath. Outside, footsteps crunched through the snow and then died away.

'Sorry about that,' said Macro, helping Cato to his feet. 'But I needed to shut you up for a moment. No harm intended. You all right?'

'N-no!' Cato gasped. 'Feel sick!'

'Save it for later. We've got better things to do. Come here.'

Cato was shoved through a doorway into a small room lit by a single lamp. Two women were sitting on a pair of seedy looking beds, and they smiled as Macro appeared through the door.

'Cato, this is Broann and Deneb. Say hello girls.'

'Hello, girls,' Cato mumbled. 'Who are they?'

'Don't really know. Only just met them. As it happens, the girls are free at the moment. Broann's mine. You get Deneb. Enjoy.'

Macro went over to Broann who smiled with trained warmth, an effect somewhat marred by several missing front teeth. With a wink at Cato, Macro withdrew with Broann behind a tattered curtain.

The optio turned to face Deneb and saw a woman whose face was so painted with make-up that her age was anybody's guess. A few wrinkles at the corners of her mouth hinted at a maturity in years nearby double that of her customer. She smiled and took his hands, pulling him down to her bed. As Cato knelt between her legs, Deneb raised a hand to her loose silk gown and parted it down the length of her body, revealing a large pair of breasts with dark brown nipples and a sparse, wiry brush of pubic hair. Cato looked her up and down for a moment. She beckoned him closer. As he learned forward towards her purple painted lips, the wine finally got the better of him and he pitched forward, unconscious.

Chapter Four

General Plautius was looking old and very tired, reflected Vespasian as he watched his commander stamp his ring seal on a series of documents handed to him by a headquarters clerk. The sharp smell of the smoke rising from the sealing wax irritated his nose and Vespasian leaned back in his seat. That he and Plautius were meeting at this late hour on a dark winter night was typical of the Roman army. While other armies might spend the winter growing soft in their billets, the men of Rome stayed fit with regular exercise and their officers saw to it that detailed preparation was made for the renewal of operations in the spring.

The previous campaigning season had ended well enough. Plautius's legions had landed on a hostile shore and fought their way up through the lands of the Cantii, across the Mead Way and the Tamesis, before taking Camulodunum, the capital of the Catuvellauni tribe heading the confederation opposed to Rome. Despite the considerable talents of the enemy commander, Caratacus, the legions had crushed the British forces in two bitterly contested battles. Unfortunately, Caratacus had not fallen into their hands, and even now the British chief was making his own preparations to continue opposing Rome's attempt to add Britain to its vast empire.

Despite the harsh winter conditions of this northern climate, Plautius had kept his cavalry active and sent them on long marches deep into the heart of the island, with strict orders to observe and not engage the enemy. Nevertheless, some patrols had run into ambushes, leaving only a few frightened survivors to report on their fate. Other patrols had disappeared entirely. Such losses were a serious matter for an army already deficient in cavalry, but the need for intelligence of Caratacus and his forces was urgent. As far as General Plautius and his staff could discover, Caratacus had retreated up the Tamesis valley with what was left of his army. There the King of the Catuvellauni had set up a number of small forward bases from which detachments of chariots and light horse were raiding into the territory held by the Romans. A number of supply columns had been intercepted and their food and equipment carried off, leaving behind only the smouldering remains of wagons and the butchered bodies of the escorting troops. The Britons had even succeeded in sacking a fort guarding the crossing on the Mead Way, and burning the pontoon bridge erected there.

These raids would have a minimal impact on the ability of the legions to fight the coming campaign, but they boosted the morale of the Britons and this was a concern at headquarters. Many of the tribes who had so eagerly embraced a treaty with Rome the previous autumn were now cooling their relationship. Large numbers of their warriors had joined with Caratacus, sickened by the alacrity with which their leaders had bowed to Rome. Spring would find Plautius and his legions facing a fresh British army.

His experiences the previous year had taught Caratacus much about the strengths and weaknesses of the Roman forces. He had seen the iron firmness of the legions and would no longer hurl his brave warriors headlong onto a wall of shields they could not hope to break. The hit-and-run tactics he was currently employing were a worrying indication of the shape of the coming conflict. The legions might well be masters of the battlefield, but their slowness would make it easy for the British forces to slip round and through them and create merry havoc with their supply lines. The Britons would no longer be so foolish as to stand and fight the legions. Instead they would sidestep each thrust and whittle away at the flank and rear of the Roman forces.

How, Vespasian wondered, could the legions deal with such tactics? Pinpointing and destroying Caratacus and his men would be rather like trying to sink a cork with a hammer. He smiled bitterly at the simile; it was too accurate a comparison for comfort.

'There!' General Plautius pressed his ring down on the last document. The clerk whisked it away from the table and tucked it under his arm with all the others.

'Get those ready for dispatching straightaway. The courier's to board the first ship leaving on the morning tide.'

'Yes, sir. Will that be all for tonight, sir?'

'Yes. As soon as the dispatches are ready, you can send your clerks back to barracks.'

'Thank you, sir.' The clerk saluted and hurried from the office before the general changed his mind. The door closed and Plautius and the commander of the Second Legion were alone in the office.

'Wine?' offered Plautius.

'That'd be welcome, sir.'

31

General Plautius rose stiffly from his chair and stretched his arms as he made his way over to a brass jug set in a small retaining stand over the delicate flame of an oil lamp. Thin wisps of steam curled up from the jug as Plautius lifted the wooden handle, and then poured two generous portions into silver goblets. He returned to his desk and set them down, smiling contentedly as he wrapped his hands round his warm goblet.

'I don't think I could ever come to love this island, Vespasian. Wet and boggy for most of the year, short summers and bitter winters. It's not a fit climate for civilised men. Much as I enjoy soldiering, I'd rather be home.'

Vespasian smiled, and nodded. 'No place like it, sir.'

'I'm determined to make this my last campaign,' continued the general in a more sombre tone. 'I'm getting too old for this life. It's time a new generation of generals took over. I just want to retire to my estate near Pompeii and spend the rest of my days savouring the view out across the bay towards Caprae.'

Vespasian doubted that Emperor Claudius would be keen to dispense with the services of a general of such great experience, but kept his silence so that Plautius might enjoy his reverie. 'Sounds very peaceful, sir.'

'Peaceful?' The general frowned. 'I'm not sure I even know what the word means any more. I've been in the field too long. If I'm honest I'm not really sure if I could stand being retired. Maybe it's just this place. Hardly been here a few months and I'm already sick of the sight of it. And that bloody man Caratacus is tasking me every step of the way. I really thought we'd beaten him once and for all in that last battle.'

Vespasian nodded. It was what they had all thought. Even though the battle had almost been lost, thanks to the Emperor's foolish tactics, the legions had finally overwhelmed and crushed the native warriors. Caratacus, and what remained of his best troops, had fled the field. In the normal course of events the barbarians would have accepted that Rome had defeated them, and sued for peace. But not these confounded Britons. Far better, it seemed to them, to fight on and be slaughtered and have their lands laid waste, than to be pragmatic and come to terms with Rome. Most hostile of all were the Druids.

A handful of them had been taken alive after the last battle and were now held in a special compound under heavy guard. Vespasian felt a tremor of revulsion as he recalled his visit to see the Druids. There were five of them, dressed in dark robes and wearing charms of twisted hair on their wrists. Their own hair was knotted back and stiffened with lime; the reek of it offended the legate's nostrils as he eyed them curiously from the other side of the wooden bars. Each man had a black tattoo of a crescent moon on his forehead. One Druid stood apart from the others, a tall, thin man with a gaunt face and a long white beard. Strikingly, his eyebrows were a mass of thick black bristles, beneath which dark eyes glinted from deep sockets. He did not speak in Vespasian's presence, only stood glowering at the Roman, arms crossed and feet planted slightly apart. For a while Vespasian was content to observe the other Druids, conversing in sullen low tones, before his gaze was drawn back to their leader, who was still staring at him. The Druid's thin lips had parted in a grin, revealing sharp yellow teeth that looked as if they had been filed. A dry rasping laugh stilled his followers who ceased their muttering and turned to look at Vespasian. One by one, they joined in the mocking laughter. Vespasian suffered it for a while, then angrily turned away and marched from the compound.

These Britons were childish fools, decided Vespasian, recalling the demeanour of the tribal leaders that had come before Claudius to pledge their good will following the defeat of Caratacus. Arrogant and stupid, and far too self-indulgent and self-regarding. Already, the emptiness of their words of friendship was becoming obvious, and much more of their blood, and that of the legions, would be shed before this island was conquered.

Such a terrible waste. As always, the worst suffering would be borne by those natives at the very bottom of this barbarian society. Vespasian doubted that they would be unduly concerned if the warrior class that ruled them was swept away and replaced by Rome. All they wanted was a decent harvest to see them through the next winter. That was the limit of their ambition, and while their overlords resisted Rome, their precarious existence would be battered by the tides of war sweeping across the land. Coming from a family only recently elevated to the aristocracy, Vespasian was sensitive to the realities of those who lived beyond the sight of the high and mighty, and readily empathised with their plight. Not that this helped him in any way; he saw it as yet more evidence of his unsuitability for the social position he held. He was quietly envious of the automatic assumption of superiority so evident in the attitude and bearing of those descended from the ancient families of the aristocracy.

Yet it was those very same qualities that had almost resulted in the destruction of Claudius and his army. Rather than take note of the skill with which Caratacus had resisted Rome thus far, the Emperor had

33

dismissed the British commander as little more than a savage, with the most rudimentary grasp of tactics, and none of strategy. Such a woeful underestimation of his enemy had nearly proved fatal. Had Caratacus been in command of a more disciplined army, a different emperor would be ruling in Rome now. Maybe the world would be better off without these perpetually preening aristocrats, mused Vespasian, then quickly dismissed the idea as fanciful.

Having learned the limitations of throwing an untrained army against the disciplined ranks of the legions, Caratacus had reorganised his forces into small flying columns with strict orders to settle for small victories, won as cheaply as possible. In this way Rome might be persuaded that the Britons were too troublesome to bother with and quit the island. But Caratacus had not reckoned on the tenacity of the legions. No matter how long it took, no matter how many men it cost, Britain would be added to the empire – because the Emperor had ordered it. That was the simple truth of things. As long as Claudius lived.

Plautius refilled his cup and stared down into the spiced wine. 'We must still deal with Caratacus. The question is how? He won't want to risk another pitched battle, no matter how many more men he has recruited. And we can't afford to bypass him and move deeper into the heart of this island. He'd bleed us white before the end of the next campaign season. Caratacus must be eliminated before the province can be settled. That is our immediate goal.' Plautius looked up and Vespasian nodded his agreement.

The general reached to the side of the desk for a large vellum roll and carefully spread the map open between himself and the legate. Much of the ink notation was crisp and black, steadily added to over the winter as the cavalry patrols provided more and more information about the lie of the land. Vespasian was impressed by the detail on the map, and said so.

'It's good, isn't it?' responded the general with a smile of satisfaction. 'Copies are being prepared for you and the other legates. I'll expect you to notify my headquarters at once of any additional significant features that you encounter.'

'Yes, sir,' said Vespasian, before he grasped the full implications of the order. 'I take it that the Second will be operating independently of the rest of the army once we've crossed back over the Tamesis?'

'Of course. That's why I'm moving you as soon as possible. I want you and your legion in place to march against Caratacus the moment the campaign season starts.'

'What are the orders?'

General Plautius smiled again. 'I thought you'd appreciate the chance to show me what you and your men can achieve. Very well, it's good to see that you're keen.' He pointed a finger south of the Tamesis estuary. 'Calleva. That's where you'll be based until spring. I've assigned elements of the channel fleet to your command. They'll join you once summer begins. You are to use them to keep you supplied during the campaign, and to sweep the river clear of the enemy. And while you cut Caratacus off from the southern part of the island, I'll be forcing him out of the Tamesis valley to the north of the river. By the end of the year we should have pushed the front forward to a line stretching from the west coast to the fens of the Iceni.

'To that end I'll take the Fourteenth, Ninth and Twentieth Legions north of the Tamesis and advance up the valley. Most of the native raiding columns have come from that direction. Meanwhile, you'll take the Second Legion back across the river and move up along the south bank. You are to fortify any bridges or fords you come across. It will mean crossing into the territory of the Durotriges, but we were going to have to tackle them at some point anyway. Intelligence reports say that they're in possession of quite a few hill forts, some of which you will need to take, and take quickly. Think you can manage that?'

Vespasian considered the prospect. 'Shouldn't present too much of a problem, provided I have enough artillery. More than I have now.'

Plautius smiled. 'That's what all my legates say.'

'Maybe, sir. But if you want me to take those forts, and guard the crossing places on the Tamesis, then I need artillery.'

Plautius nodded. 'Very well. Your request is noted. I'll see what can be done. Now then, back to the plan. The aim is to close Caratacus in bit by bit, so that he must come to battle, or continually fall back – away from our supply lines, and the territory we already occupy. Eventually he'll run out of land and be forced to fight us, or surrender. Any questions?'

Vespasian looked over the map, projecting onto it the movements the general had just described. Strategically the plan looked sound, albeit ambitious, but the prospect of dividing the army was worrying, especially as they no longer had any accurate intelligence about the size of Caratacus's re-formed army. There was no guarantee that Caratacus would not switch back to more conventional operations to take on an isolated legion. If Caratacus was to be prevented from slipping across the Tamesis, there had to be a force ready to deny him any crossing points, and that role had fallen to the Second. Vespasian looked up from the map.

'Why us, sir? Why the Second?'

General Plautius stared at him for a moment before replying. 'I don't have to give you my reasons, Legate. Just my orders.'

'Yes, sir.'

'But you would rather I did?'

Vespasian said nothing, wishing to give the correct impression of soldierly imperturbability, even as his curiosity demanded an answer. He shrugged.

'I see. Well then, Legate, your written orders will be delivered to your headquarters tomorrow morning. If the weather's clear I expect you'll be wanting to make an early start.'

'Yes, sir.'

'Good. Now then, let's finish this wine.' Plautius filled both goblets and raised his for a toast. 'Here's to a quick end to the campaign, and a well-deserved leave in Rome!'

They sipped the lukewarm wine. Plautius grinned at his subordinate. 'I expect you're keen to get back to that wife of yours.'

'I can't wait,' Vespasian replied quietly, conscious of the emotion any mention of his wife caused him. He tried to shift the general's attention away from himself. 'I expect you want to get back to your family just as much.'

'Ah! There I have the advantage over you.' Plautius's eyes glinted mischeivously.

'Sir?'

'I don't have to return to Rome to see them. They're travelling out to join me. As a matter of fact, they should be arriving here any day now . . .'

Chapter Five

A hard frost covered the ground as the Second Legion marched out of the gates of the sprawling camp. The sea of churned mud that had formed beyond the turf ramparts during the wet months of early winter had frozen as hard as rock, and was now covered with a thick blanket of snow that had compacted into ice under the feet of the legionaries. The stumps of felled trees glinted under their sparkling coat of frost, and lined the route leading from the camp towards the west and the distant Tamesis. Above the sharply defined horizon at the legion's back, the sun shone in a sky of intense blue that only the clearest winter day can produce.

So cold was the air that a deep breath caused some of the men to cough as they stepped out with their full loads of equipment. Snow crunched and ice cracked under their nailed boots. The less footsure at the rear of the column slithered and struggled to retain their balance as they followed the dense mass of the legion. Far to the front, cavalry scouts fanned out and trotted across the rolling white landscape, kicking up small showers of glistening snow in their wake. The horses, invigorated by the sharp air and the prospect of exercise, champed at their bits and were frisky. Little clouds of steamy breath rippled into nothingness up and down the columns of men and beasts as they followed the sharply defined shadows slanting across the snow ahead of them.

For Cato, there was an inexpressible joy at being alive at such a moment. After the long months immured in the vast camp with the other legions, with only short patrols, mindless drill and weapons training to dispel the boredom of the daily routine, today's march was a liberation. His eyes swept the landscape, drinking in the stark beauty of the British countryside in late winter. With his cloak wrapped tightly round him, and woven mittens on his hands, the steady pace of the march soon warmed him. Even his feet, which had ached bitterly while the legion assembled at first light, felt comfortable after the first mile on the track. The light-heartedness of his mood was only slightly tempered by the sullen expression on the face of his centurion marching beside him at the head of the Sixth Century of the Fourth Cohort. Macro was already missing the drinking houses and fleshpots of Camulodunum.

The feeling was mutual. At a stroke, nearly a quarter of the customers who had patronised those establishments were now gone. The entrepreneurs who had flooded into the town from the ports of Gaul would soon drift back to the continent once the rest of the army began its preparations to renew the war against Caratacus and his allies. Macro's depression was not wholly caused by the denial of the pleasures offered by purveryors of drink and women. He had not parted from Boudica on very good terms.

After the night when Boudica and Nessa had evaded Prasutagus, her relatives had been determined to restrict any further encounters with Roman soldiers. Only once had Boudica and Macro been able to meet again, and then only very briefly. A quick clinch in the back of a stable while curious ponies and cattle gazed on, munching their winter feed. Macro had attempted to make the most of it – too much so, for the taste of the Iceni maiden. When she sensed his fingers being rather more intimate than she would have preferred, Boudica wriggled from his passionate embrace, leaned back on the straw and slapped him.

'What the fuck was that for?' asked a startled Macro.

'What kind of a girl do you think I am?' she spat back. 'I'm not some cheap tart!'

'Never said you were. Just making the most of the situation. Thought you were up for it.'

'Up for it? What kind of invitation is that?'

Macro shrugged. 'Best I can manage.'

'I see.' Boudica glared at him for a moment, and Macro shifted away from her, sulking and moody. Boudica relented, reached over and stroked his cheek. 'I'm sorry, Macro. I just don't fancy it with all these animals looking on. Bit too public for my taste. It's not that I don't want to, but I'd envisaged something a little more romantic.'

'What's so bloody unromantic about a barn?' grumbled Macro.

And that was where things cooled off rather suddenly. Without another word, Boudica quickly rearranged her tunic and cloak, tucking her breasts back out of sight. With a last angry look at Macro, she rose to her feet and stormed out of the barn. He had been furious to be left in such a manner, and refused, on principle, to run after her. Now he regretted it bitterly. Before Camulodunum dipped out of sight, as the track passed down the far side of a low ridge, Macro glanced back ruefully. She was there, somewhere amongst the snow-covered thatch roofs that lay under the long, low smudge of woodsmoke. He had developed such deep feelings for the feisty native woman that his blood burned with desire at the merest recollection of her physical closeness. He cursed himself for being a romantic fool, and shifted his gaze away from the town and across the glinting helmets of his century, coming to rest on his optio.

'What are you bloody grinning at?'

'Grinning, sir? Not me, sir.'

The ranks of the Second Legion were rife with speculation about their mission. Some men even wondered if the legion was being withdrawn from the island now that Caratacus had been soundly beaten. The more experienced legionaries grunted their contempt at such rumours; the small-scale raids with which the Britons had been plaguing the Roman forces since autumn proved that the natives were not yet defeated. The veterans well knew the nature of the campaign that lay ahead: a vicious and exhausting period of advance and consolidation in the face of a wily foe who knew the lie of the land intimately and who would only emerge from cover to fight when the advantage was fully theirs. The threat of attack would never leave them. As likely as not, those legionaries doomed to die in the campaign would never hear the arrow that killed them, never see the spear thrown, or the dagger thrust from behind as they patrolled their picket lines. The enemy would be no more than shadows skirting round the ponderous legions, rarely seen, but with a presence that was always felt. This kind of warfare was far more difficult than a hard march and a desperate battle. It required a tenacity that only the legions could provide. The prospect of several years of campaigning across the misty wilderness of Britain soured the minds of the veterans as the Second Legion marched towards its new base of operations.

The bitter March weather did not ease for two days, but at least the skies remained clear. At the end of each day, Vespasian insisted on the construction of a 'marching camp in the face of the enemy', entailing the digging of a twelve-foot deep outer ditch and an inner ten-foot earth rampart to enclose the legion and its baggage train. At the end of the day's march, the tired legionaries had to toil into the night to break up the frozen soil with their entrenching tools. Only when the defences were completed could the men, huddled in their cloaks, line up for their steaming ration of barley and salt pork gruel. Later, bellies full, and limbs warmed in the glow of camp fires, the men crept into their goatskin tents and curled up under as many layers of clothing as they had. They re-emerged in the pale blue light of dawn, to face a world blanketed with frost that sparkled along the folds of their tents and down the guy ropes. The men tried to fold into themselves to keep warm against the raw winter mornings until their officers chivvied them into life with orders to strike the tents and prepare for the day's march.

On the third day the fickle weather of the island became more mild and the thick white mantle of snow slowly began to release its hold on the landscape. While the legionaries welcomed the sun's warmth, the meltwater quickly turned the track into a glutinous bog that sucked at the wagon wheels and the booted feet of the infantry. It was with some relief that they marched down the shallow incline into the Tamesis valley on the fourth day and came in sight of the ramparts of the huge army base constructed the previous summer when the legions had first forced their way across the great river. The base was now garrisoned by four cohorts of Batavian auxiliaries. The Batavian infantry had been left at the base while the cavalry squadrons patrolled up the valley, searching out and chasing off any of Caratacus's raiding parties they might encounter. Within the base, supplies had been stockpiled all winter as the shipping from Gaul continued to cross the channel to Rutupiae whenever the weather permitted. From there, smaller barges carried provisions up the Tamesis estuary to the base that straddled the river. The final link in the supply chain was provided by small columns of wagons which made their way under heavy guard to the advance forts, manned by small detachments of auxiliary troops.

This line of defence had been erected by General Plautius to keep Caratacus at bay. A futile attempt, it had turned out. Small bodies of enemy troops regularly slipped through, under cover of darkness, to harass the Roman supply lines and wreak havoc on those tribes who had gone over to the invaders. Once in a while a more daring attack was attempted, and a handful of outposts had had their small garrisons slaughtered. Barely a day passed without some distant smudge against the clear winter sky telling of yet another attack on a supply column, native village or Roman outpost. The commanders of the auxiliary cohorts charged with defending the area could only gaze in despair at the evidence of their failure to contain Caratacus and his men. Not until spring arrived, and the weather improved, could the ponderous weight of the Roman legions be thrown at the Britons once again.

The Second Legion's arrival at the Tamesis camp gave them only a brief respite from the daily grind of constructing a marching camp. The following day, the legate gave the order to cross the bridge to the south bank. Only now did the more strategically minded in the ranks begin to understand what the role of the legion would be in the coming campaign. Once across the river, the legion swung to the west and advanced upriver for two more days along a track that the engineers had crudely surfaced with a mix of tree trunks and thick branches. The track then turned south, and early on the afternoon of the third day the legion arrived in the lee of a long hill. It was from here that the Second Legion would launch their thrust into the territory of the Durotriges once the campaigning season started.

While the baggage train and the artillery carts were painstakingly manoeuvred up the muddy slope, the main body of the legion was marched up to the broad crest of the hill. The order was given to down packs and begin entrenching. While the men of the Sixth Century started on their section of the defensive ditch, Centurion Macro gazed south.

'Here, Cato! Isn't that some kind of town over there?'

His optio joined him and followed his pointing finger. Several miles away some thin trails of smoke eddied up, just visible against the thick gloom of the approaching winter evening. It might be a trick of the light, but Cato thought he could see the faint lines of a substantial native settlement.

'I'd imagine that's Calleva, sir.'

'Calleva? Know anything about it?'

'Got talking to a trader in Camulodunum, sir. He's got a share in a trading post on the south coast. Supplies wine and pottery to the Atrebates. It's their land we're in now. Calleva's their tribal capital, sir. The only place of any size, according to the trader.'

'So what was he doing in Camulodunum?'

'Looking for a chance to expand his business. Like the rest of his kind.'

'Did he tell you anything useful about our friends over there?'

'Useful, sir?'

'Like how loyal they are, what they're like in a fight. That kind of useful.'

'Oh, I see. Only that the Atrebates seemed friendly enough to him and the other traders. And now that the general's reinstalled Verica to their throne, they should be loyal enough to Rome.'

Macro sniffed. 'That'll be the day.'

Chapter Six

The following day was spent building up the fortifications of the main legion camp, and constructing a series of outposts to the north, overlooking the Tamesis, and to the west, to guard against incursions by the Durotriges. The morning after their arrival a party of horsemen approached the camp from the direction of Calleva. The duty cohort was instantly summoned to the walls, and word of the horsemen passed to the legate. Vespasian hurried to the guard tower and, breathing hard from the climb up the ladder, stared down the slope. The small column of horsemen was casually trotting up towards the gate, and just behind the head of the column fluttered a pair of standards, one a British serpent, the other bearing the insignia of a Roman vexillation detached from the Twentieth Legion.

A creaking on the ladder announced the arrival of the legion's senior tribune. Gaius Plinius had recently been appointed to the position, replacing Lucius Vitellius, now well on the road to Rome and a glittering career as a favourite of the Emperor.

'Who is it, sir?'

'Verica, I'd imagine.'

'And our lot?'

'His bodyguard. General Plautius sent a cohort of the Twentieth to lend some weight to Verica's cause when he reclaimed the throne.' Vespasian smiled. 'Just in case the Atrebates decided they'd be happier without their new ruler. Better see what they want.'

The roughly hewn timber gate swung inwards to admit the horsemen. On the muddy ground to one side of the churned track a hastily assembled century lined up to greet the guests. At the head of the column rode a tall man with flowing grey hair. Verica had been an imposing man in his prime, but now age and years of fretting in exile had reduced him to a frail, stooping figure who wearily dismounted from his horse to greet Vespasian.

'Welcome, sire!' Vespasian saluted, and after the briefest hesitation

Plinius followed his legate's example, swallowing his distaste for such deference to a mere native, albeit a king of his people. Verica walked stiffly up to the legate and clasped the forearm extended towards him.

'Greetings, Legate! I trust the winter has been kind to you and your men?'

'It hasn't quite finished with us.' Vespasian nodded at the slick mud lying all around them.

'Goes with the turf!' Verica grinned, pleased with his joke. Then he turned back to the horsemen, whose excitable beasts were champing and snorting at the unfamiliar surroundings. 'Centurion! If you'd be good enough to give the word for the men to dismount. Then please join us!'

Beside the vexillation standard bearer a Roman officer saluted and quickly gave the order.

Vespasian turned to his senior tribune. 'Plinius, see to it that they're given something to warm them up.'

'Yes, sir.'

'My thanks, Legate.' Verica smiled. 'I'd appreciate a drink as well. I seem to recall a certain fondness for Falernian you had when we last met.'

'Indeed, sire. I still have a drop.' Vespasian forced himself to smile. Only a meagre supply of this superior vintage remained in his private stores, and he resented having to share it. But his orders from General Plautius had been explicit: every effort was to be made to remain on the best terms with the allies Rome had won amongst the tribes of this island. The success or failure of the invasion was finely balanced due to Rome's parsimony in allocating troops to the task. Plautius dared not advance without being sure that his flanks were guarded by tribes loyal to Rome. So every man in his army, regardless of rank, was to behave with the greatest courtesy to those tribes allied to Rome, or suffer the wrath of the general. That included supplying Falernian to those who judged drink purely by its capacity to inebriate.

'I assume you already know Centurion Publius Pollius Albinus?' Verica waved a hand at the officer striding towards them. The centurion snapped a salute at the legate and stood to attention at the king's shoulder.

'Centurion.' Vespasian nodded a greeting, before turning back to his guest.

'Albinus is one of our best. I trust he has been giving you good service.'

'Can't complain.'

Vespasian glanced at Albinus, but the centurion's expression didn't flicker at the less than fulsome praise, justifying the general's selection of him for a duty that required a high degree of diplomatic tact and tolerance.

'How's the training of your men coming on, sire?'

'Well enough.' Verica shruged, clearly not terribly concerned by Rome's efforts to provide his regime with a stable backbone. 'I'm too old to take much interest in military matters. But I dare say Centurion Albinus is doing a good job. With the quality of manpower provided by the Atrebates you shouldn't have too much trouble producing an effective body of men to enforce my will. Eh, Centurion?'

'Can't complain, sire.'

Vespasian shot him a warning glance, but the centurion stared straight ahead, expressionless.

'Yes, well, I think we might retire to the warmer comforts of my tents. If you'd follow me.'

Seated around a bronze brazier, a fresh log crackling on the glowing embers, Vespasian and his two guests sipped wine from silver goblets and soaked up the warmth. Around them, clumps of mud soiled the fine patterns of the woven rugs scattered across the wooden floor panels, and Vespasian inwardly cursed the need to be so utterly faithful to his commander's orders concerning hospitality towards the natives.

'How is General Plautius?' asked Verica, leaning closer to the brazier.

'He's fine, sire. He sends his warm regards and trusts that you are in good health.'

'Oh, I'm sure he is most concerned about that!' Verica chuckled. 'It wouldn't be very helpful of me if I went and died. The Atrebates shed no tears when Caratacus kicked me out, and hardly welcomed my return, accompanied by Roman bodyguards, with affection. Whoever succeeds me might do well to claim allegiance with Caratacus rather than your Emperor Claudius, if he wants to win the hearts of our people.'

'Would the Atrebates really want to risk the terrible consequences of allowing such a man to claim your throne?'

'My throne is mine because your Emperor says so,' came the quiet response.

Vespasian thought he detected a trace of bitterness in the old man's tone. If Verica had been younger, it would have caused the legate some concern. But old age seemed to have bred a desire for peace and quashed the fiery ambition that had fuelled the glittering achievements of Verica's youth. The British king sipped his wine before continuing.

'Rome will have peace with the Atrebates as long as Centurion Albinus and his men are here to ensure that the Emperor's word is respected. But with Caratacus at large, and freely slipping through your legions to punish those tribes whose leaders have gone over to Rome, you can understand why some of my people might challenge my loyalty to Rome.'

'Of course I understand that, sire. But surely you can make them see that the legions will eventually crush Caratacus. There can be no other outcome. I'm certain of it.'

'Oh really?' Verica raised his eyebrows, and shook his head mockingly. 'Nothing in this life is certain, Legate. Nothing. Perhaps least of all the defeat of Caratacus.'

'He will be defeated soon enough.'

'Then see to it, or I cannot answer for the loyalty of my people. Particularly with those bloody Druids stirring things up.'

'Druids?'

Verica nodded. 'There have been a number of raids on small villages and trading settlements on the coast. At first we thought it might be a small band of the Durotriges. That is, until we heard a more detailed report. It appears that these raiders were not content with a little bit of theft and slaughter. Nothing was spared. Not one man, woman or infant. Not even their livestock. Every house, every hut, no matter how mean, was put to the torch. And worse was to come.' Verica paused to take another draught of his wine, and Vespasian noted that the hand clasping the goblet quavered. Verica drained the cup, and quickly gestured to Albinus to refill it. He nodded only when the red wine had almost reached the rim.

'You'd better tell him, Albinus. After all, you were there. You saw it.'

'Yes, sire.'

Vespasian switched his attention to the centurion, a scarred and weathered man well on in his career. Albinus was thin, but the muscle in his forearms was clearly defined. He had the look of a man who would not shock easily, and spoke with the brisk tonelessness of a hardened professional.

'After word of the first raids reached Calleva, the king here sent me and one century down to investigate, sir.'

'Only one century?' Vespasian was horrified. 'Hardly the kind of caution the army encourages, Centurion.'

'No, sir,' replied Albinus with a slight tilt of this head towards Verica who was busy taking another deep gulp of the legate's Falernian. 'But I thought it would be best if the rest of the cohort remained to look after the king's interests.'

'Well yes, quite. Carry on.'

'Yes, sir. Two day's march from Calleva we found the remains of a village. I scouted thoroughly before we approached. It was like King Verica says, not a thing left alive, not a single building left standing. Only, we didn't find more than a handful of bodies, all men, sir.'

'Must have taken the others prisoner.'

'That's what I thought, sir. There was some snow on the ground, and we could follow their tracks easily enough.' Albinus paused to look directly at the legate. 'I had no intention of trying anything stupid, sir. Just wanted to see where they'd come from, then report back.'

'Fair enough.'

'So we followed the tracks for another day, until just before dusk we caught sight of some smoke rising above a small ridge. I thought it might be another village being sacked. We crept up the slope, quiet like, and then I ordered the men to stay back while I went on alone. At first I could hear women and children screaming, then the fire itself – not far over the crest of the ridge. It was well into dusk when I had crept far enough forward to see what was going on.' He paused, not quite sure how to continue under the scrutiny of his superior, and quickly glanced at Verica, who had stopped drinking and eyed the centurion with a fearful expression, even though he had heard the tale before.

'Well, spit it out, man!' ordered Vespasian, in no mood for any dramatics.

'Yes, sir. The Druids had built themselves a huge wicker man, made from twisted withies and branches. It was hollow, and they'd packed it with all the women and children. It was well ablaze by the time I could see what was going on. Some of them who were inside were still screaming. Not for much longer though . . .' He pursed his lips, and his gaze dropped for a moment. 'The Druids watched for a while longer, then mounted up and rode off, into the night. Like shadows, in black robes they were. So, I rejoined my men and we marched straight back to Calleva to report.'

'These Druids. In black, you say?'

'Yes, sir.'

'Any other distinctive features, or insignia?'

'It was getting dark, sir.'

'But there was a fire.'

'I know, sir. I was watching it . . .'

47

'All right.' Vespasian could understand that, but it was disappointing that a veteran centurion could lose his attention to the important details so readily. He turned to Verica. 'I've read about the Druids' human sacrifices, but there must be more to this. A warning of the fate waiting for those who side with Rome, perhaps?'

'Perhaps.' Verica nodded. 'Nearly every one of the Druid cults has gone over to Caratacus. And now, it seems, even the Lodge of the Dark Moon.'

'The Dark Moon?' Vespasian frowned for an instant, before the memory of the prisoner compound outside Camulodunum resolved into a vivid image in his mind. 'These Druids bear a dark crescent on their foreheads, don't they? A kind of tattoo. A black moon.'

'You know of them?' Verica's eyebrows rose.

'I've met some.' Vespasian smiled. 'Guests of General Plautius. We took them prisoner after Caratacus was defeated outside Camulodunum. Now I think of it, they were the only Druids we took prisoner. The others were all dead, mostly by their own hand.'

'I'm not surprised. You Romans are not renowned for your tolerance of Druids.'

'Depends on who is Emperor at the time,' Vespasian responded irritably. 'But if Druids prefer death to capture, why did the Dark Moon allow themselves to be taken?'

'They believe they are the chosen ones. They are not allowed to take their own lives. They're the servants of Cruach – the night-bringer. In time, so the legend goes, he will rise and smite the day into a thousand pieces and will rule a world of night and shadow forever.'

'Sounds nasty.' Vespasian smiled. 'Can't say I care to meet this Cruach.'

'His servants are terrible enough, as Albinus has discovered.'

'Indeed. I wonder why the tribes of this island tolerate them.'

'Fear,' Verica admitted readily. 'If Cruach ever comes, the suffering of those who worship him will be as nothing to the eternal torments of those who have abused his servants and made light of his name.'

'I see. And where do you stand on this, sire?'

'I believe what it is important for my people to think I believe. So I offer prayers to Cruach, along with the other gods, as often as I need to. But his priests, these Druids, are a different matter. As long as they raid my villages and slaughter my people I can portray them as extremists. Perverted fanatics worshipping the most terrible of our gods. I doubt if many of the Atrebates, or any other tribe, would shed any tears over the ruthless suppression of this particular lodge of Druids.' He looked away from Vespasian, into the heart of the glowing fire. 'I hope Rome will see to it as soon as possible.'

'I have no specific orders concerning Druids,' countered Vespasian. 'But the general has made it clear that he wants your lands to be secured before the spring campaign begins. If that means dealing with these Dark Moon Druids, then our interests coincide.'

'Good.' Verica eased himself to his feet, and the Romans politely rose from their seats. 'Now, I'm tired, and I'm returning to Calleva with my men. I expect you'll want a word with the centurion.'

'Yes, sire. If that's no trouble.'

'None. I'll see you later then, Albinus.'

'Yes, sire.' The centurion saluted as Vespasian led his guest out of the tent, responding to the British king's leave-taking with as much display of respectful formality as possible. Then Vespasian returned, casting a resentful eye into the empty jug resting on the table, before waving the centurion back into his chair.

'I take it that Verica is finding the resumption of his rule something of a challenge.'

'I suppose so, sir. We've not had too many problems with the Atrebates themselves. They seem more sullen than rebellious. The Catuvellauni were pretty hard masters. The change in rule might not have improved matters much, but it hasn't made things worse.'

'Wait until they meet some Roman land agents,' muttered Vespasian.

'Well, yes, sir.' The centurion shrugged; the depredations of the civil bureaucracy following in the wake of the legions was not his concern. 'Anyway, Calleva, and the immediate area are pacified. I keep two centuries out on local patrols all the time. A third is doing a wider sweep through the villages that border on the Durotriges.'

'Have any patrols encountered the Druids?'

The centurion shook his head. 'Apart from that time I saw them, we've never come into contact, sir. All we've found is the remains of the villages and the bodies. They're mounted, of course, and that means they have us at an immediate disadvantage since pursuit is out of the question.'

'Then I'll lend you half my mounted force while we're stationed near Calleva. I need the rest for my own scouting.'

Sixty of the legion's cavalry scouts were not going to make much of an impact on the Druids' raids, but it was better than nothing and Albinus nodded his thanks.

'How's the training of the locals coming on?'

A flicker of despair showed in the centurion's expression as the mask of stolid professionalism momentarily slipped.

'I wouldn't say it's hopeless, sir. But I wouldn't say I'm very hopeful either.'

'Oh?'

'They're tough enough,' Albinus said grudgingly. 'Tougher than many of the men who serve with the eagles. But the moment you try and make them drill in a formal and disciplined way, it's an utter fucking shambles. Pardon my Gallic, sir. They can't co-ordinate; it's every man for himself in a mad charge at the enemy. About the only thing they will do is individual weapons practice. Even then they use the swords we've equipped them with like bloody meat cleavers. Keep telling 'em that six inches of point is worth any amount of edge, but I'm not getting through. They just won't be trained, sir.'

'Won't be?' Vespasian raised his eyebrows. 'Surely a man of your experience can make them train? You've dealt with difficult cases before.'

'Difficult cases, sir. But not difficult races.'

Vespasian nodded. All the Celts he had met shared the same arrogant belief in their culture's innate superiority, and affected a profound contempt for what they considered the unmanly refinements of Roman and Greek civilisations. These Britons were the worst of the lot. Too stupid by half, Vespasian concluded.

'Do what you can, Centurion. If they won't learn from their betters they'll never be a threat to us.'

'Yes, sir.' Albinus's gaze dropped despondently.

The muffled blaring of a signal trumpet sounded beyond the tent. Moments later they could hear orders being shouted. The centurion glanced towards the legate but Vespasian refused to be seen as a man who would be ruffled by any stray distraction. He leaned back in his chair to address the centurion.

'Very well, Centurion. I'll send a report back to the general to let him know about your situation, and these Druid raids. In the meantime, you're to carry on with the training, and keep the patrols going. We might not keep the Druids out but at least they'll know we're looking for them. The scouts should make that job easier. Anything else to tell me?'

'No, sir.'

'Dismissed.'

The centurion picked up his helmet, saluted and marched smartly out of the tent.

Vespasian was aware that the shouting had increased, and the chinking of weapons and armour indicated that a large body of men was on the move. It was difficult to resist the impulse to rush from the tent to discover what was happening, but he would be damned if he allowed himself to behave like some excitable junior tribune on his first day in the army. He forced himself to pick up a scroll and start reading the latest strength reports. Footsteps sounded on the floorboards immediately outside the tent.

'Is the legate there?' someone shouted to the sentries guarding the entrance flap to Vespasian's tent. 'Then let me pass.'

The folds of leather parted and Plinius, the senior tribune, pushed through, panting for breath. He swallowed anxiously. 'Sir! You have to see this.'

Vespasian looked up from the lines of figures on the scroll. 'Calm yourself, Tribune. This is no way for a senior officer to act.'

'Sir?'

'You don't go belting about the camp unless there is the gravest of emergencies.'

'Yes, sir.'

'And are we in grave danger, Tribune?'

'No, sir.'

'Then keep a cool head and set a good example for the rest of the legion.'

'Yes, sir. I'm sorry, sir.'

'All right then. What have you come to report that is so urgent?'

'There are some men approaching the camp, sir.'

'How many?'

'Two men, sir. And a few more are holding back at the treeline.'

'Two men? So what's all the fuss about?'

'One of them's a Roman . . .'

Vespasian waited patiently for a moment. 'And the other?'

'I don't know, sir. I've never seen anything like it before.'

Chapter Seven

The Sixth Century had pulled the second watch of the day. After a hurried breakfast of steaming porridge, they relieved the century patrolling the walls of the fortified camp. The centurion coming off duty briefly informed Cato of the arrival of the horsemen from Calleva. Mid-morning sunlight streamed over the ramparts. Cato squinted, having climbed up from the cold shadows around the neat lines of tents. He was forced to shield his eyes for a moment.

'Nice morning, Optio!' a legionary greeted him. 'Might actually get warm today.'

Cato turned to the man; a large, round youth with a jolly face and a handful of crooked teeth that looked like the remains of one of the stone circles the legion had marched past the previous summer. Being thin with little fat on him, thanks to his nervous disposition, Cato found it difficult to keep warm and was still shivering inside his tightly belted wool cloak. He simply nodded at the legionary, not wanting to let the man see his teeth chatter. The legionary was one of the recent replacements, a Gaul by the name of Horatius Figulus. Figulus was an adequate enough soldier, and the youngster's cheerful nature had made him popular with the century.

With a sudden jolt of awareness, Cato recalled that Figulus was the same age as he was. The same age, and yet the few months longer he had served with the eagles made him look upon this recruit with the cool gaze of a veteran. Certainly, a casual onlooker might well imagine the optio to be a veteran; the scars of the terrible burns he had suffered the previous summer were clearly visible. And yet the hair on his cheeks was still so sparse that it would be risible for him to even consider a shave. Figulus, by contrast, shared the hairy physiognomy of his Celt forebears; the fine growth of light hair across his cheeks and chin needed almost daily attention from a carefully whetted blade.

'Watch this, Optio!' Figulus leaned his javelin against the rampart and fumbled inside his cloak for a moment, before pulling out a walnut. 'I've been practising this one all week.'

Cato stifled a groan. Ever since the century had been entertained by an itinerent Phoenician conjurer several weeks earlier, young Figulus had attempted to copy the conjuror's repertoire of tricks – with little success. The would-be magician was holding out the walnut for his inspection.

'What's this?'

Cato stared at him a moment, and then rolled his eyes to the heavens with a faint shake of his head.

'It's an ordinary walnut, right, Optio?'

'If you say so,' replied Cato through gritted teeth.

'Now as we know, walnuts are not in the habit of just up and disappearing. Am I right?'

Cato nodded, once.

'Now watch!' Figulus closed his hands and flourished them about each other as he chanted the sound that best approximated the spells of the Phoenician. *'Ogwarz farevah!'* With a final sweep he flicked his empty hands open in front of his optio's face. Out of the corner of one eye Cato saw the walnut sailing up in an arc before it dropped over the side of the rampart.

'Where do you suppose that walnut has gone?' Figulus winked. 'Well, let me show you!'

He reached behind Cato's ear, and frowned. Cato sighed in exasperation. The legionary tilted his head to examine the space behind Cato's ear.

'Half a mo, the bloody thing's supposed to be there.'

Cato slapped his hand aside. 'Get on duty, Figulus. You've wasted enough time.'

With a last confused glance at Cato's ear, the legionary took up his javelin and faced out across the white wilderness of Atrebate territory. Although frost had gilded the world with its sparkling lace, the snow underneath was slowly melting away and clear ground showed on the south-facing slopes of the surrounding hills. The recruit's face showed a mixture of embarrassment and confusion and Cato was moved to take pity on him.

'Nice try, Figulus. Just needs a little more practice.'

'Yes, Optio.' Figulus grinned, and Cato instantly wished he hadn't – purely on aesthetic grounds. 'More practice, I'll see to it.'

'Right, fine. But that's for later. Keep an eye out for the enemy meanwhile.'

'Yes, sir!'

Cato left him and continued his rounds of the sector of the fort entrusted to him. Over the other side, Centurion Macro was supervising the rest of the century. Across the ranks of tent ridges basking in the glow of the rising sun, Cato could see the short powerful figure strutting along the opposite rampart, hands clasped behind his back, his head turned towards the distant Tamesis, and Camulodunum far beyond. Cato smiled as he imagined where his centurion's thoughts lay. In spite of his laddish, hard-drinking, womanising nature, Macro had let the statuesque Boudica get under his skin. It had never occurred to the centurion that a woman could be such a complete companion, one who equalled him in almost every sphere of manly behaviour, and the affection he had for her was all too apparent to his optio, and those other men who knew him best. While other centurions and optios winked at each other and joked in low voices about life lived under the thumb of such a woman, Cato was quietly pleased for his centurion.

'Call out the guard!' cried a voice.

Cato instantly turned in the direction of the shout and saw Figulus pointing away to the west, where a forest crept up the far end of the ridge. The angle of the rampart obscured Cato's view. He swore, and ran round the walkway to Figulus's position.

'What's up?'

'Men, sir! There!' Figulus jabbed his finger along the crest of the ridge towards the forest. Cato saw nothing unusual as his eyes swept the landscape.

'Use your drill!' he shouted. 'Indicate the direction properly!'

The recruit swung his javelin up and carefully sighted along it in the direction of the forest. 'There, sir.'

Cato moved behind Figulus and looked along the javelin's length. Past the wavering point, amid the trees at the edge of the forest, dark figures on horseback slowly emerged from the sylvan shadows within and picked their way onto the snow-patched open ground before the legion's ramparts. There they halted; ten men on horse, clothed in black, heads hidden in great hoods.

All around Cato the rest of the centuries from the stand-to cohort piled up onto the ramparts and dispersed along this side of the fortified camp, armed and ready to meet any sudden attack. A trumpet was blowing the signal for the cohort, and Macro sprinted along the walkway to join them.

The distant horsemen parted, and from within the group a man on the ground staggered forward, his arms tightly bound behind him. A

54

rope curved up from a halter round his neck and into the hand of the rider walking his beast alongside. The mounted man, like his companions, was thickly robed in black and wore a strange headpiece that bore an elaborate pair of antlers that made him look like a thin tree stripped for winter. The two figures approached the fort, the man on foot stumbling to retain his balance without choking on the tether held tightly by his captor.

'What's going on?' Macro had arrived, breathing hard. 'Who are they?'

'Don't know, sir.'

'Who called out the guard?'

'Figulus, sir.'

Macro turned and looked for the recruit. 'Figulus! Over here! Smartly does it, lad!'

Figulus doubled along the rampart and drew up in front of his centurion with a thud as he grounded his javelin and stood stiffly at attention. Macro surveyed him with a harsh expression. 'Did you call out the guard cohort?'

'Yes, sir.' The legionary steeled himself for a stiff bollocking from his centurion. 'Sorry, sir.'

'Sorry? What are you fucking sorry for, lad? You've done well. Now back to your position.'

It took a moment for the slow-witted youngster to realise that he had been praised, and his face split into a gap-toothed grin.

'Today, Figulus! Today!'

'Oh, right, sir!' He turned and trotted away, leaving his centurion shaking his head in thin-lipped wonder at the quality of some of the men he had been forced to take into his century to bring it up to strength. Beyond Figulus he caught sight of the red crest of a tribune bobbing above the cluster of helmets, brightly gilded in the sunlight. Plinius pushed his way through the throng on the rampart and leaned up against the palisade, staring at the two figures now little more than half a mile from the outer ditch. The man on foot wore the tattered remains of a red tunic fringed with gold thread. Plinius turned and caught sight of Macro.

'That man in front's a Roman! Pass the word for the cavalry scouts to be mounted and ready for pursuit. I'm going to get the legate.'

'Yes, sir!' Macro turned to Cato. 'You heard him. Go find the scouts' centurion and give him his orders. I'll take charge of the men up here. Can't have them behaving like a bunch of louts at a chariot race.'

As Macro started bawling out curses and orders to the men milling along the rampart, Cato made for the stables, up by the legate's tent. By the time he returned, the men on the wall were evenly dispersed and watching the distant figures making their way across the snow towards the fort. The legate and the breathless senior tribune had arrived moments before, and were staring silently at the spectacle.

'What the bloody hell has that man got on his head?' muttered Vespasian.

'Antlers, sir.'

'I can see they're bloody antlers. But why has he got them on his head? Must be awkward.'

'Yes, sir. Some kind of religious apparatus.' Plinius shrank back from the glare his superior shot at him. 'Probably . . .'

Just beyond the range of slingshot, the horseman yanked hard on the halter and those on the wall could clearly hear the sharp cry of pain from his prisoner. The rider climbed down from his horse and tossed the halter aside. The Roman sank to his knees. He was clearly exhausted, and his head slumped forward onto his breast. But his respite was momentary. The rider struck him on the head and pointed towards the fort. The men on the rampart could hear shouted words, but could make no sense of them. The Roman raised his head, steadied himself and cried out to those on the wall.

'Hear me! . . . I have a message for the commander of this legion . . . Is he there?'

Vespasian cupped his hands and called back, 'Speak! Who are you?'

'Valerius Maxentius . . . prefect of the naval squadron at Gesoriacum.'

The men on the rampart gasped in surprise that so senior an officer was in the hands of the Druids, and anxious exchanges rippled out along the palisade.

'Silence!' Vespasian roared. 'The next man to speak will be flogged! Centurion, make sure you get their names!'

'Yes, sir.'

Beyond the wall, Maxentius was calling out to them again, his voice strained and thin, deadened by the snow lying on the ground. 'I have been told to speak for the Druids of the Dark Moon . . . My ship was wrecked on the coast, and the survivors, a woman, her children and myself, were taken by a Durotrigan raiding party . . . They handed us over to the Druids. In exchange for the release of these prisoners, the Druids want some of their comrades returned to them. Five Druids of the first ring were taken by the general last summer . . . This man, the

High Priest of the Dark Moon, is their leader. He gives you until the Feast of the First Budding – thirty days from now – to respond to his demand . . . If the Druids are not released by the time of the feast, he will burn his prisoners alive as a sacrifice to Cruach.'

Vespasian recalled the words of Centurion Albinus and shuddered. The thought of his own wife and son screaming amid crackling flames filled his mind's eye and his fingers gripped the palisade tightly as he fought off the terrible image.

The rider leaned down, close to Maxentius's head, and appeared to be saying something to him. Then he stepped back and parted his black cloak. Maxentius called out to them once more.

'The Druid wishes you to have a . . . token of his determination in this matter!' Behind him, something flashed in the sunlight. The Druid had pulled a huge, broad-bladed sickle from the folds of his cloak. He gripped it with both hands, braced his feet widely, and swung the sickle back.

At the last moment, Maxentius sensed the terrible fate the Druid intended for him, and started to twist round. The sickle flashed through the air, into and through the side of the prefect's neck. It was so quickly done that for a moment some of those watching from the ramparts thought the Druid must have missed. Then the prefect's head rolled to one side and fell into the snow. An arterial spray gushed from the stump of his neck and splattered the white ground. The Druid wiped his bloodied blade in the snow. Then, sheathing it beneath his cloak, he kicked the prefect's torso over, casually mounted his horse, and spurred it back towards his comrades waiting at the edge of the forest.

Chapter Eight

Vespasian swung round, hands cupping his mouth as he bellowed, 'Send out the scouts! Get me those Druids!'

The legion's mounted men had not seen the beheading and were more alert than their stunned comrades lining the palisade. In a moment the gate was open and a dozen mounted scouts galloped out. The decurion quickly spotted the Druids on the fringe of the forest and gave the order to charge. Pounding hooves plucked up sprays of snow as the scouts fanned out, wool capes whipping out behind them. The Druid who had killed Maxentius turned his antlered head to look, then kicked his heels into the flanks of his mount, spurring his beast towards his comrades who were already melting back into the shadows of the forest.

Vespasian did not linger to observe the pursuit; he ran to the gate and out across the softly crunching snow towards the body of the navy prefect. Behind him followed the men of the Sixth Century, urged on by Macro, who feared for the safety of his commander. But some way short of the body the legionaries hung back, disgust and superstition making them uneasy, for the Druids were held in awe and dread. Many of the folk tales heard at the knees of their fathers had featured the dark and sinister powers of the Celtic magicians, and the legionaries were loath to approach too closely. They stood in silence, their breath swirling mistily in the cold air; the only sound was the distant thrum of hooves and crash of undergrowth as the cavalry scouts chased after the Druids.

Vespasian stood over the torso, lying twisted on its side. Blood still oozed from the severed blood vessels of the neck. Maxentius had worn only a belted tunic, the tattered remnants of which were now drenched and dark. A large leather pouch had been tied to his belt. Biting back the nausea that was filling his throat from the pit of his stomach, Vespasian leaned down and fumbled with the knot that held the pouch. His fingers trembled as he tried to work the cord free. He was desperate to get away from the blood glistening on the snow, and the awful presence of the prefect's head, scarcely six feet away. Mercifully, the head had rolled in such a way that it faced away from the legate and all he was aware of at the periphery of his vision was the dark, matted hair.

At last the knot slipped free. Vespasian stood up and stepped back several paces before he examined the pouch. A drawstring held the end closed and in the soft folds only a few lumps indicated that it contained anything at all. He tried not to imagine what the Druids might have left in the pouch, and forced himself to loosen the drawstring. In the dark interior of the pouch he saw a dull gleam of gold and reached inside. His fingers closed on a scrap of cloth and a pair of rings, which he drew out into the sunlight. One was quite small and plain, but broad. Inscribed on the inside, in neat block capitals, was the legend 'Filius Plautii'. The other ring was far more ornate, and bore a large onyx stone on which lay a cameo of an elephant, bone white against the polished background of dark brown. The cloth was finely spun wool, maybe from the hem of a toga. Along one edge ran a thin line of purple dye, the ancient sign that the wearer came from a senatorial family.

Vespasian suddenly felt very cold, far more so than the late winter morning warranted. Cold and sick, as the connection between the prefect and the contents of the bag registered. He must send a message to General Plautius at once. Carefully he placed the cloth and the rings back in the pouch and cleared his throat. He looked up at Macro.

'Centurion!'

'Yes, sir!'

'Have the body taken back to camp. Take it to the hospital tent. I want it prepared for cremation as soon as possible. And make sure that it . . . he, is treated with respect.'

'Of course, sir.'

The legate walked towards the gate, head down in silent contemplation as he thought through the awful implications of what he had discovered in the pouch. The general's family were now in the hands of the Druids. The same Druids who were spreading such terror through the border villages and trading settlements of the Atrebates. How had they been taken? The Britons boasted no ships that could overwhelm those of the imperial navy. In any case, Maxentius and his passengers would have been making the crossing from Gesoriacum to Rutupiae, well over a hundred miles from the land of the Durotriges and their Druid allies. A storm must have blown the ship far off course. But why hadn't the prefect made an attempt to reach the shores of the Atrebates, rather than let himself be swept so far down the coast to territory ruled by enemies of Rome? For an instant Vespasian cursed the prefect for his folly, before such unworthy feelings for a man who had died so terribly made him feel guilty. Perhaps Maxentius had tried to beach his ship on friendly soil after all, but had been prevented from doing so by the wildness of the storm.

The faint noises of pursuit from the forest abruptly took on a new note. Distant shouts and screams were accompanied by the sharp ring of clashing weapons. Vespasian, and the legionaries of the Sixth Century, turned towards the forest. The sounds of fighting quickly intensified and then died away.

'Form square!' Macro bellowed. 'Close order.'

The men reacted at once, and hurried into formation around the body of the prefect. Vespasian pushed his way into the centre and drew his sword. He caught Macro's eye and motioned towards the body and head still lying on the snow. The centurion turned to his men.

'You two! Figulus and Sertorius! Over here.'

The selected men broke ranks and trotted over to their centurion.

'Figulus, put him on your shield. The two of you'll have to carry him back to the gate. I'll carry the other shield.'

Figulus looked down at the prefect's bloody body with a look of disgust on his face.

'Don't worry, lad, the blood will come out of the shield lining easily enough. It'll just need a good scrub. Now get to it!'

While the two men bent to their grisly work, Macro turned to Cato. 'You can carry the head.'

'The head?' Cato went pale. 'Me?'

'Yes, you. Pick it up,' Macro snapped, then recalled the legate's presence. 'And, er, make sure you carry it with respect.'

He ignored Cato's glare and hurried over to the legate who was now standing at the edge of the square to get a better look at the forest.

Gritting his teeth, Cato leaned down and reached out a hand towards the prefect's head. At the first touch of the dark wavy hair his fingers recoiled. He swallowed nervously and forced himself to grasp enough hair to ensure a good grip. Then he slowly straightened up, holding the head away from his body, face out. Even so, the glutinous tendrils of sinew and clotting blood hanging from the severed neck made the bile rise in his throat and Cato quickly looked away.

A riderless horse burst out of the trees and galloped back towards the Second Legion's camp. Two more followed, and then another, this time with a scout in the saddle, bent low and kicking his heels, urging his beast towards the Sixth Century. Nothing else emerged from the trees, which remained still and silent.

'I shouldn't have ordered a pursuit,' Vespasian said quietly.

'No, sir.'

The legate turned towards Macro, eyebrows clenched together angrily at the implied criticism. But he knew the centurion was right. He should have thought. Vespasian felt sickened by the ease with which he had ordered the scouts to their doom.

Just short of the shields of the Sixth Century the surviving scout savagely reined in his horse, which reared up with a terrified whinny and kicked up a spray of snow. The scout released the reins and tumbled from his saddle.

'He's wounded!' shouted Macro. 'Get him behind the shields! Quickly!'

The nearest men ran out, grabbed the scout and dragged him inside the square. He slumped down, clasping a hand to his stomach where the bloody tear in his tunic revealed a long slash, cutting deep enough to expose some intestines. Macro knelt down to examine the injury. He grabbed the hem of the scout's cloak and made a cut in it with his dagger. Then he sheathed the blade and tore off a broad strip. Hurriedly, he worked it round the scout and tied the ends tightly. The man cried out and then clamped his teeth shut.

'There! That'll do until we can get him to the surgeons.'

'What happened?' Vespasian bent over the scout. 'Report, man! What happened to you?'

'Sir, there was scores of 'em . . . waiting for us inside the forest . . . We was following them down a trail . . . then suddenly they came at us on all sides, shrieking like wild animals . . . Didn't stand a chance. . . Cut us to pieces.' For a moment the scout's eyes widened in terror at the vivid memory of the terrifying enemy. Then his eyes refocused on the legate. 'I was at the back of the column, sir. Soon as I saw we'd had it, I tried to turn my mount. But the trail was narrow, my horse was scared and wouldn't turn. Then one of them Druids burst out of the forest and swung his sickle into me . . . I got him with my spear, sir! Got him good!' The scout's eyes gleamed with savage triumph before twisting shut as a wave of pain wracked him.

'That's enough now, lad,' Vespasian said gently. 'Save the rest for your official report, once the surgeons have sorted you out.'

Eyes tightly clenched, the scout nodded.

'Centurion, give me a hand here.' Vespasian reached under the scout's shoulders and carefully lifted the man. 'Help me get him onto my back.'

'On your back, sir? Shall I get one of the men to do it instead, sir?'

'Damn it, man! I'll carry him.'

Macro shrugged, and did as he was told. The scout put his arms round the legate's neck and Vespasian leaned forward and supported the man's legs.

'That's it. Macro! Detail a man to lead that horse, then let's get moving.'

Macro gave the order for the century to move towards the camp. In close formation, the century's pace was necessarily slow, however much the men wished to hurry back to the shelter of the camp. In the centre of the square the legate staggered under his burden. To one side Figulus and Sertorius carried the body of Maxentius on Figulus's shield. Beside them walked Cato, staring directly ahead, his aching arm outstretched to keep the head he held as far from his body as possible. Macro, marching at the rear of the square, kept looking back towards the forest, watching for any sign of the Druids and their followers. But nothing moved along the dark treeline and the forest remained absolutely silent.

Chapter Nine

Three days later the snow had almost melted and only the odd patch still gleamed in hollows and crevices where the low winter sun could not reach. The first days of March brought a little more warmth to the air and the rutted track became slick with mud beneath the booted feet of the Fourth Cohort. They were marching south from Calleva, patrolling along the border with the Durotriges, in an attempt to discourage any more raids. The mission was more of a gesture of Roman support for the Atrebates than a realistic attempt to discourage the Durotriges and their sinister Druid allies. The reports reaching Verica of the devastation being wreaked on the smaller villages had so unnerved him that he had begged Vespasian to act. So the Fourth Cohort and a squadron of scouts, accompanied by a guide, were dispatched on a tour through the frontier villages and settlements to demonstrate that the threat from the Durotriges was being taken seriously.

At first the villagers were nervous of the strange uniforms and foreign tongues of the legionaries, but the cohort had been ordered to behave in an exemplary manner. Shelter and rations were paid for in gold coin and the Romans respectfully observed local customs, which were explained to them by Verica's guide, Diomedes. He was an agent acting for a trader in Gaul and had been living amongst the Atrebates for many years. He spoke their Celtic dialect fluently. He had even married into a warrior clan that had been just liberal enough to tolerate letting one of their less prized daughters become the wife of the dapper little Greek. With his olive complexion, oiled ringlets of dark hair, carefully trimmed beard and fine continental wardrobe Diomedes could not look less like the crude natives he had chosen to live among for so long. Yet he was well enough regarded to be warmly greeted in every settlement the cohort passed through.

'What use have this lot got for cash?' grumbled Macro as the cohort's senior centurion counted out coins for a village headman in exchange for several bundles of salted beef – dark withered strips strung together by lengths of leather thong. The centurions of the cohort had gathered to be introduced to the headman and now stood to one side with the Greek guide while business was concluded.

'Oh, you'd be surprised.' Diomedes grinned, flashing his small stained teeth. 'They drink as much wine as they can afford. They've got a real taste for the stuff from Gaul – it's made me a small fortune over the years.'

'Wine? They drink wine?' Macro looked round at the motley scatter of round huts and small animal pens within a flimsy palisade that was only intended to keep wild animals out.

'Of course. You've tried their local brews. All right if you have to get drunk, but not much fun to drink otherwise.'

'You've got a point there.'

'And it's not just wine,' continued Diomedes. 'Cloth, pottery, cooking utensils and so on. They've taken to the empire's exports in a big way. A few more years and the Atrebates will almost be on the first rung of civilisation.' Diomedes sounded wistful.

'Why so glum?'

'Because then it'll be time for me to move on.'

'Move on? I thought you'd settled here.'

'Only while there's money to be made. Once this place becomes part of the empire it'll be flooded with traders and my profit margins will disappear. I'll have to move on. Maybe further north. I hear the Queen of the Brigantes has developed a taste for civilised living.' The Greek's eyes flashed with excitement at the prospect.

Macro regarded Diomedes with the special distaste he reserved for salesmen. Then something occurred to him.

'How can they afford all of this stuff you import?'

'They can't. That's the beauty of it. There's not much coinage about – only a handful of these tribes have started their own mints. So I let them barter instead. I get a much better deal that way. In exchange for my goods I take furs, hunting dogs and jewellery – anything that commands a high price back in the empire. You'd be astonished at the price Celtic jewellery commands in Rome right now.' He looked at the torc round Macro's neck. 'Take that little trinket, for example. I could get a fortune for that.'

'Not for sale,' Macro said firmly, and automatically reached for the gold torc with one hand. The heavy ornament had once been worn round the neck of Togodumnus, a chief of the Catuvellauni and brother

64

of Caratacus. Macro had killed him in single combat shortly after the Second Legion had landed in Britain.

'I'd give you a fair price.'

Macro snorted. 'I doubt it. You'd rip me off just as soon as you would one of these natives.'

'You shame me!' Diomedes protested. 'I'd never dream of it. For you, Centurion, I would pay a good price.'

'No. I'm not selling.'

Diomedes pressed his lips together and shrugged. 'Not now. Maybe later. Sleep on it.'

Macro shook his head, and met the gaze of one of the other centurions who raised his eyes in sympathy. These Greek merchants had spread right across the empire, and well beyond its frontiers, yet they were all the same – chancers on the lookout for financial gain. They viewed everyone in terms of what they could make out of them. Macro suddenly felt repulsed.

'I don't need to sleep on it. I'm not selling it, particularly not to you.'

Diomedes frowned and his eyes narrowed for an instant. Then he nodded slowly and smiled his salesman's smile again. 'You Roman army types really think you're better than the rest of us, don't you?'

Macro didn't answer, just raised his chin a little, causing the Greek to explode with laughter. The other centurions stopped their quiet chattering and turned towards Macro and Diomedes. The Greek raised his hands placatingly.

'I'm sorry, really I am. It's just that I'm so familiar with the attitude. You soldiers think that you alone are responsible for expanding the empire, for adding new provinces to the Emperor's territorial inventory.'

'That's right.' Macro nodded. 'That's about the size of it.'

'Really? So where would you be without me right now? How would your superior over there manage to buy provisions? And that's not the end of it. Why do you think the Atrebates are so well-disposed towards Rome in the first place?'

'Don't know. Don't really care. But I expect you'll tell me anyway.'

'Glad to oblige, Centurion. Long before the first Roman legionary ever shows his face in the more uncivilised corners of this world, some Greek trader like me has been travelling and trading with the natives. We learn their languages and their ways, and introduce them to the goods of the empire. More often than not they're pathetically keen to get their hands on the accessories of civilisation. Things we take for granted they treat as status objects. They develop a taste for it. We feed the taste, until they become dependent on it. By the time you turned up these barbarians were already part of the imperial economy. A few more generations and they'd have begged you to let them become a province.'

'Bollocks! Utter bollocks,' Macro replied, jabbing his finger at the Greek, and the other centurions nodded. 'Expanding the empire depends on the sword, and having the guts to wield it. You people just peddle tat to these ignorant fools for your own profit. That's all there is to it.'

'Of course we do it for profit. Why else would one risk the dangers and privations of such a life?' Diomedes smiled in an attempt to lighten the tone of the discussion. 'I merely wished to point out the benefits to Rome of our dealings with these natives. If, in some small way, my kind has helped smooth the path for the all-conquering legions of Rome then we are gratified beyond all measure. I apologise if this modest ambition in any way offends you, Centurion. I did not intend it to.'

Macro nodded. 'All right then. Apology accepted.'

Diomedes beamed. 'And if you should change your mind about the torc . . .'

'Greek, if you mention it again, I swear I'll—'

'Centurion Macro!' the senior centurion, Hortensius, called out.

Macro instantly turned away from Diomedes and stiffened to attention. 'Sir?'

'Cut the chatter and get your men formed up. Same for the rest of you – we're moving on.'

While the centurions hurried back to their units, bawling out their orders, the villagers quickly loaded the salted beef into the back of one of the supply wagons. As soon as the column was formed up, Hortensius waved the cavalry scouts on ahead and then gave the order for the infantry to advance. The haunted faces of the Atrebate villagers were eloquent testimony to their dread of being left un-defended once again, and the headman begged Diomedes to persuade the cohort to stay. The Greek had his orders and politely but firmly made his apologies and hurried after Hortensius. As the Sixth Century, on rearguard duty behind the last of the wagons, marched out of the village gate, Cato felt ashamed to be deserting them while the Druids and their Durotrigan henchmen were still raiding along the frontier.

'Sir?'

'Yes, Cato.'

'There must be something we can do for these people.'

Macro shook his head. 'Nothing. Why do you ask? What would you have us do?'

'Leave some men. Leave one of the centuries behind to guard them.'

'One less century makes the cohort that much weaker. And where would you stop? We can't leave a century in every village we pass through. There's not enough of us.'

'Well, weapons then,' Cato suggested. 'We could leave them some of our spare weapons in the wagons.'

'No we couldn't, lad. We might need them. In any case, they're not trained to use them. It'd be a waste. Now then, let's hear no more about it. We've a long march ahead of us today. Save your breath for that.'

'Yes, sir,' Cato replied quietly, his eyes avoiding the accusing glare of villagers standing beside the village gate.

For the remainder of the day the Fourth Cohort trudged along the muddy track leading south to the sea and a small trading settlement which nestled beside one of the channels leading into a large natural harbour. Diomedes knew the settlement well – he had helped to build it when he had first landed in Britain many years earlier. Now it was his home. Noviomagus, as it had come to be known, had grown rapidly and acquired a happy mixture of traders, their agents and their families. The incomers and their native neighbours had lived side by side in relative harmony over the years, according to Diomedes. But now the Durotriges were raiding their land, and the Atrebates blamed the foreigners for provoking the Druids of the Dark Moon and their followers. Diomedes had many friends, and his family, at Noviomagus, and was concerned for their safety.

As the cohort marched, the dull sun struggled across the leaden grey sky in a low arc. As the gloom of the day's end began to thicken about the cohort, a sudden shout came from the head of the column. The men looked up from the track where they had been fixing their gaze, as tiredness and the weight of their marching packs bent their backs. A handful of cavalry scouts galloped down the track from the brow of a hill. Centurion Hortensius's voice carried clearly to the rear of the column as he gave the order for the cohort to halt.

'There's trouble,' said Macro quietly as he watched the scouts make their report to Hortensius. The cohort commander nodded and then sent the scouts forward again. He turned to the column, cupping a hand to his mouth.

'Officers to the front!'

Cato shifted the yoke from his shoulder and laid it beside the track and trotted after Macro, feeling a thrill of anticipation race up his spine.

As soon as all his centurions and optios were present Hortensius quickly outlined the situation.

'Noviomagus has been attacked. What's left of it is just over that hill.' He jerked a thumb over his shoulder. 'The scouts say they can't see any movement, so it looks like there're no survivors.'

Cato glanced at Diomedes, standing aside from the Roman officers, and saw the Greek guide staring at his feet, a deep frown on his forehead. His jaw suddenly clenched tightly and Cato realised the man was close to tears. With a mixture of compassion and embarrassment at witnessing the private grief of another, he turned his eyes back to Hortensius as the cohort commander gave his orders.

'The cohort will form a line just below the crest of the hill, we'll advance over the crest and down the far slope towards the settlement. I'll give the order to halt a short distance from Noviomagus and then the Sixth Century will enter the settlement.' He turned towards Macro. 'Just give it a once-over and then make your report.'

'Yes, sir.'

'It'll be dark soon, lads. We haven't time to construct a marching camp so we'll have to repair the settlement's defences as best we can, and camp there for the night. Right then, let's get to it.'

The officers returned to their centuries and called their men to attention. Once the lines of men were formally dressed, Hortensius bellowed out the command to form line. The First Century faced right, then smoothly pivoted round to form a line two men deep. The following centuries followed suit and extended the line to the left. Macro's century was the last to move into position and he called a halt as soon as his right flank marker came abreast of the Fifth Century. The cohort was held still for a moment to steady the men, and then the order was given to advance. The double ranks rippled up the gentle slope and over the crest. Before them in the distance stretched the sea, grey and unsettled. Closer in was a large natural harbour, from which a wide channel led inland to where the settlement had stood. The surface of the channel was made choppy by a chilly breeze. There were no ships at anchor, and only a handful of small craft were drawn up on the shore. Every man was tense in anticipation of what the far side of the hill would reveal and as the ground started to slope down, the remains of Noviomagus came into sight.

The raiders had been as thorough in their destruction as time had allowed. Only the stark blackened lines of the surviving timber frames showed where the huts and houses of the settlement had stood. Around them lay the charred remnants of the walls and thatched roofs. Much of the surrounding palisade had been torn up and hurled into the ditch below. The lack of any smoke indicated that some days had passed since the Durotriges had razed the place to the ground. Nothing moved amongst the ruins, not even an animal. The silence was broken only by the raw cries of ravens nesting in a nearby copse. On either flank of the cohort the cavalry scouts fanned out, searching for any sign of the enemy.

The chinking of the legionaries' equipment seemed unnaturally loud to Cato as he marched down towards the settlement. While concentrating on keeping in step with the others, no mean feat with his lanky gait, his eyes swept over the land surrounding Noviomagus, searching for any sign that this might be a trap. In the failing light the cold winter landscape was filled with gloomy shadows and he tightened his grip on the handle of his shield.

'Halt!' Hortensius had to strain his voice to be clearly heard above the wind. The double line drew up, and stood still for a beat before the next order was called out. 'Down packs!'

The legionaries lowered the yokes to the ground and stepped forward five paces to stand well clear of their marching equipment. Now their right hands held only a javelin, and they were ready to fight.

'Sixth Century, advance!'

'Advance!' Macro relayed the order, and his men marched out of the line, approaching the settlement from an oblique angle. Cato felt his heart quicken as they neared the blackened ruins, and a flighty ripple of nervous energy flowed through his body as he prepared himself for any sudden encounter. Just beyond the ditch, Macro halted the century.

'Cato!'

'Yes, sir!'

'You take the first five sections and enter through the main gate. I'll take the rest and enter from the seaward side. See you in the centre of the settlement.'

'Yes, sir,' Cato replied, and a sudden chill of fear caused him to add, 'Be careful, sir.'

Macro paused, and looked at him scornfully. 'I'll try not to twist my ankle, Optio. This place is as still as a grave. The only thing left moving in there will be the spirits of the dead. Now get moving.'

Cato saluted, and turned back towards the ranks of legionaries. 'First five sections! Follow me!'

Without a pause he strode up towards what was left of the main gate, his men hurrying to keep up. A rutted track led gently up to the huge timbers that formed the main gate and the fortified walkway that had once protected the entrance. But now the gates had gone, savagely cut from their rope hinges and smashed into pieces. Cato picked his way over the splintered fragments. On either side, the defensive ditches curved out round the low rampart and smashed palisade. The legionaries followed silently, eyes and ears straining for any sign of danger in the tense atmosphere that enveloped them.

On the other side of the ruined gateway the full extent of the Durotriges' destruction was evident. The place was littered with smashed pots, shredded clothing and the debris of all that had made up the worldy possessions of the people who had lived here. As the men fanned out on either side of him, Cato looked around and was surprised to see no sign of any bodies; not even the remains of animals. Apart from small eddies of ash disturbed by the breeze, nothing moved in the eerie silence.

'Spread out!' ordered Cato, turning back to his men. 'Search thoroughly. We're looking for any survivors. Report back to me once we reach the centre of the settlement!'

Weapons at the ready, the legionaries cautiously picked their way through the destroyed buildings, using the points of their javelins to test any mounds of debris. Cato watched their progress for a moment before slowly walking up the ash-strewn route that led from the gateway towards the heart of Noviomagus. The lack of bodies disturbed him. He had braced himself for the horrors he might see, and the absence of any sign of the people and beasts who had lived here was almost worse, for his imagination took over and filled him with a terrible foreboding. He cursed himself angrily. It was possible that the raiders had surprised the settlement, taken it without a fight, and carried off the people and their beasts as booty. It was the most likely answer, he assured himself.

'Optio!' A voice called out close by. 'Over here!'

Cato ran towards the voice. Near the remains of a stone animal pen the legionary was standing by a large pit, covered with a hide cover. He had drawn back one side and was pointing down with his javelin.

'There, sir. Have a look at this.'

Cato joined him and looked into the pit. It was ten feet or so across and as deep as a man. The earth along the edges was loose. In the gloom he saw a pile of dried haunches of meat, scores of grain baskets, some Greek silverware and a few small chests. It was clear that the pit had been dug recently, no doubt to store the spoils the raiders had selected. They had covered the pit with the tarpaulin to keep wild animals out. Cato slipped off his shield and lowered himself down by the chests. He flipped open the lid of the nearest one. Inside he found a selection of Celtic ornaments fashioned from silver and bronze. He picked up a mirror and flipped it over, admiring the fine workmanship of the spiralling patterns on the reverse. He placed it back in the chest and took in the assorted torcs, necklaces, cups and other vessels, all of the highest craftsmanship. Little of this would have been used by the inhabitants of Noviomagus. It would have been gained from trade with native tribes and stockpiled during the winter before it was shipped to Gaul where a high price could be fetched by agents of dealers in Rome. Now the Durotriges had seized and hidden it, no doubt intending to pick it up on their way back from raiding deep into the territory of the Atrebates.

Cato trembled as he realised the full implication. He slammed down the lid of the chest and scrambled out of the pit.

'Find the others, and get them to the centre of the village as fast as possible. I'm going on ahead to find the centurion. Get moving!'

Cato hurried through the brittle remains of the burned-out buildings where only the stoutest timbers and blackened stone walls still stood. He heard Macro calling out orders, and made for his centurion's voice. Emerging between the walls of two of the more substantial buildings arranged around the heart of Noviomagus, he caught sight of Macro, and a few of his men, standing beside what looked like a covered well, about ten feet across. A waist-high stone parapet encircled it and the whole was covered with a conical hide roof. Strangely, the roof had been left intact by the raiders, apparently the one thing they had not tried to destroy.

'Sir!' Cato called out as he ran towards them. Macro looked up from the well, a distracted expression on his face. Seeing Cato, he stiffened his posture and strode to meet him.

'Found anything?'

'Yes, sir!' Cato could not restrain his nervous excitement as he made his report. 'There's a pit filled with spoils near the main gate. They must be intending to come back this way. Sir, we might have a chance to spring a trap on them!'

Macro nodded solemnly, apparently unmoved by the prospect of ambushing the raiders. 'I see,' he said.

Cato's impulse to run on about his discovery was stilled by the peculiar deadness in the face of his superior.

'What's the matter, sir?'

Macro swallowed. 'Did you find any bodies?'

'Bodies? No, sir. None. It's a funny thing.'

'Yes.' Macro pursed his lips and jabbed a thumb towards the well. 'Then I guess they must all be in there.'

Chapter Ten

In the failing light Centurion Hortensisus formed a dull silhouette, almost devoid of detail as he leaned his hands on the stonework and peered into the well. Macro and his men hung back, keeping as far from any lingering spirits of the dead as possible. Diomedes sat alone, his back against the blackened stonework of a ruined building. His head was bowed, face buried in his arms, body wracked with grief.

'He's taking it a bit hard,' muttered Figulus.

Cato and Macro exchanged a look. Both had seen the twisted pile of mutilated bodies that almost filled the well. Given the extent of the settlement, there must have been hundreds of them. What horrified Cato more than anything was that no living thing had been spared. The tangle of bodies included even the villagers' dogs and sheep, as well as women and children. The raiders had made it clear what fate would befall those who sided with Rome. The young optio had reeled before the dark vision in the well, and had felt a chilling pang of horror and despair as his eyes fell on the face of a young boy, barely more than an infant, sprawled on top of the heap. Beneath a wild thatch of straw-blond hair, a pair of startling blue eyes stared up in wide-eyed terror. The boy's mouth hung open to reveal tiny white teeth. He had been killed with a spear thrust to the chest and his coarse wool top was stained black with dried blood. Recoiling from the charnal pit, Cato had turned, bent over and thrown up.

Now, half an hour later, he felt cold and weary with the profound sorrow of those who have seen the utter grimness of life for the first time. Violent death was something he had lived with ever since he had joined the eagles. That was barely more than a year ago. So little time, he reflected. The army had succeeded in hardening him without his really being aware of it, but in the face of the bloody handiwork of the Druids of the Dark Moon cult, he was consumed with horror and despair. And as his mind tried to come to terms with the actions of men who so outraged every civilised standard, a steadily swelling urge to wreak savage revenge upon them threatened to over-whelm him. The image of the boy's face flashed through his mind once more and instinctively his hand twisted and tightened on the pommel of his sword. Now the same Druids had their hands on a Roman family, no doubt destined for the same fate as the inhabitants of Noviomagus.

Macro noticed the movement. For a moment he was almost moved to place a fatherly hand on his optio's shoulder and try to comfort him. He had grown used to the optio's presence and tended to forget that Cato lacked experience of the absolute brutality of war. It was hard to believe that the clumsy bookworm who had turned up with the other bedraggled recruits back in Germany was the same man as the scarred junior officer standing silently beside him. The lad had already won his first decoration for bravery; the polished phalera gleamed on the optio's harness. There was no doubting his courage and intelligence, and if he survived the harsh life of the legions for long enough, a good future lay ahead of him. Yet he was still little more than a boy, inclined to a painful degree of self-consciousness that Macro could not understand. Any more than he could understand the depths of the lad's occasional moods, when he seemed to shrink into himself and wrap himself up in a tangle of unfathomable threads of thought.

Macro shrugged. If the boy would only stop thinking so much, he'd find life a lot easier. Macro had little time for introspection, it merely confused the issue and prevented a man from doing things. Best left to those idle intellectuals back in Rome. The sooner Cato accepted that, the happier he'd be.

Figulus was still tutting at Diomedes's shameless display of emotion. 'Bloody Greeks! They turn everything into a drama. Too much tragedy and not enough comedy in their theatres, that's their problem.'

'The man's lost his family,' Macro said quietly. 'So do him a favour before he overhears you, and fucking shut up.'

'Yes, sir.' Figulus waited a moment, and then casually wandered off, as if looking for something else to divert his attention while the century waited for orders.

Centurion Hortensius had seen enough, and briskly strode over to join Macro.

'Bloody mess in there.'

'Yes, sir.'

'Best get your lads to fill it in. We haven't got time for a proper burial. Anyway, I don't know what the drill is for the local version.'

'You could ask Diomedes,' suggested Macro. 'He'd know.'

They both turned to look at the Greek guide. Diomedes had raised his head, and was staring towards the well, his features twisted and trembling as he struggled with his grief.

'I don't think so,' decided Centurion Hortensius. 'Not for a while at least. I'll take care of him while you see to the well.'

Macro nodded, before another thought occurred to him. 'What about the loot my optio discovered?'

'What about it?'

Cato looked up irritably at the senior centurion's failure to grasp the significance of his find. Before he could give voice to any insubordinate explanation, Macro intervened.

'The optio reckons the raiders intend to return for their spoils.'

'Oh, does he?' Hortensius glared at the young optio, angered that so young and inexperienced a soldier should presume to understand the enemy's intentions.

'Otherwise, what would be the point of putting them to one side, sir?'

'Who knows? Maybe it's some kind of offering to their gods.'

'I don't think so,' Cato responded quietly.

Hortensius frowned. 'If you've got something to say, you say it properly, Optio,' he snapped.

'Yes, sir.' Cato stood to attention. 'I merely wished to suggest that it looks to me as if the raiders have put aside anything they can carry with them when they retreat back into the territory of the Durotriges. That's all, sir. Other than the fact that they could pass back this way at any moment.'

'Any moment, eh?' Hortensius mocked him. 'I doubt it. If they've any sense they're already safely tucked up back where they came from.'

'Even so, sir, the lad might have a point,' said Macro. 'We ought to post a watch on some high ground.'

'Macro, I wasn't born yesterday. It's taken care of. The cavalry scouts are screening the approaches to the village. If anyone comes, they'll be spotted long before they threaten us. Not that I believe the raiders are still out there.'

He had barely stopped speaking when a thrumming of hooves sounded in the dusk. The three officers turned, and moments later a scout galloped his horse into the centre of the settlement. He reined his beast in and slipped from its side. 'Where's Centurion Hortensius?'

'Over here. Make your report!'

The man ran over, saluted and took a deep breath. 'Column of men approaching, sir! Two miles off.'

'Which direction?'

The scout turned and pointed towards the east, beyond a dip between two hills, where a track wound its way along the coast.

'How many?'

'Two hundred, maybe more.'

'Right. What's your decurion doing?'

'He's pulled the squadron back into the trees on the nearest hill. Except for two men, unmounted. They're keeping an eye on the column.'

'Good.' Hortensius nodded with satisfaction and dismissed the scout. 'Off you go. Tell the decurion to stay under cover. I'll send a runner with orders as soon as I can.'

The scout ran back to his mount and Hortensius turned to his officers. He forced himself to smile slightly.

'Well, young Cato. Seems you might be right. And if you are, then those Druids and their friends are in for a great big fucking surprise.'

Chapter Eleven

'And just for a change it's snowing,' grumbled Cato as he looked up into the first flurry descending from the night sky. A cold wind was blowing in from the sea and brought a swirling mass of white flakes down on the men of the Fourth Cohort as they lay hidden in and around the ruined settlement. The clear weather of the last few days had left the ground dry and the snow began to settle at once, speckling the dark cloaks and shields of the legionaries as they shivered in silence.

'Won't last long, Optio,' Figulus whispered. 'Look there!' He indicated a clear patch of sky to one side of the dark looming clouds. Stars, and the dim crescent of a half-moon, glimmered faintly in an almost black sky.

It seemed a long time since night had fallen, and the tense anticipation of the men sharpened their senses as they waited for the raiders to fall into the trap. The Sixth Century was concealed in the ruins around the centre of the settlement. Peering over the waist-high stonework of a hut, Cato could not see any of the other men of the century but their presence was palpable. As was the presence of the dead piled up in the well close by. The image of the dead boy came unbidden into Cato's mind and his bitter appetite to exact a terrible revenge on the Druids and their followers was given a new edge.

'Where the hell are those bloody British bastards?' he muttered, then immediately clenched his jaw, furious with himself for displaying his impatience in front of his men. With the exception of Figulus, they had sat in silence, according to their orders. Most of them were seasoned veterans who had been posted to the Second Legion the previous autumn to bring the unit up to strength. Vespasian's unit had suffered grievous losses in the early battles of the campaign and had been fortunate enough to have first pick of the replacements from the reserves shipped in from Gaul.

'Want me to go and look, sir?' Figulus asked.

'No!' snapped Cato. 'Sit still, damn you. Not another sound.'

'Yes, sir. Sorry, sir.'

As the recruit shuffled off a short distance, Cato shook his head in despair. Left to his own devices that idiot would wreck the hurriedly laid plans of Centurion Hortensius. In the short time before the enemy column came within sight of the settlement, two centuries had been deployed in the settlement itself, the other four hidden in the defensive ditch, ready to close the circle that would snare the raiders. The cavalry scouts were concealed along the fringes of a nearby wood and had been detailed to emerge as soon as the signal to attack was given. They would then watch for and chase down any of the Britons that managed to escape from the settlement. Not that Cato intended to give them much chance of that.

The charred remains of the settlement were already disappearing under a thin mantle of snow. As Cato watched for the enemy, the loom of the fallen snow reminded him of the finest white silk, and suddenly he was thinking of Lavinia – young, fresh and filled with an infectious enthusiasm for life. Too soon the image faded and was replaced by her startled expression in death. Cato forced the vision from his mind and tried to focus on something else. Anything else. He was surprised, then, to find himself thinking about Boudica – her face fixed with one arched eyebrow in the gently mocking expression he had become peculiarly fond of. Cato smiled.

'Sir!' Figulus hissed, half rising to his feet. The other men of the section glared at him.

'What?' Cato looked round. 'Thought I told you to still your tongue.'

'Something's happening!' Figulus jabbed his finger towards the opposite side of the settlement.

'Shut your mouth!' Cato growled through clenched teeth, raising a fist to emphasise the order. 'Get down!'

Figulus squatted back under cover. Then, as cautiously as he could, Cato looked out on the open space before the well. His eyes strained for any sign of movement. The low moan of the wind frustrated his hearing, and so it was that in spite of the darkness he saw the enemy before he heard them. The dark outline of one of the ruins opposite shifted its shape, then a shadow slowly emerged from between two stone walls. A horseman. On the threshold of the open space he reined in, and sat quite still on his mount, as if sniffing the air for signs of danger. At length the horse whinnied and raised a hoof, scraping a dark gash through the snow. Then, with a clearly audible click of the tongue, the Briton urged his beast forward, towards the well. The dark shape moved slowly through the speckled swirl and Cato got a clear sense that the man's eyes were scouring the silent ruins. He hunched down behind the wall as far as he could go and still see over the blackened stonework. As the horseman reached the well, he reined in again, then edged alongside the rim for a better view down the well shaft. Cato's hand tightened on the handle of his sword, and for a moment the temptation to draw the weapon was almost unbearable. Then he forced himself to release his grip. The men around him were tense enough to jump into action at the slightest hint that he was preparing to rush into the attack. They must wait for the trumpet. Hortensius was watching from the top of a burial mound outside the settlement and would only give the signal to spring the trap when all the raiders had passed inside the ruins of the main gate. The orders were clear: no man must move an inch until the signal was given. Cato turned towards his men, silently waving them down. From the way they were crouched and holding their shields and javelins ready, he could see that they were ready to move.

By the well, the horseman casually leaned to the side, hawked up some phlegm and spat down the shaft. The cold ache for revenge inside Cato was momentarily fanned into a terrible burning rage that set the blood pounding through his veins. He fought back against the impulse, clenching his fists so tightly that he could feel the fingernails biting painfully into his palms. The Durotrigan seemed satisfied that no danger threatened him or his companions and casually turned his horse and trotted out of the settlement's centre back towards the main gate. Cato faced his men.

'The signal will be coming soon,' he told them, his voice low. 'Once that scout gives the all-clear, the Druids and their mates will march in through the gate. They're going to retrieve their loot and probably intend to spend the night here. They'll be tired and longing to get some rest. That'll make 'em careless.' Cato drew his sword and pointed it towards his men. 'Remember, lads . . .'

Some of the veterans could not help chuckling at being referred to as a lad by the young optio, but they were respectful of rank and quickly stilled their amusement. Cato drew a sharp breath to hide his annoyance.

'Remember, we go in hard. We've been ordered to take prisoners, but don't take any unnecessary risks to get them. You know how much the centurion hates having to write bereavement messages for the families back home. He's not likely to forgive you in a hurry if you get yourself killed.'

Cato's words produced the desired effect and the awful tension of waiting to fight was eased as the men chuckled again.

'Now then. On your feet, shields up and javelins ready.'

The dark shapes of the men rose and amid the sweep of large snowflakes their ears strained to hear the trumpet signal above the low moan of the wind. But before the signal came, the first of the Britons appeared from the direction of the main gate. Men on foot, leading their horses and talking in contented tones now that their day's march had come to its end. They slowly emerged from the greater darkness of the burned buildings and gathered in the open space before the well. As Cato watched nervously, the raiders grew in number until over twenty of them were milling around, and still more were trudging out of the night. The champing and pawing of the horses mingled with the cheerful tones of the Britons and seemed unbearably loud after the long period of enforced silence. Cato feared his men might not hear the trumpet signal above the noise. Despite their stillness, he was acutely aware of their growing anxiety. If the signal did not come soon, the scattered men of the Sixth Century might be outnumbered by those they were set on ambushing.

There was a sudden harsh shout from the centre of the milling mass of raiders. A mounted man forced his way through and issued a string of orders. The Britons fell silent and at once the loose rabble turned into soldiers ready to act on the word of command. A handful of men assigned as horse holders began to take their charges in hand while the others formed up in front of the mounted man. To Cato's intense frustration, the best moment to launch an attack was slipping away. Unless Hortensius gave the signal immediately, the enemy might yet be sufficiently organised to offer effective resistance.

Even as he cursed the delay, Cato became aware of a man walking directly towards him. The optio silently lowered himself, staring anxiously at the outline of the stonework above his head as the Briton approached, stopped and fumbled with his cloak. There was a pause before a dull splashing sound caught the optio's ears. The Briton let out a long sigh of satisfaction as he relieved himself against the stone wall. Someone called out to him, and Cato heard the man laugh as he turned to answer, clumsily knocking the loose stones at the top of the ruined wall. A large rock tipped inward and toppled down towards Cato's head. Instinctively he ducked and the rock glanced off the side of his helmet with a dull metallic clang. The raider's head appeared above the wall, looking for the source of the unexpected sound. Cato held his breath, hoping that he and his men would not be seen. The Durotrigan warrior sucked his breath and yelled a warning to his comrades that split the darkness and carried above the other sounds with startling clarity.

'Get up!' Cato bellowed. 'Get 'em!'

Springing to his feet, he thrust his short sword at the dark shape of the Briton's face and felt the shock of impact travel down his arm as the raider's shrill scream rang in his ears.

'Use your javelins!' Macro's voice called out from nearby. 'Javelins first!'

The dark shapes of legionaries rose up from the ruin surrounding the Durotrigan raiders.

'Release javelins!' Macro bellowed. With grunted effort the men around Cato threw their spear arms forward at the low angle of point-blank range, and the long deadly shafts flew into the dense mass of the enemy. The thud and clatter of impact instantly gave way to the cries of wounded men and the high-pitched whinny of terrified horses struck by the vicious iron points of the javelins.

Cato and his men scrambled over the wall, short swords drawn and ready to thrust.

'Keep close to me!' Cato shouted, anxious to keep his men distinct from the Britons. Hortensius had drilled into his subordinates that their men must be kept under tight control during the ambush. The Roman army had a healthy aversion to fighting night actions, but this opportunity to trap and kill the enemy was too providential for even a by-the-book centurion like Hortensius to resist.

'Close up!' Macro shouted a short distance off, and the order was repeated by all the section leaders as little knots of legionaries closed in on the Britons. Behind their large rectangular shields the eyes of the Romans darted about, searching for the nearest exposed enemy body to thrust their short swords into. Cato blinked as a gust blew several large flakes into his face, momentarily obscuring his sight. A large shadow reared up in front of him. Fingers closed over the top his shield rim, inches from his face, and wrenched it to one side. Instinctively Cato thrust his arm forward, throwing his full weight behind it. The Briton's grip held firm and the bottom of the shield pivoted up so that it caught him a crunching blow between the legs. He groaned, eased his grip and began to double up. Cato smashed the pommel of his sword onto the back of the man's head to help him on his way. He stepped over the

81

prone form, glancing round to make sure that his section was still with him. Behind their dark rectangular shields, the legionaries thrust forward on each side, fighting shoulder to shoulder as they cut down the struggling mass of Britons. There was no organised resistance to the ambush, the Britons simply fought to free themselves of their dead and wounded, and of the tangle of equipment and bent javelin shafts that encumbered them. Those who had broken free of this chaos desperately tried to smash a way through the closing ring of shields and deadly flickering blades of the Roman short swords. But very few escaped, and with a cold, ruthless efficiency the legionaries pressed forward, killing all before them.

Then, above the shouts and cries of men and the clatter and clash of weapons, a strident brass note carried across the settlement as, belatedly, Hortensius gave the signal for attack. To make best use of what was left of the element of surprise, Hortensius threw his men onto the dark column of British warriors entering the settlment. The loud roar of the cohort's battle cry swelled up on all sides and the Durotrigan raiding party stopped in its tracks, momentarily too stunned to react. The remaining centuries rose from the settlement's defence ditches and swarmed over the gleam of freshly fallen snow towards their enemy. The Druid leaders tried to rally their men and form them up to face the threat, but in no time the legionaries were in amongst them, quickly cutting the tribesmen to pieces.

With renewed fervour the Sixth Century dealt with the few remaining Britons still alive amid the carnage around the settlement's well. Cato's blade was wedged in the ribcage of one of the raiders and with a frustrated growl he stamped a boot down on the man's stomach and wrenched the sword free. Looking up, he just had time to jump back as the rearing head of a horse surged towards him, nostrils flaring and eyes wide with terror at the screams and clash of weapons that filled the night. Above the head of the horse loomed the silhouette of the warrior who had tried in vain to form his men up and fight the Romans. He brandished a long sword in one hand, raised high and clear of his frightened horse. He fixed his gaze on Cato and swung his blade with all his might. Cato went down on his knees and threw his shield up in the path of the sword. The blow landed with a shattering crash just above the shield boss and would have cut clean through had it not caught on the reinforced metal rim of the side nearest the horse. Instead, the blade stuck, and when the warrior tried to draw it back, he wrenched the shield back with it. Snarling in wild frustration, the man lashed out at Cato with his boot, connecting with the side of the optio's helmet.

Cato was dazed for only a moment, then he stabbed his sword into the leggings above the boot. The Briton howled in anger and rage, and urged his horse to trample the Roman. Unused to horses in his civilian life, and with an infantryman's respect for the dangers posed by cavalry, Cato flinched away from the lethal hooves. But the press of legionaries behind him left no room for retreat. With all his might Cato wrenched his shield away from the Briton, and with a splintering crack, sword and shield parted. The Briton kicked his heels in and savagely jerked back on his reins, causing his beast to rear up, hooves thrashing dangerously. Cato rolled under the horse's belly, protecting his body with the badly damaged shield, and thrust his short sword up into the animal's vitals.

The horse struggled wildly to free itself of the blade, rearing back so far that it rolled over onto its back and crushed its rider. Before the Briton could try to free himself of the mortally wounded beast, a legionary sprang forward and finished him off with a quick stab to the throat.

'Figulus! See to the horse as well!' ordered Cato as he crept back from the flailing hooves of the stricken animal. The young legionary worked his way round to the head and opened an artery with a quick slash of his sword. Cato was back on his feet, glancing round to find a new enemy, but there were none. Most of the Britons were dead. A few of the wounded cried out, but they would be ignored until there was time to end their suffering with a merciful thrust. The rest had fled, running pell-mell through the remains of the settlement in a bid to escape the wicked blades of their attackers.

The legionaries were surprised at the speed with which they had overwhelmed the enemy, and for a moment they remained tense and crouched, ready to fight.

'Sixth Century! Form up!'

Cato saw the squat form of his centurion march off to one side of the pile of bodies by the well.

'Come on, lads! Form up! We're not on a fucking exercise! Move!'

The well-disciplined men responded instantly, hurrying over to their centurion, forming a small column on the snowy ground. Macro saw no gaps in the ranks and nodded with satisfaction. The enemy had had too little time to injure more than a handful of the men in Macro's century. He nodded a greeting at Cato as he took his place in front of the men.

'All right, Optio?'

Cato nodded, breathing heavily.

'Back towards the gate then, lads!' Macro shouted. He clapped Figulus on the shoulder. 'And don't spare the horses!'

Chapter Twelve

As the snow billowed softly about them, the legionaries moved down the track towards the remains of the gate, from where the wind-muted sounds of battle drifted back to them. Cato noticed that the wind had slackened a little. Silvery patches were opening up in the clouds above to admit the light of the stars and the dim crescent moon. In the baleful glow reflecting off the blanket of snow, the fleeing shapes of the Britons could be seen amongst the ruins. For a moment Cato felt a welling up of rage and frustration at the sight. They might yet escape before the legionaries' thirst for revenge was slaked. Then Cato smiled grimly. Maybe he was the only one who desired to make the enemy pay for what he had seen in the well. Maybe the veterans marching down the track with him just saw the enemy in professional terms. A foe to be overcome and destroyed; no more, no less.

As they approached the ruined gateway, they could see a great dark mass of Durotrigan raiders surging around the ruins with little sense of order. Individual figures were scrambling along the remains of the earthen rampart, seeking a means of escape through the shattered wooden palisade and the iron cordon of the legionary skirmish line waiting beyond. A few of the raiders might escape, but only a few, Cato thought to himself with cold satisfaction.

'Halt!' Macro ordered. 'There they are, lads, ripe for killing. Keep close and make sure you look before you thrust. There's enough of 'em to go round without you having to kill any of our lads! Form line!'

While the front rank of the column stood still, the following files took position on each side until the century formed a line two men deep, across the ruins. As Cato waited for his centurion to give the order to advance, he noticed a small knot of Durotrigans break away from their comrades and slip into the shadows of some ruined huts.

'Sir!'

'What is it?'

Cato thrust his sword arm out, pointing towards the huts with his blade. 'Over there. Some of them are making a break for it.'

'I see 'em. We can't have that,' Macro decided. 'You take half the men and see to them.'

'Yes, sir.'

'Cato, no heroics.' Macro had noted the dark mood that had possessed his optio since the lad had witnessed the grim horror inside the well and wanted it known that he would not tolerate any foolishness. 'Just hunt them down and then bring the men straight back.'

'Yes, sir.'

'I'll advance first. Once I'm clear, you can carry on.'

Cato nodded.

'Squads to my left . . . advance!'

With Macro setting the pace, the first five sections stepped forward, shields facing the enemy, short swords at the ready. The dark mass of the Britons shrank back from the approaching shield wall, and their cries of despair and panic reached a new pitch of terror as the silent line of Romans closed on them. A few of the more stout-hearted among the Durotriges broke free of the mob and stood, weapons raised, prepared to go down fighting, true to their warrior code. But they were too few to make any difference and were quickly overwhelmed and cut down. Moments later came the dull crash of shields and the ringing of swords as Macro and his men carved their way into the heaving mob.

Cato turned away and drew a deep breath of the cold air. 'The rest of you, follow me!'

He led the men around the fringe of the fighting by the gate, into the winding lane down which the small group of Durotriges had disappeared. Here the huts of the settlement were not so badly gutted by fire. Chest-high walls of stone and the skeletal remains of timber frames rose up all around them as they pursued the enemy at the trot. Their leather harnesses creaked and their scabbards and loin guards chinked as the snow softly crunched under their boots. Ahead of him the path was disturbed by the passage of the Durotriges only moments before, and they had left a clear trail for the Romans to follow. It quickly became obvious to Cato why the small party had made off in this direction as he recalled the storage pits that had been uncovered earlier. They were after whatever loot they could carry with them.

The narrow lane turned a sharp corner and a faint low hiss warned Cato to duck under his shield just in time. The double-headed axe glanced off the rim of his shield and straight into the face of the legionary immediately behind him. With a sickening crunch the heavy

86

blade took the top of the man's helmet and head clean off. He didn't even cry out as he fell back, splashing bloodied brains over his nearest comrades. A huge Durotrigan warrior rose above Cato. The man let out a savage cry as he saw the damage his weapon had wreaked. The blade continued its arc and buried itself deep in a wooden beam. The Durotrigan warrior snarled, then yanked the axe free with an explosive gasp at the effort. The action left him exposed for a brief moment and Cato thrust his short sword into the man's midriff and felt the solid impact of a good strike. But instead of falling back mortally wounded, the huge Briton just seemed to be further enraged by the blow. He bellowed out a war cry and moved out from the shadow of the wall he had been using for concealment to stand astride the lane where he had room to wield his broadaxe freely. He swung it in a double-handed loop and dared the Romans to approach him.

For a moment Cato did shrink back, and his men with him, as the blade hissed through the air. The optio regarded it with horror, well imagining the bone-shattering impact it would have on any man foolish enough to venture within its sweeping arc. Every instant he delayed Cato knew that the Briton's companions would be making good their escape. But he was seized in the grip of an icy dread that sent shivers rippling up his backbone and turned his guts to water. He was shocked to find himself shaking. Every fibre of his being told him to turn and run and leave his men to deal with this terrifying giant of a man. And with that thought came a wave of bitter self-contempt and revulsion.

Cato tensed, watching the sweep of the axe, waiting for it to pass him by. As it swooped past his shield, he gritted his teeth and threw himself on the Briton, thrusting his sword into the man's body once again. The man grunted at the impact then raised his knee and kicked out at Cato. His boot slammed into Cato's thigh and almost toppled him. Cato struck again, this time thrusting his shield into the man's face while he twisted the blade inside his opponent, trying for a vital organ. Blood, hot and sticky, poured over his sword grip and hand, yet the Durotrigan warrior still kept coming, bellowing with pain and defiance. He dropped the axe and grabbed at Cato's face and throat with his huge powerful hands. The optio gasped in agony as his windpipe was crushed in the Briton's grip. With one arm trapped by his shield strap, Cato let go of his sword and snatched at the hand clenched round his throat. Other men were alongside him now, smashing their shields into the giant and thrusting their swords in from all sides. He took it all, growling from deep in his chest, a sound of pure animal rage, and still he kept his grip on his foe, throttling him. Cato, close to blacking out, thought he must surely die, but suddenly the grip slackened. Dizzily he heard the wet thud of sword strikes as the legionaries brutally finished off the Briton.

With a deep rasping sigh, the man slumped to his knees, his hands fell away from Cato's throat and dropped to his side. One of the legionaries warily kicked him in the chest and he fell back on the disturbed snow, quite dead.

'You all right, Optio?'

Cato was leaning against the stonework, gasping for air as blood pounded through his neck. He shook his head to try and clear the dizziness.

'I'll live,' he croaked painfully. 'Have to keep after the others . . . Let's go.'

Someone handed him the ivory-handled sword bequeathed to him by Centurion Bestia, and Cato continued up the lane. The terror of another ambush weighed heavily against the desire to rush forward and yet he forced himself to run, determined not to let his men realise how much he felt like a scared little boy lost in the midst of a terrifying nightmare. Every shadow on either side of the lane ahead became the darkest depths of hell from which unspeakable horrors threatened to emerge.

Then the lane turned a corner, and there ahead lay the storage pits. The covers had been pulled back, and beyond the pits a handful of the enemy were still in view, weighed down by booty and struggling to catch up with their comrades who had placed good sense above greed.

'Get 'em!' rasped Cato.

The legionaries ran forward in open order. This fight would be man to man – the shield wall would not be necessary. Shouting the legion's battle cry, 'Up the Augusta!' they fell on the Britons as if they were hunting rats in a granary. Immediately ahead of Cato a Roman caught up with a Durotrigan warrior who was dragging a huge bundle through the snow. The Briton sensed the danger behind him and turned, raising an arm in terror as the short sword rose up above him. Cato found himself cursing the legionary's lapse of training – the short sword was designed for stabbing, not cutting, and the man really should know better than to let his bloodlust overwhelm his training. Bad as a fucking one-day-wonder recruit. The expletive jumped unbidden into his mind, and shocked him for an instant, until he realised with a wry smile, just how far he had become immersed in the military world.

The Briton screamed as the short sword hacked through his forearm and shattered the bone so that the limb flopped like a freshly caught fish.

As Cato ran past the legionary, he shouted, 'Use your weapon properly!'

The legionary nodded guiltily then turned back to finish off his shrieking victim with the point of his sword.

Cato passed more bodies sprawled in the snow, their booty scattered around them – dark bundles of cloth from which spilled silver goblets and plates, pieces of personal jewellery and, bizarrely, a pair of carved wooden dolls. A Durotrigan warrior no doubt looking for a gift to carry home to his children, Cato guessed. He was startled by the thought that the men who had wrought such terrible destruction on this settlement and were capable of massacring even its youngest infants might have children of their own. He looked up from the dolls and saw dim shapes slipping through the remains of the palisade, pursued by Romans panting hoarsely from the chase and excitement of battle.

Cato clambered up the steep turf slope to the roughly hewn wooden stakes of the palisade. On the far side, spread out across the ditch and the white landscape beyond, were the dark shapes of those who had managed to escape the slaughter of their comrades back in the settlement. A number of his men joined him, anxious to get after the enemy.

'Hold still!' Cato managed to cry out hoarsely, despite the pain in his throat. Some of the men continued forward, and Cato had to shout again, straining to make his order louder. 'Hold!'

'Sir!' someone protested. 'They're getting away!'

'I can bloody well see that for myself!' Cato cursed angrily. 'There's nothing we can do. We'd never catch them now. Have to hope the cavalry scouts see 'em.'

Discipline and good sense halted the men. Chests heaving from their exertions, and steamy breath whipping around their heads, they watched the enemy flee into the darkness. Cato was shaking, partly from the cold wind that blew even more keenly up on the ramparts, and partly from the release of nervous tension.

Had so little time passed since they had rushed the enemy in the centre of the settlement? Forcing himself to concentrate, he realised that the whole affair could only have lasted little more than quarter of an hour. No sounds of fighting carried on the wind, so the skirmish at the gate must be over as well. All finished with as quickly as that. He recalled the first ever battle he had fought in. A village in Germania, not so very different to this one. But that desperate fight had lasted an afternoon and through the night until the first rays of dawn. Short though this fight might have been, the same burning exultation at

89

having survived fired his veins and made him feel somehow older and wiser.

His throat ached abominably, and it was an agony to swallow or move his head too far in any direction. That huge Durotrigan warrior had almost done for him.

Chapter Thirteen

The faint pink glow in the sky cast a paler shade over the snow lying across the ruined settlement. As if the very earth itself had bled during the night, thought Cato as he rose stiffly from the corner of a wall where he had been resting under his army cloak. He had not slept. It had been too uncomfortable for that; his thin frame meant he felt the cold more keenly than the more muscled and hardened veterans of the legion, like Macro. As usual the centurion's full-throated snore had filled the night, until awakened for his century's turn on guard duty. Then, having woken the next officer on the rota, he had slipped instantly back into a deep sleep with a guttural rumbling that sounded like a distant earthquake.

A light layer of snow cascaded silently from the folds of Cato's cloak as he stood up. Wearily he brushed the remainder off and stretched his limbs. Picking his way over the rubble, he approached the huddled form of Figulus and gently poked him with the toe of his boot. The legionary grumbled and turned away without opening his eyes and Cato had to deliver a kick.

'On your feet, soldier.'

New to the army though he was, Figulus knew when he had been given an order and his body responded quickly enough, though his somewhat slower mind struggled to catch up.

'Get a fire lit,' ordered Cato. 'Make sure it's on clear ground away from anything combustible.'

'Sir?'

Cato gave the legionary a hard look, unsure if the lad was taking the piss. But Figulus stared back blankly, not a trace of guile in his simple features, and Cato smiled. 'Don't build the fire too close to anything that might catch light.'

'Oh, I see.' Figulus nodded. 'I'll get on with it, Optio.'

'Please.'

Figulus ambled off, scratching his numb backside. Cato watched him and clicked his tongue. The lad was too dim and too immature for the legions. It ought to feel strange to be making that kind of a judgement about someone who was a few months older than he was, and yet it didn't. Experience brought more wisdom than age ever could, and that was what counted in the army. A sense of well-being flowed through Cato's body at this further evidence that he was becoming fully attuned to the life of a soldier.

Clutching his cloak tightly about him, Cato made his way out of the ruined huts where the Sixth Century had spent the night. A few men had already stirred and were sitting in bleary-eyed semi-consciousness, watching dawn break in a clear sky. Some of them bore the marks of the previous night's skirmish; bloodstained rags tied round heads and limbs. Only a handful of men in the cohort had been mortally wounded. By contrast, the Britons had been cut to pieces. Nearly eighty of their band lay stiffening down by the gate and over twenty more were heaped by the well. The wounded and prisoners numbered over a hundred, packed in the remains of a barn under the wary gaze of half a century assigned to guard them. A few Druids had been taken alive, and were lying, tightly bound, in one of the storage pits.

As he crunched across the frost-hardened snow towards the pits, Cato saw Diomedes squatting to one side, staring fixedly at the Druids. A strip of cloth was wound round his head and dried blood stained the side of his face. He did not look up as the optio approached and gave no sign of life apart from the regular curling wisp of exhaled breath. Cato stood a few paces to one side for a moment, waiting for the Greek to acknowledge his presence, but he did not move, just stared at the Druids.

For their part, the Druids lay on their sides, hands securely fastened behind them and ankles bound. Although they were not gagged, they made no attempt to talk and just glared angrily at their guards as they shivered on the snowy ground. Unlike the other Britons that Cato had encountered, these men wore their hair long, with no attempt at lime-styling. Thick and matted, it was tied back in a long unkempt ponytail, while their beards were left free. Each man bore a dark moon tattoo on his forehead and wore black robes.

'Nasty looking bunch,' Cato said quietly, for some reason not wishing to be overheard by the Druids. 'Never seen anything like them.'

'Then count yourself lucky, Roman,' Diomedes muttered.

'Lucky?'

'Yes,' Diomedes hissed, and turned towards the optio. 'Lucky. Lucky not to have such bloody, evil scum living on the fringes of your world, never knowing when they might appear in your midst to spread terror.

I'd never imagined they would have the guts to strike so deep into Atrebates territory. Never. Now the people who lived here are all dead, every man, woman and child. All slaughtered, and dumped in that well.' Dimoedes's brow creased and his lips pressed tightly together for a moment. Then he rose to his feet and reached a hand inside his cloak. 'I don't see why these bastards should be allowed to live. Vermin like them deserve only one fate.'

Even allowing for the fact that Diomedes had helped found the settlement and had family among those whose bodies were heaped in the well, Cato was taken aback by the chilling intensity of his words. The Greek began to withdraw his arm from within the folds of his cloak and Cato, realising what he intended to do, instinctively raised his hands to restrain Diomedes.

'Morning!' a cheery voice hailed.

Cato and Diomedes turned and saw Centurion Hortensius striding up towards them. Cato stiffened to attention and saluted; Diomedes frowned and slowly took a pace back from the edge of the pit. Hortensius stood beside them, looking down at the Druids and smiling with satisfaction. 'A good haul! A small fortune for the cohort from the proceeds of selling the prisoners, and a clap on the back from the legate for capturing these beauties. One of the lowest butcher's bills I've ever had after a fight. And now a fine clear morning for marching back to the legion. We're lucky men, Optio!'

'Yes, sir. How many did we lose in the end?'

'Five dead, twelve wounded and a few scratches.'

'The gods were kind, sir.'

'Kinder to some than others,' Diomedes added quietly.

'Well, yes, that's true.' Hortensius nodded. 'Still, we've got the buggers now. That'll be an end to their games.'

'No, it won't, Centurion. There are plenty more Druids and Durotrigan warriors hovering on our borders, waiting to continue the "game". Many more of these people are going to die before you Romans finally wipe out the Druids.'

Hortensius ignored the slight. The legions would only begin campaigning when it was prudent to do so. No amount of enemy provocation or appeals to Rome to honour the integrity of their alliance with the Atrebates would change that. But when the time came to take the sword to the Durotriges and their Druid leaders, there would be no mercy as the iron-shod legions rolled forward the new frontier of the empire. Hortensius smiled sympathetically at the Greek and laid a firm hand on his shoulder.

93

'Diomedes, you'll have your revenge, in time.'

'I could have my revenge now...' Diomedes nodded his head towards the Druids, and Cato saw the murderous darkness in the Greek's expression. If the cohort's commander allowed him to have his way, Diomedes would be sure that his revenge was as protracted and painful as possible. For a moment the memory of what he had seen in the well made Cato incline to support the man's thirst for bloody vengeance, but then he recoiled from the prospect with disgust. A fearful awakening of self-knowledge caused him to shudder at this will to violence he had discovered in himself.

Hortensius shook his head. 'Not possible, Diomedes. We're taking them back to the legate for questioning.'

'They won't talk. Believe me, Centurion, you'll learn nothing from them.'

'Maybe.' Hortensius shrugged. 'Maybe not. We've got some lads at headquarters trained in the art of loosening tongues.'

'They won't achieve anything.'

'Don't be so sure.'

'I'm telling you, they won't. Better to make an example of the Druids here and now. Kill them, mutilate them as they have mutilated others. Then we can leave their heads on stakes as a warning to their followers of what they can expect.'

'Nice idea,' Hortensius agreed. 'It might discourage their mates, but we can't do it. I've got orders concerning these lads. All Druids who fall into our hands are to be taken back for questioning. The legate needs 'em in good condition if he's thinking of trading them for that Roman family the Druids have got. Sorry, but there it is.'

Diomedes moved closer to the centurion. Hortensius raised his eyebrows in surprise but did not flinch or recoil at the fierce expression on the face now inches from his own.

'Let me kill them,' Diomedes said quietly through clenched teeth. 'I can't bear to live while those monsters still draw breath. They must die, Centurion. I must do it.'

'No. Now be a good fellow and calm down.'

Cato watched as Diomedes glared into the centurion's face, lips trembling as he tried to control his rage and frustration. Hortensius, by contrast, calmly returned the look with no hint of any emotion in his expression.

'I hope you won't live to regret your decision, Centurion.'

'I'm sure I won't.'

Diomedes's lips shifted into a thin smile. 'An ambiguous choice of words. Let's hope the gods are not tempted by your carelessness.'

'The gods will do as they please.' Centurion Hortensius shrugged, then turned to Cato. 'Get back to your century. Tell Macro to get his men ready to march as soon as possible.'

'After breakfast, sir?'

Hortensius stabbed a finger into Cato's chest. 'Did I say anything about fucking breakfast? Well, did I?'

'No, sir.'

'Right. Never interrupt an officer before he's finished giving orders,' Hortensius spoke in the low menacing tones of a drill instructor, and continued to stab his finger to emphasise his point. 'Do it again and I'll have your fucking balls for paperweights. Got that?'

'Yes, sir.'

'Good. Now then, I want the cohort formed up outside the gate as soon as the sun has fully risen.'

'Yes, sir!' Cato saluted, turned and trotted away. He glanced back once, and saw Hortensius having one last quiet word with Diomedes.

'There you are, Optio!' Figulus grinned as he stood up. By his feet a thin trail of smoke curled gently into the chill morning air. 'Fire's going nicely. Weren't easy though.'

'Leave it,' Cato snapped. 'We're on the move.'

'But what about breakfast?'

For an instant Cato was sorely tempted to subject Figulus to the same roasting he had just had from Hortensius. But that would have been churlish, and against the odds the legionary had managed to get a fire started.

'Sorry, Figulus. No breakfast. Put the fire out and get ready to move.'

'Put the fire out?' Figulus's expression took on the kind of pained expression usually associated with the death of a cherished family pet. 'Put out my fire?'

Cato sighed, and then quickly used the side of his boot to scrape a small mound of snow over the heap of smouldering twigs. With a spit of steam and a hiss the tiny lick of flame was extinguished.

'There. Now get moving, soldier.'

Macro had only just awakened when Cato returned to the Sixth Century's billet. He nodded in response to the orders, and then stretched his shoulders with a deep growl before he turned to bellow at his men.

'Up, you idle bastards! On your feet! We're moving out!'

A low chorus of groans and complaints rippled round the ruins.

'What about breakfast?' someone piped up.

'Breakfast? Breakfast is for losers,' Macro replied irritably. 'Now move!'

As the men raised themselves and wearily pulled on their armour, Macro stamped around delivering encouraging kicks to those whose lack of haste was most obvious. Cato hurried back to his marching yoke. Once his mess tin and the rest of the field equipment was securely fastened to the yoke, Cato struggled into his chain mail vest and was fastening his sword belt when a man from one of the other centuries came running up.

'Where's Macro?' the man panted.

'Centurion Macro is over there.' Cato pointed over the remains of a wall and the runner began to move.

'Wait!' Cato shouted. He was angry at the way some of the men of the other centuries were inclined to let their resentment of his youth override the respect due to his rank.

The man paused, then reluctantly turned round to face the optio and came to attention.

'That's better.' Cato nodded. 'You address me as Optio, or sir, next time you speak to me. Understand?'

'Yes, Optio.'

'Very well. You can carry on.'

The man disappeared round the end of the wall and Cato continued to put on his equipment. Moments later the runner reappeared, heading back towards the gate, and then came Macro, looking for his subordinate.

'What's the matter, sir?'

'It's that bloody fool Diomedes. He's done a runner.'

Cato smiled at the apparent foolishness of the statement. Where would the Greek run to? More importantly, why would he flee the safety of the cohort?

'That's not all,' Macro continued with a grim expression. 'He knocked out one of the lads guarding the Druids, and then gutted them before he disappeared.'

Chapter Fourteen

'Hmmm. Not a pretty sight,' Centurion Hortensius muttered. 'Diomedes made a pretty thorough job of it.'

The robes of the Druids had been wrenched aside and each man savagely slashed from groin to ribcage. A tangle of glistening guts and viscera lay in a pool of blood by each man. With a convulsive heave, vomit rose up in Cato's throat and he choked on the bitter taste of it. He turned away as Hortensius began to brief the other centurions.

'There's no sign of the Greek. Shame, that.' Hortensius's brow creased in anger. 'I'm looking forward to kicking seven shades out of him. No one kills my prisoners unless they've bought them off me first.'

The other officers grumbled their agreement. Prisoners who were to be sold as slaves were won at great personal risk, and were too infrequently come by to be wasted in such a profligate manner, even when vengeance was an issue. If Diomedes reappeared, Hortensius would be sure to insist on compensation.

He raised a hand to still the angry undertone. 'We're heading back to the legion with the other prisoners. There's too many of them to send back under guard – the cohort would be too weak. And without the Greek to speak for us, I doubt we'd get much of a welcome from the other Atrebate villages we're supposed to visit. So we go straight back.'

It was a breach of orders, but the situation merited it and Macro nodded with approval.

'Now then,' continued Hortensius. 'A few of those bastards and their mounts managed to slip away and you can be sure that they'll be running back to their little mates as quick as boiled asparagus. The nearest Durotrigan hill fort is a good day's ride away. If they're going to mobilise a force to come after us, we shouldn't be seeing them for at least another day. Let's make the most of it. Drive your men hard – we've got to put as much distance between this place and ourselves as possible before tonight. Any questions?'

'What about the bodies, sir?'

'What about 'em, Macro?'

'Are we just going to leave them?'

'The Durotriges can look after their own. I've made arrangements for our dead and the locals. The cavalry squadron has orders to place our men in the well with the locals and fill it in before they set off after us. That's the best we can do. There's no time for any funeral pyres. Besides, I believe the local preference is for burial.'

The Romans shuddered with distaste at the thought of subjecting the dead to gradual decay. It was one of the more disgusting practices employed by the less civilised nations of the world. Cremation was a neat and tidy end to corporeal existence.

'Back to your units. We leave at once.'

The sun inscribed a shallow parabola across a clear sky on the second day of the cohort's march back to the Second Legion. The previous night had been spent in a hastily erected marching camp and despite the exhausting effort of breaking up the frozen ground to make the ditch and inner rampart, the cold and fear of the enemy denied sleep to the men of the cohort. From first light Hortensius permitted no rest stops and watched the men like a hawk, swooping to bawl out any legionary who showed signs of slackening his pace, and freely wielding his vine cane if further encouragement was required. Even though the air was cold, and the snow compacted to ice underfoot, the men soon broke into a sweat under the burden of their equipment yokes. The British prisoners, though chained, were unburdened and had the best of it. One, who was wounded in the legs, had dropped out of the column towards the end of the first day. Hortensius stood over him and laid into the Briton with his vine stick, but the man just curled up in a protective ball and would not get up. Hortensius nodded grimly, stuck his vine into the ground and in one sweeping movement drew his sword and cut the Briton's throat. The body was left by the track as the column moved on. No more prisoners had fallen out of line since then.

Without any rest periods to relieve the pressure of the hard yoke poles on the men's shoulders, the march was an agony. The men in the ranks grumbled about their officers in increasingly bitter undertones as they forced themselves to place one foot in front of the other. Not many had slept since the night before the attack on the Durotriges. By early afternoon on the second day, as the sun began to dip towards the smudgy grey of the winter horizon, Cato wondered how much longer he could bear the strain. His collarbone was being rubbed raw under its burden, his eyes were stinging with weariness and every pace sent shooting pains up from the soles of his feet.

Looking round at the rest of the century, Cato could see the same strained expressions etched on every face. Even when Centurion Hortensius called a halt to the march at the end of the afternoon, the men would have to begin the back-breaking work of preparing a marching camp. The prospect of having to tackle the frozen soil with his pickaxe filled Cato with dread. As so often before, he cursed himself for being in the army and his imagination dwelt on the relative comforts of the life he had previously enjoyed as a slave in the imperial palace in Rome.

Just as he surrendered to the need to shut his eyes and savour the image of a neat little desk close by the warm, flickering glow of a brazier, Cato was snapped back to reality by a sudden cry. Figulus had stumbled and fallen and was scrabbling to retrieve his scattered equipment. Gratefully dropping out of the column, Cato dumped his pack and helped Figulus back onto his feet.

'Pick up your stuff and get back in line.'

Figulus nodded and reached for his yoke.

'Sweet mother! What the fuck is going on here?' Hortensius bawled as he raced down the column towards the two men. 'You ladies are not being paid by the fucking hour! Optio, is he one of yours?'

'Yes, sir.'

'Then why aren't you giving him a bloody kicking?'

'Sir?' Cato blushed. 'A kicking?' He looked up the column towards Macro, in the hope of support from his centurion. But Macro was veteran enough to know when not to intervene in a confrontation and did not even glance back.

'Deaf as well as dumb?' Hortensius roared into his face. 'Only dead soldiers are allowed to fall out of line in my cohort, understand? Any other bastard who gives it a try will fucking wish he was dead! Get it?'

'Yes, sir.'

To one side, Figulus quickly continued hooking his equipment to the yoke. The senior centurion spun round. 'Did I say you could move?'

Figulus shook his head and the senior centurion's vine cane instantly lashed out and smashed onto the side of the legionary's helmet with a sharp clang. 'Can't hear you! You've got a bloody mouth. Use it!'

'Yes, sir,' Figulus snapped back, clenching his teeth against the ringing pain in his head. He dropped his equipment and stood to attention. 'No, sir. You did not say I could move.'

'Right! Now pick up your shield and javelin. Leave the rest. Next time you'll think twice about dropping your equipment.'

Figulus burned with the injustice of the order. It would cost him several months' pay to replace the equipment. 'But, sir. I was tired, I couldn't help it.'

'Couldn't help it!' Hortensius shouted. 'Couldn't help it? YOU CAN FUCKING HELP IT! One more word out of you and I'll cut your hamstrings and leave you here for the Druids. Now get back in line!'

Figulus snatched up his fighting equipment, and with a pained glance at his yoke and his scattered belongings, ran back towards the gap in the Sixth Century where he had been marching. Hortensius turned his wrath back onto Cato. He leaned closer, speaking in a menacing whisper.

'Optio, if I have to step in and discipline your men for you again I swear it'll be you I beat senseless and leave for the enemy. How do you think it looks to the other men if you bloody go and act like his nursemaid? Before you know it, they'll all be dropping like flies and whining that they're too tired. You've got to make 'em too terrified to even think of resting. Do that and you can save their lives. But if you piss around like I just saw you do, every straggler the enemy slaughters will be down to you. Got it?'

'Yes, sir.'

'I fucking hope so, sunshine. Because if there's one thing—'

'Enemy in sight!' a distant voice called out, and from beyond the head of the cohort one of the horsemen from the cavalry squadron was galloping down the line, looking for Hortensius. The beast slewed to a halt in front of the centurion. To the side, on the track, the men of the cohort continued to march past as no order to halt had been given, but the horseman's cry had raised every head and the men looked around for sign of the enemy.

'Where?'

'Ahead, across the track, sir.' The cavalry scout pointed up the track to where it curved round a low forested hill. The rest of the squadron, tiny dark figures set against the snowy landscape, were forming up in a line at the point where the track began to bend round the hill.

'How many?'

'Hundreds, sir. And they've got chariots and some heavy infantry.'

'I see.' Hortensius nodded, and bellowed the order to halt the cohort. He turned back towards the scout. 'Tell your decurion to keep them under observation. Let me know the moment they make a move.'

The scout saluted, wheeled his horse round and pounded back

towards the distant figures of the squadron, hooves spraying snow into the faces of the infantry as he passed.

Hortensius cupped his hands. 'Officers! To me!'

'Not much light left,' Cato muttered, gazing anxiously at the sky.

Macro nodded but kept his eyes on the thick line of enemy warriors barring the track ahead where it passed through a narrow vale. Unusually for the Britons, these men stood still and silent, heavy infantry drawn up in the centre, light infantry to each side and a small force of chariots on each flank. Well over a thousand men, he estimated. Set against the four hundred and fifty effectives of the Fourth Cohort the odds did not look good. The cavalry squadron was no longer with them; Hortensius had ordered them to slip round the enemy and make best speed to the legion's headquarters and beg the legate to send out a relief column. The legion was nearly twenty miles distant but the scouts should reach them during the night, if all went well.

The cohort had another problem as it stood to in a hollow box astride the track. In the centre, ringed by half a century of nervous legionaries, squatted the prisoners taken at the settlement. They were excited, and craned their necks for sight of their comrades, whispering urgently to one another until a harsh shout and a brutal blow of a shield stilled their tongues. But it was like damming an irresistible current and as soon as one section was silenced, the whispering flowed elsewhere.

'Optio!' Hortensius shouted to the officer in charge of the prisoners. 'Get 'em to shut their fucking mouths! Kill the next Briton who opens his trap.'

'Yes, sir!' The optio turned back to the prisoners and drew his sword, daring them to utter a sound. His posture was eloquent enough and the natives shrank back in sullen silence.

'What now, I wonder,' said Macro.

'Why don't they attack us, sir?'

'No idea, Cato. No idea.'

As the light in the sky thinned and the gloom of late afternoon thickened, the two forces stood in silent confrontation. Each waited for the other to surrender to the imperative need to do something to end the tension wearing away at their nerves. Macro, veteran though he was, found that he was rapping his fingers on the rim of his shield and was only made aware of it by the curious sidelong glance of his optio. He withdrew his hand, cracked his fingers loudly enough to make Cato wince, and rested his palm on the handle of his sword.

101

'Well, I've never seen the like before,' he began conversationally. 'The Durotriges must either have the best self-control I've ever seen in a Celtic tribe or they're even more nervous of us than we are of them.'

'Which do you think it is, sir?'

'I don't think I'd bet much on them being scared.'

As he spoke, the enemy line parted to let a handful of men through. With a thrill of terror Cato saw that their leader wore an antlered headpiece and that he and his mounted followers were swathed in the same black robes they had worn before the ramparts of the Second Legion when their leader had beheaded the navy prefect, Maxentius. With a slow, deliberate and menacing gait, the Druids walked their horses up towards the cohort and gently reined in, just out of javelin range. For a moment the only movement came from their horses gently pawing the ground. Then their leader raised a hand.

'Romans! I would speak with your leader!' The accent was marked, betraying the Druid's Gallic origins. His deep voice echoed flatly off the snow-covered slopes of the vale. 'Send him forward!'

Macro and Cato turned to look at Hortensius. His lips curled with contempt for an instant, before realisation of the cohort's peril restored his self-control. The nearest men saw him swallow, stiffen his spine and then step out from the cohort's ranks and stride confidently towards the Druids. As he watched, Cato felt a cold tingle of dread at the back of his neck. Surely Hortensius would not be so foolish as to risk ending up like Maxentius? Cato leaned forward, biting on his lip.

'Easy, lad,' Macro said in a low growl. 'Hortensius knows what he's about. So don't let your feelings show – you'll make the womenfolk nervous.' He tipped his head towards the nearest men of the Sixth Century and those within earshot grinned. Cato blushed, and stood still, forcing all expression from his face as he watched Hortensius approach the Druids.

The senior centurion stopped a short distance from the horsemen and stood with his feet planted apart, his hand on the pommel of his sword. The two sides conversed, but the words were too faint to make out. The exchange was brief. The horsemen remained where they were while Hortensius moved back several paces, before slowly turning and making his way to the safety of the cohort. Once inside the wall of shields, he called for his officers. Macro and Cato trotted over to join the others, all of them burning to know what had passed between Hortensius and the dark Druids.

'They say they'll let us march on unhindered,' Hortensius paused, and gave his officers a wry smile, 'provided we set our prisoners free.'

102

'Bollocks.' Macro spat on the ground. 'They must think we were born yesterday.'

'My sentiments exactly. I told 'em I might release their mates only when we were behind the walls of the Second Legion's camp. They weren't impressed with that, and suggested a compromise. That we free the prisoners once we're in sight of the camp.'

The officers considered the offer, each weighing up the likelihood of the cohort being able to reach the camp, unencumbered by prisoners, before the Britons reneged on the deal and tried to cut them to pieces.

'There'll be plenty of chances to take more prisoners later in the campaign,' one of the centurions suggested, and then stopped speaking as Hortensius laughed and shook his head.

'That bastard Diomedes has stitched us up nicely!'

'Sir?'

'They don't want that sorry lot over there!' Hortensius jabbed his thumb towards the Britons squatting on the ground. 'They're talking about the Druids we took back at the settlement. The ones that little shit Diomedes killed.'

Chapter Fifteen

'Back to your units.' Hortensius gave the order quietly. 'Tell them to prepare to advance. As soon as I give the signal.'

The officers trotted over to their centuries. Cato glanced over at the Druids waiting for Hortensius's response to their offer. They'd get their answer soon enough, he reflected, and found himself desperately hoping the cohort would manage to kill them before they could wheel their mounts and escape.

The men of the Sixth Century had forgotten their exhaustion and listened intently as Macro and his optio passed down the line, quietly readying the men for the order to advance. Even in the dying light Cato could see the determined glint in the eyes of the legionaries as they checked their helmet ties and made sure of their grip on their shields and javelins. This would be a straight fight, unlike the mad rush of the trap they had sprung in the ruined settlement. Neither side would have the advantage of surprise. Nor would tactical skill play a part. Only training, equipment and raw courage would determine the outcome. The Fourth Cohort would cut its way through the Britons, or be cut to pieces in the attempt.

The Sixth Century formed the left-hand side of the front face of the box formation. To its right was the First Cohort, and three other cohorts formed the sides and rear of the box. The last cohort acted as reserve, with half its strength guarding the prisoners. Macro and Cato moved to the centre of the front rank of their century and waited for Hortensius to give the order. On the track ahead of them the Druids were now aware that something was amiss. They craned their necks to peer over the wall of shields for any sign of their comrades. The leader kicked his heels and urged his mount closer to the legionaries. He raised one hand to cup his mouth.

'Romans! Give us your response! Now, or die!'

'Fourth Cohort!' Hortensius roared. 'Advance!'

The cohort stepped forward, booted feet crunching over the frozen snow as they closed on the silent mass of the Durotriges waiting for them. As the wall of shields moved forward, the Druids wheeled their mounts and galloped back to the safety of their followers. Behind the metal trim of his shield, Cato's eyes scanned the dark figures barring the cohort's route, and then looked longingly beyond them to where the track led towards the safety of the Second Legion's camp. His right hand tightened its grip round the handle of his sword and the blade rose to the horizontal poise.

As the distance closed between the two sides, the Druids barked out orders to the Durotrigan warriors. With a crack of reins and cries of instruction and encouragement to their horses, the charioteers on the flanks began to move further out, ready to charge down on any gaps that opened in the Roman formation. Axles squeaked and the heavy wheels rumbled as the chariots moved off under the anxious gaze of the legionaries. Cato tried to reassure himself that they had little to fear from these outdated weapons. As long as the Roman lines held firm, the chariots could be regarded as little more than an unpleasant distraction.

As long as the formation held firm.

'Hold the line steady!' Macro shouted, as some of the more nervous men in the century began to outpace their comrades. Chastened, the men adjusted their stride and lines evened out to present an unbroken wall of shields to the enemy. The Durotriges were no more than a hundred paces away now and Cato could pick out the individual features of the men he would kill or be killed by in the next few moments. Most of the enemy's heavy infantry wore chain mail over their brightly coloured tunics and leggings. Shaggy beards and pigtails hung down beneath polished helmets and each man carried a war spear or long sword. Although they had been organised into a discreet unit, it was clear from the unevenness of their line of shields that they had been poorly trained in formation drill.

Cato was aware of a strange whirring sound rising above the crunch of snow and chink of equipment, and glanced to the light infantry on each side of the enemy centre.

'Slingers!' someone shouted out from the Roman ranks.

Centurion Hortensius reacted at once. 'First two ranks! Shields high and low!'

Cato adjusted his grip and crouched slightly so that the bottom rim of his shield protected his shins. The legionary immediately behind raised his shield above Cato. The action was repeated all along the first two ranks so that the front of the Roman formation was sheltered from the coming volley. A moment later and the whirring abruptly rose in pitch and was accompanied by a whipping sound. A deafening rattle filled the air as the deadly volley of shot struck the Roman shields. Cato flinched as a corner of his shield was hit by a lead shot. But the Roman line did not falter and remorselessly advanced as the slingshot continued to crash off the shields with a sound like a thousand hammer blows. Yet several cries told of shots that had found their targets. Those men who fell out of line were quickly replaced by the legionaries in the next rank and their writhing forms left to be scooped up by a handful of men acting as casualty bearers and dumped in one of the cohort's wagons, rumbling along inside the square.

Thirty yards out from the heaving mass of the enemy line, Hortensius ordered the cohort to halt.

'Front ranks! Ready javelins!' Those who still had a javelin to throw after the fight in the settlement swept their right arms back, planting their feet apart in readiness for the next order. 'Javelins, release!'

In the dying light it appeared as if a fine black veil rose up from the Roman ranks and arced down onto the milling mass of the Durotriges. A shattering clatter and crash was quickly followed by screams as the heavy iron heads of the Roman javelins punched through shields, armour and flesh.

'Draw swords!' bellowed Hortensius above the din. A metallic rasp sounded from all sides of the box formation as the legionaries drew their short stabbing swords and presented the tip to the enemy. Almost at once the harsh blare of war horns sounded from behind the Durotriges and with a great roar of battle rage they swept forward.

'Charge!' Hortensius cried out, and with shields held firmly to the front and swords held level at the waist, the Roman front lines threw themselves at the enemy. Cato's heart pounded against his ribs and time appeared to slow – enough for him to imagine being killed or terribly wounded by one of the men whose savage faces were mere feet away. An icy sensation flowed through his guts before he filled his lungs and gave vent to a wild cry of his own, determined to destroy everything in his path.

The two lines hurtled against each other with a rolling clatter of spear, sword and shield that sounded like a huge wave crashing on a stony shore. Cato felt his shield jar as it thumped into flesh. A man gasped as the air was driven out of his lungs and then again in agony as the legionary next to Cato drove his sword into the Briton's armpit. The man dropped and Cato kicked him to one side as he in turn thrust towards the unprotected chest of a Briton wielding his axe above

Macro's skull. The Briton saw the blow coming and threw himself back from the point of Cato's sword so that it merely tore open his shoulder instead of dealing a mortal blow. He did not cry out as blood poured down his chest. Nor did he cry out when Macro rammed his sword in so ferociously that it went straight through and burst bloodily from the small of the man's back. A startled expression flashed onto his ruined face, then he fell amongst the other dead and injured littering the churned-up snow, now stained with blood.

'Press forwards, lads!' Cato shouted. 'Keep it close, and stick it to 'em!'

Beside him Macro smiled approvingly. The optio was finally acting like a soldier in battle. No longer coy about shouting out encouragement to men far older and more experienced than him, and cool-headed enough to know how the cohort must fight in order to survive.

The heavily armed Britons hurled themselves on the Roman shield wall with a fanatical savagery that horrified Cato. On either side of the box formation, the more lightly armed natives closed in on the flanks, screaming their battle cries and urged on by the Druids. The priests of the Dark Moon stood a little behind the fighting line, pouring curses on the invaders and calling upon the tribesmen to sweep this small knot of Romans from the British soil they defiled with their eagle standards. But religious fervour and blind courage provided no protection for their unarmoured breasts. They fell in large numbers before the lethal thrusts of swords designed to make short work of such foolish heroics.

At length the British heavy infantry became aware of the grievous losses that were piling up at the front of the armoured square, and still the Roman line remained unbroken and unwavering. The Durotriges began to shrink back from the terrible blades that stabbed out at them from between shields that all but hid their enemy from view.

'We've got 'em!' Macro bellowed. 'Forward! Keep forcing them back!'

The Durotriges, brave as they were, had never before encountered such a ruthless and efficient foe. It was like fighting a great iron machine, designed and built for war alone. It rolled forward without pity, impressing upon all who stood in its path that there could be only one outcome for those who dared to defy it.

A cry of anguish and fear grew in the throats of the Durotriges and flowed through their milling ranks as they realised the Romans were prevailing. Men were no longer willing to throw themselves uselessly at this moving square of impenetrable shields that was cleaving its way through ranks of swords and spears. As the Durotriges at the front recoiled, the men in the rear began to step back, at first just to keep their balance, and then their feet picked up speed, as if of their own will – carrying them away from the enemy. More men followed and scores, then hundreds of Britons peeled away from the dense mass of their comrades and fled down the track.

'Don't fucking stop!' Hortensius roared from the front rank of the First Century. 'Keep advancing. If we stop we're dead! Forward!'

A less experienced army would have drawn up right there, flushed with excitement at having bested their enemy, trembling with the thrill of having survived and awed by the carnage they had wrought. But the men of the legions continued their advance behind a solid shield wall, swords poised and ready to strike. Most had grown into manhood under the iron will of a military discipline that had stripped away the soft malleable material of humanity and fashioned them into deadly fighters, wholly subordinate to the will and word of command. After only the briefest pause to dress their lines, the men of the Fourth Cohort steadily advanced down the track leading through the vale.

The sun had settled beyond the horizon and the snow took on a bluish tinge as dusk closed in. On either side, the slopes were loosely covered by the broken ranks of the Durotriges, watching in silence as the square trudged past. Here and there their leaders, and the Druids, were busy re-forming their men by force of will and cruelly wielded blows from the flat of their blades. War horns brayed out their rallying cries and the warriors gradually began to recover their wits.

'No slacking!' Macro ordered. 'Keep up the pace!'

The first enemy units to re-form began to march after the cohort. The square formation was designed for protection, not speed, and the lightly armed units easily outpaced the Romans. As night fell, the men of the Fourth Cohort were uncomfortably aware of the dark mass of men flowing past them along the slopes in a bid to head off the legionaries once again. And this time, Cato reflected, the Durotriges would have prepared a more effective line of attack.

Night marches are difficult in the best of circumstances. The ground is largely invisible and lays plenty of traps for the unwary foot: a concealed rabbit hole or entrance to a sett can easily twist an ankle or break a bone. The unevenness of the ground quickly threatens to break up a formation and its officers have to move up and down the ranks tirelessly to ensure that a steady pace is maintained and that no gaps appear in the unit. Beyond these immediate difficulties lies the larger problem of route finding. With no sun to guide the men and, in overcast conditions, no stars, there is little more than faith to act upon in setting the line of march. For the men of the Fourth Cohort the problems of night marching were particularly acute. Snow had buried the track they had marched south on some days earlier and Hortensius could only follow the course of the vale, warily assessing each dip and rise in case the cohort was blundering off course. On either side, the sounds of the unseen Britons wore down the exhausted nerves of the men as they dragged their feet forwards.

Cato was more tired than he had ever been in his life. Every sinew in his body cried out for rest. His eyelids were almost too heavy to keep open and the cold was no longer the numbing distraction it had been earlier in the day. Now it fuelled the desire to slip into a deep, warm sleep. Insiduously, his mind entertained the idea and slowly drained the resolve that strove against the demand of every aching muscle for rest. He withdrew his attention from the world around him, away from watching the ranks of legionaries and the danger of the enemy lurking invisibly beyond. The monotonous pace of the advance aided the process and at length he succumbed to the desire to shut his eyes, just for a moment, just to take away the awful stinging sensation for a moment. He blinked them open to make sure of his bearings, and then they closed again, almost of their own will. Slowly his chin dipped towards his chest . . .

'On your fucking feet!'

Cato's eyes snapped open, his body filled with the chilling tremor that comes with being forcibly wrenched from sleep. Someone held his arm in a tight, painful grip.

'What?'

'You were falling asleep,' Macro whispered, not wanting his men to overhear. He dragged Cato forward. 'Nearly fell on top of me. Happens again and I'll cut your balls off. Now, stay awake.'

'Yes, sir.'

Cato shook his head, reached down for a handful of snow and wiped it across his face, welcoming the restorative effect of its icy sting. He fell into place alongside his centurion, feeling ashamed of his physical weakness. Even though he was at the end of his endurance he must not show it, not in front of the men. Never again, he promised himself. Cato forced himself to keep his attention focused on the men as the cohort continued to trudge forward. More regularly than before he moved up and down the dark lines of his men, snapping out orders to those who showed any sign of lagging.

Several hours into the night, Cato became aware that the vale was narrowing. The dark slopes on either side, only fractionally darker than the sky above, began to rise more steeply.

'What's that ahead?' Macro suddenly asked. 'There. Your eyes are better than mine. What do you reckon?'

Across the snow stretching out in front of the cohort an indistinct line extended across the vale. There was some movement there, and as Cato strained his eyes to try and make out more detail, a low whirring sound filled the freezing night air.

'Shields up!'

Cato's warning came moments before the slingshot came whipping out of the darkness and struck the cohort with a splintering clatter. The aim was understandably poor and much of the volley passed over the legionaries or struck the ground short of the target. Even so, a number of cries and a scream sounded above the din.

. 'Cohort, halt!' shouted Centurion Hortensius. The cohort drew up, each man shrinking into the shelter of his shield as the whirring started again. The next volley was as ragged as the first and the only casualties this time came from the huddle of prisoners under guard in the centre of the formation.

'Ready swords!'

The order was followed by a rasping clattering chorus from the dark lines of the legionaries. Then the cohort was still again.

'Advance!'

The formation rippled forward a moment before settling into a more measured stride. From the front rank of the Sixth Century, Cato could now make out more detail of what lay ahead. The Durotriges had constructed a rough barrier of felled trees and branches that stretched across the narrow floor of the vale and a little way up the slope on each side. Behind this light cover swarmed a dark horde of men. The slingers were no longer shooting in volleys and the whirring of slings and sharp crack of shot were almost constant. Cato flinched from the sound and ducked his head below the rim of his shield as the cohort advanced on the barrier. There were more cries from the ranks of legionaries as the range decreased and the enemy slingers were able to aim more accurately. The gap between the cohort and the felled trees steadily closed until at last the men of the front rank came up against the tangle of branches. On the other side, the enemy had stopped using their slings and now brandished spears and swords, screaming their war cries into the Romans' faces.

'Halt! Clear the barricades away! Pass the word!' Macro shouted, aware that his order would barely carry above the noise.

The legionaries quickly sheathed their swords and began pulling at the branches, desperately tugging and shaking the tangle loose. As the men set about the Durotriges' makeshift defences, a wild roar of voices from behind the century carried across the vale. Cato glanced back and saw a dark mass swarming across the snow towards the two centuries at the rear of the square formation. Hortensius bellowed out the order for those centuries to turn and face the threat.

'Nice trap!' Macro grunted as he heaved a thick limb free of the barricade and fed it back to the men behind him. 'Get rid of this stuff as quick as you can!'

As the Durotriges crashed into the rear of the formation, the legionaries at the front tore at the barrier, driven to desperation by the knowledge that unless the cohort could continue to advance, it would be trapped and annihilated. Slowly, the barrier was wrenched apart and small gaps opened that a man could squeeze through. Macro quickly passed the word that no one was to take the enemy on single-handed. They must wait for his order. Some of the Durotriges, however, were not so prudent and dashed forward to get at the Romans the moment an opening appeared. They paid dearly for this impetuousness and were cut down the moment they reached the Romans. But in death they at least delayed the legionaries in their work. At last there were a number of openings large enough for several men to get through and Macro shouted an order to draw swords and form up at the gaps.

'Cato! Get down to the left flank and take charge. Once I give the order, get through and form the men back into line as soon as you can on the far side. Got that?'

'Yes, sir!'

'Away with you!'

The optio eased his way back through the ranks of the century and then ran down to the left-hand corner of the formation.

'Make way there! Make way!' Cato shouted, pushing his way to the front. He saw an opening in the barricade, slightly to one side. 'Close up on me! When the centurion gives the order, we go through together!'

The legionaries bunched up on either side of their optio and joined shields so that the enemy would have little chance to strike at them as they forced their way through. Then they waited, swords poised, ears straining for Macro's order above the war cries and screams of the Durotriges.

'Sixth Century!' The centurion sounded very distant to Cato. 'Advance!'

'Now!' Cato shouted. 'Stay with me!'

Pushing his shield out a little way to absorb any impact, Cato led off, making sure that the others kept close and retained the integrity of the shield wall. Although the larger branches had been cleared away, the ground beneath was littered with twisted remnants of wood and every step had to be taken carefully. As soon as the Durotriges became aware of the Roman thrust, their shouting reached a new pitch of rage and they hurled themselves onto the legionaries. Cato felt someone slam into his shield and quickly thrust his sword, sensing a glancing contact with his foe before he whipped his blade back ready to deliver the next blow. On both flanks, and behind, the men of the century pressed through, thrusting deeper into the dark mass of Britons on the far side of the barricade.

The Druids had obviously counted on the volleys of slingshot and the barricade to stop the Roman advance and had manned it with their light infantry while the remains of the heavy infantry assaulted the rear of the Roman square. The well-armoured legionaries easily cut a series of wedges into the enemy's ranks and as more legionaries pushed through the barricade, they spread out on either side. The lightly armed Durotriges were totally outclassed. Even their reckless courage could do little to effect the outcome. Before long the leading centuries of the Roman square had formed a continuous line on the far side of the ruined barricade.

Once before, the Britons had faced the relentless killing machine of Rome, and once again they broke before it, streaming away into the night. As he watched them flee, Cato lowered his sword and found that he was shaking. Whether from fear or exhaustion he no longer knew. Strangely, his sword hand was so tightly clenched round the handle that it was almost unbearably painful. Yet it took all the force of will he could summon to make his hand slacken its grip. Then awareness of his surroundings became more rational and he saw the line of bodies stretched out along the barricade, many still writhing and crying out from their injuries.

'First and Sixth Centuries!' Hortensius was shouting. 'Keep going! Advance a hundred paces and halt!'

The Roman line moved forward, and slowly the flank centuries and supply wagons slipped through the gaps and resumed their place in the square formation, shepherding their surviving prisoners along with them. Only the rear two centuries remained on the far side of the barricade, steadily giving way under the onslaught of the Durotriges' best warriors. While his century was halted, Macro ordered Cato to make a quick tally of their strength.

112

'Well?'

'Fourteen lost, best as I can say, sir.'

'All right.' Macro nodded with satisfaction. He had feared the butcher's bill would be higher than that. 'Go and report that to Centurion Hortensius.'

'Yes, sir.'

Hortensius was not difficult to locate; a stream of orders and shouts of encouragement were ringing out across the sound of battle, even though the voice now carried the rasp of extreme exhaustion. Hortensius received the strength report and did a quick mental calculation.

'That makes our losses over fifty, and there's the rear cohorts to go yet. How long until dawn, do you think?'

Cato forced himself to concentrate. 'I'd guess four, maybe five hours.'

'Too long. We'll need every man on the formation. Can't spare any more for guard duties . . .' The senior centurion realised he had no alternative. 'We're going to have to lose the prisoners,' he said with unmistakable bitterness.

'Sir?'

'Get back to Macro. Tell him to round up some men and kill the prisoners. Make sure the bodies are left with those we've just killed on the far side of the barricade. No sense in giving the enemy any greater cause for grievance. What are you waiting for? Go!'

Cato saluted and ran back towards his century, A wave of nausea swept up from the pit of his stomach as he passed the kneeling forms of the prisoners. He cursed himself for being a weak sentimental fool. Hadn't these same men killed all their prisoners? And not just killed, but tortured, raped and mutilated them. The face of the flaxen-haired boy staring lifelessly from the bodies heaped in the well swam back before his eyes and bitter tears of confused rage and a sense of injustice welled up. Much as he had wished death on every member of the Durotrigan nation, now that it came to killing these prisoners, some strange reserve of morality made it seem wrong.

Macro, too, hesistated on hearing the order.

'Kill the prisoners?'

'Yes, sir. Right now.'

'I see.' Macro looked into the young optio's shadowed expression and made a quick decision. 'I'll see to it then. You stay here. Keep the men formed up and ready, just in case that lot get it into their thick British heads to try it on again.'

Cato fixed his eyes on the churned-up snow stretching out ahead of the cohort. Even when pitiful cries and screams rose up from a short distance behind him, he refused to turn and acknowledge the sound.

'Keep your eyes to the front!' he shouted at the men closest to him, who had turned to seek out the source of the awful noise.

At length it died down and the last cries were drowned out by the sound of the fight from the rear of the formation. Cato waited for fresh orders, numb with the cold and exhaustion, his spirit weighed down by the bloody deed Centurion Hortensius had ordered done. No matter how hard he tried to justify the execution of the prisoners in terms of the cohort's survival, or the well-deserved retribution for the massacre of the Atrebate inhabitants of Noviomagus, it felt wrong to kill their captives in cold blood.

Macro slowly threaded his way back through his men to take up position in the front rank of his century. He stood beside Cato, grim-faced and silent. Cato glanced at his superior, a man he had come to know well over the last year and a half. He had quickly learned to respect Macro for his qualities as a soldier, and more importantly his integrity as a human being. While he would hesitate to call the centurion a friend to his face, a certain intimacy had grown between them. Not quite father and son, more that of a much older, worldy-wise brother and his younger sibling. Macro, he knew, regarded him with a degree of pride and smiled on his achievements.

For Cato's part, Macro embodied all those qualities he aspired to. The centurion lived at ease with himself. He was a soldier through and through and had no other ambition in life. Not for him the tortuous self-analysis that Cato inflicted on himself. The intellectual pursuits he had been encouraged to indulge in when he was raised as a member of the imperial household were no preparation for life in the legions. No preparation at all. The lofty idealism Virgil lavished on his vision of Rome's destiny to civilise the world had no relevance to the naked terror of this night's fight, or the bloody horror of military necessity that had caused the prisoners to be killed.

'It happens, lad,' Macro muttered. 'It happens. We do what we must if we are to win. We do what we must to see the light of the next day. But that doesn't make it any easier.'

Cato stared at his centurion for a moment, before nodding bleakly.

'Cohort!' Hortensius bellowed from the rear of the formation. 'Advance!'

The rearmost centuries had passed through the barricade and re-formed on the far side, all the while fighting off the increasingly desperate assault of the Durotriges' heavy infantry. But once it was clear that the attempt to trap and destroy the cohort had failed, the fight went out of the Durotriges in that strange indefinable way that kindred sentiment spreads through a crowd. Warily, they disengaged from the Romans and simply stood in silence as the cohort tramped away from them. The defiant ranks of legionaries remained unbroken, and had left a trail of native bodies in their wake. But the night was far from over. Long hours remained before dawn stretched its first faint fingers over the horizon. Long enough to settle the score with the Romans.

The cohort moved on through the darkness, the square formation tightly compacted about its supply wagons bearing their load of casualties. The moans and cries of the wounded chorused with every jolt and grated on the nerves of their comrades still fit enough to march. They were straining to hear any sound of the enemy's approach and cursed the wounded and the squeak and rumble of the wagon wheels. The Durotriges were still out there, and they dogged the cohort. Slingshot whirred in from the darkness, mostly rattling off the shields but now and then finding a target and reducing the cohort's strength by one more each time. The ranks closed up and the formation steadily shrunk as the night wore on. Nor was slingshot the only danger. The chariots the cohort had last seen at dusk now rumbled along the slopes, and every so often charged in on the cohort with blood-chilling war cries. Then at the last moment they veered away, having hurled their spears into the Roman ranks. Some of these, too, found their mark and inflicted even more terrible injuries than the slingshot.

Throughout it all Centurion Hortensius shouted out his orders, and threatened terrible punishments to those he knew were best motivated by fear, while offering encouragement to the rest. When the Durotriges yelled abuse from the darkness, Hortensius returned it in kind at top parade-ground volume.

Finally the sky began to lighten over to the east, slowly gathering pale luminescence, until there was no mistaking the approach of dawn. To Cato it seemed that the morning was being drawn across the horizon almost by the willpower of the legionaries alone as each man gazed longingly towards the growing light. Slowly the dark geography around them resolved itself into faint shades of grey and the legionaries could at last see the enemy once again, faint figures stretching out on either flank, shadowing the cohort as it struggled on, exhausted and battered but still intact and ready to summon up enough strength to resist one last onslaught.

Ahead the ground gently rose up to a low crest and as the front ranks of the century reached the ridge, Cato looked up and saw, no more than three miles away, the neatly defined outline of the ramparts of the Second Legion's fortified encampment. Over the thin dark line of the palisade hung a dirty brown haze of woodsmoke and Cato realised how hungry he felt.

'Not long now, lads!' Macro called out. 'We'll be back in time for breakfast!'

But even as the centurion spoke, Cato saw that the Durotriges were massing for another attack. One last attempt to obliterate the enemy who had managed to evade destruction all night. One last effort to exact a bloody revenge for their comrades whose bodies lay scattered along the line of march of the Fourth Cohort.

Chapter Sixteen

'Yesterday afternoon, you say?' Vespasian raised his eyebrows as the cavalry decurion finished making his report.

'Yes, sir,' replied the decurion. 'Though more dusk than afternoon, sir.'

'So why has it taken you until dawn to get back to the legion?'

The decurion's gaze flickered down for an instant. 'At first we kept running into them, sir. Seemed that they were everywhere, horsemen, chariots, infantry – the lot. So we swung back and circled round during the night. I realised I'd lost my bearings after a while and had to make a best guess. Before first light, we were way over to the east, sir. Took us a while before we even sighted Calleva. Then we made the best time we could, sir.'

'I see.' Vespasian scrutinised the decurion's expression for any sign of guile. He would not tolerate any officer who put his personal safety before that of his comrades. Covered in mud and clearly exhausted, the decurion stood to attention with all the dignity he could muster. There was a tense silence as Vespasian stared at him. At last he said, 'What was the Durotriges' strength?'

He was pleased to see the decurion pause to consider the question before replying, rather than impulsively trying to gratify his legate with a hurried guess.

'Two thousand . . . maybe as many as two and a half thousand, but no more than that, sir. Perhaps a quarter were heavy infantry. The rest were light troops, some armed with slings, and possibly thirty chariots. That's all I could see, sir. More of them may have turned up during the night.'

'We'll find out soon enough.' Vespasian nodded towards the tent's entrance. 'You and your men are dismissed. Get 'em fed and rested.'

The decurion saluted, turned smartly and marched away from the legate's desk. Vespasian shouted past him for the duty staff officer. An instant later one of the junior tribunes, a younger son of the Camilli clan – all expensively braided tunic and no brains – burst into the tent, brushing the decurion to one side as he passed.

'Tribune!' Vespasian roared. Both the decurion and the tribune flinched. 'I'll thank you not to treat your fellow officers in such an unmannerly fashion!'

'Sir, I was just responding to—'

'Enough! If it happens again I'll have the decurion here take you on an extended patrol you won't forget in a hurry.'

The decurion grinned with delight at the thought of that fine young aristocratic arse rubbed raw by a cavalry saddle. Then he ducked out of the tent to go and see to his men.

'Tribune, give the order for the legion to stand to. I want the First, Second and Third cohorts ready to move as soon as possible. The rest are to man the ramparts. It'll be a quick action, no marching rations need to be issued. I want them formed up on the track outside the south gate. Got that?'

'Yes, sir!'

'Then please see to it.'

The young man turned and ran to the entrance.

'Tribune!' Vespasian called after him.

The tribune turned back, and was surprised to see a faint smile on Vespasian's face.

'Quintus Camillus, try to exude a calm professionalism as you go about your duties. You'll find it helps in your relations with the career officers, and will be less alarming to the men under your command. No one likes to think their fate is in the hands of an overgrown schoolboy.'

The tribune flushed bright red but managed to bite back his embarrassment and anger. Vespasian tilted his head towards the entrance and the tribune turned and stiffly marched away.

It had been a harsh put-down, but Camillus would think more carefully about his demeanour from now on. How one appeared in front of career officers and the other ranks determined the esteem with which the latter would regard the highest social classes of Roman society. Vespasian was keenly aware that the young aristocrats serving their tour of duty with the legions were generally held in contempt by the rank and file. This regrettable state of affairs was only made worse by the arrogant immaturity of young gentlemen like Camillus. Social distinctions within the military were already a touchy issue, without the situation being made any worse. If in future Camillus affected the bearing of a calm professional, it would go some way towards easing the resentment of the men he might have to command in battle one day.

Vespasian's thoughts returned to the matter he had been pondering before news of the Fourth Cohort's predicament reached him. There had still been no response to the message he had sent General Plautius. The courier might have been delayed, of course. The native tracks were of poor quality even in the best weather. But, even allowing for that, he should have heard from the general by now.

One more day, he decided. If he had heard nothing by the following morning he would send the general another message. Meanwhile, the trumpets were sounding the assembly; the legionaries would be tumbling out of their tents, cursing as they struggled to get their armour and weapons strapped on. Every man had been drilled to respond instantly to the trumpet call, and the legate was no exception.

'Pass the word for my body slave!' Vespasian shouted.

The climb up the ladders to the lookout tower above the southern gate served to remind Vespasian how unfit he had become in recent months. He hauled himself through the hatchway and stood against the sentry rail for a moment, breathing heavily. He should have done this before strapping on his muscled cuirass. The dead weight of the silvered bronze together with the rest of his equipment doubled the effort required to climb the ladders. Too much paperwork and too little exercise, Vespasian reflected, would be the ruin of him as a soldier. At thirty-five he was beginning to feel the onset of middle-age and was human enough to prefer domestic comforts over the physical hardships of campaigning. Vespasian's tour of duty would be coming to an end next year, and the prospect of a return to Rome, with all the opportunities for self-indulgence that implied, was very comforting. Any escape from the awful climate of this perpetually damp and bedrizzled island would be worth losing a limb for. Yet none of the natives he had met socially in Camulodunum had registered the slightest complaint about Britain's climate when he had raised the issue. The damp must have got to their brains, Vespasian decided with a wry grin.

He looked up, cleared his mind, and concentrated on the situation opening up before him in the light of the early morning sun. Below, the stout timbers of the south gate had been swung inwards and through the gate tramped the double-strength First Cohort. Behind them would march two other cohorts, nearly two thousand men in all. Vespasian was confident that this force would be more than enough to frighten off the Durotriges swarming about the distant ranks of the Fourth Cohort, barely visible on the crest of a distant hill. He estimated that the Fourth was still nearly three miles off, which meant the relief column would not reach them for an hour or so yet. The Fourth Cohort should be able to keep the Durotriges at bay for that long at least. Vespasian was pleased at the way things had worked out. Rather than having to spend fruitless weeks consolidating the Atrebates' defences and attempting to hunt down the Durotrigan raiding parties, their Druid leaders had obligingly delivered them up to the Seond Legion. If a quick defeat could be inflicted on them today then the coming campaign would get off to a fine start indeed.

A creaking on the ladder caused him to turn his head. A massive man was squeezing through the hatchway. Over six feet tall, and broad-shouldered to match, the Second Legion's camp prefect was a grey-haired veteran with a livid scar from forehead to cheek. As the senior career officer of the legion he was a soldier of immense experience and courage. In Vespasian's absence, or death, Sextus would assume command of the legion.

'Morning, Sextus. Come to see the fight?'

'Of course, sir. How're the lads of the Fourth doing?'

'Not too bad. Still formed up and heading this way. By the time I get over there with the relief I imagine it'll all be over.'

'Maybe,' Sextus replied with a shrug as he squinted at the distant fight. 'Are you sure you should be leading the relief column, sir?'

'You think I shouldn't?'

'Frankly, sir, no. Legates should look after the legion as a whole, not arse around on minor details.'

Vespasian grinned. 'That's your job, I suppose.'

'Yes, sir. As it happens.'

'Well, I need the exercise. You don't. So be a good chap and look after things here for an hour or so. I'll try not to make a mess of your First Cohort.'

Both men chuckled; camp prefects were promoted from the rank of senior centurion of the First Cohort, and they were notoriously protective about the last field command of their career.

Vespasian turned and swung himself onto the sentry ladder, slipping easily through the hatchway. Back on the ground, he paused by the gate where his body slave carefully slipped on his helmet and tied the chin thongs securely. The men of the Third Cohort were tramping by, heading through the gates to join the column formed up on the track outside. Vespasian felt a thrill of excitement flow through his body at the prospect of leading the relief column to the aid of the Fourth Cohort.

After the tedium of the long winter, most of it snugged down in temporary barracks, here was a chance to get back to some proper soldiering again.

Vespasian allowed his body slave a final tweak of the red ribbon fastened about his cuirass and then turned to march out of the camp and take up his position at the head of the column. Before he made it through the gate, a shrill cry from the top of the watchtower stopped him in mid-stride.

'Horsemen approaching from the north-east!'

'Now what?' muttered Vespasian, angrily slapping his hand against his thigh. Through the gate he saw the three cohorts waiting to go to the aid of their comrades. But he could hardly leave the legion until he had ascertained whether the camp was being threatened on another front. Equally, any delay in sending help to the Fourth Cohort would cost lives. The relief column had to set off at once. And since he had to investigate the sighting to the north-east, it would need a new commander. He looked up at the watchtower.

'Camp Prefect!'

A face, dark against the sky, appeared above the palisade. 'Yes, sir?'

'Take charge here.'

By the time Vespasian had run across the camp and climbed the watchtower on the northern gate, he was desperately out of breath again. Clutching the sentry rail and taking great gulps of air, he took a last glance at the relief column snaking its way across the rolling countryside towards the dark mass of tiny figures that represented the Fourth Cohort. Sextus could be trusted to see that the rescue operation was carried out with as little loss of life as possible. Camp prefects, as a rule, had long outgrown the distasteful – and dangerous – thirst for glory that some of the junior officers espoused. If he was honest, the men of the relief column were probably safer with Sextus in charge rather than himself. That thought did little to relieve the frustration he felt at having to pass the command over to the camp prefect.

As soon as he was breathing more easily, Vespasian turned and walked over to the sentry keeping watch to the north.

'So where are these bloody horsemen?'

'Can't see them right now, sir,' the sentry replied nervously, not wanting his legate to suspect that it might be a false alarm. He continued hurriedly, 'They rode down into that dip there, sir. Just a moment ago. Should be coming back into view any time now, sir.'

Vespasian looked in the direction indicated, a shallow valley running parallel to the camp barely a mile away. But the only sign of life was a thin trail of smoke rising from a small group of thatched huts. They waited in silence, the sentry growing ever more twitchy as he willed the horsemen to reappear.

'How many of them did you see?'

'Thirty or so, sir.'

'Ours?'

'Too far off for me to be sure, sir. They might have had red cloaks.'

'Might have?' Vespasian turned to look at the sentry, an older man who must have served quite a few years with the eagles. Certainly long enough to know that a sentry should only ever report details they were sure of. The legionary stiffened under the legate's gaze and was astute enough to refrain from any further comment. Vespasian seethed internally at having been diverted to the watchtower. If he'd known the number of the approaching horsemen earlier he could have left Sextus to deal with the matter. Well, it was too late now, he reflected, and it would be bad form to take it out on this nervous sentry. Better to keep an air of imperturbability, and enhance the image of the unflappable commander he presented to the men of his legion.

'Look, sir!' The sentry jabbed his hand over the palisade.

A line of plumed helmets bobbed up over the side of the valley. Above them flapped a purple pennant.

'The general himself!' The sentry whistled.

Vespasian's heart felt heavy. The general had got his message, then. He now knew of the terrible danger his family was in. Reminded of his own pregnant wife and young son, Vespasian could sympathise with his general. But sympathy did not allay his apprehension about the general's state of mind.

Vespasian was suddenly aware that the sentry was watching him.

'What's the matter, soldier? Never seen a general before?'

The sentry coloured, but before he could respond, Vespasian sent him down the ladder to alert the duty centurion of General Plautius's approach. The usual formalities due to a commanding general would have to be organised quickly. Vespasian stayed in the watchtower until the sentry returned, watching the approaching column canter towards the northern gate. The general's mounted guard came first, followed by Plautius himself and a handful of staff officers. With them rode two hooded figures, and then came the rearguard section, riding either side of five Druids who were tied to their mounts. As they neared, Vespasian could see the foam on the flanks of the horses; the beasts had obviously been driven to the limits of their endurance in the general's bid to reach the Second Legion as swiftly as possible.

Vespasian quickly descended from the tower and took position at the end of the honour guard formed up on either side of the gateway. It would create a good impression if he greeted the general in person. The pounding of hooves was clearly audible now, and Vespasian gave a nod to the centurion in command of the honour guard.

'Open the gates!' shouted the centurion. The locking bar was lifted and carried to one side and then with a deep groan the gates were hauled open as widely as possible. It was neatly timed, as moments later the first of the general's personal guard reined in to one side of the gateway and waited for Plautius to enter the camp first. The general, followed by his staff, slowed to a walk as the guard centurion bellowed his orders.

'Honour guard . . . present!'

The grounded javelins of the legionaries were thrust forward at an angle, and the general responded with a salute in the direction of the headquarters tents where the Second Legion's standards were housed in a temporary shrine. Plautius came to a halt beside Vespasian and dismounted.

'Good to see you, General!' Vespasian smiled.

'Vespasian.' Plautius nodded curtly. 'We need to talk, at once.'

'Yes, sir.'

'But first, please see to it that my escort . . . and my companions,' he indicated the staff officers and the two cowled figures, 'see to it that they're made comfortable, somewhere quiet. The Druids can be tied up with the horses.'

'Yes, sir.' The legate waved the duty centurion over and passed on the instructions. The horses, badly blown by the effort they had been put to, bellowed with deep breaths from their flared nostrils.

The general's escort led the horses off in the direction of the stables and the duty centurion conducted the mud-stained staff officers towards the tribunes' mess tent. The two cloaked and hooded figures silently followed the others. Vespasian watched them curiously, and Plautius gave a thin smile.

'I'll explain about them later. Right now we need to talk about my wife and children.'

Chapter Seventeen

As soon as the exhausted men of the Fourth Cohort came in sight of the camp of the Second Legion a spontaneous cheer burst from their lips. The Durotriges, and their Druid leaders, might yet be frustrated in their efforts to wipe out the cohort. A scant hour's march away lay the security of the ramparts and an end to the nightmare of endurance that Centurion Hortensius had driven them through. But if the Romans' spirits were raised by the sight of the camp, then so was the determination of the enemy to obliterate the men of the cohort before any of their comrades came to their aid. With a savage howl the Durotriges fell upon the tightly packed ranks of the Roman formation.

Cato's shield and sword had long since become intolerable burdens and the muscles in his arms burned with the agony of bearing their weight. Even though he had shared the cheer of the other men at sight of the camp, the distance that lay between filled him with despair. The same despair that a drowning man feels when he views a distant shore in a rough sea. The thought was no sooner with him than a great roar of rage swelled up on either side and to the rear of the square as the Durotriges charged. The rippling thud of shields and metallic ring of weapons sounded with greater intensity than ever. The Roman formation faltered, and then halted under the impact of the charge and took a moment to firm up their shield wall once again.

As soon as Hortensius was satisfied his cohort was holding its own, he gave the order for the advance to continue. The hollow square crept forward once again, fending off the frenzied warriors clinging to their heels. Roman casualties had grown so numerous that there was little room left in the wagons packed into the small space at the centre of the square. With gaunt expressions the injured watched their comrades make the best of the uneven fight. Each jolt of a wagon brought fresh groans and cries from those inside, but there was not time to stop and tend to their wounds. Under these desperate circumstances Hortensius could spare few men to take care of the casualties and only the worst wounds had been roughly bandaged.

The Sixth Century, at the front of the square, had a clear view of the legion's camp. Cato was tantalised by the sight but the snail's pace of the cohort only served to convince him that they would never make it. The Durotriges would whittle down the exhausted legionaries long before they could reach the safety of the ramparts.

'What the hell are they doing down there?' Macro's eyes blazed with bitter frustration at the sight of the peaceful stillness of the camp. 'Fucking sentries must be blind. Just wait until I get my hands on them . . .'

To one side, the Durotriges' heavy infantry, rallied after the night's ferocious fighting, were hurrying past the square. Cato could only look on in despair, for the Britons' plan was clear. When a hundred paces lay between themselves and the cohort, the enemy column moved obliquely across the face of the Roman square and quickly deployed into a battle line, with a small group of slingmen on each wing. And there they stood their ground, shouting their defiance at the cohort as the shield wall approached.

The legionaries had bested the Durotriges all night but they were now beyond the limits of their endurance. They had had scarcely an hour of sleep in nearly three days of hard marching. Bleary, aching eyes peered out of filthy faces matted with several days' growth of beard. The younger Romans of Cato's age had little facial hair, but their gauntness of expression made even them look years older. The rear and sides of the square no longer formed a steady line and began to concede ground under the relentless pressure from their less weary foes, who now at last scented victory. Soon the square was no longer a square, but a misshapen block of men struggling for their very survival. Centurion Hortensius's voice, harsh and cracked, again rose above the din of battle.

'They're coming, lads! The legion's coming for us.'

At the front of the square Cato looked over the ranks of the Britons – scarcely forty paces off now – and saw the cohorts trickling out of the camp's southern gate, polished helmets glinting in the early morning sun. But they were miles off, and might not make it in time to save the men of the Fourth.

'Keep moving!' shouted Hortensius. 'Keep moving!'

Every step forward closed the distance between the two Roman columns. Cato clenched his teeth and raised his sword towards the writhing mass of the Durotriges' heavy infantry.

'Watch it!' Macro yelled. 'Slingshot!'

The Romans only just managed to shelter behind their shields in time as the first volley flew in diagonally from the flanks of the enemy line. With a roar the Durotriges charged home behind the volley. The sharp rattle and crack of the slingshot on the front of the square showed that the slingers had made sure of their aim. But one shot flew over Cato's head and struck one of the mules harnessed to a wagon in the centre of the formation. It pulverised the eye and the bone surrounding the socket and with a shriek of agony the mule plunged about in its traces, terrifying the other three beasts harnessed to the same wagon. In an instant the wagon swerved into its neighbour and with a protesting groan from the straining axle, it slowly tilted to one side and overturned. The injured were thrown out, scattered beneath the thrashing hooves of the panicked mules. One man, crushed by the side of the wagon, let out a terrible groan before choking on the blood that gushed from his mouth. He fell back lifeless. The shrill braying of the injured mule split the air and made Cato shudder. The wounded on the ground desperately tried to crawl out from under the terrified mules but many were trampled before they could get free. Then another wagon went over and fresh cries of terror and pain rent the air.

'Cohort! Halt!' Hortensius shouted. 'Get those fucking mules sorted out!'

He dived towards the injured animal who had started the chaos and plunged his sword deep into the mule's throat before tearing the blade free. The blood gushed out. For a moment the mule stood stupidly hanging its head, looking at the crimson pool splashing about its hooves. Then its knees went and it collapsed into the blood, mud and snow.

'Kill 'em all!' Hortensius yelled, and thrust the nearest soldiers towards the terrified animals.

It was all over in a moment and the surviving injured were hauled back into the scant shelter of the undamaged wagons. The cohort could not move any more, not without abandoning its wounded to the bloody savagery of the Durotriges. For a moment Cato wondered if Hortensius was cold-blooded enough to save what was left of his cohort and try to break out towards the relief column. But he remained true to the credo of the centurionate.

'Close ranks! Close ranks around the wagons!'

The legionaries engaged to the rear and sides slowly backstepped, thrusting out with their swords as the Durotriges stabbed and slashed against the shield wall, driving it back until the Romans compacted into a small knot round the surviving wagons. Those legionaries who stumbled and fell as they gave ground were crushed underfoot and then hacked to death by the Britons. Cato stuck close to Macro, tucked in behind his shield and striking out at the sea of enemy faces and limbs in front of him.

'Careful, lad!' Macro called out. 'We're right by the mules!'

Cato's foot splashed into the animals' blood and he felt the rasp of mule hide against the back of his calf. On either side of him, men of the Sixth Century were backing up against the bodies of the mules, too hard pressed by the Durotriges to clamber round or over them. With a roar of defiance Macro stabbed the tip of his sword into an enemy's face. As the man fell, he seized the chance to scramble over the flank of the mule.

'Come on, Cato!'

For a moment the optio stood facing two Britons, young men like himself, but thicker set with hair limed into crazy white spikes. One carried a broad-leafed war spear, while the other had armed himself with a short sword he had snatched up from a Roman body. Both of them made a feint, hoping to distract the optio enough for a fatal thrust, but he kept his shield moving, presenting it first one way, then the other, his eyes darting from spear to sword and back again. He dared not try to get over the dead mule while the two warriors waited for his guard to slip. Suddenly the spear tip flickered forward. Cato instinctively swung his shield to counter the threat, sending the tip glancing down. Seizing his chance, the other Briton leaped forward and thrust at Cato's stomach. A rough hand grasped Cato by a harness strap and bodily yanked him over the mule's body. The sword missed him and Cato sprawled on the ground, winded and gasping.

'They nearly had you there!' Macro laughed and jerked Cato back to his feet. Struggling to draw breath and clutching at his chest, Cato could not help wondering at the way his centurion seemed to exult at the prospect of imminent death. A strange thing, this madness – this euphoria – of battle, Cato reflected. Shame he would not live long enough to consider the phenomenon more fully.

The men of the Fourth Cohort instinctively closed ranks in an uneven ellipse around their wounded comrades. The enemy swarmed round them, hacking and chopping at the Roman shields in a rising frenzy as they sought to destroy the cohort before it could be reached by the relief column quick-marching towards them, but still far off. In the savage intimacy at the heart of the struggle Cato's mind was wonderfully cleared of any thoughts but the need to take the life of his enemy and preserve his own. His shield and his sword felt like natural extensions to his body. Warding off blows with one then striking with the other, Cato moved with the deadly efficiency of a well-trained machine. At the same time, tiny sensory details, frozen images of the fight burned themselves into his memory: the acrid stink of mule sweat and the sweeter odour of blood; the churned-up ground about his muddy boots; the blood-spattered faces of friend and foe, feral and snarling; and the aching cold of the winter morning shuddering through his exhausted body.

The Durotriges whittled away the men of the cohort one by one. The wounded were drawn back into the centre while the dead were thrown out of the formation to stop their bodies being a hazard underfoot to their surviving comrades. And still the cohort lived on; the enemy dead piled up in front of their shields so that the Durotriges had to clamber over them to get at the legionaries. They presented perfect targets for the short swords as they balanced precariously on the uneven, yielding mass of dead and dying flesh, from which the terrified cries of the still living rang out above the thud of shields and sharp ring of metal on metal.

The intensity of the moment robbed Cato of any sense of the passage of time. He stood shoulder to shoulder with his centurion on one side, and young Figulus on the other. But Figulus was no longer Figulus the soft-featured lad perpetually fascinated by a world that was so very different from the squalid slum he had been born into in Lutetia. Figulus had been slashed above one eye; the torn flesh was hanging from his brow and half his face was dripping with blood. The gentle lips were drawn back in a savage snarl as he hissed and spat with the effort of battle. The months of training might never have taken place; as agony and rage took hold of him, he slashed and hacked with his short sword in a manner it had never been designed to be used. Even so, the Durotriges shrank back from him, awed by his terrible wrath. He drew back his blade for another lunge, and his elbow smashed into Cato's nose. For an instant the optio's head burst with white light before the pain rushed in.

'Steady there!' Cato shouted into his ear.

But Figulus was totally lost to any appeal to reason. He frowned and shook his head once, then threw himself back into the fray with a guttural snarl. A Briton wielding a long-shafted battleaxe came at Cato. He threw his shield up and dropped down to his knees, gritting his teeth in expectation of the impact. The blow splintered the wood and swept on down into the chest of a body lying at Cato's feet. The warrior's momentum carried him forward, straight onto the point of Cato's sword which passed through his collarbone and into his heart. He dropped to one side, taking Cato's blade with him. Cato snatched up the nearest weapon, a long Celtic sword with an ornately decorated handle. The unfamiliar weapon felt awkward and clumsy in his hand as he tried to wield it as if it were a Roman short sword.

'Come on, you bastards!' Macro growled and presented the point of his sword to the nearest enemy. 'Come on, I said! Who's next? Come on, what're you waiting for, you fucking pansies!'

Cato laughed, and quickly stopped as he heard the hysterical edge to the laugh. He shook his head to try and clear a sudden dizziness, and made ready to fight on.

But there was no need. The ranks of the Durotriges were visibly thinning before his eyes. They were no longer shouting their war cries, no longer brandishing their weapons. They simply melted away, falling back from the ring of Roman shields, until a gap of thirty or so paces had opened up between the two sides, littered with bodies and abandoned and broken weapons. Here and there injured men moaned and writhed pathetically. The legionaries fell silent, waiting for the Britons' next move.

'What's happening?' Cato asked quietly in the sudden hush. 'What are they up to now?'

'Haven't got a bloody clue,' replied Macro.

There was a sudden rush of feet, and slingers and bowmen took up position in the enemy line. Then a moment's pause before an order was shouted from behind the ranks of the Durotriges.

'Now we're for it,' muttered Macro, and then quickly turned to the rest of the cohort to shout a warning. 'Cover yourselves!'

The legionaries crouched down and sheltered under their splintered shields. The wounded could only press themselves down into the bottom of the carts and pray to the gods to be spared the coming fusillade. Risking a peek through a gap between his shield and that of Figulus, Cato saw the bowmen draw back their bowstrings, accompanied by the rising note of whirring slings. A second order was shouted and the Durotriges' volley was unleashed at point-blank range. Arrows and slingshot hurtled towards the huddled ranks of the cohort, together with spears and swords picked up from the battlefield – even stones, such was the burning desire of the Durotriges to destroy the Romans.

Under his wrecked shield Cato crouched as low as he could, wincing at the terrific din made by the barrage of missiles cracking and thudding against shields and bodies. He looked round and met Macro's gaze under the shadow of his own shield.

'It never rains but it pours!' Macro smiled grimly.

'Story of my life in the army so far, sir,' Cato replied, attempting a grin to match his centurion's apparent fearlessness.

'Don't worry, lad, I think it's passing.'

But the fire suddenly renewed in intensity and Cato cringed into himself as he waited for the inevitable – the searing agony of a slingshot or arrow wound. Every moment he remained unscathed seemed nothing short of a miracle to him. Then, all at once, the barrage stopped. The air became strangely still. The enemy's war horns sounded and Cato was aware of movement, but did not dare glance out in case yet more missiles came their way.

'Get ready, lads!' Hortensius croaked painfully from nearby. 'There'll be one last attempt to rush us. Any moment now. When I say, get back on your feet and prepare to receive the charge!'

There was no charge, just a jingling of equipment and clatter of spear butts as the Durotriges drew back from the ring of Roman shields and marched off in the opposite direction to the Second Legion's camp. The enemy gradually picked up speed until they were quick-marching away. A thin screen of skirmishers formed up at the rear of the column and hurried along in its wake, casting frequent nervous looks behind them.

Macro cautiously rose to his feet and started after the retreating enemy. 'Well, I'll be . . .' Quickly he sheathed his sword and cupped a hand to his mouth. 'Oi! Where are you wankers off to?'

Cato started in alarm. 'Sir! What do you think you're doing?'

Macro's cries were taken up by the other legionaries and a chorus of jeers and catcalls pursued the Durotriges as they marched over the crest of the shallow ridge and into the vale beyond. The Roman taunts continued for a moment longer before turning to shouts of joy and triumph. Cato turned round and saw the front of the relief column rising up the track towards them. He felt sick as a wave of delirious happiness washed over him. Sinking down to the ground, he lowered his sword and shield and let his head rest heavily in his hands. Cato closed his eyes and breathed deeply a few times before, with great effort, he opened them again and looked up. A figure detached itself from the head of the column and jogged up the track towards them. As the man approached, Cato recognised the craggy features of the camp prefect. When Sextus drew near to the survivors of the cohort, he slowed down and shook his head at the dreadful scene before him.

Scores of bodies were strewn across the ground and lay in mounds around the cohort. Hundreds of arrow shafts spiked the ground and protruded from bodies and shields, nearly all of which were battered and splintered beyond repair. From behind the shields rose the filthy, bloodied forms of exhausted legionaries. Centurion Hortensius pushed his way through his men and strode towards the camp prefect, arm raised in greeting.

'Good morning, sir!' Despite his best efforts, the strain showed through in his voice. 'You took your fucking time.'

Sextus shook his hand, ignoring the blood congealing in a wound on the centurion's palm. The camp prefect stood, hands on hips, and nodded towards the survivors of the Fourth Cohort. 'And what kind of a bloody shambles do you call this? I ought to put the lot of you on fatigues for a month!'

Beside Cato, Figulus watched the centurion and the camp prefect exchange their greetings. He was silent for a moment before he spat on the ground. 'Bloody officers! Don't you just fucking hate 'em?'

Chapter Eighteen

The general eased himself onto a cushioned chair with a momentary wince. Several days in the saddle had not been kind to his backside and the slightest pressure was painful. His expression gradually relaxed, and he took the cup of heated wine that Vespasian offered him. It was slightly too hot for comfort but Plautius needed a drink and something warm in his belly to counter the numbness in the rest of his body. So he drained the cup and gestured for a refill.

'Any further news?' he asked.

'None, sir,' Vespasian replied as he poured more wine. 'Just the details I sent to you at Camulodunum.'

'Well then, any useful intelligence of any kind?' Plautius continued hopefully.

'Not just yet, but I've a cohort returning from patrol of the border with the Durotriges. They might have gathered some useful information. They seem to have run into a little trouble on their way back. I've sent a few cohorts out to see them home safely.'

'Ah yes. That would be the skirmish I saw on the far side of the camp as we rode up.'

'Yes, sir.'

'Have the cohort commander debriefed immediately he returns to camp.' The general frowned for a moment, staring into the faint coils of steam rising from the cup clasped in his hands. 'You see . . . I have to know as soon as possible.'

'Yes, sir. Of course.'

Vespasian took a seat opposite his general, and an awkward silence grew. For almost a year Aulus Plautius had been his commanding officer and he was not certain how to respond on a more personal level. For the first time since he had met Plautius – commander of the four legions and twelve auxiliary units charged with invading and conquering Britain – the general was revealing himself as just an ordinary man, a husband and father consumed with fear for his family.

'Sir?'

Plautius continued looking down, one finger gently stroking the rim of his cup.

Vespasian coughed. 'Sir.'

The general's eyes flickered up, tired and despairing. 'What am I to do, Vespasian? What would you do?'

Vespasian did not reply. He couldn't. What can a man say in the face of another's awful predicament? If the Druids had been holding Flavia and Titus, he little doubted that his first, and most powerful, instinct would be to take a horse and find them. To set them free or die in the attempt. And if he were too late to save them, then he would wreak the most terrible revenge he could upon the Druids and their folk, until he too was killed. For what was life without Flavia and Titus – and the child that Flavia was carrying? Vespasian's throat tightened uncomfortably. To distract himself from this train of thought he rose abruptly and went to the tent flap to shout an order for more wine. By the time he returned to his seat, he had composed himself, though inwardly he raged at what he saw as his weakness. Sentimentality was not permitted in an ordinary ranker; in a legion commander it was tantamount to a crime. And in a general? Vespasian gave Plautius a guarded look and shuddered. If someone as high and mighty as the army's commander had so much trouble keeping his private grief from view, what hope was there for a lesser man?

With a visible effort Aulus Plautius stirred from his introspection and met the legate's gaze. The general frowned for an instant, as if unaware of precisely how long he had been drowning in his own despair. Then he nodded emphatically.

'I must do something. I need to make arrangements to have my family rescued before time runs out. There's only twenty-three days left before the Druids' deadline.'

'Yes, sir,' replied Vespasian, framing his next question carefully to avoid any hint of censure. 'Are you going to exchange the Druid prisoners for your wife and children?'

'No . . . not yet at least. Not until I've tried to rescue my family. I won't let a bunch of superstitious murderers dictate terms to Rome!'

'I see.' Vespasian was not quite convinced. Why else would the general bring the Druids with him from Camulodunum? 'In that case, what plan do you have in mind to recover your family, sir?'

'I haven't decided yet,' Plautius admitted. 'But the main thing is to act quickly. I want the Second Legion ready to move as soon as possible.'

'Ready to move? Move where, sir?'

'I want to start the campaign early. At least, I want the Second Legion to start early. I've prepared orders for your legion to move into the territory of the Durotriges. You're to crush every hill fort, every fortified settlement. There are to be no enemy warriors or Druids taken prisoner. I want every tribe in this island to know the cost of murdering a Roman prefect and taking Roman hostages. If the Druids and their Durotrigan friends have any sense they will return my wife and children at once, and sue for peace.'

'And if they don't?'

'Then we'll start killing our Druid captives, saving their leader for last. If that doesn't move them, we'll kill every living thing in our path.' The dreadful determination in Plautius's voice was unmistakable. 'Nothing will be allowed to survive, do you understand?'

Vespasian did not reply. This was madness. Madness. Understandable, but madness all the same. None of it made any strategic sense. But he knew he had to handle the general carefully.

'When do you want my legion to advance?'

'Tomorrow.'

'Tomorrow!' Vespasian almost laughed at the ridiculous notion. Almost, until he caught the intense gleam in the eyes of his superior. 'It's out of the question, sir.'

'Why?'

'Why? Where shall I start? The ground is not yet firm enough for my artillery carriages and heavy wagons to move. That means we can only carry food for three, maybe four days. And I haven't the slightest idea about enemy capability.'

'I've anticipated that. I've brought along a Briton who knows the area well. He was once a Druid initiate. He and his translator will act as your guides. As for your supplies, you can march on half rations to start with. Later on you can use the fleet to supply you by river, and I'll send you all the light carts I can spare. You might even find some enemy food caches. Winter is almost over, but they're bound to have stockpiles you can forage. And to enable you to assault enemy hill forts, I've arranged for the transfer of the Twentieth's artillery to your unit . . .'

'Even if we find their hill forts, we'll have no fire support for any attack on the ramparts if the artillery gets bogged down. Our men will be slaughtered.'

'How formidable could the defences be?' Plautius snapped bitterly. 'After all, these savages haven't even heard of siegecraft. All their ramparts and stockades are fit for is deterring the odd hungry wolf and itinerant trespasser. I'm sure a man of your ingenuity could manage to storm such defences without much loss of life. Or do you find commanding a legion too onerous, or dangerous, a duty?'

Vespasian gripped the arm of his chair tightly to prevent himself from leaping up and angrily denouncing such a slur. The general had gone too far. To order the Second Legion on a wild-goose chase was madness enough, but to counter his reasoned protests with accusations of incompetence and cowardice was a rank insult. Plautius's eyes coldly mocked him for a moment, then the general frowned and looked down into his cup once again.

'Forgive me, Vespasian,' Plautius said quietly. 'I'm sorry. I should not have said that. No one in this army would doubt your qualities as a legate. As I say, forgive me.'

Plautius looked up, and the apologetic expression that Vespasian sought was not there; the general's regret was merely a form of words intended to steer them both back to consideration of his lunatic plans.

Vespasian could barely keep the icy derision out of his voice when he replied. 'My forgiveness is meaningless compared to the forgiveness you would need from the five thousand men of this legion, and their families, should you insist on the Second Legion carrying out this ill-conceived plan of yours. Sir, it would be nothing short of a suicide mission.'

'Don't exaggerate.' Plautius placed his cup on a side table and leaned closer to his legate. 'Very well then, Vespasian. I will not order you to do this. I will ask you to do it. Have you not a family of your own? Do you not understand the demons that drive me to this? Please agree to do as I ask.'

'No.' Vespasian shook his head. 'I cannot permit it. What afflicts you, Plautius, is a private tragedy. Do not make it a public tragedy. The empire can only afford so many Varian disasters. You are a general on active service. In the field your family is the army all around you. The men are as sons to you. They trust you to lead them wisely, and not expose them to needless risk.'

'Please spare me the cheap rhetoric, Vespasian. I'm not some fickle pleb in the forum.'

'No, you're not . . . Let me try another argument. Consider your feelings for your wife and children. As you say, I have a family too, and even imagining what it would be like for them to be in the hands of the Druids is torment enough. But you have it as a reality, and against that my tortured imagination is only a pale imitation. Now, magnify that a thousandfold and more. That is the measure of the suffering you will inflict on the families and friends of the men you would send to their deaths if you order the Second Legion to march tomorrow, without adequate supplies or artillery support.'

Plautius shut his eyes and rubbed his creased brow, as if that might somehow ease his inner suffering. Vespasian watched him closely, searching for any sign that his arguments had hit home. If the general did not change his mind, Vespasian knew he would have to refuse to lead the Second out tomorrow. That would utterly damn his career. But he would have no part in the general's reckless and futile plan. He would challenge Plautius to find another man to appoint as legate. As soon as Vespasian considered this he realised that his replacement would be chosen for his willingness to do the general's bidding, not for his leadership qualities. Such an appointment would only make the inevitable disaster far worse. Vespasian realised he was trapped. To quit his command would be to increase the already terrible risk to his men. To stay in command would at least present him with a chance to limit the damage. Silently he cursed his fortune.

The general opened his eyes and looked up. 'Very well then, Vespasian. How soon can the Second Legion be ready to attack the Durotriges?'

'With supply wagons and artillery?'

Plautius nodded reluctantly, and Vespasian's despair receded. He had won the crucial concession. Foolish though the rest of the plan might be, at least the Second Legion would have a fighting chance. Looking at Plautius, he judged that the general had given as much ground as he was prepared to give.

'I need twenty days.'

'Twenty! That's cutting it too fine.'

'I grant you it gives us twenty days less to find them, but weigh that against the loss of a legion. Besides . . .' Vespasian's mind raced ahead for a moment.

'Besides what?'

The legate rushed to fit the pieces together in his mind before he continued. 'Well, sir, it might take the legion twenty days to be ready to move, but why wait to start looking for your family until then?'

'I'm not in the mood for cryptic clues. Speak your mind, Legate, and make it good.'

'Why not send a few men out to scout the villages and hill forts while the legion prepares to advance? That man you brought with you – the Druid initiate. You said he knows the Durotriges. He can lead them, and try to discover where your family is being held. Who knows?

They might even manage a rescue on their own. It's got to be better than having the Second Legion bludgeoning its way through the countryside; the Druids would have plenty of advance warning and just keep moving your family.' Vespasian paused. 'We'd probably never get them back if we relied on such a blunt strategy. If they're being held in a hill fort and we laid siege to it, the Druids would more than likely kill them before they allowed us a chance to succeed.'

General Plautius considered the proposal for a moment. 'I don't like it. I can't risk any botched rescue attempt by a handful of men in the middle of enemy territory. That's more likely to lead to my family being killed than anything else.'

'No, sir,' Vespasian countered firmly. 'I'd say it's the best chance we have. If your Briton really knows the lie of the land and its people, we stand a good chance of finding the hostages before the enemy is alerted to the Second's advance.'

Plautius frowned. 'Your best chance has just been downgraded to a good chance.'

'Better than little or no chance, sir.'

'Did you have anyone in mind for this mission?'

'No, sir,' Vespasian admitted. 'Haven't thought that far ahead. But we'd need some men with plenty of initiative. They'd have to be resourceful, good in a fight – if it came down to it . . .'

Plautius looked up. 'What about that centurion you sent to retrieve Caesar's pay chest, just after we landed? Him and that optio of his. Did a pretty good job, as I recall.'

'Yes, they did,' mused Vespasian. 'A very good job indeed . . .'

Chapter Nineteen

'Come on, you dozy beauties!' roared Centurion Hortensius as he stuck his head into Macro's tent. Macro was fast asleep on his camp bed, snoring with a deep bass rumble. To one side Cato slumped over a desk where he had been compiling the Sixth Century's strength return when the irresistible need for rest had finally overwhelmed him. Outside, in the century's line of tents, the men were also fast asleep, and so it was with the rest of the Fourth Cohort. Except Senior Centurion Hortensius. After seeing to the injured and giving orders that a hot meal be prepared for the cohort, he had gone to make his report.

To find himself in the presence of not only the legate but also the commander of all the Roman forces in Britain was something of a surprise. Tired as Hortensius was, he stood to attention and stared rigidly ahead as he outlined the short history of the Fourth Cohort's patrol. Giving the bare details, without embellishment, Hortensius delivered his report with the formal tonelessness of a long-serving professional. He answered their questions in the same style. As the debriefing proceeded, Hortensius became aware that the general seemed to want far more from his answers than he could possibly provide. The man seemed to be obsessive about even the smallest details concerning the Druids, and was horrified when told of Diomedes's slaughter of the Druid prisoners.

'He killed all of them?'

'Yes, sir.'

'What did you do with the bodies?' asked Vespasian.

'Dumped them in the well, sir, then filled it in. Didn't want to give their mates any further excuse to give us a hard time.'

'No, I suppose not,' Vespasian replied, with a quick glance at the general. The questions continued for a little while before the general relented and curtly waved him towards the door. Vespasian was angered by the general's casual dismissal of the veteran centurion.

'One final thing, Centurion,' Vespasian called out.

Hortensius halted and turned round. 'Sir?'

'You did an excellent job. I doubt many men could have led the cohort as you did.'

The centurion inclined his head slightly in acknowledgement of the praise. But Vespasian was unwilling to let the matter rest there. He placed heavy emphasis on his next words. 'I imagine there will be some kind of commendation or award for your performance . . .'

General Plautius looked up. 'Er, yes . . . yes, of course. Some kind of award.'

'Kind of you, sir.' Hortensius addressed his reply to his legate.

'Not at all. It's well-deserved,' Vespasian said crisply. 'Now, one last thing. Would you be kind enough to send Centurion Macro and his optio to see us? At once, if you please.'

Cato had dipped his head into an icy butt of water in an attempt to be more wakeful in front of his legate, and he looked a sorry state as he and Macro entered the headquarters tent. His dark hair was plastered across his forehead and beads of water trickled down either side of his nose and dropped in dark spatters on his tunic. Macro looked sidelong at him and frowned, largely oblivious of his own appearance. Since returning to the camp they had removed only their belts and armour and, still wore the soiled, bloodstained and torn tunics of the last three days of marching and fighting. Nor were their shallow cuts and scratches dressed in any way; dried blood still crusted their arms and legs. The legate's chief clerk curled his lip at the sight of them as they approached his desk outside the general's day tent; these two were hardly likely to do the legion's reputation much good in the eyes of the general. The clerk added a wrinkled nose to his expression of distaste as the two men came to a halt in front of him.

'Centurion Macro? Couldn't you have presented yourself in a more respectable condition, sir?'

'We were told to be here as soon as possible.'

'Yes, but even so . . .' The chief clerk looked disapprovingly at Cato, dripping perilously close to his paperwork. 'You might have let the optio dry out first.'

'We're here,' said Macro, too tired to be angry with the clerk. 'Better tell the legate.'

The clerk rose from his stool. 'Wait.' He slipped through the tent flap and pulled it to behind him.

'Any idea what this is about, sir?' Cato rubbed his eyes – the refreshing shock of the cold water had already worn off.

139

Macro shook his head. 'Sorry, lad.' He tried to think of any misdemeanour he or his men might have unwittingly committed. One of the recruits had probably been caught taking a dump in the tribunes' latrine again, he mused. 'I doubt we're in any kind of serious trouble, so take it easy.'

'Yes, sir.'

The clerk reappeared. He stood to one side of the tent flap and held it open for them.

'Anyway, we'll find out soon enough,' mumbled Macro as he led the way. Inside, he raised his eyebrows at the sight of the general, just as Hortensius had done before him. Then he marched up to the senior officers and stood to attention. Cato, younger and lacking the toughness of the veteran centurion, shambled to his side and stiffened into the appropriate posture as best he could. Macro saluted his legate.

'Centurion Macro and Optio Cato reporting as ordered, sir.'

'At ease,' ordered Plautius. The general cast a disapproving eye over them before he turned to Vespasian. 'These are the men we were talking about?'

'Yes, sir. They're just back from that patrol. You haven't caught them at their best.'

'So it seems. But are they as reliable as you say?'

Vespasian nodded, uncomfortable at discussing the two men as if they were not present. He had noticed that those of aristocratic descent, like Aulus Plautius, were inclined to regard the lower orders as part of the scenery without a moment's consideration of how crushing it was to be treated that way. Vespasian's grandfather had been a centurion, like this man standing before them, and it was only due to the social reforms of Emperor Augustus that men from more humble lineages could now rise to the highest offices in Rome. In due course Vespasian, and his elder brother Sabinus, might become consuls, the highest post a senator could achieve. But those senators from the oldest families would still look down their fine noses at the Flavians and mutter snide remarks to each other about the arrivistes' lack of refinement.

'You're sure of them?' Plautius persisted.

'Yes, sir. Definitely. If anyone can do the job, it's these two.'

Despite his exhaustion, Cato's curiosity was aroused and it sharpened his concentration. He barely managed to restrain a glance towards his centurion. Whatever this 'job' was, it came right from the top and had to be a chance to distinguish himself and prove to the other men of the legion, and more importantly to himself, that he was worthy of the optio's white strap he wore on his shoulder.

'Very well,' said the general. 'You'd better brief them.'

'Yes, sir.' Vespasian quickly collected his thoughts. As things stood, the Second was to redirect its thrust into the heart of the Durotriges' territory rather than support the main campaign north of the Tamesis. Vespasian's troubled mind was plagued by the perils this posed for himself and his men, two of whom he must now send to an almost certain death. A death, moreover, at the hands of the Druids, who would be sure to extract every last measure of torment in the process.

'Centurion, you will recall the death of the fleet prefect, Valerius Maxentius, some days back.'

'Yes, sir.'

'You may remember the demands he was forced to make before he was murdered.'

'Yes, sir,' Macro repeated, and Cato nodded, vividly recalling the scene.

'The hostages he mentioned, the ones who were offered in exchange for the Druids we took at Camulodunum, they're the wife and children of General Plautius.'

Both Cato and Macro were astonished and could not help shifting their gaze to the general. He sat staring into his lap, quite motionless. Cato saw the weary stoop of the man's shoulders and his troubled expression. For a moment Cato felt pity for the general, until the shamefulness of that emotion embarrassed him. When Aulus Plautius looked up and caught his eye, it was as if he sensed that he had revealed more of himself than he should have. The general straightened his shoulders and concentrated on the legate's briefing with a stern and alert expression.

'General Plautius has authorised me to send a small party out into the territory of the Durotriges to search for and, if the opportunity presents itself, to rescue his family, Lady Pomponia and the two children, Julia and Aelius. He recalls the discreet manner with which you two retrieved that pay chest of Caesar's last year and I agree with his choice for the job.' Vespasian allowed a moment for his words to sink in. 'Centurion, I know your worth, and the optio here has no more need to prove himself to me. I won't deceive you; this task is more dangerous than anything you've ever been asked to do before. I will not order you to go, but I can think of no two men in the legion more likely to succeed in this mission. The decision is yours. But, if you do succeed, the general and I will be sure to reward you generously. Isn't that right, sir?'

General Plautius nodded.

141

Macro frowned. 'Like we were rewarded after we got that pay chest back—'

'You mentioned a small party, sir,' Cato quickly interrupted. 'I take it the centurion and I won't be alone in this.'

'No. There are two others, Britons, who know the area. They'll act as your guides.'

'I see.'

'One of them is a woman,' the general intervened. 'She will be your interpreter. The other was once a Druid initiate, in the order of the Dark Moon.'

'The same as those bastards we ran into then,' said Macro. 'How can we be sure this one can be trusted, sir?'

'I don't know that we can trust him. But he's the only one I could find who knows the area well and was willing to guide Romans inside Durotrigan territory. He's aware of the risks. If he, and the woman, get discovered in the service of Rome then they'll surely be killed.'

'Unless they were to lead us into a trap, sir. Hand the Druids two more hostages to bargain with.'

Plautius gave the centurion a grim smile. 'If they were prepared to murder a prefect of the navy to make a point then I doubt they would bother to treat two rankers as hostages. Centurion, make no mistake about this; if you're taken by the enemy the very best you can hope for is a quick death.'

'Put like that, sir, I'm not sure that I want to volunteer me and the lad for this mission of yours. It'd be plain madness.'

Plautius said nothing, but Cato could see that he was gripping the arms of his chair so hard that the tendons on his arm stood out like knotted wooden rods. When his fury had subsided a little, he spoke in a strained voice.

'This isn't easy for me, Centurion. The Druids are holding my family . . . Have you got a family?'

'No, sir. Families get in the way of soldiering.'

'I see. Then you can have little idea how much this affair torments me and how demeaning I find it having to ask you and the optio to find them for me.'

Macro pressed his lips tightly together to bite off his instinctive response. Then his usual calmness under pressure reasserted itself. 'Permission to speak freely, sir?'

The general's eyes narrowed. 'Depends what you want to say.'

'Very well, sir.' Macro lifted his chin and stiffened to attention, still and silent.

'All right, Centurion. Speak freely.'

'Thank you, sir. I understand what you're saying all right.' His tone was brittle with fatigue and ill-concealed contempt. 'You're in a fix and you want me and my optio to stick our necks out for you. And because we're plebs, we're expendable. What chance have we got wandering around in the middle of enemy territory with a bloody woman and some quack magician? You're sending us to our deaths, and you know it. But at least you will have tried something, to make yourself feel better. Meanwhile, the lad and I will have been parted from our heads, or burned alive. Does that sum the situation up . . . sir?'

Cato blanched at the uncharacteristic outburst, and glanced anxiously at the senior officers. The outraged expression on Vespasian's face was far less frightening than the dark gleam blazing in the eyes of the general.

'I volunteer to go, sir!' Cato blurted out.

The other three looked at him in surprise, instantly diverted from the tense confrontation that could only have ended in disaster for Macro. Cato quickly licked his lips and nodded to emphasise his words.

'You?' The general's eyebrows rose.

'Yes, sir. Let me go. I'll do the best I can.'

'Optio,' Vespasian said. 'I don't doubt your courage, and your intelligence. And you have a certain amount of resourcefulness. All that I can't deny. But I think it's too much to ask of one man.'

'Barely a man at that,' added the general. 'I won't send a boy to do a man's job.'

'I'm no boy,' Cato replied coldly. 'I've been a soldier for over a year now. I've been decorated once already, and I've proved my reliability. Sir, if you really think this mission has almost no chance of success, then surely the loss of one man is better than the loss of two or more?'

'You don't have to do this,' Macro muttered.

'Sir, my mind's made up. I'll go.'

Macro glared at Cato. The boy was mad, quite mad; he was bound to come a cropper at the first obstacle. The thought of Cato, undeniably bright and courageous but still a little naive and rough around the edges, in the hands of some devious Briton and his woman filled Macro with dismay. Damn the boy! Damn him! There was no way he could leave the lad to his own devices.

'All right then!' Macro turned back to the general. 'I'll go. If we're going to do it, might as well do it properly.'

'Thank you, Centurion,' the general said quietly. 'You will not find me ungrateful.'

'If we return.'

Plautius merely shrugged.

Before the situation could degenerate again, Vespasian stood up and shouted an order for more wine to be fetched. Then he stepped between his general and the two rankers and motioned towards some seats to one side of the tent.

'You must be tired. Sit down and we'll have something to drink while I pass the word for our British scouts. Now that you've agreed to go, it's best that you meet them. Time's short; there are only twenty-two days before the Druids' deadline. You'll leave tomorrow, at dawn.'

Macro and Cato walked over to the seats and eased their tired bodies down onto the comfortable cushions.

'What the fuck was that all about?' Macro whispered angrily.

'Sir?'

'What have I told you about volunteering? Don't you listen to a bloody word I say?'

'What about the pay chest, sir? You volunteered us for that.'

'No I bloody didn't! Bloody legate ordered me to do that one. But even he wouldn't have the heart to order anyone to do this. What the fuck have you got us into?'

'You didn't have to volunteer, sir. I said I'd go alone.'

Macro snorted with contempt at the idea, and shook his head in despair at the alacrity with which his optio seemed to embrace the chance to die a grim and lonely death in some dark corner of a barbarian field. Cato, for his part, wondered what else he could have done in the circumstances. The Roman army did not tolerate the sort of insubordination Macro had displayed – and to a general no less. What the hell had come over him? Cato cursed his centurion and himself in equal measure. He had said the first thing that had entered his mind and now felt sick at the prospect of venturing into the land of the Druids, sick at the certainty of his own death. Beyond that there was only a cold anger directed at that part of him which had so wanted to spare the centurion the wrath of his general.

A light rasp of leather made Cato look up. A slave had entered the tent, carrying a bronze tray with six goblets and a slender bronze jug filled with red wine. The slave set the tray down and, at a nod from Vespasian, filled the goblets without spilling a drop. Cato was watching him and so he did not see the Britons enter the tent until they had almost reached the table. The former Druid initiate was huge, and towered over the Roman officers. At his side was a tall woman in a dark riding cloak with the hood pulled back to reveal a tightly braided arrangement of red hair. The general nodded a greeting and Vespasian unconsciously straightened his shoulders as he looked over the woman appreciatively.

'Fuck me!' Macro whispered as the woman turned slightly and they saw her face. 'Boudica!'

She heard her name and looked towards them, eyes widening in surprise. Her companion turned to follow her gaze.

'Oh no!' Cato shrank back from the giant's withering glare. 'Prasutagus!'

Chapter Twenty

When Cato woke he had a nagging headache that pounded against the inside of his forehead. It was dark outside and only a faint chink showed where the tent flap had fallen shut but not been tied. With no idea of the time, he closed his eyes and tried to sleep again. It was futile; thoughts and images crept back from the margins of his consciousness, refusing to be disregarded. He had still not recovered from the sleepless nights of march and battle, and now he was about to embark on this crazy new venture, just when he should be resting his body. Despite his anxieties after last night's lengthy briefing, he had fallen asleep very quickly once he had curled up under his blanket. The other men of his section were already out for the count, with Figulus grumbling away to himself amid his dreams as ususal.

By the time the men of the Sixth Century rose at dawn, their centurion and his optio would have left the camp. That would be the least of the changes to their immediate world. It would be the last morning that they would rise as comrades within the same unit. The Sixth Century was to be broken up and what remained of its men distributed to the other centuries in the cohort to make good their losses.

Macro had been mortified when Vespasian informed him. The Sixth Century had been his ever since he had been promoted to the centurionate and Macro had developed the customary fierce pride and protectiveness typical of an officer's first command. Since landing in Britain he and his men had fought numerous bloody battles and bitter skirmishes together. Many had been killed, others crippled and sent back to Rome for early discharge. The gaps in the ranks had been filled with a stream of new recruits. Few of the faces remained from the original eighty men he had faced on the parade ground for the first time a year and a half ago. But while men came and went, the century – his century – had endured, and Macro had come to regard it as an extension of himself, responsive to his will, and he was proud of its hard-fighting efficiency in battle. To lose the Sixth Century felt like losing a child and Macro was angry and bereft.

But what else could be done? the legate had reasoned with him. The century could not be left leaderless while it waited for its commander to return, and the other centuries needed seasoned replacements. General Plautius had already drawn on all of the replacements ear-marked for the legions in Britain and no more would be forthcoming for several months. When the mission was over and Macro returned to the legion, he would be given the first command that fell vacant.

Cato had glanced at Macro, and the centurion had shrugged regret-fully. The army was no respecter of well-forged teams and there was nothing to be done if the legate had made up his mind.

'What about my optio, sir?' Macro had asked. 'If we make it back.'

Vespasian had looked at the tall, slender youth for a moment, and then nodded. 'He'll be looked after. Perhaps a temporary post on my staff while we wait for a vacancy on the optios' list.'

Cato had tried not to let his disappointment show; being posted to a different century to Macro's was not an appealing prospect. It had taken months to win the centurion's grudging respect and to convince him that he was worthy of the rank of optio. When he had joined the legion, Cato, a former imperial slave, had been the target of bitter resentment and much jealousy because of his instant promotion, for which he had the Emperor himself to thank. Cato's father had served with distinction on the imperial staff, and when he died, Emperor Claudius had freed the boy and sent him to join the eagles, with a kindly lift onto the first rung of the promotional ladder. It had been a well-meant gesture, but no one as lofty as the Emperor had any inkling of the bitterness with which men at the bottom of society reacted to blatant nepotism.

Cato was loath to recall his early experiences of life in the Second Legion: the harsh discipline of the drill instructors, laid more heavily upon him than any of the other recruits; the bullying at the hands of a cruel ex-convict named Pulcher; and perhaps worst of all the frank disapproval of his centurion. That had hurt him more than anything else, and driven him to prove himself on every possible occasion. Now, that struggle for recognition of his worth would begin all over again. In addition, he had a certain personal regard for Macro, at whose side he had fought through the most terrible battles of the campaign so far. It would not be easy to adjust to the style of another centurion.

Vespasian had noticed the optio's expression and tried to offer him some words of comfort. 'Never mind. You can't carry on being an optio forever. Someday, sooner than you think perhaps, you will have a century of your own.'

That he spoke to the lad's inmost ambitions, Vespasian had no doubt. Every young man he had ever known dreamed of honour and promotion, however unlikely they knew it to be. But this one just might make it. He had proved his courage and his intelligence, and with a little help from someone placed high enough to make a difference, he would be sure to serve the empire well.

Since there was little chance of either himself or Macro ever returning to the Second Legion, these kindly words from Vespasian had a distinctly hollow ring. They were so typical of the well-worn encouragement that all commanders offer to those facing certain death, and Cato had felt contempt for himself for having been momentarily taken in by the legate's guile. The bitterness of the thought stayed with him through the night.

'Fool!' he muttered to himself, turning over on his bracken-filled bedroll. He pulled the thick army blanket tightly about him and round his head to keep the chill out. Once again he tried to get to sleep, banishing all thought from his mind, and once again the subtle wiles of insomnia nudged his mind back to the previous night's encounter.

Surprise at seeing Boudica and her dangerous cousin was mirrored in the faces of General Plautius and Vespasian as they realised that the new arrivals were known to the centurion and his optio.

'I see you're already acquainted.' Plautius smiled. 'That should make things easier all round.'

'I'm not so sure, sir,' replied Macro, warily sizing up the British warrior towering over him. 'Last time we met, Prasutagus here didn't seem to have much affection for Romans.'

'Really?' Plautius looked steadily at Macro. 'Not much affection for Romans, or not much for you?'

'Sir?'

'You should know, Centurion, that this man volunteered to help in any way that he could. Once I made known to the Icenian elders that my family was being held, this man came forward and volunteered to do all in his power to help me recover them.'

'Do you trust him, sir?'

'I have to. What other choice do I have? And you will work closely with him. That's an order.'

'I thought we'd volunteered, sir.'

'You have, and now that you have, you'll obey my orders. You're to co-operate fully with Prasutagus. He knows the country and customs of the Durotriges, and a great deal about the practices and secret places of the Dark Moon Druids. He's the best chance we have. So look after him, and pay close heed to what he tells you – or rather to what the lady here translates for you. You appear to have met her before as well.'

'You might say that, sir,' Macro replied quietly, and nodded his head formally at Boudica.

'Centurion Macro,' she acknowledged him. 'And your charming optio.'

'Ma'am.' Cato swallowed nervously.

Prasutagus glared at Macro for a moment, and then helped himself to a goblet of the legate's wine which he drank so fast that from either side of the rim drops of red liquid spilled down the thick blond hair of his ornate moustache.

'How quaint,' Vespasian muttered, eyebrows rising anxiously as the Briton went back to the glass jug for a third goblet.

'Since you seem to approve . . .' Boudica joined Prasutagus and poured herself a goblet, filling it to the brim. 'To a safe return.'

She raised the goblet to her lips and drank until the last drop had been drained, then thumped the goblet down. Boudica grinned at the scandalised expressions of the general and his legate. This was a world away from the prim codes of behaviour they were used to among the better class of Roman women.

Prasutagus muttered something and nudged Boudica to translate.

'He says the wine's not bad.'

Vespasian gave a tight-lipped smile and sat down.

'Well then, enough of the formalities. We haven't much time. Centurion, I will brief your team as fully as I can, and then you need to rest. I'll have some horses, provisions and weapons made ready so that you can leave the camp before dawn. It's important that your party is not seen leaving the legion. You'll be travelling by night mostly, and laying up during the day. If you happen to run into anyone you'll need a cover story. Your best chance is to pretend to be travelling entertainers. Prasutagus will play the part of a wrestler, offering to take on all-comers, for a fee. She will pose as his wife. You two are going to be a pair of Greek slaves, ex-soldiers bought to provide protection in this wild land. The southern tribes of Britain are used to the comings and goings of merchants, traders and entertainers.'

An image of the slaughtered victims of the burned village flickered into Cato's mind. 'Excuse me, sir, given the way they treat the Atrebates, what makes you think they won't just kill us out of hand?'

149

'It's a tribal convention; you don't piss on your own doorstep. By all means raid other tribes, but you don't want to discourage trade from outside. That's how it works with all the tribes on the edges of the empire. However, you're right to be cautious. The Druids are an unknown element in this. We don't know what the Durotriges will do under their influence. Prasutagus is best placed to deal with any situations you encounter. Watch him carefully, and follow his lead.'

'I'll be watching carefully right enough,' Macro said quietly.

'You really think that'll work, sir?' asked Cato. 'Aren't the Durotriges going to be just a little suspicious of strangers, now that there's a Roman army camping on their doorstep?'

'I admit it won't stand up to much scrutiny, but it might buy you time, should you need it. Prasutagus may be remembered in some parts, which should count for something. You and the optio should stay out of sight as far as possible and let Prasutagus and Boudica approach the Durotriges or any settlements you come across. They'll listen for news of my family. Follow up any leads for as long as it takes, and find them.'

'I thought we only had twenty odd days left, sir. Before the Druids' deal is off.'

Plautius answered him. 'Yes, that's right. But once the deadline has passed and . . . and if the worst has happened, I'd like to be able to give them a decent funeral. Even if all that's left is ash and bone.'

A hand grasped Cato's shoulder and shook him roughly. His eyes flickered open and his body, stiffened at the sudden waking.

'Shhh!' Macro hissed from the darkness. 'Keep it quiet! It's time to go. Got your equipment?'

Cato nodded, then realised that it was still too dark for Macro to see him. 'Yes, sir.'

'Good. Then let's go.'

Still tired, and reluctant to quit the relative warmth of the tent, Cato shivered as he quietly crept outside, dragging the bundle he had prepared before going to sleep. Wrapped inside a spare tunic was his mail armour and leather harness, together with sword and dagger. Helmet, shield and everything else would be collected by the headquarters staff and kept safe fom pilfering until they returned. Cato had little doubt that they would become someone else's property in the near future.

As he followed Macro through the dark lines of tents towards the stables, fear of what lay ahead began to unravel his determination to

150

see the mission through. It was tempting to make himself trip over a guy rope and fake a twisted ankle. In the darkness it might pass for a credible excuse. But he could imagine the contemptuous doubt that Macro and the legate would be sure to feel, if not express. This shaming prospect made him dismiss the plan and tread more warily in case the accident happened for real. Besides, he couldn't let Macro go blundering about in the depths of enemy territory with only Prasutagus and Boudica for company. It would be all too easy for the Iceni warrior to slit Macro's throat while he slept. But not so easy if they took turns to watch over each other. There really was no way out of this, he concluded glumly. If only Macro hadn't been so rude to the general, then he wouldn't have had to intervene. Now they were both for the chop, thanks to Macro.

Grumbling silently to himself, Cato forgot to pay attention to where he was putting his feet. The guy rope caught his shin and he tumbled head first with a sharp cry. Macro whipped round.

'Quiet! You want to wake up everyone in the fucking camp?'

'Sorry, sir,' Cato whispered as he struggled back to his feet, the heavy bundle in both arms.

'Don't tell me, you've gone and twisted your ankle.'

'No, sir! Of course not!'

Someone stirred inside the tent. 'Who's there?'

'No one,' snapped Macro. 'Get back to sleep . . . Come on, lad, and watch your step.'

Beside the horse pen, a dim light glimmered inside the large tent where the riding tack and cavalry weapons were stored. Cato followed Macro through the flap into the dull glow of a hanging oil lamp. Prasutagus, Boudica and Vespasian stood waiting.

'Best change right now,' said Vespasian. 'Your horses and pack animals are ready.'

They dropped their bundles and stripped down to their loincloths. Under the curious gaze of Boudica, Cato hurriedly covered himself with a fresh tunic and pulled his mail shirt over the top. He slipped into his harness, attached the sword and dagger scabbards and reached for his military cloak.

'No!' Vespasian interrupted the gesture. 'Not that. Wear those.' He indicated a pair of grimy brown cloaks, well-worn and spattered with mud. 'Best not look too much like a pair of squaddies when you reach Durotrigan territory. And wear these thongs round your heads.'

He handed them two lengths of leather, broad at the front and tapering at the ends. 'The Greeks wear them to hold their hair back. Your military cut is an instant giveaway, so keep these on, and your hoods up, and you might just pass muster as a couple of Greeks – from a distance. Just don't try and engage anyone in conversation.'

'All right, sir.' Macro grimaced at the thong, then tied it round his head. Prasutagus watched Macro while Boudica grinned at Cato.

'Somehow you look more convincing as a Greek slave than you've ever done as a legionary.'

'Thank you. Much appreciated.'

'Save it for later,' ordered Vespasian. 'Come with me.'

He beckoned to Prasutagus and led them outside. Over at the tethering posts stood four horses with plain blankets spread across their backs, covering the legion's brand. Saddlepacks hung over each flank, and to one side stood two ponies carrying more provisions.

'Right then, you'd best be off. The watch officer on the gate is expecting you, so you can slip out without some idiot shouting a challenge.' The legate looked them over one last time and then quickly slapped Macro on the shoulder. 'Good luck!'

'Thank you, sir.'

Macro took a breath and threw his leg up over his horse, swinging his body after it. A graceless moment of subdued curses followed before he was properly seated and had a good grasp of the reins. Being taller, Cato managed to mount his horse with a little more style.

Prasutagus muttered something to Boudica and Macro swung round. 'What did he say?'

'He wondered if it might be better if you and your optio travelled on foot.'

'Oh really? Well, you tell him—'

'That's enough, Centurion!' Vespasian snapped. 'Just go.'

The Iceni warrior and woman mounted with familiar ease and turned their horses towards the camp gate. Behind them, Macro and Cato tugged on the long reins of the pack animals and followed on. As the hooves thudded on the frosted mud of the track, Cato took a last look over his shoulder. But Vespasian was already marching back towards the warmth of his quarters and was quickly swallowed up by the darkness.

Ahead loomed the gate, and at their approach a quiet order was given. The locking bar squealed back into its receiver and one gate swung inwards. As they passed through, a handful of legionaries watched them in silence, curious but obedient to the strict instructions not to utter a word. Beyond the ramparts, Prasutagus twitched his reins and led them down the slope towards the forest from which the Druids had emerged with the fleet prefect several days earlier.

Without his helmet and shield, and the comforting security of the camp around him, Cato suddenly felt horribly exposed. This was worse than going into battle. Much worse. Ahead lay enemy territory. And the enemy was unlike any other that the Romans had faced. Looking to the west, where the land was so dark it almost merged with the night, Cato wondered if his eyes were deceiving him, or was the blackness there made yet more black by the shadows of the Druids of the Dark Moon?

Chapter Twenty-One

By the time the sun had risen above the milky horizon into a dull grey sky, they had passed deep into the forest. They rode along a well-used trail that wound past the gnarled trunks of aged oak trees whose twisted branches showed even more starkly as the light increased. Some of the highest boughs were well nested, and the raw croaking call of crows filled the air as the dark birds watched the small party passing beneath with greedy speculative eyes. The forest floor was covered with dark, dead leaves. The snow had almost disappeared and the air felt cold and damp. The gloomy atmosphere was oppressive and Cato glanced anxiously from side to side, alert for any sign of the enemy. He rode at the rear, with only a pack pony behind him, rustling through the damp leaves. Immediately ahead was the other pony, tethered to Macro's saddle. The centurion himself, bare-headed and swaying uneasily atop his cavalry mount, seemed unconcerned by the dismal surroundings. He had far more interest in the woman ahead of him. Boudica wore her hood up and, as far as Cato was aware, had not looked back since they had left the camp.

This puzzled him; he had assumed that Boudica would be keen to see Macro once again. But there had been a marked coolness in her attitude to them both during the previous evening's briefing. And now this long silence since they had left camp. At the front rode Prasutagus, looming larger than ever on the saddle of the biggest horse that could be found for him. He led the way at a calm, unhurried pace, nonchalantly regarding the track ahead. He had ignored them at the briefing, only listening and speaking to the legate through Boudica.

Cato looked at the great mane of hair on Prasutagus's head and wondered how much the giant recalled of that night back in Camulodunum when, drunk and angry, he had caught up with his cousin drinking in an alehouse full of Romans. Whatever had happened after that night seemed to have worked some change in Boudica and strained her friendship with Macro. Perhaps Nessa had been right. Boudica and Prasutagus might be more to each other than mere cousins.

Of all the Britons that might have offered to help the general, it seemed typical of the perverse fates that governed Cato's life that it had to be Prasutagus and Boudica. This mission was dangerous enough already, Cato reflected, without having to deal with tensions arising out of Macro and Boudica's fling, and the consequent affront to Prasutagus's aristocratic pride in every root and branch of his family.

Then there was Prasutagus's particular knowledge of the Durotriges and the Dark Moon Druids. Nearly every Roman child was reared on garish tales of the Druids and their dark magic, human sacrifices and blood-drenched sacred groves. Cato was no different, and had seen such a grove for himself the previous summer. The terrible atmosphere of the place still endured, in vivid detail, in his memory. If this was the world in which Prasutagus had once immersed himself, then how much of the man was still Druid, and not fully human? What lingering loyalties might Prasutagus harbour for his former masters and fellow initiates? Was his eagerness to aid the general merely a treacherous ploy to deliver two Romans into the hands of the Druids?

Cato reined in his imagination. The enemy would hardly go to such elaborate lengths to capture a mere centurion and his optio. He scolded himself for thinking like a paranoid schoolboy and monstrously inflating his own importance.

It reminded him of a time in the imperial palace, many years earlier, when he had been little more than an infant and had taken a fancy to a small carved ivory spoon he had seen on a banqueting table. It had been easy enough to pinch, and then conceal in the folds of his tunic. In a quiet spot in the garden he had examined it, wondering at the ornate work on the handle with its sinuously twisting dolphins and nymphs. Suddenly he heard shouting and the sound of running feet. He chanced a look round the side of a bush and saw a squad of Praetorians run from the doors of the palace into the garden and begin searching the topiary. Cato had been terrified that the theft of the spoon had been discovered, and now the Emperor's men were hunting the thief down. Any moment he would be taken, evidence in hand, and hurled to the ground before the cold eyes of Sejanus, the commander of the Praetorian Guard. If only a little of what the palace slaves whispered to each other was true, Sejanus would have had his throat cut and his body thrown to the wolves.

The Praetorians came closer and closer to the hiding place where Cato trembled, biting his lip in case a whimper should attract attention.

Then, just as a thick, muscled arm groped into the bush where he crouched, there was a distant shout.

'Caius! They've found him! Come on.'

The hand withdrew, and feet pounded away across the marble flagstones. Cato nearly fainted with relief. As quietly as he could, he slipped back into the palace and replaced the spoon. Then he returned to the small chamber he shared with his father and waited, praying that the spoon's return would be noticed soon and the hue and cry would die away and the world would return to safe normality.

It was late in the evening before his father returned from the offices of the imperial secretariat. By the faint glow of an oil lamp Cato saw the anxious expression in his lined face, and then the grey eyes flickered towards his son, registering surprise that the boy was still awake.

'You should be asleep,' he whispered.

'I couldn't sleep, Daddy. Too much noise. What's happened?' Cato asked as innocently as he could. 'The Praetorian Guards were running about all over the palace. Has Sejanus caught another traitor?'

His father gave a grim smile in response. 'No. Sejanus will never catch any more traitors now. He's gone.'

'Gone? Left the palace?' A sudden anxiety sparked in Cato's mind. 'Does that mean I can't play with little Marcus any more?'

'Yes . . . yes, it does. Marcus . . . and his sister . . .' His father's face twisted into a grimace at the appalling outrage that had been wrought on the innocent children of Sejanus during the day's bloodletting. Then he leaned over his son and kissed his brow. 'They've gone with their father. I'm afraid you won't be able to see them again.'

'Why?'

'I'll tell you later. In a few days, maybe.'

But his father never did explain. Instead, Cato heard it all from the other slaves in the palace kitchen the following morning. At the news of Sejanus's death, Cato's first reaction was great relief that the previous day's events had had nothing to do with his theft of the spoon. All the anxiety, the dreadful anticipation of capture and punishment lifted from his childish shoulders. That was all that was important to him that morning.

Now, over ten years later, his face burned with embarrassment at the memory. That moment, and several others like it, frequently reached out to torment him into helpless self-loathing. Just as his present self-important fear did, and doubtless would again in the future. He seemed unable to escape these wearing rounds of harsh self-examination and he wondered if he would ever be able to live at ease with himself.

The sky remained a dismal grey for the rest of the day and there was not a whisper of breeze in the forest. The still and silent trees provoked a brooding nervousness in the riders. Cato persuaded himself that in less dangerous circumstances the harsh aesthetics of winter might lend the forest a kind of beauty. But for now, every rustle in the undergrowth or crack of a twig made him jump in his saddle and anxiously scan the shadows.

They followed a bend in the trail and began to pass the spiky tangle of a blackberry thicket. Without warning a great cracking and thrashing sounded from within. Cato and Macro flipped back their capes and drew their swords. The horses and ponies, nostrils flaring and eyes wide with fright, reared and retreated from the brambles. The thicket shook and bulged, and a stag burst out onto the track. Bloodied from numerous scratches and snorting its steamy breath into the clammy air, the stag dipped its antlers at the nearest horse and shook them threateningly.

'Keep clear!' shouted Macro, eyes on the sharp white ends of the antlers. 'Get out of its way!'

In the commotion of wheeling horses and ponies, the stag saw a gap and bounded through it. As the riders strove to control their mounts, the stag pounded into the depths of the forest on the opposite side of the track, kicking up great divots of fallen leaves.

Prasutagus mastered his horse first, then looked round at the Romans and burst into laughter. Macro scowled at him, then noticed he was still holding his short sword, poised and ready to thrust. In a sudden release of tension, he returned the Iceni warrior's laugh and sheathed his sword. Cato followed suit.

Prasutagus muttered something then tugged on his reins and headed down the track again.

'What'd he say?' Macro asked Boudica.

'He's not sure who jumped highest, you or the stag.'

'Very funny. Tell him he didn't do so bad himself.'

'Better not,' cautioned Boudica. 'He's a bit prickly on the pride front.'

'Is he? Then we've got something in common after all. Now tell him what I said.' Macro's gaze did not waver as he challenged Boudica to defy his will. 'Well, go on then, tell him what I said.'

Prasutagus looked back over his shoulder. 'Come! We go!' he shouted, and then continued in his own tongue, having exhausted his knowledge of Latin.

'Sir,' Cato intervened quietly. 'Please don't push the matter. He's the only one who knows the way ahead. Just humour him.'

'Humour him!' Macro snorted. 'Bastard's begging for a fight.'

'Which we can't afford to have,' said Boudica. 'Cato's right. We mustn't let petty rivalries brew up if we're to rescue your general's family. Calm down.'

Macro clamped his lips together and glared at her. Boudica just shrugged and turned her horse to follow Prasutagus. Knowing only too well how quickly Macro's temper came and went, Cato kept his silence and stared vaguely to one side, until with a muttered oath Macro kicked his horse forward and the small company continued on its way.

They emerged from the forest as dusk fell. The shadows and dark ancient trees fell behind and Cato's spirits lifted a little. Before them the ground dipped gently into a band of wetlands bestride a river that snaked away to the horizon on either side. A few sheep dotted the meadows, busily feeding on the green shoots exposed by the melting snow. The track wound down and away to the right. A mile away a thin column of smoke rose from a large round hut set to the back of a stockade. Prasutagus pointed it out and said a few words to Boudica.

'That's where we'll spend the night. There's a ford not much further on where we can cross the river in the morning. We should be safe enough for the night. Prasutagus knew the farmer a few years ago.'

'A few years ago?' said Macro. 'Things can change in a few years.'

'Maybe. But I don't want to spend the night in the open before I really have to.'

As Boudica's mount stepped forward, Macro leaned from his saddle and held her shoulder.

'Wait a moment. We have to talk sometime.'

'Sometime.' Boudica nodded. 'But not now.'

'When?'

'I don't know. When the time's right. Now, let go of me please, you're hurting me.'

Macro searched her eyes for some sign of the affection and lightness of spirit he had once known, but Boudica's expression was weary and empty of any emotion. His hand fell away and with a quick kick Boudica urged her horse on.

'Bloody women,' Macro muttered. 'Cato, my lad, a word of advice.

Don't ever get too closely involved with them. They can do funny things to a man's heart.'

'I know they can, sir.'

'Of course. Sorry, I forgot.'

Reluctant to dwell on the painful memory of Lavinia, Cato tugged the reins of his pony and headed down the track towards the distant farm. The leaden skies grew ever darker in the failing light and the landscape faded into hazy shades of grey. The stockade and the hut became indistinct, except for a brilliant pinprick of orange showing through the doorframe of the hut, which beckoned to them with a promise of warmth and shelter against the chill of night.

At their approach the stockade gates quickly swung shut and a head emerged from the shadows above the sharpened stakes to shout a challenge. Prasutagus bellowed a reply, and when they were close enough for his identity to be confirmed, the gates were opened again and the small party urged their beasts inside. Prasutagus dismounted and strode over to a short, thickset man who did not seem to be much older than Cato. They grasped each other by the forearms in formal but friendly greeting. It emerged that the farmer Prasutagus had once known was three years dead and buried in a small orchard behind the stockade. His eldest son had died the previous summer, fighting the Romans in the battle for the Medway crossing. The younger son, Vellocatus, now ran the farm, and remembered Prasutagus well enough. He glanced at Prasutagus's companions and said something quietly. Prasutagus laughed, and replied with a quick jerk of his head at Boudica and the others. Vellocatus stared at them for a moment before nodding.

Beckoning them all to follow him, he led the way across the muddy interior of the stockade towards a line of crudely constructed pens. Two other men, much older, were busy forking winter feed into cattle byres and paused for a moment to watch the newcomers as they led their mounts into a small stable. Inside, the riders wearily removed the saddles from their mounts, taking care to leave the blankets strapped over the legion's brand. Once the tack, provisions and equipment had been carefully stowed to one side of the pen, their host provided them with some grain and soon the horses were champing contentedly, their steamy breath curling about them in the cold air.

It was fully dark before they picked their way across to the large round hut with its thick, insulating thatch. The farmer ushered them inside and drew a heavy leather cover across the entrance. After the sharp freshness of the air outside, the smoky stench of the interior

159

made Cato cough. But at least it was warm. The floor of the hut sloped towards the hearth where wood cracked and hissed amid flickering orange flames rising from the wavering glow of the fire's base. Above the flames a blackened cauldron hung from an iron tripod. Bending towards the steam rising from the cauldron was a heavily pregnant woman. She supported her back with a spare hand as she stirred the contents with a long wooden ladle. At their approach she looked up and smiled a greeting to her husband before her eyes flashed towards their guests and her expression became wary.

Vellocatus indicated the comfortably wide stools arranged to one side of the hearth and invited his guests to sit. Prasutagus thanked him and the four travellers gratefully eased their stiff and aching limbs down. While Prasutagus talked to the farmer, the others gazed contentedly into the flames and absorbed the warmth. The rich aroma of stewing meat rising from the cauldron made Macro feel desperately hungry and he licked his lips. The woman noticed and raised the ladle. She nodded towards him and said something.

'What's she saying?' he asked Boudica.

'How should I know? She's Atrebatan. I'm Iceni.'

'But you're both Celts, surely?'

'Just because we're from the same island doesn't mean we all speak the same language, you know.'

'Really?' Macro adopted a look of innocent surprise.

'Really. Does everyone in the empire speak Latin?'

'No, of course not.'

'So how do you Romans make yourselves understood?'

'We talk more loudly.' Macro shrugged. 'People usually get the gist of what you're saying. If that fails, we lay into them.'

'I don't doubt it, but for the Lud's sake don't try that approach here.' Boudica shook her head. 'So much for the sagacity of the master race ... As it happens, I know this dialect well enough. She's offering you some food.'

'Food! Well, why didn't you say so?' Macro nodded vigorously at the farmer's wife. She laughed and reached into a large wicker basket by the hearth and lifted out some bowls which she set down on the hard earth floor. She ladled the steaming broth into the bowls and handed them round, guests first, as custom dictated. The wicker basket yielded up some small wooden spoons and moments later a hush fell over the hut as they all set to their meal.

The broth was scalding hot, and Cato had to blow over each spoonful before putting the spoon into his mouth. Looking more closely at the bowl he realised that it was Samian ware, the cheap crockery manu-factured in Gaul and exported across most of the western empire. And beyond, it seemed.

'Boudica, could you ask her where these bowls came from?'

The two women struggled to converse for a moment before the question was fully understood and an answer given.

'She traded for them with a Greek merchant.'

'Greek?' Cato nudged Macro.

'Eh?'

'Sir, the woman says she got these bowls off a Greek merchant.'

'I heard, so?'

'Was the merchant's name Diomedes?'

The woman nodded and smiled, then spoke quickly to Boudica in the singsong tones of the Celtic tongue.

'She likes Diomedes. Says he's a charmer. Always has a small gift for the women and a quick enough wit to pacify their menfolk afterwards.'

'Beware Greeks bearing gifts,' mumbled Macro. 'That lot'll jump anything that moves, male or female.'

Boudica smiled. 'From my own experience I'd say you Romans are only marginally more discriminating. Must be something they put in all that wine you southern races are so fond of drinking.'

'You complaining?' asked Macro, watching Boudica closely.

'Let's just say it was an education.'

'And you've learned all you need about the men of Rome, I suppose.'

'Something like that.'

Macro's eyes glinted angrily at Boudica, before he returned to his broth and continued eating in silence. An awkward tension filled the air. Cato stirred his broth and brought the conversation back to the less touchy subject of Diomedes.

'When was the last time she saw him?'

'Only two days ago.'

Cato stopped stirring.

'Came through on foot,' Boudica continued. 'Just stayed for a meal and passed straight on, heading west into Durotrigan territory. Doubt he'll find much trade there.'

'He's not after trade,' Cato said quietly. 'Not any more. Did you hear, sir?'

'Of course I heard. This bloody mission is dangerous enough as it is, without that Greek stirring things up. Just hope they find him and kill him quickly, before he causes us any trouble.'

They continued eating in silence, and Cato made no further attempt to keep the conversation going. He pondered the implications of the news about Diomedes. It appeared that killing the Druid prisoners was not enough for the Greek. His thirst for revenge was leading him towards the Dark Moon Druids' heartland. On his own he stood little chance, and he might alert the Durotriges to be on the lookout for strangers. That could only magnify the risk the four of them already faced. Gloomily Cato ate another spoonful of broth, chewing hard at a lump of gristle.

The hospitality of Vellocatus and his wife extended to a silver platter of honeyed cakes when they had eaten their fill of broth. Cato lifted a cake and noticed a geometric pattern on the platter beneath it. He dipped his head to look more closely.

'More of the Greek's trading, I imagine,' said Boudica as she helped herself to a cake. 'Must be making a fine living out of it.'

'I bet he is,' said Macro and took a bite of cake. His eyes instantly lit up and he nodded approvingly at their hostess. 'Good!'

She beamed happily and offered him another.

'Don't mind if I do,' said Macro, spilling crumbs down his tunic. 'Come on, Cato! Fill up, lad!'

But Cato was lost in thought, staring fixedly at the silver platter, until it was taken away and returned to the wicker basket. He was certain he had seen it before, and was greatly disturbed to see it again. Here, where it had no reason to be. While the others happily ate the cakes, he had to force himself to chew his. He watched Vellocatus and his wife with a growing sense of unease and anxiety.

'Are you sure they're asleep?' whispered Macro.

Boudica took a last glance at the still forms huddled beneath their furs on the low bier and nodded.

'Right, you'd better let Prasutagus have his say.'

Earlier, the Iceni warrior had quietly asked Boudica to let the others know he wanted a word before they passed into Durotrigan territory the next day. Their host had insisted on broaching a cask of ale and had made enough toasts to ensure his happy inebriation before he staggered over to his wife and fell asleep. Now he breathed with the regular deep rhythm of one who would not wake for many hours yet. Against the occasional rumbling of snores from the shadows, Prasutagus briefed the rest of his party in low, serious tones. He watched the others closely as Boudica translated, to make sure that the gravity of his words sank in.

'He says, once we cross the river, we must be seen as little as possible. This may well be the last night we can enjoy shelter. There will be no fires at night if there is any chance of them being seen by the enemy and we will make as little contact with the Durotriges as possible. We will search for another twenty days, until the Druids' deadline has passed. Prasutagus says that if we find nothing by then we head back. To stay any longer would be too dangerous, given that your legion will be marching against the Durotriges in only a few days' time. The moment the first legionary sets foot on Durotrigan soil, every stranger travelling their lands will be regarded as a potential spy.

'That wasn't the deal,' Macro protested quietly. 'The orders were to find the general's family, alive or dead.'

'Not if the deadline has passed, he says.'

'He'll follow his orders, like the rest of us.'

'Speak for yourself, Macro,' said Boudica. 'If Prasutagus goes, then I go, and you're on your own. We didn't agree to suicide.'

Macro glared angrily at Boudica. 'We? Who is this "we", Boudica? The last time we were together this one was just some lunk of a relative who couldn't resist playing the father figure to you and your mate. What's changed?'

'Everything,' Boudica replied quickly. 'What's past is past, and whatever's to come must not be tainted by the past.'

'Tainted?' Macro's eyebrows rose. 'Tainted? Is that all I was to you?'

'That's all you are to me now.'

Prasutagus hissed. He nodded his head towards their hosts and wagged his finger at Macro, warning him to lower his voice. Then he spoke quietly to Boudica, who relayed his words.

'Prasutagus says the route he has planned will take us through the heart of Durotrigan territory. That's where we'll find the bigger villages and settlements, the most likely places where your general's family might be held.'

'What if we're caught?' Cato asked.

'If we're caught, and handed over to the Druids, then you two and I will be burned alive. He'll face a far worse death.'

'Worse?' Macro sniffed. 'What could be worse?'

'He says he'll be skinned alive, and then fed piece by piece to their hunting dogs while he still draws breath. His skin, and head, will be nailed to an oak outside their most sacred glade as a warning to Druids of all levels of the fate that will befall any who betray the brotherhood.'

'Oh . . .'

A short silence fell. Then Prasutagus told them to get some sleep.

Tomorrow they would be in enemy country and would need all their wits about them.

'There's just one more thing,' Cato said softly.

Prasutagus had started to rise to his feet, and shook his head at the optio. 'Na! Sleep now!'

'Not yet,' Cato insisted, and with a hiss of anger Prasutagus sat down again. 'How can we be sure this farmer can be trusted?' whispered Cato.

Prasutagus explained impatiently, and nodded to Boudica to translate.

'He says he has known Vellocatus since he was a young boy. Prasutagus trusts him and will stand by that trust.'

'Oh, that's reassuring!' said Macro.

'But I don't understand why Vellocatus can live here, right on the doorstep of the Durotriges, and not be afraid of cross-border raids,' Cato persisted. 'I mean, if they wipe out an entire settlement well inside Verica's lands, why leave this place alone?'

'What's your point?' Boudica asked wearily.

'Just this.' Cato reached into the wicker basket by the hearth and quietly withdrew the silver platter, careful not to disturb the crockery. He showed the platter to Macro. 'I'm almost certain I've seen this before, in the storage pit at Noviomagus. We left the booty there, if you recall, sir. No space in the wagons.'

'I remember.' Macro sighed regretfully. 'But if this is the same platter, how did it get here?'

Cato shrugged, reluctant to voice his suspicions. If he accused Vellocatus of working for the enemy, Prasutagus might not react too well. 'I suppose it might have been traded by Diomedes. But if it is the same platter, then Vellocatus can only have been given it by the raiding party. Once we had moved out, I imagine the surviving Durotriges went back for their spoils.'

'Or maybe Vellocatus was in the raiding party himself,' Macro added.

As Boudica translated from the Latin, Prasutagus looked hard at the platter, and then suddenly rose to his feet, turned towards Vellocatus and started to draw his sword.

'No!' Cato jumped up and clasped Prasutagus by his sword hand. 'We've no proof. I might be wrong. Killing them serves no purpose. It'll just alert the Durotriges to our presence if they find him dead.'

Boudica translated and Prasutagus frowned, softly uttering a string of oaths. He released his grip on the sword handle and folded his arms.

'But if you're right about this Vellocatus,' Macro pointed out 'then

164

we can't let him live to tell any passer-by that he's seen us. We'll have
to kill him and the rest of them here before dawn.'

Cato was shocked. 'Sir, we don't have to do that.'

'You get a better idea?'

The young optio thought fast under the cool gaze of the others.

'If Vellocatus is working with the Durotriges, we might yet turn that
to our advantage by making sure that whatever he tells anyone else
serves our ends.'

Chapter Twenty-Two

They set off again in darkness, following Vellocatus down a track to the ford. The party had breakfasted on the unwarmed remains of the broth, which was scant comfort in the clammy mist that hung over the icy water and shrouded the willow trees lining the bank. At the edge of the ford Vellocatus stood to one side, watching them mount. When all was ready, Prasutagus leaned down from his saddle and quietly thanked their host, clasping him by the hand. Then as the farmer stepped back into the black shadows of the willows, Prasutagus spurred his horse and the quiet was broken by the churning splash of the horses entering the river. The shock of the freezing water startled the animals and they whinnied in protest. The water rose up the horses' flanks and over Cato's boots, adding to his misery. He tried to console himself with the thought that at least the flow would wash away some of the filth that had caked his feet for several days now. Not for the first time, Cato wished himself a slave again, in the service of the imperial palace in Rome. Liberty he might not have, but at least he would be free of the endless discomfort of being a legionary on campaign. Right now he would have given his soul in exchange for a few hours' sweating in one of the public baths back in Rome. Instead, he was shivering uncontrollably, his feet were going numb and the immediate future seemed to promise only a terrible death.

'Are we happy?' grinned Macro, riding beside him.

'Are we fuck!' Cato completed the army saying with feeling.

'This was your idea, remember? Bloody well should have let you go on your own after all.'

'Yes, sir.'

The river bed gradually sloped up to the far bank, and the horses eagerly emerged from the freezing water. Looking back across the disturbed surface they could see almost nothing of the far side, their last sight of friendly land. In case Cato's suspicion of Vellocatus was justified, they first went upriver, away from the strongholds of the

Durotriges, and increased their pace to a quick trot so that the sound of their hoofbeats on the beaten track would carry across the water back to the farmer, if he was waiting and listening beneath the willows.

A mile down the track, they halted, turned south-west, and quietly walked their horses through the cold wetland until they rejoined the track leading inland from the ford. As the first light of day began to filter through the darkness, Prasutagus quickened the pace, anxious not to be caught in the open once dawn had broken. At a gentle canter they followed the track until the surrounding land became more firm and the wetlands gave way to meadows, and then clumps of more substantial trees. Before long they had entered a small forest. Prasutagus followed the trail a short distance and then branched off along a twisting side path that led deep into an area where pine trees grew, evergreen and straight-trunked. As the lower branches closed in on either side, they had to dismount and lead their horses on foot. At length, the narrow path opened out into a small clearing. Cato was surprised to see a small timber hut faced with turf to one side. All around it stood bare wooden frames. Above the lintel over the hut's door hung the skull of a stag with a spectacular set of antlers. Nothing moved.

'I thought we were supposed to be avoiding the locals,' Macro hissed at Boudica.

'We are,' she relayed the answer back. 'This is a Druid hunting lodge. We'll spend the day here, resting. We'll continue along the main track at dusk.'

Once the horses had been relieved of their baggage and tethered, Prasutagus pushed aside the heavy leather flap that served as a door to the hut and they went inside. There was the usual beaten earth floor and a framework of pine branches held up the tightly packed thatch of the roof. A rich scent of pine and mustiness filled their nostrils. A small hearth stood at one end below an opening in the roof, and a line of simple wooden cots lined the rear wall. The bracken in the cots was slightly damp but serviceable.

'Seems comfortable enough,' said Macro. 'But how safe are we here?'

'We're safe,' Boudica replied. 'The Druids only use the lodge in summer, and most of the Durotriges are too scared of the Druids to venture anywhere near this place.'

Macro tested one of the cots with a hand, then stretched out on the rustling bracken. 'Ahhh! Now that's what I call comfortable.'

'Better get as much rest as you can. We've quite a way to go when it gets dark.'

'Fair enough.'

Cato eased himself into the next cot, eyes already heavy at the prospect of slumber. A nagging anxiety over the trustworthiness of Vellocatus had robbed him of sleep the night before and his mind was dull with exhaustion. He lay back and pulled his cloak tightly about him. His aching eyes closed and his mind quickly drifted away from the harsh discomforts of the real world.

Prasutagus regarded the Romans with a faint look of contempt, then turned back towards the low doorway. Macro quickly propped himself up.

'Where do you think you're going?'

Prasutagus made a quick gesture towards his mouth. 'Find food.'

Macro stared at the Briton, wondering how far he could be relied on.

Prasutagus held his gaze for a moment then turned and ducked out of the lodge. A flash of pearly daylight filled the interior before the leather curtain fell back across the doorway and all was still and silent in the lodge. With his veteran's instinct to snatch whatever rest he could, Macro fell asleep almost at once.

He awoke with a start, eyes snapping open, perplexed by the tangle of pine branches above his head. Then a sense of location returned and Macro remembered he was in the lodge. From the pale quality of the light filtering in from a narrow slit in the wall it was clear that dusk was approaching. He had been asleep for almost the entire day then. A snapping crackle of twigs sounded from the end of the lodge and Macro twisted his head round. Boudica was squatting down next to the hearth with a pile of kindling at her side. She reached for another handful as he watched. There was no sign of Prasutagus, and no sound from outside. Cato was still deeply asleep and lay with his mouth open, his breathing accompanied by an occasional clicking at the back of his throat.

'It's time we talked,' said Macro quietly.

Boudica appeared not to have heard him, and continued snapping twigs, arranging them in a nest around the clump of dry bracken she had pulled from one of the cots.

'Boudica, I said it's time we talked.'

'I heard you,' she replied without turning round. 'But what's the point? It's over between us.'

'Since when?'

'Since I was betrothed to Prasutagus. We're to be wed as soon as we return to Camulodunum.'

Macro sat up and swung his legs over the side of the cot. 'Married? To him? When was all this decided? It's been less than a month since we last saw each other. You couldn't stand the sight of him then. At least, that's how you behaved. So what are you playing at, woman?'

'Playing?' Boudica repeated the word with a faint smile. Then she turned and faced him. 'There are no more games for me, Macro. I am a woman now, and I'm expected to behave like one. That's what they told me.'

'Who told you?'

'My family. After they finished beating me.' Her eyes fell to the floor. 'Seems that I caused them some embarrassment after that last night we had in the inn. When I got home to my uncle's house they were all waiting for me. Somehow, they'd found out. My uncle took me out to his stable and whipped me. He kept shouting that I had shamed him, shamed my family and shamed my tribe. And all the time he whipped me. I-I've never known a person could feel such pain . . .'

Macro had been beaten a few times in his younger days – at the hands of a centurion wielding a vine staff with all the brutality the officer could muster. He remembered the agony well enough, and understood what she must have endured. Rage and pity welled up inside him. He rose from the cot and went to sit beside her.

'I thought he was going to kill me,' whispered Boudica.

Macro put his arm round her shoulder and gave her a comforting squeeze. He felt her body flinch at his touch.

'Don't, Macro. For pity's sake don't touch me. I can't bear it.'

The chilling despair of rejection turned Macro's guts to ice. He frowned, angry with himself for having let this woman work her way into his heart so completely. He could imagine the other centurions laughing contemptuously into their cups if they ever got wind of his infatuation with some native girl. Screwing them was one thing; forming an emotional attachment was quite another. It was just the sort of pathetic behaviour he himself had once been so critical of. He recalled the jibes he had given Cato when the lad had fallen for the slave girl Lavinia. But that had been a harmless teenage fling; just the kind of thing to be expected of youngsters before the harsh demands of adulthood closed down such experimentation with all that life had to offer. Macro was thirty-five, nearly ten years older than Boudica. True, there were relationships with greater differences in age, but they were rightly derided by most people. The gap in age that had charmed him so utterly a few months earlier now mocked him. The centurion felt like one of the pathetic old gropers who haunted the Circus Maximus, trying their hand with women young enough to be their grandchildren. The comparison made him burn with shame. He stirred uncomfortably.

'So they forced you never to see me again?'

Boudica nodded.

'And you went along with it.'

She turned her face to him, twisted with bitterness. 'What else could I do? They said if I was ever caught with another Roman I'd be beaten again. I think I'd rather die than face that. Truly.' Her expression softened. 'Sorry, Macro. I can't risk it. I have to think about my future.'

'Your future?' Macro was scornful. 'You mean marriage to Prasutagus? I must admit, that came as a bloody big surprise. Why did you agree to it? I mean, he's not exactly the sharpest arrow in the quiver.'

'No. He's not. But he is well-positioned for the future. An Iceni prince with a household in Camulodunum and a growing reputation in the tribe. Now he's developing a useful relationship with your general. With this mission he will win Plautius's gratitude.'

'I wouldn't put too much faith in that,' muttered Macro. He had experience of just how short-lived the general's gratitude could be.

Boudica gave him a curious glance. When he did not elaborate, she continued, 'If we manage to find the general's family, Prasutagus will have more influence with Rome than almost any other Briton. And if Rome does eventually conquer this island, those people who helped her do so are bound to be rewarded.'

'Those people, and the wives of those people.'

'Yes.'

'I see. Well, you've come a long way over the last month. I hardly recognise you.'

Boudica was injured by his cynical tone and looked away. Macro did not regret his remark, but at the same time he could not make himself dislike Boudica enough to enjoy insulting her. He wished he could find some hint of the brassy, affectionate girl he had fallen for back in Camulodunum. 'Are you really so cold-blooded?'

'Cold-blooded?' The idea seemed to surprise her. 'No. I'm not cold-blooded. I'm just making the most of what has been forced on me. If I was a man, if I had power, then things would be very different. But I'm a woman, the weaker sex, and I have to do what I'm told. That's the only choice I have, for now.'

There was a pause before Macro summoned the courage to speak. 'No, you had another choice. You could have chosen me.'

Boudica turned and looked at him closely. 'You're serious, aren't you?'

'Very.' Macro's heart soared as he saw Boudica smile. Then her eyes fell away and she shook her head.

'No. It's out of the question.'

'Why?'

'It would be no life for me. I'd be an outcast from my tribe. What if you tired of me after a while? I'd have nothing left. I know what becomes of such women, pathetic hags who follow the army and live off the legion's scraps, until disease or some violent drunk does for them. Would you wish that on me?'

'Of course not! It wouldn't be like that. I would provide for you.'

'Provide for me? You don't make it sound very appealing. I'd be rootless, and at your mercy, in your world. I couldn't bear that. Despite what I've learned of life beyond the lands of the Iceni, I'm still Iceni through and through. And you're Roman. I might speak your language well enough, but that's as far as I want Rome to penetrate my being – and none of your filthy innuendo, please!'

They both smiled for a moment, and then Macro raised his rough soldier's hand to her cheek, marvelling at its softness. Boudica remained still. Then, very tenderly, her lips brushed his palm in a soft kiss that sent tingles up Macro's arm. He slowly leaned forward.

There was a heavy thud outside the lodge. The leather flap hanging across the entrance was flung to one side. Macro and Boudica sprang apart. The centurion snatched up some kindling and began snapping it into pieces and thrusting it at Boudica, who resumed laying the fire. A dark figure blotted out the light from the doorway. Macro and Boudica, squinted at the silhouetted figure.

'Prasutagus?'

'Sa!' He moved inside the lodge, dragging the gutted carcass of a small deer after him. The light fell on the Iceni warrior's face, revealing a faint look of amusement in his eyes.

Chapter Twenty-Three

For the next five days they travelled deeper into Durotrigan territory, cautiously riding along trails by night and finding somewhere to hide and rest during the day. Prasutagus seemed tireless, never sleeping more than a few hours. Each stage of their journey was planned by him to bring them close to a village. He rested until midday, and then slipped into each village to look for any signs of Roman hostages. A dusk he returned with meat for the others, which they cooked over a low fire, huddling round to draw as much warmth as they could from the flames in the bitter night air. Once they had eaten, they put the fire out and followed Prasutagus as he picked his way along well-used trails. Every farmstead and small settlement was carefully circumvented and there were frequent stops while the Iceni warrior made sure that the way ahead was clear before they continued. Just before dawn he led them off the tracks into the nearest woodland, and would not let them stop until they had discovered a dip in the forest floor where the party could rest for the day unobserved.

They covered themselves with cloaks and the blankets from their mounts and slept as well as they could in such uncomfortable conditions. A watch was kept throughout the day, and all four of them took their turn, standing quietly in the shadows of the forest, a short distance from the camp.

Cato, younger and thinner than the others, suffered most from the cold, and his sleep was fitful and broken. The temperature had dropped below freezing on the second day and the penetrating cold of the frozen earth made his hip joints so stiff that he could barely move his legs when he woke up.

On the fifth day, a mist closed in. Prasutagus left them as usual to scout round the next village. While they waited hungrily for him to reappear with the day's meal, Boudica and the two Romans prepared a small fire. A light breeze was blowing through the forest, and they had to build a turf windbreak round the fireplace. Cato collected some fallen branches from beneath the nearest trees, every so often pausing to rub his hips and ease the stiffness in his joints. When he had amassed enough fuel to maintain the fire for the few hours it would be needed, he slumped down between Boudica and his centurion, who sat opposite each other on either side of the fireplace. At first no one spoke. The wind steadily strengthened and they clutched their cloaks more tightly about them against the biting cold. A few paces away the horses and ponies stood in sullen silence, lank manes lifting and flapping with each gust.

There were now only fifteen days left before the Druids' deadline. Cato doubted that they would find the general's family in time. There was no point in their being here. There was nothing they could do to prevent the Druids from murdering their hostages. Nothing. Five nights of tense scrambling through enemy territory had taken their toll and Cato did not think he could cope with much more. Cold and filthy, exhausted in mind and body, he was in no condition to keep looking for the hostages, let alone to rescue them. This was a fool's errand, and the hostile glances Macro increasingly threw his way convinced Cato that he would never be forgiven for his stupidity – assuming they ever made it back to the Second Legion.

Above the dark interlace of tossing branches, the sky dimmed into dusk, and still there was no sign of Prasutagus. At length Boudica rose to her feet and stretched her arms behind her back with a deep grunt.

'I'll just go a little way down towards the track,' she said. 'See if there's any sign of him.'

'No,' Macro said firmly. 'Sit tight. We can't take the risk.'

'Risk? Who in their right mind would be abroad on a day like this?'

'Besides us?' Macro chuckled mirthlessly. 'I dread to think.'

'Well, I'm going anyway.'

'No, you're not. Sit down.'

Boudica remained on her feet and spoke quietly. 'I really thought you were a better man than this, Macro.'

Cato shuffled himself deeper inside his cloak and stared into the unlit fire, wishing he could make himself disappear.

'I'm only being careful,' Macro explained. 'I expect your man will be back soon enough. You don't have to worry about him. So sit still.'

'Sorry, I need a shit. Can't wait any longer. So, if you won't let me go somewhere discreet, I'll have to do it here.'

173

Macro went red with embarrassment and anger, knowing it would be foolish to accuse her of lying. In frustration he balled his hands into fists.

'Go on then! But don't go far and come straight back.'

'I'll be as long as it takes,' she spat back and stamped off into the shadows of the forest.

'Bloody women!' mumbled Macro. 'Bloody liabilities, all of 'em. Want a word of advice, lad? Never have anything to do with them. They're just trouble.'

'Yes, sir. Shall I get the fire started?'

'What? Oh, yes. Good idea.'

As Cato struck the flints in his tinder pan, Macro continued to watch for the return of Boudica and Prasutagus. A small lick of orange flame caught the dry shreds of moss in the pan and Cato carefully transferred it to the fire, taking care to shield the delicate flame from the wind with his body. The kindling caught quickly and soon he was warming his hands in front of a crackling blaze as the fire got to work on the larger pieces of wood he had fed into the flames. A faint orange glow wavered on the surrounding trees as night began to close in.

Boudica did not reappear and Cato began to wonder if anything had happened to the two Britons. Even if nothing had happened, would Boudica be able to find her way back to them in the dark? What if they had been captured by the Durotriges? Would they be tortured for information about accomplices? Were the Durotriges already looking for him and his centurion?

'Sir?'

Macro turned his face away from the dark woods. 'What?'

'Do you think anything's happened to them?'

'How should I know?' snapped Macro. 'They might have gone off to negotiate a price for us with the locals as far as I know.'

It was a foolish thing to say, and Macro regretted it almost immediately. He spoke out of anxiety for Boudica, and concern for what would happen to them if Prasutagus never returned. The prospects were not hopeful for two Roman legionaries stranded in a dark forest in the middle of enemy territory.

'He seemed trustworthy enough to me,' Cato said anxiously. 'Don't you trust him, sir?'

'He's a Briton. These Durotriges may be from a different tribe to our man but he has far more in common with them than he does with us,' Macro paused. 'I've seen people sell out their countrymen to Rome on almost every frontier I've served. I tell you, Cato, you've seen nothing

174

until you've served in Judaea. They'd sell their own mothers if they thought it might help them score the smallest point against some rival or other. This lot aren't much better. Look how many of those exiled British nobles have done a deal with Rome in order to regain their kingdoms. They'd prostitute themselves to anyone in exchange for a bit of power and influence. Prasutagus and Boudica are no different. They'll stay loyal to Rome only as long as it's in their interests to do so. Then you'll see their true value as friends and allies. You mark my words.'

Cato frowned. 'You really think so?'

'Maybe.' Macro's weathered face suddenly broke into a good-humoured grin. 'But I'd be more than happy to be wrong!'

A twig snapped nearby. The Romans were on their feet, swords drawn, in an instant.

'Who's there?' Macro called out. 'Boudica?'

With a rustling of dead leaves and further cracking of twigs, two figures emerged from the dark shadows and into the wavering amber glow of the fire. Macro relaxed and lowered his sword.

'Where the bloody hell have you two been?'

Prasutagus was grinning, and he talked excitedly as he strode up to the fire and clapped Macro on the shoulder. True to form he had brought some meat with him – a butchered suckling pig hung from a thong on his belt. Prasutagus flung the carcass down by the fire and continued talking. Boudica translated as quickly as she could.

'He says he's found them – the general's family!'

'What? Is he sure?'

She nodded. 'He got talking to the local chief. They're being held in another village only a few miles away. The chief of that village is one of the Druids' most loyal followers. He trains their personal bodyguard. Recruits the most promising of the young boys from all the outlying settlements, then trains them to be fanatically loyal to their new masters. By the time he's finished with them they'd rather die than disappoint the chief. A few days ago he was in the village Prasutagus just visited. He'd come to claim his quota of new recruits. He was drinking with the local warriors, and that's when he let slip that he was guarding some important hostages.'

Prasutagus nodded his head, eyes blazing with excitement at the prospect of action. He put a broad hand on Macro's shoulder.

'Is good, Roman! Yes?'

For a moment Macro stared up into the Iceni warrior's beaming face, and all the discomfort of the last few days was swept away in a wave of relief that their mission had achieved its first goal. The next step would be far more perilous. But for the moment Macro was content and he returned Prasutagus's excited expression with a warm smile.

'Is good!'

Chapter Twenty-Four

Cato gently eased the tall reeds apart and crept forward, making for the low hummock where he had left Macro earlier in the day. Around him, the cold damp air was thick with the smell of rotting vegetation. His feet squelched through dark mud, staining his calves black as he progressed as quietly as he could, dragging the cut bough of a holly bush behind him. At last the ground became firm underfoot, and he crouched low, picking his way up the bank, eyes and ears straining for any sign of his centurion.

'Pssst! Over here.'

A hand reached through the reeds at the top of the hummock and beckoned. Cato eased himself forward, taking care not to disturb the reeds, in case anyone in the village was looking their way. Just beyond was the small patch they had quietly cut before dawn. Macro was lying on a bed of rushes, peering through the dried brown remains of the previous summer's growth. Cato dropped the end of the holly branch and stretched out on the ground beside him. On the other side of the hummock, the reeds stretched out along a slowly flowing river that curled round a Durotrigan village and provided it with a natural defence. On the opposite side of the village rose a high rampart topped with a stout palisade that crossed a narrow gateway. The village itself was the usual dismal affair that seemed to be the best the more rustic of the Celts could construct. A loose muddle of round wattle and daub huts topped with a thatch of rushes cut from the river bank. From the slight elevation of the hummock Macro and Cato had a good view over the village.

The biggest of the huts stood on the bank directly opposite Cato and Macro and had its own palisade. The ring of posts was lined on the inside with smaller huts. A number of thick posts rose on one side of the compound. They were familiar enough to the two Romans – sword practice posts. Even as they watched, a small group of black-cloaked men emerged from one of the smaller huts, stripped off their cloaks,

177

and drew their long swords. They each picked a post and began to lay into them with well-honed swinging cuts. Sharp cracks and dull thuds carried clearly across the glassy surface of the river. Cato's gaze shifted to a peculiar structure built onto the side of the large hut. It appeared to be a small cabin of some kind. But there were no windows, and the only visible opening was filled by a small timber door, fastened on the outside by a stout bar. Another black-cloaked figure stood guard by the entrance, a war spear in one hand, the other hand resting on the rim of a grounded kite shield.

'Any sign of the hostages, sir?'

'No. But if they're anywhere in the village, that hut looks like our best bet. Saw someone take a jug and some bread in there not long ago.'

Macro turned away from the village and eased himself back on the rustling mass of cut reeds.

'Everything sorted?'

'Yes, sir. Our horses are safe in that dell Prasutagus showed us. I've agreed a signal with Boudica in case there's any trouble.' Cato indicated the holly bough.

'If they leave it much longer it'll be dark before we get started,' said Macro quietly.

'Prasutagus said he'd give me enough time to get back to you and then they would move.'

'You left them in the dell?'

'Yes, sir.'

'I see.' Macro frowned, then heaved himself back into position to continue watching over the village. 'Then I expect we'll have to wait a while longer before they turn up.'

Even though the winter months had nearly come to an end, it was still cold and the steady light drizzle had thoroughly penetrated their clothes. After a little while Cato's teeth were chattering and his body trembled. He tightened his muscles to try and fight off the sensation. These last few days had been the most uncomfortable of his life. Apart from the physical discomforts they had endured, the constant fear of discovery, and terror of the consequences, had made every moment a nervous torment. Now, as he lay on a damp river bank, legs caked in foul-smelling muck, chilled to the bone and starving for a decent warm meal, he began to fantasise about fixing himself an honourable discharge from the legion. It was not the first time the thought of quitting the army had come to his mind. Not the first by a long way. The train of thought was familiar and primarily focused on the task of discovering a means by which he could quickly acquire a pensioned discharge without sustaining a disabling injury. Unfortunately teams of sharp-minded imperial clerks had pored over the regulations long before Cato was born and had managed to close nearly every loophole. But somewhere, some way, there had to be a means by which he could beat the system.

Macro suddenly grunted. 'Here they come. Must have satisfied himself with a quickie.'

'Pardon?'

'Nothing, lad. There they are, on the track in front of the gate.'

Cato looked beyond the village and saw two tiny grey shapes on horseback emerging from the forest. As they boldly trotted down the track towards the village, the watchman above the gate turned and called down to a small knot of men huddled round a glowing fire. They responded to his summons at once and scrambled up the crude wooden steps inside the rampart. Prasutagus and Boudica disappeared from sight as they rode up to the gate. Watching the villagers on the palisade brandishing their weapons, Cato felt a momentary pang of concern. But a moment later the gates swung inwards and the two Iceni entered.

At once they were surrounded and the reins of their mounts seized. Even from across the river Macro and Cato could hear Prasutagus bellow in outraged indignation and issue his challenge in his role as itinerant wrestler. One of the villagers ran off, disappearing among the huts before he burst into the compound surrounding the largest hut. He hurried inside and quickly re-emerged in the company of a tall erect figure whose black cloak was fastened at the shoulder with a large gold brooch. In an unhurried manner he followed the watchman back to the main gate. Meanwhile Prasutagus continued to shout his challenge to the villagers in his deep booming voice and by the time the village chief appeared, a large crowd had gathered at the foot of the rampart. The chief pushed his way through and strode up to the visitors, who were still on horseback. Prasutagus showed just the right amount of arrogance by folding his arms and staying put for a moment. Then he casually flung his leg across his beast and slipped to the ground. He still towered over the chief, and lifted his chin to emphasise his contemptuous gaze.

Prasutagus made his challenge again. This time he undid the clasp of his cloak and tossed it to Boudica, who had also dismounted and stood with the horses, having seized the reins back from the villagers. The Iceni warrior pulled his tunic off and stood bare-chested, arms raised and fists clenched, bunching his muscles for the delectation of the crowd.

'Bloody show-off!' muttered Macro. 'Poncing around like some rich old tart's gladiator playmate! One more of those poses and I'll puke.'

'Easy, sir. It's all part of the plan. Look there, at the compound.'

The men training at the sword posts had stopped, and were hurriedly sheathing their swords and pulling on their black cloaks. As they left the compound, the guard on the door of the cabin took a few steps towards them and called out. The response was a harsh shout and with a sullen expression the guard went back to his post at the door of the cabin.

'Now's our chance!' Macro slipped back down from the crest of the hummock and started to pull off his clothing. He glanced at Cato. 'Come on, lad! Let's be having you.'

With a resigned sigh, Cato slithered down over the rushes and began to strip. Off came the cloak, the harness and chain mail, and lastly his under tunic. As he peeled the last layer of wet material from his body, the cold air brought his skin up in tight goose pimples and he shivered terribly. Macro looked over his thin frame with disapproval.

'You'd better get some decent food inside you and do some fitness training when we get back to the legion. You look like shit.'

'Th-thank you, sir.'

'Come on, boots off. The only thing you need is your sword, and your float.'

Cato's swimming skills were rudimentary at best, the result of lack of practice and a deep-rooted fear and hatred of water. Macro passed him an inflated wineskin. 'Cost me the last drop of the decent stuff, that did.'

'You didn't throw it away?'

'Course not. It was Massic. Can't be throwing that away, so I finished it off. Helps to keep the cold out. Anyway, here. Take it, and don't bloody drown on me.'

'Yes, sir.'

Cato fastened his leather scabbard belt tightly round his waist and followed Macro down the far side of the hummock, careful not to disturb the reeds as he passed. He took a last glance towards the village gate where Prasutagus and one of the villagers were already squaring up. Then they rushed at each other and the villagers let out an excited roar.

'Fucking move yourself!' Macro hissed at Cato.

The still and stagnant water amongst the reeds was bitterly cold and Cato gasped as he squatted down beside Macro. The freezing water stung his skin, almost as if it was burning him. The two Romans rustled through the reeds to the edge of the river. As the far bank came into sight, they lowered themselves into the water until just their heads were exposed. Under the surface Cato's arms were wrapped tightly about the inflated wineskin.

'Right, off we go,' whispered Macro. 'Keep it as quiet as you can. Not one splash or we're dead.'

The centurion eased himself out into the slow current and gently stroked through the water. With a deep breath, Cato pushed himself away from the bank and followed Macro, using his legs to propel himself after his centurion.

The river was perhaps fifty paces wide at this point, but for Cato the distance seemed insurmountable. He felt certain that either the wineskin would deflate and he would drown, or that the terrible aching cold would freeze him to death. The danger of being spotted by the enemy and being killed by a spear was the least of his concerns. It would bring an end to the awful misery of being up to his neck in this icy current.

They paddled towards the back of the large hut, the maddening slowness of their progress a necessary agony if they were not to be discovered. By the time they emerged from the water, Cato's fingers and toes had become quite numb. Macro, too, was suffering and shivered uncontrollably as he helped Cato up onto the river bank and then rubbed his optio's limbs vigorously, trying to restore some sensation in them. Then they made their way up the bank and round the hut to the cabin. Macro nodded to Cato to make ready, but Cato could not stop shaking and had barely enough feeling in his hands to draw his sword and hold it with a firm grip.

'Ready?'

Cato nodded.

'Let's go.'

The cheers and shouts from the fight reached an abrupt crescendo, then there was a deep collective groan. Prasutagus had floored their first champion. In the sudden quiet Macro held his hand out to stop Cato. The Iceni warrior bellowed another challenge. Someone replied, and the shouting rose again.

'Come on.' Macro crept forward, crouching low and using his spare hand for balance. They climbed a small lip of earth at the top of the bank and then pressed up against the back wall of the main hut. Lungs still aching from the effort of swimming the river, and shivering with cold, Macro eased himself along the wall. Behind him Cato strained his ears for any sound of an approaching tribesman. Macro caught sight of the corner of the log cabin and stopped, flattening himself against the wall. Above the low bark roof he could see the guard's spear tip, and below that the top of his bronze helmet. Macro bent low, barely breathing, and eased his way into the angle where the cabin leaned up against the hut. With his back to the cabin, he beckoned to Cato. For a moment they listened, but no noise came from the front of the cabin. Macro indicated that Cato should stay put, then he inched his way along the rough timber towards the corner.

Sword ready, he slowly peered round and saw the guard standing six feet away, outside the low entrance. Despite his spear, helmet and flowing black cape, he was little more than a boy. Macro moved his head back round the corner and with his eyes searched the ground by his feet. He picked up a hard clod of earth and stone and made ready to lob it.

Suddenly the guard started speaking. Macro froze. Someone responded to the guard – a low voice close at hand, and with a start Cato realised it came from within the cabin. He jabbed his finger towards the wall of the cabin behind him and Macro nodded. Someone else must have been imprisoned with the general's family. Before the guard could reply, Macro threw the clod in a low arc across the roof of the cabin. The moment it landed with a soft clump, he rose and dived round the corner. As he had hoped, the guard had turned to investigate the sound, and before he could react to the soft pad of feet, Macro had clamped a hand over the guard's mouth. He yanked the guard's head back and rammed his sword through the black cape, the tip angled up under the Briton's ribcage into his heart. The guard jerked and thrashed a moment, powerless in the centurion's tight grip. The movements quickly became feeble, and then stopped. Macro held him a moment longer to make certain, and then quietly lifted the body round the corner of the cabin and laid it down against the wall of the hut.

The voice from inside the hut called out.

'We'd better put a stop to that,' whispered Macro. 'Before someone hears.'

Leading the way, Macro hurried to the bar locking the cabin door, slid it out and tossed it to the ground. With a powerful heave he pushed the sturdy wooden door inwards. The light from outside fell on the blinking face of another black-caped man. He had raised himself on one arm and now scrambled for the sword lying beside him. Macro lunged forward, smothering the Briton with his body, and smashed the

182

pommel of his sword into the side of the man's head. With a grunt the Briton went limp, knocked cold by the blow.

'Sir!' Cato called out, but before Macro could respond to the warning, a figure charged out of the gloom at the end of the cabin, spear held ready to thrust into Macro's naked side. There was a sharp crack as Cato smashed his sword down on the shaft of the spear and the leaf-shaped blade bit into the hard-packed earth a few inches from Macro's heaving chest. As the Briton's momentum carried him forwards, Cato flicked his blade round and the man tumbled throat first onto the point. The blade penetrated his brain and the Briton died instantly.

'Shit! That was close!' Macro blinked at the spear embedded in the ground close to his chest. 'Thanks, lad!'

Cato nodded as he worked his sword free of the second man's skull. With a soft crunch the blade came out, stained with blood. Despite all the death he had seen in the brief time he had served with the eagles, Cato winced. He had killed before, in battle, but that was instinctive, and there was no time to reflect on the matter. Unlike now.

'Is there anyone here?' Macro called out, straining his eyes into the gloom of the cabin. There was no reply. One end was piled with split logs. At the other some indistinct shapes lay huddled on the ground around the pitcher and what was left of the loaves Macro had seen enter the cabin a while earlier.

'My lady?' Cato called out. 'Lady Pomponia?'

There was no movement, no sound, no sign of life in the cabin. Cato hefted his sword and slowly approached, a sick feeling of despair welling up in his guts. They were too late. With the point of his sword he lifted the top layer of rags and swept them to one side. Underneath lay a pile of wool capes and fur skins. Bedding, not bodies. Cato frowned for a moment, then nodded.

'It's a trap,' he said.

'Eh?'

'The general's family were never here, sir. The Druids must have guessed we'd attempt a rescue, and wanted to divert us from where they're really keeping the prisoners. So they spread a rumour that the captives were being held in this village. Prasutagus got word of it, and here we are. They set us up.'

'And we fell for it,' Macro replied, the instant relief he had felt at not finding bodies now turned just as quickly to an icy dread. 'We have to get out of here.'

'What about the others?'

'We can signal them when we get back to the hummock.'

'And if the Durotriges discover the bodies of their men before we can show the signal?'

'Then that's too bad.'

Macro pushed Cato out of the cabin, shut the door and hurriedly replaced the locking bar. Keeping low, they ran round the back of the hut and slithered down the bank to the river. Cato retrieved his wineskin float from the reeds at the water's edge and waded in, gritting his teeth as the freezing water rose up his bare chest. Then he was kicking out, desperately trying to keep up with his centurion. The return crossing seemed to take longer. Cato listened for the first shouts indicating that the enemy had discovered the bodies, but mercifully the cheering from the village gate continued unabated and at last, numb with cold, he waded after Macro into the reeds on the far bank.

Moments later they were sitting by their equipment and clothing, each with their heavy wool cloaks clenched tightly about their shivering bodies. Macro turned towards the village where Prasutagus and his latest challenger were locked in an awkward stumbling hold. To one side, halfway up the rampart, stood Boudica.

'She's there. Make the signal,' Macro ordered. 'Quick as you can.'

Cato grabbed the holly bough and held it upright in the soft ground just below the top of the hummock. 'Has she seen it, sir?'

'I don't know . . . No. Oh shit.'

'What's happening, sir?'

'Someone's come back into the compound.'

As Macro watched, the black-cloaked figure passed the cabin without a glance and strode down the line of practise posts before turning into one of the smaller huts and disappearing from sight. Macro breathed deeply with relief, then turned his gaze back to the village gate. Boudica remained still, as if she was watching the fight. When Prasutagus brought his foe crashing to the ground, Boudica still did not react. Then suddenly she raised her hand to her hood and lifted it.

'She's seen it! Get that thing down now!'

Cato quickly lowered the branch and wriggled up to join his centurion. By the gates Prasutagus stood erect, his magnificent arrogance evident even at this distance. The villagers were clamouring for another challenger. When Boudica stepped up to Prasutagus's side and held out his tunic and cloak, the crowd's roar became angry. The warrior chief, black feathers adorning his helmet, confronted Prasutagus. The Icenian shook his head and held out his hand for the purse owed him for defeating his opponents. The chief shouted angrily, and stripped off his cape, challenging Prasutagus in person.

'Don't you fucking dare!' Macro hissed.

'Sir!' Cato pointed at the compound. The man they had seen earlier had re-emerged from his hut and was walking towards the compound gate, a purse swinging from his hand. Just before he turned into the narrow gateway he stopped and looked over towards the cabin. He shouted something, waited, and shouted again. When there was no response, he headed over towards the cabin, tying the purse to his belt.

Macro switched his gaze back to the village gate, where Prasutagus still stood, head raised haughtily, apparently considering the chief's challenge. Macro thumped his fist down on the ground.

'Get moving, you fool!'

In the compound the Durotrigan warrior had reached the cabin. He called out again, angrily this time, hands on hips, cloak swept back behind his elbows. Then he happened to glance down at the ground. An instant later he was crouching, fingers probing something by his feet. He looked up, and his hand went for his sword. Rising to his feet, the Durotrigan cautiously crept round the cabin. He stopped when he saw the body wedged into the corner by the hut.

'That's done it,' muttered Cato.

Back by the village gate, Prasutagus finally gave way and pulled on his tunic and cape. The crowd shouted their contempt. The chief turned to his people and punched his fists into the air triumphantly, now that his foe had backed down. In the compound, the Durotrigan unbarred the cabin door and went inside. A moment later he burst out and ran towards the compound gate, shouting for all he was worth.

'Prasutagus, you bastard, get moving!' Macro growled.

The Icenian, swung up onto the back of the horse Boudica held ready for him. Then, amid jeers from the villagers, the two of them rode out through the village gates, trying not to look too hurried. They were fifty paces down the track towards the forest when the Durotrigan warrior sprinted into the crowd and pushed his way through to the chief. Moments later the chief was bellowing out orders. The crowd fell silent. Men hurried towards the compound and the chief strode after them, then halted, whipped round and pointed through the gate after Prasutagus and Boudica. Whatever he shouted, it was heard by the Icenians and immediately they kicked their heels and galloped for their lives into the forest.

Chapter Twenty-Five

'Someone bloody well told them!' Macro snapped. 'I mean, it's not the kind of trap you set up on the off chance. And if it's him, I'll have his balls for breakfast.' He jabbed his finger at Prasutagus, who was sitting on a fallen tree, chewing a strip of dried beef.

Macro glared at Boudica. 'Tell him.'

She raised her eyes in weary frustration. 'Tell him yourself. You really want a fight? With him?'

'Fight?' Prasutagus stopped chewing and his right hand casually slipped down to his sword belt. 'You fight me, Roman?'

'You're beginning to get your tiny little mind round the world's greatest language, aren't you, sunshine?'

Prasutagus shrugged. 'You want fight?'

Macro thought about it for a moment, and then shook his head. 'It can wait.'

'It doesn't make any sense,' said Cato. 'Prasutagus is in as much danger as the rest of us. If anyone told the Durotriges that we were coming, it has to be someone else That farmer, for instance. Vellocatus.'

'It's possible,' admitted Macro. 'He was a shifty looking sod. So what now? The enemy knows what we're up to. They'll be on their guard everywhere we go. Numbskull here won't be able to go anywhere near any of the locals to pick up news of the general's family. I'd say that we've almost no chance of finding them now. Mounting a rescue is out of the question.'

Cato had to agree. The rational side of his mind knew they should abandon the mission and return to the Second Legion. Cato was confident that Vespasian possessed enough intelligence to see that they had done all they could before turning back. It would be foolhardy to continue while the Durotriges were hunting for them. As things stood, it would be dangerous enough trying to make it back into friendly territory. But as the thought of danger sidled into his consciousness, Cato could not help thinking of the vastly greater danger the general's family was in. Cursed with a vivid imagination, he could picture Plautius's wife and children living in daily terror at the prospect of being tied up inside one of those giant wicker effigies the Druids liked to construct. There they would be burned alive, and the mental image of their screaming faces struck Cato with such sharpness that he flinched. The general's son, whom he had never met, assumed the features of the blond child he had seen in the well . . .

No. He couldn't let that happen. To turn back and live with the knowledge that he had not acted to prevent the child's death would be unbearable. This was the irreducible truth of the situation. No matter how much he chided himself for being prey to his emotions, for being too sentimental to act according to objective reasoning, he could not swerve from the course of action demanded by some perverse instinct so deep inside him that it evaded any kind of analysis.

Cato turned towards Macro. 'Are you saying we should turn back, sir?'

'Makes sense. What do you reckon, Boudica? You and him?'

The Icenians exchanged a few words. Prasutagus did not appear very interested in the centurion's proposal, and only Boudica seemed to have a point of view, apparently urging him towards one course of action. At length she gave up, and looked down into her lap.

'Well? What's the opinion of our resident Druid?'

'He doesn't care either way. It's your people we're supposed to be saving. Makes no difference to him if they live or die. If you want to leave them to burn then that's up to you. Says it'll be an interesting test of character.'

'Test of character, eh?' Macro stared coldly at the Icenian warrior. 'Unlike you lot, we Romans can make difficult decisions. We don't just charge in and die out of sheer stupidity. Look where your dumb heroics have got you Celts over the years. We've done what we can here. Now we get some rest and start marching back to the legion once night falls.'

Macro looked towards Cato. The optio returned his gaze without expression. It unsettled Macro.

'What is it, lad?'

'Sir?' Cato stirred, as if from some kind of trance, and Macro recalled that they had had little sleep over the past few days. That must be it. 'I was just thinking . . .'

Macro felt a heavy weight drag his spirits down; when Cato started sharing his thoughts, he had a tendency towards complication that made it very wearing for those trying to keep up with him. Why the hell

Cato refused to see the world as plainly as it appeared to other men was one of the great frustrations Macro had to suffer in his dealings with his optio.

'You were thinking what, exactly?'

'That you're right, sir. Best thing for us to do is turn tail and get as far away from those Druids as possible. No sense in taking any unnecessary risks.'

'No. There isn't.'

'The general's sure to understand your line of thinking, sir. He'll make sure no one accuses you of lacking – how can I put it? – lacking moral fibre.'

'Lacking moral fibre?' Macro didn't like the sound of the phrase. Made him sound like some civvy idler. Macro was the kind of man who resented being described as lacking anything, and he glared accusingly at his optio. 'None of your high-flown nonsense now, lad. Just speak your mind nice and clear. You say we might be accused of cowardice once we get back to the legion? Is that it?'

'We might be. It'd be an understandable mistake, of course. Some people might say we had one near scrape and that was enough for us. Naturally the general will appreciate the implications of having Prasutagus's cover story blown. Even though it meant the certain death of his family he'd be sure to try and persuade others that we had no alternative. In time everyone would see the point and come round to your way of thinking.'

'Hmmm.' Macro nodded slowly, pressing a thick knuckle to his forehead as if that might help him concentrate his tired mind. He needed time to think this through.

'We'll be riding light, won't we, sir?' Cato continued cheerfully. 'I suppose I'd better offload anything we don't need. Anything that might slow us down when we run back to the legion.'

'Nobody's running back anywhere!'

'Sorry, sir. I didn't mean it to sound that way. Just keen to get moving.'

'Oh, are you? Well, you can just stop right there. Leave the packs alone.'

'Sir?'

'I said leave 'em. We're not going back. Not yet at least. Not until we've searched a little longer.'

'But you just said—'

'Shut it! I've made my decision. We keep looking. Anyone else got any objections?' Macro turned to the Icenians, jaw thrust out, daring them to challenge him. Boudica struggled to hide a grin. Prasutagus, as usual, grasped the wrong end of the stick and nodded his head vigorously.

'We fight now, Roman?'

'No. Not now!' Macro snapped, exasperated. 'When we've got a little more time on our hands, and only if you're a good boy until then. All right? Better make sure he gets that clear, Boudica.'

Prasutagus looked disappointed, but his natural good humour overcame any inclination to sulk. He reached over to Macro and gave the centurion a hearty slap on the shoulder with his huge paw.

'Ha! You good man, Roman. We friends, maybe.'

'Don't count on it.' Macro smiled as sweetly as his scarred veteran's face would permit. 'Meanwhile, we need to decide what to do next.'

Cato coughed. 'Sir, it occurs to me that the Druids might have some sacred place, somewhere secret, known only to themselves.'

'Yes. So?'

'So we might want to press Prasutagus on that point. After all, he was a novice once. You might want to ask him if the Druids have such a place, somewhere where the general's family could be held safely.'

'True.' Macro eyed the Icenian warrior thoughtfully. 'Strikes me our man might just have been holding out on us. Ask him, Boudica.'

She turned to her kinsman and translated. The warrior's expression changed completely. He shook his head.

'Na!'

'Someone's not very happy. What's the matter?'

'He says there is no such sacred place.'

'He's lying. And he's no good at it. You better tell him. And tell him I want the truth, right now.'

Prasutagus shook his head again, and started to shuffle away from Macro, until the centurion's hand shot out and trapped the Iceni warrior's wrist in an iron grip.

'No more of your bullshit! I want the truth.'

For a while the two men stared at each other, faces taut and uncompromising. Then Prasutagus nodded, and began to speak quietly, his tone resigned and fearful.

'There is a sacred grove,' Boudica translated. 'He was trained there for a while . . . It's where he failed the initiation into the second ring. The Druids call it the grove of the sacred crescent. It's the place where Cruach will rise and reclaim the world for himself one day. Any day. Until then his spirit hangs like a black shadow over every stone, leaf and blade of grass in the grove. You can hear the cold rasp of his breath through the limbs of the trees. Prasutagus warns you that Cruach will sense your presence at once and will show no mercy to the enemies of his servants. No mercy.'

'I've seen enough of this world to know that the only thing anyone needs to be afraid of is other men, said Macro. 'If your cousin's afraid, tell him I'll hold his hand for him.'

Boudica ignored the last comment and continued with Prasutagus's warning. 'He says that the grove is on an island at the centre of a large marsh two days' ride from here. There's a small causeway leading to the main entrance, and that's always heavily guarded. We'd never make it in that way.'

'Then there's another way in,' Cato guessed shrewdly. 'A way in that Prasutagus discovered?'

'Yes.' Boudica glanced quickly at her kinsman, and he nodded for her to continue. 'He used it to visit the daughter of the man commanding the Druids' guards. She got pregnant and as soon as the Druids discovered he had broken his oath of celibacy he was thrown out of the order.'

Macro roared with laughter, causing the others to glance anxiously around, but nothing stirred in the surrounding trees.

'Oh dear!' Macro wiped his eyes and grinned at Prasutagus. 'You just can't resist a bloody challenge, can you? You got kicked out on account of a piece of tail – what a prat! You know, I think we might just get on after all.'

'This way in.' Cato leaned closer to Boudica. 'Does anyone else know about it?'

'Prasutagus doesn't think so. It's a series of shallows through the water. It ends in a thicket on the bank of the island close to the grove. Prasutagus says he marked it out with a line of coppice stakes, placed quite far apart.'

'Can he find it again? After all these years?'

'He thinks so.'

'I'm not reassured,' said Macro.

'Maybe not,' said Cato. 'But it's the only chance we've got left, sir. We take it or go home empty-handed. We face the consequences either way.'

Macro stared at Cato a moment before replying. 'You've got such a cheerful way with words, haven't you?'

Chapter Twenty-Six

'Your Druid friends have found a good place to hide from the world,' Macro muttered as he squinted through the dusk. At his side Prasutagus grunted conversationally and cocked an eye at Boudica, who whispered a quick translation of the centurion's words.

'Sa!' Prasutagus agreed vigorously. 'Safe place for Druids. Bad place for Romans.'

'That's as maybe. But we're going in there all the same. What d'you think, lad?'

Cato's dark eyes took in the scene through the tangle of coppice branches. They were on a slight rise, looking across a wide expanse of brackish water towards a large island. Some of it appeared to be natural, the rest was manmade, and held in place by substantial log tresses and stout piles driven deep into the soft bottom of the lake. A thick growth of mixed willow and ash towered up a short distance from the shore of the island. Under their boughs a tall stockade was visible. Beyond that, their gaze could not penetrate. Away to their right, a long, narrow causeway stretched out across the lake towards a substantial towered gate leading into the Druids' most sacred and secret grove.

'It's a good set-up, sir. The causeway is long enough to keep them out of arrow and sling range and it's narrow enough to restrict any attackers to a two- or three-man front. Even against an army, with the right men the Druids could hold out for several days, maybe a month or so.'

'Good assessment.' Macro nodded approvingly. 'You've learned a lot over the last year or so. What would you recommend, in the absence of an attacking army?'

'The main entrance is out of the question under any circumstances, now that they've been alerted to the presence of Prasutagus. Looks like we've no choice. We have to try his way in, sir.'

Macro looked at the gloomy water between them and the Druids' island. There was no shore on the near ground, only a tangle of reeds

191

and low trees rising above dark peaty mud. If they were caught wading through that lot there would be no chance of escape. He wondered at the Iceni warrior's confidence that he could find his trail again in the dark. Yet Prasutagus had sworn by all his most sacred gods that he would lead them safely across to the island. But they must trust him, and follow him precisely.

'We'll go as soon as it's dark enough,' decided Macro. 'The three of us. The woman stays.'

'What?' Boudica turned angrily towards him.

'Hush!' Macro nodded towards the island. 'If we find the general's family but don't make it back, someone has to ride to the legion and let them know.'

'And how precisely would you let *me* know?'

Macro smiled. 'You don't make centurion unless you can be heard at a distance.'

'He's right enough there,' muttered Cato.

'But why me? Why not leave Cato here. You'll need me to translate.'

'There won't be much need for talking. Besides, Prasutagus and me are coming to an understanding of sorts. He can speak a few words now. A few words of a proper language, that is. Ain't that right?'

Prasutagus nodded his shaggy head.

'So, keep your ears pricked. If I call your name, or if any of us does, that's the signal. We've found them. You don't wait a moment. You get back to the horses, take one and ride like the wind. Report everything to Vespasian.'

'What about you?' asked Boudica.

'If you hear any of us shout, chances are those will be our last words.' Macro raised a hand and gently held her shoulder. 'Are you clear about all that?'

'Yes.'

'Right then, this is as good a place as any to wait. Stay here. As soon as it's dark enough, we'll strip down to tunics and swords and follow Prasutagus over to the island.'

'And just for a change,' said Macro softly, 'we're up to our balls in freezing water.'

The smell of decay that rose from the disturbed waters about their legs was so pungent that Cato thought he might throw up. This was worse than almost anything he had ever smelt before. Even worse than the tannery outside the walls of Rome he had once visited with his father. The hardy tanners, long immune to the stench, had laughed themselves silly at the sight of the small boy in the neat livery of the imperial palace heaving his guts up into a tub of sheep entrails.

Here in the mangrove the pungency of decayed vegetation combined with the odour of human waste and the sweet stench of rotting flesh. Cato covered his nose with his hand and swallowed the bile rising in his throat. At least the darkness concealed the detritus floating about his knees. Ahead of him, beyond the broad dark bulk of Macro, he could just see the tall figure of Prasutagus leading the way through the rushes. The stalks rustled as the Briton slowly waded from one coppice stake to the next. Most were still in place, and Prasutagus had lost his way only once, suddenly splashing down into deeper water with a sharp cry. All three had frozen, ears straining for any indication of alarm from the dark mass of the Druids' island above the slopping of the water. When the disturbed water had stilled again, Prasutagus gently eased himself back onto more solid ground and flashed a dim grin at the centurion.

'Long time gone before I here,' he whispered.

'All right,' Macro said softly. 'Now just keep your mouth shut and your mind on the job.'

'Huh?'

'Get a fucking move on.'

'Oh. Sa!'

At length they emerged from the rushes and Prasutagus halted. The island still seemed some distance away but Cato noted that the rushes reached most closely towards it at this point and could see why Prasutagus had picked this route for his night-time assignations. The open water contained no more stakes to guide them. Prasutagus was shifting his position and staring hard at the island. Following his gaze, Cato could see two dead pine trunks standing out above the rest of the trees on the island. They were so close together that from certain angles they looked like a single trunk, and Cato realised that their alignment was how Prasutagus guided himself across the open water to the island. The Icenian shuffled to his left and then motioned to the others to follow him.

Moving slowly, the water gently swirling around their knees, the small party headed across towards the dark foreboding shadow of the Druids' island.

The stench slackened as they moved further out from the rushes. Cato allowed himself a few deep breaths as he carefully followed in line behind the others. Underfoot, the bottom felt strangely soft and yielding, with the occasional firmness of a branch. For a moment he wondered how Prasutagus could possibly have constructed this

193

underwater walkway. Then he decided it must just be the tangled accumulation of dead and fallen matter which the Briton must have found by chance, and put to good use. Cato smiled to himself. Good use, maybe. But it had caused him to be expelled from the order of the Dark Moon.

Thought of the Druids drew his mind sharply back to the present. The dark outline of the island loomed closer against the fainter shadow of the night sky, and it seemed that the island floated not on water but on the ethereal mist rising from the lake. It certainly seemed sinister enough, Cato reflected. The dread in Prasutagus's expression whenever he had talked of this place over the last two days suggested there was worse to come. But what, in this world, could be terrible enough to frighten the huge warrior? Cato's imagination went to work to provide an answer and he felt a chill finger of horror trace its way up his spine. He cursed himself for this superstitious self-indulgence but as they silently glided through the dark waters, his heightened senses continued to magnify every sound and shift of shadow. It took a great effort of will to prevent his imagination conjuring up the demons lurking invisibly on the shores of the sacred Druid isle.

They were now close enough to the shore for the outermost boughs of its ancient trees to overhang them. Looking up through the twisted black tendrils of the outermost branches, Cato gazed up at the stars, cold and unblinking above the mist. Then he turned and gazed back across the gloomy water to where Boudica waited for them. He wondered if he would ever see her again, and found himself desperately wanting to see her face once more. The unbidden longing was quite shocking and Cato wondered at this instance of self-revelation.

He started as Macro grasped his arm, flinching backwards and splashing the water.

'Keep still!' hissed Macro. 'Want to let every bloody Druid in Britain know we're here?'

'Sorry.'

Macro turned back to Prasutagus, who was muttering something under his breath. The whispered words flowed with a cadence and rhythm that was not like everyday speech and Macro realised this must be some kind of charm. When the Briton paused, Macro gently touched his shoulder.

'Let's go, mate.'

Prasutagus stared at him for a moment, silent and still as a stone, before nodding gravely and then creeping forward once again. This section of the shore was lined with wicker reinforced with timber piles and stood two feet above the icy water. They heaved themselves across it as quietly as possible, but inevitably water dripped and splashed, sounding dangerously loud. Prasutagus glanced anxiously into the shadows beneath the trees, certain that they must be heard. But nothing stirred, no breath of air even lifted the lightest of the dark branches. All three were still for a while, squatting and listening. Cato shivered as he waited for Prasutagus to wave them forward. They made their way along the shore for a short distance, until they came to a track leading into the dark trees. It seemed to Cato that the night suddenly became colder, as if a breeze was blowing, but the air about him was perfectly still.

'Down there?' Macro whispered.

'Sa. You come, but shhh!'

As they made their way silently along the track, darkness closed in on them, impenetrable as ink, and the air seemed to grow yet colder, with a clammy edge to it now. Cato counted the paces he took, trying to keep a clear mental image of the island as they penetrated further. Soon after he had counted a hundred, the trees opened out, admitting a welcome faint glow from the stars. The path ended abruptly at a wooden screen, within which was a door. It was held closed by a simple latch operated by a pull rope. For a moment Prasutagus listened, but the heart of the island was as oppressively silent as its fringes, and the only sound Cato could detect above the rapid pounding of his heart was the occasional booming of a bittern away in the marshes. Prasutagus gently pulled on the rope, the latch eased up and he nudged the door open. He stepped through, leaving the two Romans squatting at the side of the entrance; a moment later his head reappeared and he beckoned to them.

Beyond the screen, a large clearing opened out. It was roughly circular and lined with thatched huts. The ground was bare and hard; the army boots of the two Romans clumped on its surface for the first few paces before Cato and Macro took care to set each foot down as softly as possible. Dominating the centre of the clearing was a huge circular hut, in front of which was a raised platform. A carved wooden chair of immense proportions rested on the middle of the platform, and fixed to the tall backrest was the biggest pair of antlers Cato had ever seen. In front of the platform stood the remains of a fire in a huge iron grate. The dying embers imparted a faint orange hue to the wisps of smoke curling up into the night.

Nothing moved in the clearing. None of the torches was lit in the iron stands positioned in front of every hut. There was no sign of life. And yet a brooding presence seemed to hang over the clearing, as if they were being watched from every shadow. Not that Cato sensed a trap of any kind, just a feeling that their presence had been sensed by somebody, or some thing. Silently they made their way to the entrance of the first hut and crept inside. It was dark, too dark to make out any details, and Macro cursed softly.

'It's no good, we need some light,' he whispered.

'Sir, that's madness!' Cato hissed. 'We'd be seen at once.'

'Who by? There's no one here. Hasn't been for hours – look at the fire.'

'Then where are they?'

'Ask him.' Macro jerked a thumb at Prasutagus.

The Briton got the gist of the question and shrugged. 'Druids gone. All gone.'

'In that case, let's get ourselves some light to see by,' Macro insisted. 'We need to be sure we don't miss anything.'

We removed the nearest torch from its holder and thrust it into the embers, sending a swirling cloud of brilliant sparks flying into the air. The torch flared. Raising it in front of him, Macro strode back to the first hut and ducked inside. The flickering glare of the torch illuminated the interior in a wavering light. Several beds were to one side, covered with blankets and furs. On the other side was a shrine, against which leaned a pair of small harps. A set of wooden eating platters and earthenware cups was stacked by a tub of water.

'No cooking fire,' mused Cato.

'No cooking,' Prasutagus said. 'Others bring food for Druid.'

'Leeching off the common folk, eh?' Cato shook his head. 'Same the world over, as far as priests are concerned.'

Macro clicked his fingers. 'When you two have finished your fascinating theological conversation, we've got some huts to search. Look for any signs of the general's family.'

They went through each hut thoroughly, but aside from the sparse possessions of the Druids they found nothing that indicated that any Roman had ever been there.

'Let's try the big hut,' suggested Cato. 'I'd imagine that's where the chief of the Druids lives.'

'All right then,' Macro agreed.

'Na!'

The Romans turned to look at Prasutagus. He stood rooted outside the entrance of the last hut they had searched, a look of utter terror on his face. He shook his head imploringly.

'I not go in!'

196

Macro shrugged. 'Suit yourself. Come on, Cato.'

The entrance to the hut was as imposing as the hut itself. A huge timber frame, twice the height of a man, was topped by a carved lintel bearing impressions of dreadful, inhuman faces, savage and howling with jagged teeth. In their maws lay the half-consumed bodies of men and women, mouths gaping with terror. So compelling were the images that Macro paused at the threshold and raised his torch for a better look.

'What the hell is this?'

'I imagine it's what the future holds for mankind when Cruach rises up and stakes his claim, sir.'

Macro turned to Cato, eyebrows raised. 'You think so? Don't think I'd want to run into this Cruach character on a dark street.'

'No, sir.'

Just inside the entrance hung a series of heavy animal skins, totally blocking the interior from sight. Macro pushed them aside and stepped into the chief Druid's quarters. He raised the torch up and whistled.

'Quite a contrast!'

Cato nodded as his eyes swept over the furs covering most of the floor space, the great upholstered beds set to one side, and the vast oak table and ornately carved chairs. The table held the remains of a half-eaten feast. Large wooden platters lay before the chairs, covered with joints of meat still resting in their congealed juices. To the side of each platter lay chunks of bread and cheese. Drinking horns rested in intricate gold stands decorated in the Celtic style.

'Seems the senior Druids know how to live well.' Macro smiled. 'No wonder they wanted to keep prying eyes out. But what made them leave in such a hurry?'

'Sir!' Cato pointed to the far side of the hut. A small wooden cage rested on bare earth. The door was ajar. They crossed over to it. The inside was bare, apart from a piss pot, the top of which was mercifully covered. Cato looked closer, and leaned into the cage, reaching for the covering which was no more than a scrap of fabric.

'I doubt they're hiding in there,' said Macro.

'No, sir.' Cato retrieved the material and held it up for closer inspection by the light of the torch. It was silk, with an embroidered hem. The middle was soiled.

'Nice smell you've uncovered!' Macro wrinkled his nose. 'Now put it back.'

'Sir, this is the proof we're looking for. Look!' Cato held the material out for his centurion to see. 'It's silk. Patterned in Rome, and the maker has stitched a small emblem in the corner.'

Macro stared at the neat design: an elephant's head – the family motif of the Plautii.

'That's it then! They're here. Or were here, at least. But where are they now?'

'Must have gone with the Druids.'

'Maybe. We'd better just check the site for any other signs of the general's family – or what might have become of them.'

Outside the hut Prasutagus could not hide his relief at being in the company of other humans again. Macro held out the silk.

'They were here.'

'Sa! Now we go, yes?'

'No. We keep looking. Is there any other place on the island they might have been taken to?'

Prasutagus looked at him blankly. Macro tried to make his meaning simpler.

'We keep looking. Another place? Yes?'

Prasutagus seemed to understand, and turned to point at a track leading into the trees directly opposite the antlered chair.

'There.'

'What's up that way?'

Prasutagus did not answer, and continued staring towards the track. Macro saw that he was trembling. He shook the warrior's shoulder. 'What's up there?'

Prasutagus wrenched his gaze from the track and turned to face him, eyes wide with terror.

'Cruach.'

'Cruach? That dark god of yours? You're taking the piss.'

'Cruach!' Prasutagus insisted. 'Sacred grove of Cruach. His place in this world.'

'Quite talkative when you're shitting yourself, aren't you?' Macro smiled. 'Come on, mate. Let's have a little word with this Cruach. See what he's made of.'

'Sir, is that wise?' asked Cato. 'We've found what we came for. Wherever the general's family are, they're not here now. We should get moving before we're discovered.'

'Not until we check the grove,' Macro replied firmly. 'No more nonsense. Let's go.'

With Macro at their head, the three men strode across the clearing and started down the track. With the torch flickering before them, they could see the gnarled trunks of oak trees lining the route on either side.

'How far to the grove?' asked Macro.

'Near,' Prasutagus whispered, keeping close to the flickering torch.

The trees were silent all about them; nothing stirred, not an owl or any other creature of the night. It was as if the island was under some kind of spell, Cato decided. Then he realised the smell of decay was back again. With every step along the track, the scent of death and putrid sweetness grew stronger.

'What was that?' Macro stopped abruptly.

'What was what, sir?'

'Shut up! Listen!'

The three of them paused, ears straining to hear anything above the unnaturally loud crackle and hiss of the torch. Then Cato heard it: a low moan that rose and fell to a whimper. Then a voice muttered something. Strange words that he could not quite make out.

'Draw swords,' Macro ordered quietly, and the three men eased the blades from their scabbards.

Macro stepped forward, and his companions followed nervously, senses straining for any sign of the source of the noise. Ahead of them, the track began to widen, and out of the darkness loomed a stake with a lumpen shape jammed on top. As they approached, the light of the torch illuminated the dark stains running down its length, and the head impaled on the end.

'Shit!' muttered the centurion. 'I wish the Celts wouldn't do that.'

They came upon more stakes, each bearing a head, in varying stages of decay. All of them were arranged to face the track so that the three trespassers were walking under the gaze of the dead. Once again the air felt colder than it should to Cato, and he was about to comment on it when a fresh moan broke the silence. It came from the far side of the grove, beyond the wavering pool of light cast by the torch. This time the moan increased in intensity, and became a piercing wail of agony that tore through the darkness and froze the blood of the three mortals.

'We go!' Prasutagus whispered. 'We go now! Cruach comes!'

'Bollocks!' replied Macro. 'No god makes a sound like that. Come on, you bastard! Don't chicken out now.'

He half dragged the Briton towards the sound and Cato followed reluctantly. In truth, he would have gladly turned and run from the grove, but that would have meant leaving the security of the glow cast by the torch. The thought of being lost and alone in this terrible dark world of the Druids made him stick as close to the others as possible.

Another cry rose through the night, much closer now, and ahead of them loomed the flat stone of an altar, and beyond it the being giving voice to the cries of agony that seemed so much a part of this dreadful place.

'What the hell is that?' Macro cried out.

No more than fifteen paces away, on the far side of the altar, the figure of a man slowly writhed. He was suspended from a wooden beam, his forearms lashed to its rough surface. From below he was impaled on a long shaft of wood which entered his body just behind his testicles. As they watched, the man tried to raise himself, straining at the ropes that bound his arms. Astonishingly he managed to do this for a moment, before his strength gave out and he slid down again, causing him to let loose another terrible wail of agony and despair. The inhuman noise subsided into prayers and curses, in a language that was almost as familiar to Cato as his own Latin.

'That's Greek he's speaking!'

'Greek? That's not possible . . . Unless . . .' Macro strode closer to the man, raising the torch as he approached. 'It's Diomedes . . .'

The Greek stirred at the sound of his name, and forced his eyelids to open. He stared down at them with a desperate glint in his eyes.

'Help me!' he mumbled in Latin through tightly clenched teeth. 'For pity's sake, help me!'

Macro looked round at his comrades. 'Cato! Get up that beam and cut him free. Prasutagus! Keep his weight off that stake!'

The Briton tore his gaze from the terrible spectacle and stared blankly at Macro who quickly mimed a lifting action with his spare hand and pointed at Diomedes. Prasutagus nodded and hurried over. He grasped the Greek's legs and eased him up, bearing Diomedes's full weight in his powerful arms without difficulty. Meanwhile Cato, never terribly athletic, was struggling to shin up one of the supporting posts. With a sigh of impatience, Macro came over and stood with his back to the post.

'Use my shoulders to get up!'

Up on the crossbeam Cato crawled along to the first binding. His sword cut through the coarse rope with some difficulty before the Greek's left arm came free, flopping down to his side. Cato reached over to the other binding and a moment later the other arm was freed. The optio dropped down from the crossbeam.

'Now then, let's get him off the stake. Lift him up, you idiot!'

Prasutagus understood, and with straining arms he began to raise the Greek up the stake that penetrated deep into his body. There was a wet sucking sound from the wound, then a muffled grating of bone. Diomedes threw his head back and shrieked to the heavens.

'Shit! Be careful, you fool!'

With a heave Prasutagus lifted the Greek clear of the point and gently set him down on the altar. A dark gush of blood spilled out of the gaping wound where Diomedes's anus had once been and Cato winced at the sight. The Greek trembled fitfully and his eyes rolled in their sockets as he fought the terrible, mortal agony. He was very close to death.

Macro leaned close to the Greek's ear. 'Diomedes. You're dying. Nothing can stop that. But you can help us. Help us get back at the bastards who did this to you.'

'Druids,' Diomedes gasped. 'Tried to . . . make them pay . . . Tried to find them.'

'You found 'em all right.'

'No . . . Caught me first . . . Brought me here . . . and did this.'

'Did you see any of the other prisoners?'

A spasm of pain twisted his features. When it subsided a little, he nodded. 'The general's family . . .'

'Yes! You saw them?'

Diomedes clenched his teeth. 'They were . . . here.'

'Where are they now? Where have they been taken?'

'They've gone . . . Heard someone say . . . they'd take shelter in . . . the Great Fortress. They call it *Mai Dun* . . . Only safe place . . . once they found out they'd been . . . betrayed by a Druid.'

'The Great Fortress?' Macro frowned. 'When was this?'

'This morning . . . I think,' Diomedes whispered. His strength was fading fast as his blood pumped from the open wound. He convulsed as another spasm of agony ripped through his body. One of his hands grabbed the centurion's tunic.

'For pity's sake . . . kill me . . . now,' he hissed through his teeth.

Macro stared down into the wild eyes for a moment and then replied gently, 'All right. I'll make it quick.'

Diomedes nodded his gratitude and clenched his eyes shut.

'Hold the torch,' Macro ordered and passed it to Cato. Then he lifted the Greek's left arm to one side, exposing the armpit, and looked into Diomedes's face.

'Know this, Diomedes. I swear by all the gods that I'll get revenge for you and your family. The Druids will pay for all they've done.'

As the Greek's expression softened, Macro thrust his sword deep into his armpit and through to his heart with an animal grunt of effort.

Diomedes's body tensed for an instant and his mouth opened with a gasp as the impact of the blow drove the dying breath from his lungs. Then his body went limp, and his head rolled to one side, eyes glazed in death. No one spoke for a moment. Macro wrenched the blade free, and wiped it on the dirty remnants of the Greek's tunic. He raised his eyes to look at Prasutagus.

'He said the Great Fortress. Do you know it?'

Prasutagus nodded, hearing the words but unable to tear his gaze from Diomedes.

'You can take us there?'

Prasutagus nodded again.

'How far?'

'Three days.'

'Then we'd better get moving. The Druids have a day's head start on us. If we push it, we might catch them before they reach this Great Fortress of theirs.'

Chapter Twenty-Seven

'We're not going to catch them, are we?' Cato said to Boudica as he chewed on a leathery piece of hardtack.

After Diomedes had died, they had hurried back to find Boudica to begin their pursuit of the Druids at once. Even after dawn had broken, Macro had ordered that they continue; the need to catch up with the Druids and their prisoners before they could take shelter in the Great Fortress outweighed the risk of discovery. From the rushed translation provided by Boudica, it was clear that once inside the vast ramparts of the fortress, protected by a large garrison of selected warriors – the bodyguard of the King of the Durotriges – the hostages would be beyond any hope of rescue. The general's family would either be exchanged – if Aulus Plautius allowed himself to be so humbled that it would destroy his career – or they would be burned alive in a wicker effigy under the eyes of the Druids of the Dark Moon.

So the two Romans, and their Iceni guides, had ridden their horses hard all through the night and well into the next day until it was clear that the animals were spent and would collapse and die if they were pushed any further. They hobbled the horses in the ruined pen of an abandoned farm, and gave them the last of the feed carried by the ponies. Tomorrow, before first light, they would set off again.

Prasutagus stood the first watch, while the others ate and tried to sleep, huddled in their cloaks in the cold air of early spring. Macro, as usual, fell into a deep slumber almost as soon as he had curled up under his cloak. But Cato's mind was restless, tormented by Diomedes's terrible fate and the prospect of what lay ahead, and he fidgeted and fretted. When he could take no more, he threw back his cloak and stood up. He added some wood to the glowing embers of the fire and helped himself to one of the air-dried strips of beef in his saddlebag. The meat was as hard as wood and could only be swallowed after a great deal of chewing. Which suited Cato, who needed something to occupy him. He was on his second strip of dried beef when Boudica joined him in front of the fire. They had risked a small fire, concealed by the crumbling walls of an abandoned farm. The thatch roof had fallen in and now lazy flames licked around the remains of the roofing timber Cato had chopped to bits for fuel.

'We might catch them up,' she answered him. 'Your centurion thinks we will.'

'And what happens if we do?' Cato said quietly, with a quick glance towards the bundled form of his snoring centurion. 'What will three men be able to achieve against who knows how many Druids? There'll be some kind of bodyguard as well. It'll be suicide.'

'Don't always look for the dark side of a situation,' Boudica chided him. 'There's four of us, not three. And Prasutagus is worth any ten Durotrigan warriors that ever lived. From what I know of your centurion, he's a pretty formidable fighter as well. The Druids will have their work cut out with those two. I have my bow with me, and even my small hunting arrows can kill a man if I'm lucky. Which leaves you. How good are you in a fight, Cato?'

'I can handle myself.' Cato opened his cloak and tapped his fingers on the phalerae he had been awarded for saving Macro's life in a skirmish over a year earlier. 'I didn't get these for record-keeping.'

'I'm sure you didn't. I meant no disrespect, Cato. I'm just trying to work out our chances against the Druids and, well, you don't have the build or the look of a killer about you.'

Cato gave her a thin smile. 'I try not to look like a killer, actually. I don't find it aesthetically pleasing.'

Boudica chuckled. 'Appearances aren't everything.' As she said this she turned her head to look at the sleeping centurion and Cato saw her smile. The tenderness of her expression jarred with the cool tension that had seemed to exist between her and Macro over recent days and Cato realised she still bore more affection towards Macro than she was willing to admit. Still, any relationship between his centurion and this woman was no business of his. Cato swallowed the shred of beef he had been chewing and stuffed the rest into his knapsack.

'Looks can certainly deceive,' Cato agreed. 'When I first saw you back in Camulodunum, I would never have guessed you enjoyed this kind of cloak and dagger stuff.'

'I might say the same about you.'

Cato blushed and then smiled at his reaction. 'You're not the only one. It's taken me a while to gain any kind of acceptance in the legion. It's not my fault, or theirs. It's not easy to accept having a seventeen-year-old foisted on you with the rank of optio for no better reason than that his father happened to be a faithful slave in the imperial secretariat.'

Boudica stared at him. 'Is that true?'

'Yes. You don't suppose I'm old enough to have earned such a promotion through years of exemplary soldiering, do you?'

'Did you want to be a soldier?'

'Not at first.' Cato smiled sheepishly. 'When I was a boy I was far more interested in books. I wanted to be a librarian, or maybe even a writer.'

'A writer? What does a writer do?'

'Writes histories, or poetry, or plays. Surely you have them here in Britain?'

Boudica shook her head. 'No. We have some written words. Passed down to us by the ancient ones. Only a handful know their secrets.'

'But how do you preserve stories? Your history?'

'Up here.' Boudica tapped her head. 'Our stories are passed down through the generations by word of mouth.'

'Seems a pretty unreliable method of keeping records. Isn't there a temptation to try to improve the story with each telling?'

'But that's the point of it. The tale's the thing. The better it becomes – the more it is embroidered, the more it grips the audience – the greater it is, and the more enriched we become as a people. Is it not so in Rome?'

Cato silently considered the matter for a moment. 'Not really. Some of our writers are storytellers, but many are poets and historians and they pride themselves on telling the facts, plain and simple.'

'How dull.' Boudica grimaced. 'There must be some people who are trained to tell stories like our bards do. Surely?'

'Some,' admitted Cato. 'But they are not held in the same esteem as writers. They are mere performers.'

'Mere performers?' Boudica laughed. 'Truly, you are a strange people. What is it that a writer produces? Words, words, words. Mere marks on a scroll. A storyteller, a good one, mind you, produces a spell that binds his audience into sharing another world. Can written words ever do that?'

'Sometimes,' Cato said defensively.

'Only for those who can read. And how many in a thousand Romans can do that? Yet every person who hears can share a tale. So which is the better? The written or the spoken word? Well, Cato?'

Cato frowned. This conversation was becoming unsettling. Too many of the eternal verities of his world were in danger of being undermined if he should entertain the vision Boudica offered him. As far as he was concerned, the written word was the only reliable way a nation's heritage could be preserved. Such records could speak to the generations as freshly and accurately as at the time they were written. But what was the utility of such a marvellous device for the illiterate masses that teemed across the empire? For them only an oral tradition, with all its foibles, would suffice. That the two traditions might be complementary was anathema to his view of literature, and he would have none of it. Books were the ultimate means by which the mind could be improved. Folk tales and legends were mere palliatives to beguile and distract the ignorant from the true path of self-improvement.

Which thought led him to consider the nature of the woman before him. She was clearly proud of her race and its cultural heritage, and she was also educated. How else did she come to have so ready a grasp of Latin?

'Boudica, how did you learn to speak Latin?'

'The same way anyone learns a foreign language – hard practice.'

'But why Latin?'

'I speak some Greek as well.'

Cato's eyebrows rose appreciatively. This was no small achievement in so backward a culture, and he was curious. 'Whose idea was it that you should learn these languages?'

'My father's. He saw the way things were moving years ago. Even then our shores had been penetrated by traders from all over your world. For as long as I can remember, Greek and Latin have been part of my life. My father knew that one day Rome would no longer be able to resist the temptation of seizing this island. When that day came, those who were familiar with the tongue of the eagle soldiers would profit most from the new order. My father thought himself too old and too busy to learn a new language, so I was given that task and spoke for him in his dealings with traders.'

'Who taught you?'

'An old slave. My father had him imported from the continent. He'd been teaching the sons of a procurator in Narbonensis. When they had grown to manhood the procurator no longer had any use for the tutor and put him on the market.' Boudica smiled. 'I think it came as a bit of a shock when he came to our village, after his years in a Roman household. Anyway, my father was hard on him, and he in turn was hard on me. So I learned Latin and Greek, and by the time the tutor died. I was fluent enough for my father's purposes. And now yours.'

'My purposes?'

'Well, Rome's. It seems that older and wiser heads among the Iceni elders think we must tie our future to that of Rome. So we do our best to become loyal allies and serve Rome in her wars against those tribes foolish enough to resist the legions.'

Cato did not miss the resentful edge to her words. He reached out to the small pile of wood and placed another splintered length of roof beam on the small fire. The dry timber caught at once, cracking and hissing, and the flare lit up Boudica's features in a fiery red that made her look quite beautiful and terrifying at the same time, and Cato's heart quickened. He had not found her attractive before, as she had been Macro's woman, and he had been grieving for Lavinia. But now, as he gazed furtively at Boudica, he felt an unaccountable yearning for her. Almost at once he cautioned himself against such feelings. If Prasutagus suspected that he had taken a fancy to his future wife, who knew how he would react? If the unpleasant scene back in that inn at Camulodunum was anything to go by, Boudica was a woman best left alone.

'I take it you don't wholly approve of the policy of your tribal elders?'

'I've heard how Rome is inclined to treat its allies.' Boudica looked up from the fire with glinting eyes. 'I think the elders are out of their depth. It's one thing to make a treaty with a neighbouring tribe, or to grant trade rights to some Greek merchant. It's quite another to play politics with Rome.'

'Rome is usually grateful enough to its allies,' Cato protested. 'I think Claudius would like to see his empire as a family of nations.'

'Oh really?' Boudica smiled at his naivety. 'So your Emperor is a kind of father figure, and I suppose you strapping legionaries are his spoiled sons. The provinces are his daughters, fertile and productive, mothers to the empire's wealth.'

Cato blinked at the absurd metaphor, and nearly laughed.

'Don't you see what being an ally of Rome means?' Boudica continued. 'You unman us. How do you think that goes down with people like Prasutagus? Do you really think he'll meekly slip into whatever role your Emperor provides for him? He'd rather die than hand over his weapons and become a farmer.'

'Then he's a fool,' replied Cato. 'We offer order, and a better way of life.'

'On your terms.'

'They are the only terms we know.'

Boudica looked at him sharply, and then sighed. 'Cato, you have a good heart. I can see that. I'm not having a go at you. I merely question the motives of those who direct your energies. You're bright enough to do that for yourself, surely? You don't have to be like most of your countrymen, like your centurion there.'

'I thought you liked him.'

'I . . . I did. He's a good man. As fiercely honest as Prasutagus is proud. He's attractive too.'

'He is?' Now Cato was truly astonished. Never would he have described Macro as handsome. The weathered, scarred face had frightened him when he had first met the centurion as a new recruit. But there was an easy, honest charm about him that made the men of his century steadfastly loyal. But where was the attraction for women?

Boudica smiled at Cato's astonished and confused expression. 'I mean what I say, Cato. But that's not enough. He's Roman, I'm of the Iceni, the difference is too great. Anyway, Prasutagus is a prince of my people, and may one day be king. He has slightly more to offer than the billet of a centurion. So, I must do as my family wish and wed Prasutagus, and be true to my people. And I must hope that Rome is true to her word and lets the kings of the Iceni continue to rule their own people. We're a proud nation, and we can stomach the alliance our elders have negotiated with Rome only as long as we're treated like equals. If the day ever comes when we are dishonoured in any way, then you Romans will learn just how dreadful our wrath can be.'

Cato regarded her with open admiration. She would be wasted as an army wife; there was no doubt about that. If ever there was a woman born to be queen, it was Boudica, though her casual, even cynical, dismissal of Macro pained him greatly.

Boudica yawned and rubbed her eyes.

'Enough talk, Cato. We should get some rest.'

While he built up the fire, Boudica pulled her thick riding cloak about her and punched her haversack into a tight rest for her head. Satisfied that it would be comfortable enough, she winked at Cato and, turning her back to the fire, curled up and went to sleep.

The next morning they ate some biscuits and clambered stiffly onto the backs of their horses. The ponies were no longer required, and were set free to fend for themselves. To the south, several miles away, a thin haze of smoke lifted lazily into the clear sky, and below lay the dark shapes of huts in the bend of a stream. That was where the Druids had spent the night, Prasutagus told them. In the distance, a group of horsemen escorting a covered wagon was visible. It was still not clear to Cato how the four of them could take on a much larger party of Druids and still emerge from the fight victorious. Macro, for his part was frustrated by the way they could do no more than tail their enemy, passively hoping for a chance to attempt a rescue to present itself. And all the time the Druids drew closer to the impregnable earthworks of the Great Fortress.

The spring day wore on as Prasutagus led them along narrow tracks, all the while keeping the horsemen and their wagon in view, and closing the distance only when there was no risk of being spotted. It called for an exhausting degree of vigilance. By late afternoon they were still some way behind the enemy, but close enough to see that the wagon was protected by a score of mounted Druids in their distinctive black cloaks.

'Bollocks!' said Macro, squinting into the distance. 'Twenty on three isn't good odds.'

Prasutagus merely shrugged and urged his horse along an overgrown track winding up the side of a hill. The Druids were obscured for a moment behind a line of trees. The others trotted after him, until they stopped in an overgrown track just below the crest from where they could see the Druids below, still heading south-east. Macro was riding at the back, watching the column, when Cato suddenly reined in, causing Macro to yank on his reins savagely to avoid riding into the backside of Cato's mount.

'Oi! What the fuck are you playing at?'

But Cato ignored his centurion.

'Bloody hell . . .' he muttered in awe at the panorama stretching out before him.

As Macro eased his beast alongside, he too could see the vast expanse of multi-tiered earthworks rising up from the plain ahead of them. With a recently developed eye for ground, Cato took in the neatly overlapping ramps that defended the nearest gateway, and the well-placed redoubts from which any attacker would fall victim to enfilading volleys of arrows, spears and slingshot. On the highest tier of the hill fort a stout palisade ringed the enclosure. From end to end Cato estimated the hill fort must measure nearly half a mile. Below the fortress, the rolling wooded landscape was divided by a serenely meandering river.

'We've had it,' Macro said quietly. 'Once the Druids get the general's family safely inside that lot, nobody'll be able to get to them.'

'Maybe,' replied Cato. 'But the bigger the line of defence, the more thinly spread the watchmen.'

'Oh, that's good! Mind if I quote you some day? You idiot!'

Cato had the grace to flush with embarrassment at his precocious remark, and Macro nodded with satisfaction. Didn't do to let these youngsters get too full of themselves. Up ahead Prasutagus had wheeled his horse round and now raised his arm to point at the hill fort. He was grandly illuminated by a halo of bright sunshine against the blue sky as he spoke.

'The Great Fortress . . .'

'No, really?' Macro growled. 'Thanks for letting us know.'

Despite his sarcastic response, Macro was still running a professional eye over the structure and wondering if it might yet be taken, once the Second Legion set to it. Despite the clever layout of the approach route through the ramparts, there was no sign that the fortress was designed to withstand the attentions of a well-equipped modern army.

'Sir!' Cato interrupted his line of thought and Macro raised an angry eyebrow. 'Sir, look there!'

Cato was pointing away from the Great Fortress, back towards the Druids and the small covered wagon they were escorting. Only they weren't escorting it any more. In sight of their haven, the Druids had urged their mounts into a trot and already the column of horsemen had drawn well ahead of the wagon. They were making straight for the nearest gate in the ramparts. In front of them the track curved round a small forest towards a narrow trestle bridge that spanned the river. Cato's excitement rose as he quickly estimated the relative speeds of the mounted Druids, the wagon and themselves. He nodded. 'We could do it.'

'There's our chance!' Macro barked. 'Prasutagus! Look there!'

The Iceni warrior quickly grasped the situation and nodded vigorously. 'We go.'

'What about Boudica?' asked Cato.

'What about her?' Macro snapped. 'What're we waiting for? Come on!'

Macro kicked his heels into the flanks of his horse and headed down the slope in the direction of the wagon.

Chapter Twenty-Eight

As they charged down the grassy slope, the wind roared in Cato's ears and his heart thudded against his chest. Only shortly before, they had been quietly picking their way along a little-used path. Now fate had thrown them a slim chance to rescue the general's family and Cato felt the mad exhilarating terror of imminent action. Looking ahead, he saw that the hill fort was now hidden behind the trees that ran alongside the track. Barely half a mile away trundled the wagon on its solid wooden wheels, drawn by a pair of shaggy ponies. The two Druids on the driver's bench were not yet aware of the riders' approach and sat upright, craning their heads forward for the first glimpse of the ramparts of the Great Fortress. Behind them, over the axle, a leather cover hid their prisoners from view. As hooves pounded the ground beneath him it seemed impossible to Cato that they had not been noticed, and he prayed to any god that would hear him that they remain undetected a moment longer. Long enough to prevent the Druids whipping their ponies into a trot and buying them just enough time to alert their companions who had gone ahead.

But the gods were either ignorant of this tiny human drama or cruelly conspiring with the Druids. The driver's companion suddenly glanced back, and shot up from the bench, shouting and pointing at the approaching Romans. With a sharp crack that carried clearly across the open ground, the driver lashed out at the broad rumps of his ponies and the wagon lurched ponderously forward, axle groaning in protest. The other Druid fell back on the bench, then cupped his hands and shouted for help, but his comrades were screened from sight by the curve of the treeline and his cries went unheeded.

Cato was now close enough to make out each Druid's features over the flapping mane of his horse, and saw that the driver was grey-haired and overweight, while his companion was a sallow youth, thin and pinch-faced. The fight would be over very quickly. With luck they

212

would release the hostages and be racing away from the hill fort well before the mounted Druids began to wonder at the time the wagon was taking to catch up with them. Under the frantic urgings of the driver, the wagon rumbled forward at an ever increasing pace, bumping and jolting violently along the rutted track as it headed round the curve of the trees towards the bridge. Their pursuers were only a short distance away from them, kicking in their heels and urging their foam-flecked mounts on.

Their was a sharp squeal of panic from behind him, and Cato glanced back to see Boudica's horse tumble headlong, rear legs flailing at the sky before crashing over the horse's neck. Boudica was flung forwards and instinctively ducked her head and curled her body just before hitting the ground. She bounced over the grassy hummocks with a scream. Her companions reined in. The horse lay twisted, its back broken, its forelegs struggling vainly to raise the rear half of its body. Boudica had fetched up in a puddle and was rising uncertainly to her feet.

'Leave her!' Macro shouted, spurring his horse on. 'Get the fucking wagon before it's too late!'

The Druids had gained valuable distance from their pursuers. The wagon was rumbling wildly, a scant few hundred paces from the bridge; soon it would emerge in full view of the hill fort, and the Druid horsemen not far beyond. With a savage dig into the flanks of his mount, Cato raced after his centurion, with Prasutagus at his side. They were galloping parallel to the track, keeping clear of its treacherous ruts, and ahead of them they could see the tied leather flaps at the rear of the wagon. The younger Druid glanced back at them, his face filled with fear.

Round the bend in the track appeared the massive earthworks of the hill fort, and Cato spurred his horse into one last desperate effort and rapidly closed on the wagon. The huge wheels of solid oak flung clods of mud into his face. He blinked, grasped the handle of his sword and drew it, the blade rasping as it came free. Ahead of him, Macro raced past the driver and swerved his horse across the path of the ponies. With terrified whinnies they tried to halt but were pushed forward in their harnesses by the momentum of the wagon bumping along behind them. Cato held his sword low to one side, ready to thrust. As he drew up beside the driver's bench, there was a dark blur of movement and the young Druid crashed into him. Both tumbled to the ground. The impact smashed the breath out of Cato and there was a blinding flash as his head hit the earth. His vision cleared, and he found himself staring into the young Druid's snarling face, inches from his own. Then, as the spittle dripped from his stained teeth, the Druid gasped, eyes wide with surprise, and he slumped forward.

Cato thrust the limp body away from him, and saw the handguard of his sword pressed into the dark cloth of the Druid's cloak. There was no sign of the blade, only a spreading stain around the guard. The blade had been driven right up through the Druid's guts into the vital organs under his ribcage. Grimacing, Cato rolled to his feet and heaved on the handle. With a sickening sucking noise the blade reluctantly came free. The optio quickly looked round for the other Druid.

He was already dead, slumped back against the leather cover, blood pumping from a gaping wound in his throat where Prasutagus had hacked with his long Celtic sword. The Iceni warrior was off his horse and tearing at the ties binding the rear of the cover. From inside the wagon a child's muffled shriek reached their ears. The last of the ties came undone and Prasutagus swept the flaps apart and stuck his head inside. Fresh screams split the air.

'It's all right!' shouted Boudica in Latin, running up the track. She spoke angrily to Prasutagus in their native tongue and pushed him to one side. 'It's all right. We're here to rescue you. Cato! Come here! They need to see a Roman face.'

Ducking her head back into the wagon, Boudica tried to sound calm. 'There are two Roman officers with us. You're safe.'

Cato reached the back of the wagon and looked into the gloomy interior. A woman sat hunched, with her arms round the shoulders of a small boy and a slightly older girl, both whimpering in wide-eyed terror. The clothes they wore had once been of fine quality but were now soiled and torn. They looked like common street beggars, huddled and frightened.

'Lady Pomponia,' Cato, tried to sound reassuring. 'I'm an optio of the Second Legion. Your husband sent us to find you. Here's my centurion.'

Cato stepped to one side as Macro joined them. The centurion motioned to Prasutagus to keep watch up the track towards the hill fort.

'All in one piece then?' Macro glanced at the woman and two children. 'Good! Let's get moving. Before those bastards come back.'

'I can't,' replied Lady Pomponia, lifting the tattered hem of her cloak. Her bare foot was chained at the ankle to an iron ringbolt in the bed of the cart.

'The children?'

Lady Pomponia shook her head.

'All right then, kids, get out of the cart, so I can get to work on your mum's chain.'

They pressed still more closely to their mother.

'Go on, do as he says,' Lady Pomponia said gently. 'These people are here to help us and take us back to your father.'

The girl hesitantly shuffled over the grimy boards to the rear of the wagon and slid off the end, into Boudica's arms. The boy buried his face against his mother and clenched his little fists tightly in the folds of her cloak. Macro frowned.

'Look here, lad, there's no time for this nonsense. Get out now!'

'That's not going to do any good,' Boudica muttered. 'The boy's scared enough as it is.'

Holding the girl on one hip, she reached a hand out to the child. With a gentle push from his mother, the boy reluctantly allowed himself to be lifted down from the wagon. He clutched at Boudica's leg and anxiously watched Cato and Macro.

The centurion hauled himself into the bed of the wagon and examined the chain where it was attached to an ankle fetter.

'Shit! It's been iron pegged – there's no lock.'

The stout metal peg that fastened the manacle needed a special spiked tool to remove it. Macro drew his sword and carefully applied the point to one end of the pin. Lady Pomponia looked on in alarm, instinctively flinching.

'You'll need to keep still.'

'I'll try. Be careful, Centurion.'

Macro nodded, and gradually pushed the end of the iron pin. When it refused to budge, he applied more pressure, taking care to keep the point of his sword on the end of the pin. The muscles in his arms bunched and he gritted his teeth as he strained to set the woman free. The blade slipped and thudded down into the wagon bed, just missing the grimy skin of Lady Pomponia's foot.

'Sorry. I'll try that again.'

'Please hurry.'

A cry from Prasutagus made Cato glance up. The Iceni warrior was trotting back down the track to the wagon, speaking quickly. Boudica nodded.

'He says they're coming. Four of them. Walking their horses back this way.'

'How far off?' asked Cato.

'Quarter of a mile from the bridge.'

'Not much time then.'

'I'm trying to get her out as fast as I can.' Macro grunted as he applied his sword to the pin once again. 'There! I'm sure it shifted a bit.'

Cato hurried to the front of the wagon. He pulled the body of the fat Druid upright and wedged the whip between the dead man's legs. Then he gestured to Prasutagus to carry the younger Druid into the treeline. Prasutagus reached down for the body and effortlessly heaved it onto his shoulder. He trotted round the front of the cart's ponies and flung the body into the shadows at the edge of the forest.

'Get our horses out of sight! Where's Boudica's?'

'She's finished,' Boudica called out. 'The fall broke her back. I had to leave her behind.'

'Three horses . . .' Cold dread gripped Cato. 'There are seven of us. We could get two on a horse, but three?'

'We'll have to try,' Boudica said firmly, giving a reassuring squeeze to the two children. 'No one's being left behind. How's that chain coming, Macro?'

'It bloody isn't! Pin's too small.' Macro slid off the back of the wagon. 'Wait there, my lady. I'll be back in a moment. Now then . . .' He glanced up the track, squinting in the failing light. Four dark shapes were heading towards the narrow trestle bridge. 'We'll have to take on that lot first. Then have another go at the chain. I'll cut the bloody bolt out if I have to. Into the forest everyone. This way.'

Macro herded Boudica and the children away from the wagon and into the shadow of the trees. They stepped over the sprawled form of the younger Druid and crouched down close by the horses Prasutagus had tethered to a pine trunk.

'Swords out,' said Macro quietly. 'Follow me.'

He led Cato and Prasutagus to a position fifty feet on from the front of the wagon and they squatted down, waiting for the Druids to appear. The ponies harnessed to the front of the wagon stood as still and quiet as the body of their master on his bench. The three men lay in wait, senses straining for the first sounds of the Druids' approach. Then it came, the rumbling of hooves on the boards of the trestle bridge.

'Wait for me to make the first move,' whispered Macro. He raised his eyes at Prasutagus's quizzical expression and tried a simpler phrase. 'Me fight first, then you come. Got that?'

Prasutagus nodded, and Macro turned to Cato.

'Right, make it short and make it bloody. We've got to get 'em all. No one must be allowed to escape and give the alarm.'

216

A few moments later the Druids caught sight of the wagon and called out. When there was no reply, they called out again. The silence made them cautious. A hundred paces away they reined in their horses, muttering to each other.

'Shit!' Macro hissed. 'They're not going to buy it.'

The centurion made to rise, but Cato did the unthinkable and reached out a hand to restrain his superior.

'Wait, sir. Just a moment.'

Macro was so startled by his optio's effrontery that he froze for just long enough to hear the Druids' soft laughter. Then the riders continued forward. Cato tightened his grip on the handle of his sword and tensed, ready to spring up behind Macro and throw himself upon the enemy. Through the uneven mesh of the lowest branches Cato could see the approaching Druids, riding in line, strung out along the track. Beside him Macro cursed; the three of them could not spread out now without attracting attention.

'Leave the last one to me,' he whispered.

The first of the Druids passed their position, and shouted to the driver, apparently poking fun at him. Prasutagus grinned widely at the man's remark and Macro nudged him fiercely.

The second Druid passed them, just as the leader shouted out again, much louder this time. One of the ponies started at the noise and tried to back away. The wagon swivelled slightly, and as the ambushers watched, the body of the driver slowly toppled to one side and fell onto the track.

'Now!' bellowed Macro and sprang out of the shadows, screaming his war cry. Cato did the same as he threw himself at the second Druid. To his right, Prasutagus swung his long sword in a dull grey arc into the head of his Druid. The blow landed with a sickening crunch and the man slumped in his saddle. Armed with a short sword, Cato did as he had been trained and rammed it home into the side of his target. The impact drove the breath out of the Druid with an explosive gasp. Cato grasped his black cloak and savagely hauled him to the ground, where he wrestled the blade free and quickly slit the Druid's throat.

Ignoring the gurgling sound of the man's dying breaths, Cato looked round, sword held ready. Prasutagus was moving towards the leader. Having survived the immediate rush, the first Druid had drawn his sword and turned his horse. Kicking in his heels he rode straight at the Iceni warrior. Prasutagus was forced to dive to one side, ducking the sword swipe that followed. The Druid cursed, kicked his heels in again and galloped towards Cato. The optio stood his ground, sword raised.

The Druid snarled savagely at the temerity of the man who faced a mounted foe wielding a long blade, armed only with the short sword of the legions.

Blood pounding in his ears, Cato watched the horse surging towards him, its rider raising his sword arm high for the killing blow. Just as he felt a warm snort of air from the horse's nostrils, Cato snapped his blade up and smashed it down across the horse's eyes, then rolled away. The horse screamed, blinded in one eye and in agony from the smashed bone across the width of its head. It reared up, front hooves flailing, and threw its rider before bolting across the plain, head shaking from side to side, flinging dark drops of blood. Back on his feet, Cato sprinted the short distance to the rider, who desperately tried to raise his weapon. With a sharp ring of blade on blade, Cato parried it to one side and buried his sword in the Druid's chest. Terrified by the attack, the two riderless horses bolted into the dusk.

Cato turned to see how Macro was coping with the last Druid. Thirty paces away, an uneven duel was being fought. The Druid had recovered from the surprise of the attack before Macro could reach him. With his long sword drawn he now slashed and chopped at the stocky centurion who had worked his way round to block the route back to the bridge.

'Could do with some help here!' Macro shouted as he threw his sword up to block another ringing blow.

Prasutagus was already up and running to his aid, and Cato sprinted after him. Before either man reached the centurion, he tripped and fell. The Druid seized his chance and slashed down with his sword, leaning right over the centurion to make sure of his blow. The blade connected with a dull thud and glanced off Macro's skull. Without a sound, Macro pitched forward, and for an instant Cato just stared, frozen in horror. A howl of rage from Prasutagus brought him back to his senses and Cato turned on the Druid, determined to have his blood. But the Druid had more sense than to take on two enemies at once and he knew he must summon help. He wheeled his horse about and galloped back up the track towards the hill fort, shouting for his comrades.

Sheathing his bloody sword, Cato fell to his knees beside Macro's still form.

'Sir!' Cato grabbed Macro's shoulder and pulled the centurion onto his back, wincing at the savage wound to the side of his head. The Druid's sword had cut through to the bone, shearing off a large flap of scalp. Blood covered Macro's lifeless face. Cato thrust his hand inside his tunic. The centurion's heart was still beating. Prasutagus was kneeling beside him, shaking his head in pity.

'Come on! Take his feet. Get him to the wagon.'

They were struggling back with the limp centurion when Boudica emerged from the trees, leading the children by either hand. She stopped as she saw Macro's body. Beside her the young girl flinched at the sight.

'Oh no . . .'

'He's alive,' grunted Cato.

They laid Macro gently in the back of the wagon while Boudica retrieved a waterskin from under the driver's bench. She blanched at her first clear look at the centurion's wound and then removed the stopper from the skin and poured water over the bloody mangle of skin and hair.

'Give me your neck cloth,' she ordered Cato, and he quickly untied it and handed her the length of material. Grimacing, Boudica eased the strip of scalp back into place over Macro's skull and tied the neck cloth firmly round the wound. Then she removed Macro's neck cloth, already stained with his blood, and tied that on as well. The centurion did not regain consciousness, and Cato heard him breathing in shallow gasps.

'He's going to die.'

'No!' Boudica said fiercely. 'No. Your hear me? We have to get him out of here.'

Cato turned to Lady Pomponia. 'We can't leave. Not without you and your children.'

'Optio,' Lady Pomponia said gently, 'take your centurion, and my children, and go now. Before the Druids come back.'

'No.' Cato shook his head. 'We all go.'

She raised her chained foot. 'I can't. But you must get my children away. I beg you. There's nothing you can do for me. Save them.'

Cato forced himself to look into her face and saw the desperate pleading in her eyes.

'We have to go, Cato,' Boudica muttered at his side. 'We must go. The Druid that got away will fetch the others. There's no time. We have to go.'

Cato's heart sank into a pit of black despair. Boudica was right. Short of hacking off Lady Pomponia's foot, there was no way she could be released before the Druids returned in strength.

'You could make it easier for me,' said Lady Pomponia, with a cautious nod in the direction of her children. 'But get them away from here first.'

Cato's blood chilled in his veins. 'You're not serious?'

'Of course I am. It's that or be burned alive.'

219

'No . . . I can't do it.'

'Please,' she whispered. 'I beg you. For pity's sake.'

'We go!' Prasutagus interrupted loudly. 'They come! Quick, quick!'

Instinctively Cato drew his sword, and lowered the tip towards Lady Pomponia's chest. She clenched her eyes.

Boudica knocked the blade down. 'Not in front of the children! Let me get them mounted first.'

But it was too late. The boy had grasped what going on, and his eyes widened in horror. Before Boudica or Cato could react, he had scrambled into the back of the wagon and threw his arms tightly round his mother. Boudica grabbed the arm of Pomponia's daughter before she could follow her brother.

'Leave her alone!' he screamed, tears coursing down his dirty cheeks. 'Don't touch her! I won't let you hurt my mummy!'

Cato lowered his sword, muttering, 'I can't do this.'

'You have to,' Lady Pomponia hissed over the head of her son. 'Take him, now!'

'No!' the boy screamed, and he locked his hands tightly about her arm. 'I won't leave you, Mummy! Please, Mummy, please don't make me go!'

Above the boy's crying, Cato heard another sound: faint shouts from the direction of the hill fort. The Druid who had escaped the ambush must have reached his comrades. There was very little time.

'I won't do it,' Cato said firmly. 'I promise I will find another way.'

'What other way?' Lady Pomponia wailed, finally losing her patrician self-control. 'They're going to burn me alive!'

'No they're not. I swear it. On my life. I will set you free. I swear it.'

Lady Pomponia shook her head hopelessly.

'Now, hand me your son.'

'No!' the boy screamed, squirming away from Cato.

'The Druids come!' Prasutagus shouted, and all of them could hear the distant drumming of hooves.

'Take the girl and go!' Cato ordered Boudica.

'Go where?'

Cato thought quickly, mentally reconstructing the lie of the land from his memory of the day's travel.

'That wood we passed four, maybe five miles back. Head there. Now!'

Boudica nodded, grasped the arm of the girl and headed into the trees where she untied their horses. Cato called Prasutagus over and indicated Macro's still form.

'You take him. Follow Boudica.'

The Iceni warrior nodded, and lifted Macro easily into his arms.

'Gently!'

'Trust me, Roman.' Prasutagus looked once at Cato, then turned and headed towards the horses with his burden, leaving Cato standing alone at the back of the wagon.

Lady Pomponia grasped her son by the wrists. 'Aelius, you must go now. Be a good boy. Do what I say. I'll be all right. But you must go.'

'I shan't,' sobbed the little boy. 'I won't leave you, Mummy!'

'You have to.' She forced his wrists away from her and towards Cato. Aelius struggled frantically to break her grip. Cato took hold of his middle and pulled him gently out of the wagon. His mother watched with tears in her eyes, knowing she would never see her small son again. Aelius wailed and writhed in Cato's grip. A little way off, hooves pounded on wood as the Druids reached the trestle bridge. Boudica and Prasutagus were waiting, mounted, by the edge of the trees. The girl sat mute and silent in front of Boudica. Prasutagus, with one hand firmly holding the centurion's body, held out the reins of the last horse and Cato thrust the boy up on its back before he swung into the saddle, himself.

'Go!' he ordered the others, and they set off along the track away from the hill fort. Cato took one last look at the wagon, consumed with guilt and despair, and then dug his heels in.

As the horse jolted into a trot, Aelius wriggled free and slipped from Cato's grasp. He rolled away from the horse, stood up and ran back to the wagon as fast as his little legs could carry him.

'Mummy!'

'Aelius! No! Go back! For pity's sake!'

'Aelius!' Cato shouted. 'Come here!'

But it was no use. The boy reached the wagon, scrambled up and hurled himself into the arms of his sobbing mother. For an instant Cato turned his horse towards the wagon, but he could see movement down the track beyond it.

He cursed, then jerked the reins and galloped his horse after Boudica and Prasutagus.

Chapter Twenty-Nine

Cato felt more wretched than he had ever felt in his entire life. The four of them, and the girl, Julia, were sitting deep in a wood they had passed earlier that day. Night had fallen when they had found the crumbling remains of an old silver mine and stopped in the diggings to rest and let their blown horses recover from their double burden. Julia was crying softly to herself. Macro lay under his and Cato's cloaks, still unconscious, his breath shallow and rasping.

The Druids had tried to track them down, fanning out across the countryside and calling to each other every time they thought they saw something, Twice they heard the sounds of pursuit, distant cries muffled by the trees, but nothing for some hours now. Even so, they kept quiet.

The young optio was in torment over the fate of Lady Pomponia and her son. The Druids had taken too many lives in recent months, and Cato would not let them have these last two. Yet how could he possibly honour his vow to rescue then? Lady Pomponia and Aelius were even now imprisoned in that vast hill fort, with its massive ramparts, high palisade and watchful garrison. Their rescue was the kind of deed that only mythic heroes could carry out successfully, and Cato's bitter self-analysis was that he was too weak and scared to have even the remotest chance of carrying it off. Had Macro not been injured, he might have felt more optimistic. What little Macro lacked in foresight and strategic initiative he more than made up for with courage and strength. The worse the odds, the more determined the centurion became to overcome them. That was the key quality of the man who had become his friend and mentor, and Cato knew it was precisely that quality he lacked. Now, more than ever, he needed Macro at his side, but the centurion lay at his feet, on the verge of death, it seemed. The wound would have killed a weaker man outright, but Macro's thick skull and physical resilience were keeping him on this side of the Styx, but only just.

'What now?' Boudica whispered. 'We must decide.'

'I know,' Cato replied irritably. 'I'm thinking.'

'Thinking's not good enough. We have to do something. He's not going to live long without proper attention.'

The emotion in her voice was barely hidden, and reminded Cato of her personal interest in Macro. He coughed to clear his throat and ease the emotion in his own voice.

'I'm sorry, I wasn't thinking.'

Boudica laughed briefly. 'That's my boy! Now then, let's talk. We have to get Macro back to the legion if he's to stand any chance of surviving. We need to get the girl out of here too.'

'We can't all go back. The horses aren't up to it. In any case, I need to be here, close to the hill fort, where I can keep an eye on things and see if there's any chance to rescue Lady Pomponia and the boy.'

'What can you do alone?' Boudica asked wearily. 'Nothing. That's what. We've done our best, Cato. We came very close to doing what we set out to do. It didn't work out. That's all there is to it. No point in throwing your life away.' She laid a hand on his shoulder. 'Really. That's how it is. No one could have done more.'

'Maybe not,' he agreed reluctantly. 'But it's not over yet.'

'What can you do now? Be honest.'

'I don't know . . . I don't know. But I'm not giving up. I gave my word.'

For a moment Boudica stared at the barely visible features of the optio's face.

'Cato . . .'

'What?'

'Be careful,' Boudica said softly. 'Promise me that at least.'

'I can't.'

'Very well. But you should know that I'd consider the world a poorer place without you in it. Don't go ahead of your time.'

'Who says this isn't my time?' Cato replied in a grim tone. 'And this isn't the moment to philosophise about it.'

Boudica regarded him with a sad, resigned expression.

'We'll tie Macro to one of the horses,' Cato went on. 'You and the girl take the other two. Leave the forest on the opposite side we came in from – that should keep you clear of the Druids. Go east, and don't stop until you reach Atrebate territory. If Prasutagus is right, that should take you no more than a day. Get back to the legion as soon as possible and tell Vespasian everything. Tell him I'm still here with Prasutagus and that we'll try to rescue Lady Pomponia if there's a chance.'

'What then?'

'Then? I imagine Vespasian will have some instructions for me. Prasutagus and I will use this forest as our base. If there's any message for us, it's to come here. You'd better make a mental map of the route on your way back so Vespasian's man can find us.'

'If there's a message, I'll bring it.'

'No. You've risked yourself enough already.'

'True, but I doubt a Roman would be intelligent enough to follow my directions back here.'

'Look, Boudica. This is dangerous. I choose to stay here. I wouldn't want your life on my conscience as well. Please.'

'I'll be back as soon as I can.'

Cato sighed. There was no arguing with the bloody woman, and there was nothing he could do to stop her. 'As you wish.'

'Right then, let's get Macro in the saddle.'

With Prasutagus's help, Macro was gently lifted from the ground and onto the horse, where he was bound securely to the high horns of the saddle. His heavily bandaged head drooped, and for the first time since he had been injured he mumbled incoherently.

'Haven't heard him speak like that since the last time we went drinking,' muttered Boudica. Then she turned to Julia and gently steered the girl towards another horse. 'Up you go.'

Julia refused to move, and stared silently at the looming shadow of the horse. Boudica was suddenly struck by a nasty thought.

'You can ride, can't you?'

'No . . . A little.'

There was a stunned silence as Boudica took this in. Every Celt, male or female, could ride a horse almost before they could run. It was as natural as breathing. She turned towards Cato.

'Do you people really have an empire?'

'Of course.'

'Then how the hell do you get around it? Surely you don't walk?'

'Some of us ride,' Cato replied sourly. 'No more talk. Get going.'

Prasutagus lifted the girl onto the horse and pressed the reins into her uncertain hands. When Boudica was mounted, she took the reins of Macro's horse and clicked her tongue. Her mount was still tired and required a sharp dig from her's heels before it moved.

'Take care of my centurion!' Cato called after her.

'I will,' she replied softly. 'And you take care of my betrothed.'

Cato looked round at the looming hulk of Prasutagus and wondered what he could possibly require by way of care.

'Don't let him do anything stupid,' Boudica added before the horses disappeared into the gloom.

'Oh, right.'

The two of them stood side by side until the last sounds of the horses' passage through the forest had faded. Then Cato coughed and turned to the Iceni warrior, not quite certain how to impress upon Prasutagus the fact that he was now in charge.

'We must rest now.'

'Yes, rest.' Prasutagus nodded. 'Good.'

They settled back down on the soft bed of pine needles covering the forest floor. Cato pulled his cloak tightly around him and curled up, resting his head on an arm. Above him, in small gaps in the foliage, the stars twinkled through the swirling steam of his breath. Another time he would have wondered at the beauty of this sylvan setting, but tonight the stars looked as hard and cold as ice. Despite his weariness, Cato could not sleep. The memory of his enforced abandonment of Lady Pomponia and her terrified son played over and over in his mind, tormenting him with his powerlessness. When that image faded, it was replaced by the dreadful vision of Macro's wound, and much as he might pray to the gods to spare Macro's life, he had been in the army long enough to know that the wound was almost certainly fatal. It was a coldly clinical assessment, but in his heart Cato could not bring himself to believe that his centurion would die. Not Macro. Hadn't he survived that final stand in the marshes by the River Tamesis the previous summer? If he could come back from that, then surely he could survive this wound. Nearby, in the darkness, Prasutagus stirred.

'Cato.'

'Yes?'

'Tomorrow we kill Druids. Yes?'

'No. Tomorrow we watch Druids. Now get some rest.'

'Huh!' Prasutagus grunted, and gradually slipped into the deep regular breathing of sleep.

Cato sighed. Macro was gone, and now he was saddled with this mad Celt, He couldn't deny the man was good in a fight, but although he had the physique of an ox he had the brains of a mouse. Life, the optio decided, had a funny way of making an impossible situation effortlessly worse.

Chapter Thirty

Early the next morning Cato and Prasutagus crept to the edge of the forest, crawling through the cold wet grass at its fringe. The trees sprawled over a gently sloping hill, and, looking down towards the track in the vale, they saw no signs of any of the Druids who had pursued them into the darkness. On the far side of the track the land sloped up to another forested hill. Beyond that, Cato knew, lay the site of the abortive rescue attempt on the wagon. A wave of anguish rushed over him at the recollection, but he swiftly pushed the thought aside and concentrated on his memory of the landscape. From the farther hill they should have a good view of the massive ramparts of the Great Fortress. Cato motioned to Prasutagus and indicated a shallow defile in the side of the hill, overgrown with gorse bushes and occasional patches of blackberry. It would provide good cover all the way down the slope. From there they would have to chance a quick dash across to the forest on the far side of the track.

Although the sky was clear, it was still early spring and the sun gave little warmth at this time of day. The exertion of creeping through the thorny bushes, and the anxiety of being discovered, kept Cato from shivering, but as soon as they stopped at the foot of the hill, his body trembled with cold. Worried that Prasutagus might construe his shaking as fear, Cato fought to control his body's instincts and just managed to still his limbs. Keeping his head low, he scanned the surrounding landscape. Aside from a light breeze rippling the grass, no living thing moved. Beside him Prasutagus drummed his fingers impatiently on the ground and inclined his head towards the trees beyond the track.

Cato nodded his assent, and both of them bolted across the open ground, over the track and into the welcome shadows of the trees. They ducked down and Cato listened for any sign that they had been spotted but the pounding of blood in his ears drowned out anything he might have heard. He dragged Prasutagus further into the trees, through a dense tangle of undergrowth. The ground sloped upwards until it eventually levelled out on the crest. Both men slumped down on a fallen tree trunk, covered with the moss and lichen of ages. Breathing heavily, Cato suddenly felt very dizzy and braced himself with both hands to stop himself tumbling to the ground. Prasutagus reached over to Cato's shoulder to steady him.

'You rest, Roman.'

'No. I'm not tired,' Cato lied. He was exhausted, but more pressing than that was his hunger. He had not eaten property for days, and the effects were becoming apparent.

'Food. We must have food,' he said.

Prasutagus nodded. 'You stay here. I find.'

'All right. But be careful. No one must see you. Understand?'

'Sa!' Prasutagus frowned at the unnecessary warning.

'Off you go then,' muttered Cato. 'Don't be long.'

Prasutagus waved a farewell and disappeared through the trees along the crest. Cato eased himself onto the ground and leaned back against the soft moss on the tree trunk. His eyes closed and he breathed in the forest-scented air deeply. For a while his mind was clear and he rested peacefully, indulging his senses as he listened to the different bird calls from the branches above. Now and then he was jarred by the sound of other animals making their way across the forest floor, but there were no voices and the sounds receded quickly enough. It was strange to be alone for the first time in months, to savour the peculiar serenity that comes from having no other person nearby. The euphoric feeling quickly faded as his mind started working on the wider situation he found himself in. Macro was gone, so was Boudica. All that remained was himself and Prasutagus. The Iceni warrior's knowledge of the area and the customs of the Druids was vital. He even claimed to have some familiarity with the hill fort where Lady Pomponia and her son were imprisoned.

The image of the terrified boy running to his mother plagued him. Cato cursed himself for not going back for Aelius, even though the Druids were only moments away, pounding down the track towards the wagon. Cato and the boy might have got away. He doubted it, but it was still a possibility. A possibility that Vespasian and Plautius would not overlook if he ever returned to the legion to tell the tale. His harsh self-judgement was burden enough, without the sidelong scorn of the men who would question his courage.

Hours passed and, as the sun began to dip from its midday position, Cato decided he had rested enough. There was still no sign of

Prasutagus, and Cato felt a pang of concern. But there was nothing he could do to speed the man's return; he could only hope that he had not fallen into the hands of the Druids, and that he had found food.

Cato looked round at the nearest trees, and picked one that had plenty of branches, promising to be an easy climb. Limb by limb he pulled himself up the tree, until the trunk became thin enough to sway under his weight. With one arm wrapped round the rough bark, Cato parted the slender branches. He had lost his bearings and could not see the hill fort at first. Then, adjusting his footing, he tried another direction and gazed down on the grassy sward running beside the river. He could see the trestle bridge and followed the line of the track leading up to the hill fort.

Cato was awed anew by the scale of the ramparts. How many men had laboured for how many years to create this vast monument to the might of the Durotriges? How many men would it cost Rome to take this hill fort when the time came for the legions to march west? Of course it would be his legion, the Second, that would be tasked with storming those ramparts. The legion had only just managed to best the Britons in setpiece battles. Would they be able to storm their formidable fortresses? Cato had read of siegecraft as a child but had not been called upon to practise it since he had joined the eagles. The prospect of assaulting those towering ramparts of earth filled him with dread.

A heavy thump from below startled him and he nearly let go of the trunk. Cato, looked down through the branches and saw Prasutagus searching around for him. By the tree trunk lay the body of a dead pig with a bloody tear in its throat.

'Up here!' Cato called.

Prasutagus tilted his head back, then laughed as he caught sight of Cato. He reached for one of the lower branches.

'No. Stay there. I'm coming down.'

On the ground, Cato eyed the pig appreciatively. 'Where did you get it?'

'Uh?'

'Where?' Cato pointed at the pig.

'Ah!' Prasutagus pointed along the ridge, and mimed a valley, and another ridge. Then he paused, frowning, as he tried to think how to mime the next part. The word suddenly came to him. 'Farm!'

'You took this from a farm?'

Prasutagus nodded, smiling widely.

'Where was the farmer?'

Prasutagus drew a line across his throat.

'Oh great! That's all we need,' Cato said angrily.

Prasutagus raised a calming hand.

'I hide body. No one find.'

'I'm glad to hear it. But what happens when he's missed? What then, you fool?'

Prasutagus shrugged his huge shoulders, as if that was no concern of his. He turned to the pig.

'We eat?'

'Yes.' Cato's stomach rumbled. Both men laughed spontaneously at the sound. 'We eat. Now.'

With long-practised skill Prasutagus gutted the pig with his dagger, placing the inedible organs in a glistening pile. Then he shoved the lot down the hollow interior of the tree trunk, saving the liver for a little snack later. After wiping his bloodstained hands with clumps of damp moss, he started gathering branches.

'No fire,' ordered Cato. He pointed upwards, then towards the hill fort. 'No smoke.'

Prasutagus had obviously fixed his heart on roast pork and for a moment he baulked at the prospect of eating the pig raw. But then he shrugged and drew his dagger again. He hacked strips of flesh from the pig's loin and tossed one to Cato. The pink flesh had blood and white membrane on it, but Cato hungrily sank his teeth into the still warm meat and forced himself to chew.

After they had eaten their fill, Prasutagus pushed the carcass into the hollow trunk and covered the end with some branches. Then they rested in turns until nightfall, when they moved down the slope, carrying the pig with them. They headed away from the hill fort until they discovered a small hollow where an ancient oak had fallen, wrenching up the earth attached to its myriad roots. There they toiled to light a small fire with dry moss and flints from Cato's haversack. When the kindling had finally caught, they carefully built the fire up and roasted the pig. In the red glow of the warming flames, Cato sat with his arms round his knees savouring the sizzle of fat and the rich aroma of meat. At length, Prasutagus stood up and carved it, placing a large steaming pile on a stone beside Cato. They feasted till they could not eat another scrap and fell asleep with warm, full bellies.

For the next two days they took turns to keep watch on the hill fort, and saw a steady stream of tribespeople making their way towards it. There were wagons too, and small herds of animals, including sheep, driven up from their spring pastures, even though the lambing season was imminent. Clearly, the Durotriges were preparing their people for a siege, which meant they had had news of an approaching enemy. Right now that enemy could only be Rome; the Second Legion must be on the march. Cato's pulse raced at the realisation. In days, perhaps, the legionaries would throw a ring of steel round the hill fort and the Druids and their prisoners would have nowhere to flee. The general's wife and son would be used as bargaining counters to ameliorate the terms of the hill fort's surrender – unless the Durotriges were every bit as mad as the Druids and opted to fight Rome to their last breath. In that case there was little hope for Lady Pomponia and Aelius.

Cato had agreed with Prasutagus that on the third day one of them should return to the place Boudica had left them; that was the earliest she could be expected to return. So at dusk Cato slipped back across the track and headed towards the forest. Despite his certainty that he could recall the route by which he and Prasutagus had travelled, the trees seemed strange in the dark, and he failed to find the ruins of the silver mine. He tried to retrace his steps and only succeeded in becoming even more lost. As the night wore on, caution gave way to speed and the undergrowth crackled and rustled under his feet. He was on the point of calling out for Boudica when a dark figure stepped out from behind a tree directly in front of him. Cato flipped his cloak back and drew his sword.

'Why not just sound a trumpet next time you want to attract some attention?' Boudica chuckled. 'I thought I must have discovered one of Claudius's lost elephants.'

For a moment Cato just stared at Boudica's outline, then with a nervous laugh he lowered his blade and took a deep breath.

'Shit, Boudica, you scared me!'

'You deserved it. Where's my cousin?'

'He's fine. He's keeping watch on the hill fort. Unless he's gone hunting for pig farmers again.'

'What? Never mind. Explain later. Now listen to me. There's not much time, and I've got something really scary to tell you.'

Chapter Thirty-One

The edge of the night sky was washed with the pale glow of dawn by the time Cato and Boudica reached the hollow where Prasutagus was waiting. They had left her horse tied to a tree in the silver workings, with a full bag of feed to keep it company. The two Iceni embraced warmly in greeting, each obviously relieved that the other was safe and well. Although safe was pushing it a bit, Cato reflected. Being camped in a forest barely a mile from their savage enemy was not so very safe at all.

Boudica gratefully accepted some cold pork, but sniffed suspiciously before taking a bite.

'How old is this delightful morsel?'

'Nearly three days. It should be all right to eat.'

'Well, I'm hungry enough, so thanks.' She tore of a strip off the grey meat and chewed. 'Now then, my news. You'll have to excuse me if I talk while I eat.'

'Fine.' Cato nodded impatiently.

'I managed to reach an Atrebate village the night after I left you. They told me that a Roman army had passed through earlier in the day. Seemed quite awed by the experience. Anyway, I set off straight away and we caught up with Vespasian a few hours later. The Second Legion is making directly for the Great Fortress. Vespasian aims to knock it out of the campaign first, as an example to any Durotriges planning to hold him off in other hill forts.'

'Makes sense,' said Cato. 'And he'll go in hard. But how's Macro?'

'Macro was taken straight to the field hospital.'

'He's still alive?'

'For the moment. The chief surgeon didn't sound hopeful, but then I suppose they never do,' she continued quickly when she saw the look on Cato's face. 'Vespasian was delighted to see the general's daughter, but then showed me something that had been tied to an arrow and shot over the camp gate just after nightfall . . .' Boudica paused.

231

'Go on.'

'It was a finger, a small finger. There was a message from the Dark Moon Druids on the strip of cloth that tied it to the arrow. One of the legion's native scouts translated. It said that the finger was cut off the hand of the general's son as a warning not to try any more rescue attempts.'

Cato felt sick. 'I see,' he muttered.

'No, you don't. Plautius left orders with Vespasian that if any harm befell his family, then the head of the senior Druid in Vespasian's charge was to be cut off and sent to the Durotriges. The others are to be killed at two-day intervals and their heads sent back, until the surviving members of the general's family are released.'

'They're dead the moment that first head arrives, aren't they?'

'If they're lucky.'

'Has Vespasian carried out the order?'

'Not yet. He's sent the daughter back, with a request for confirmation of the orders.'

'Which Plautius will give, the moment he hears his daughter's story.'

'I'd imagine that's how he might react.'

Cato did some quick calculations. 'That was two days back. Allow two days each way for the message to reach the general and the order to be confirmed, then a day for the head to be delivered . . . That means we've got two days, three at the outside. No more.'

'That's what I reckon.'

'Oh great . . .' Cato looked down at his folded hands, then continued thoughtfully. 'Unless Vespasian delays carrying out the order.'

'He might,' agreed Boudica. 'But I think he has other plans. Your Second Legion will arrive under the walls of the hill fort in two days' time. I think he means to storm the fortress as quickly as possible and rescue the general's family himself.'

Cato was shocked. 'The Druids would never let it happen. They'd kill the hostages the moment the wall was breached. All we'd find are the bodies.'

Boudica nodded. 'But what choice does he have? They're dead either way.' She looked at Cato. 'Unless someone gets in there and gets them out before the legion turns up.'

Cato returned her gaze steadily. Just as Vespasian had no choice in his actions, neither did he.

'We have to try it. There must be a way in. Prasutagus would know.'

The Iceni warrior raised his head at the sound of his name. He had not been able to follow the discussion and was staring into the flames, with an occasional contented glance at Boudica. She turned to him and spoke in their tongue.

Prasutagus shook his head firmly. 'Na! No way in.'

'There has to be something!' Cato replied desperately. 'Some small opening. Anything. Just a way inside the palisade. That's all we'd need.'

Prasutagus stared at the optio, bemused by the look of utter despair in his face.

'Please, Prasutagus. I gave my word. If there is a way, all you need do is lead me to it. I'll go alone from there.'

After Boudica translated, Prasutagus considered a moment, spat into the fire, and nodded slowly before he replied to his cousin.

'He says there might be a way. A drainage outlet on the far side of the fort, opposite the main gate. It might be possible to climb through it and get inside. He'll take you there, tomorrow night, but that's it. Then you're on your own. He'll wait at the drain but the moment he hears any commotion, he'll go.'

'Fair enough,' agreed Cato. 'Tell him I'm grateful.'

Prasutagus laughed when Boudica translated. 'He says he doesn't want gratitude from a man he's leading to his death.'

'Thank him anyway.'

Cato knew the risk in what he planned to do was appalling. They might be discovered as they clambered up the ramparts, the drain was likely to be guarded, especially after the rescue attempt on the wagon. And once inside, then what? Where would he look inside that vast fortress filled with Durotrigan tribespeople and Dark Moon Druids? If he escaped their notice, and actually located the general's wife and son, could he really free them on his own and lead them to safety, from the very heart of the enemy's greatest fortification?

In a more rational world Cato would have dismissed the idea out of hand. But he had given his word to Lady Pomponia. He had seen the terror in the boy's eyes. He had witnessed the terrible atrocities that the Dark Moon Druids had visited on Diomedes, and on the peaceful village of Noviomagus. The blond child's face, submerged in his memories these last few days, loomed forth again, cold and beseeching. Then there was Macro. The centurion was all but dead, and he had been prepared to give his life to rescue the general's family.

The moral burden of all he had seen and experienced was overwhelming. Reason had nothing to do with it. He was driven by a compulsion far stronger. There was no reason in the world, he reflected somberly – just an endless sea of unreasonable compulsions, shifting with the tides and carrying its human flotsam where it willed. He could no more turn his back on a final attempt at rescuing the general's wife and son than he could reach up and stroke the face of the moon.

When he rose in the morning, Cato prepared himself for his fate. Numbly he chewed the last of the cold pork, then he climbed to the top of the hill. More Durotrigan warriors were streaming into the hill fort, and he marked them down in the small waxed tablet he carried in his haversack. The information might at least be of some use to Vespasian if he did not return. Boudica would carry it to the legate.

While Boudica took her turn in the tree, Prasutagus mysteriously disappeared, and for a while Cato wondered if the Iceni warrior could not face the night's impossible task. But even as he wondered, he knew this was not the case. Prasutagus had proved himself a man of his word. If he said he would lead the way to the hill fort's drainage outlet, then he would.

Shortly before the sun dipped beyond the trees and plunged the forest into gloom, Prasutagus at last reappeared, carrying a bag filled with roots and leaves. He lit a small fire and began to boil the plants in his skillet, producing a sharp odour that irritated Cato's nostrils. Boudica came and joined them.

'What's he doing?' Cato nodded towards the bubbling brew.

She spoke to Prasutagus a moment, then replied, 'He's making some dyes. If you get into the fortress you'll need to blend in with the tribesmen, as far as you can. Prasutagus is going to paint you and lime your hair.'

'What?'

'It's that or be killed on sight.'

'All right then,' Cato relented.

In the light and warmth of the fire he stripped off his tunic and stood in only his loincloth as Prasutagus knelt before him and traced a series of swirling blue patterns across his torso and arms. He completed the work with smaller, more intricate patterns on Cato's face, painting with an intensity of concentration that Cato had never seen in him before. While he worked, Boudica prepared the lime and plastered it on his hair. He flinched at the tingling sensation on his scalp and then forced himself to be still when Boudica tutted.

Finally, the two Iceni stood back and admired their handiwork.

'How do I look?'

Boudica laughed. 'Personally, I think you'd make a great Celt.'

'Thanks. Can we get going now?'

'Not quite. Take off the loincloth.'

234

'What?'

'You heard me. You need to look like a warrior. Wear my cloak fastened over your body. Nothing else.'

'I don't recall seeing any of the other Durotriges in the altogether. Can't imagine it's habitual.'

'It isn't. But spring has begun. It's the time we Celts call the First Budding. In most tribes the menfolk walk naked for ten days in honour of the Goddess of Spring.'

'Naturally the Iceni are exceptions.' Cato looked at Prasutagus.

'Naturally.'

'Bit of a voyeur, this goddess.'

'She likes to weigh up the talent,' Boudica explained light-heartedly. 'In some tribes, a young man is picked each year for his looks and becomes her groom.'

'How does that happen?'

'The Druids cut his heart out and let the blood fertilise the plants around her altar.' Boudica smiled at his horrified expression. 'Relax, I said some tribes, some of the wilder ones. Just try not to be too good-looking.'

'There are wilder tribes than the Durotriges?'

'Oh yes. That lot on the hill are nothing compared to some of the tribes of the north-west. I expect you Romans will discover that in due course. Now then, your loincloth please.'

Cato untied it, and with an embarrassed glance at Boudica, let it fall away. Her eyes could not help flickering down and she smiled. At her side Prasutagus chuckled and whispered something in Boudica's ear.

'What did he say?' Cato asked angrily.

'He wonders if Roman women ever notice they're having it off.'

'Oh, he does, does he?'

'Now then, boys, that's enough. You've got work to do. Here's my cloak, Cato.'

He took it, and handed her the loincloth. 'Look after it.'

He fastened the shoulder clasp and was given a last inspection by Prasutagus.

He nodded and punched the optio on the shoulder.

'Come! We go!'

Chapter Thirty-Two

A crescent moon had risen when Prasutagus and Cato left the forest and started out for the Great Fortress. A brisk wind carried thin strands of moon-silvered cloud across the star-sprinkled darkness. Prasutagus and Cato ran across the meadows surrounding the ramparts, going to ground and crawling as soon as the clouds cleared the moon again. The imminent arrival of the first elements of the Second Legion had meant that all surrounding flocks of sheep had been driven up into the hill fort, and Cato was grateful that the nervous animals were not around to give them away; the pale light cast by the moon was bad enough.

About two hours later, as near as Cato could estimate it, they reached the far side of the Great Fortress. Prasutagus led him directly towards the black mass of the first rampart. The faint sound of singing and cheering drifted down from the plateau on top of the hill fort. Ahead of Cato, Prasutagus crept forwards, constantly looking right and left as the ground began to slope up onto the first rampart.

He paused, and then threw himself down, and Cato did likewise, eyes and ears straining. Then Cato saw them: two men, silhouetted against the starry sky, patrolling along the top of the first rampart. Their conversation carried down the slope and the light-hearted tone suggested they were not being as diligent in their duties as they should. Clearly, the harsh discipline of sentry duty in the legions did not apply here. When the patrol had passed by, they rose from the ground and began scrambling up the grassy slope of the rampart. The gradient was severe and Cato was soon panting with the exertion of the climb, wondering how much harder this would be in full armour and with a full equipment load should the Second Legion launch an attack on the hill fort.

They reached the top of the rampart and dropped flat again. Now that he was actually on the defences, Cato was even more in awe of their scale. A narrow track ran along the first rampart, stretching out on either side as far as he could see in the moonlight. On the other side, the ground fell away steeply to form a deep trench, before rising up again to the second rampart. At the bottom of the trench there was a strange cross-hatching pattern which Cato could not quite make out. Then he realised what it was. A band of sharpened stakes, set into the ground at different angles lay in wait to impale any attacker who made it this far. No doubt the trench between the second and third ramparts contained more of the same wicked points.

'Go!' Prasutagus whispered.

Crouching low, they crossed the patrol path and half ran, half slid down the other side of the rampart, taking care to slow their descent as they neared the sharp points at the bottom. The stakes had been cleverly arranged, so that a man who managed to negotiate one stake would find himself immediately facing the point of another. Any attempt by a group to rush through would result in a bloodbath, and Cato prayed that Vespasian had the sense not to attempt a direct assault. If he survived this night it was vital that he warn the legate of the dangers that faced his legionaries.

With only their cloaks to hamper them, Prasutagus and Cato quietly picked their way through the stakes and began scaling the second rampart. It was only slightly smaller than the first, and Cato's limbs ached by the time they reached the top. Now they could see the palisade on top of the third and final rampart. It was hard to be sure in the dark, but Cato estimated the wooden wall to be at least ten feet in height; more than enough to hold back any enemy foolhardy enough to attempt a direct attack. A quick glance either way along the path revealed no enemies and they slipped over and down the other side to where more stakes waited for them at the bottom. Once through, Prasutagus did not start up the final slope, but edged along its base for a while, continually looking up towards the palisade.

They smelt the drain before they saw it; a foul odour of human waste and decaying food slops. The ground underfoot squelched and became slippery as they crept on. Dark pools of filth had collected around the stakes. Soon the pools gave way to a stinking swamp of ordure that filled the trench and glistened in the moonlight. An immense heap of rubbish and sewage grew out of it, like a huge cone with its base in, and overflowing, the trench, and its summit blending into a narrow gully leading up to the palisade high above them.

Prasutagus caught the optio's arm and pointed at the gully. Cato nodded and they began the ascent towards the hill fort's last line of defence. The higher they climbed, the more pungent the stench. The air became so thick with it that Cato choked, feeling bile rise in this throat. Desperately he fought the urge to vomit in case the sound attracted attention. At last they reached the palisade and rested beside the reeking gully. A small wooden structure had been built over the head of the gully and projected a little way from the wall. In its base was a small square opening through which the rubbish and sewage was tipped. There was no sign of life on the palisade above, only the distant din of the Durotriges drinking themselves into a stupor. Prasutagus eased himself down into the gully, making sure of his footing on the slimy ground. He positionied himself directly below the opening, grabbed the base of the palisade in front of him, and beckoned to Cato.

The image of some passing Durotrigan pausing to take a dump on the proud Icenian's head struck Cato, and he was unable to stifle a snort of laughter. Prasutagus looked at him in fury and jabbed a hand up at the opening.

'Sorry,' whispered Cato, as he scrambled over. 'Nerves.'

'Take cloak off,' ordered Prasutagus.

Cato undid the clasp and let Boudica's cloak drop. Suddenly stark naked in the cold air, he shivered violently.

'Up!' Prasutagus hissed. 'On me.'

Cato placed both his hands on the warrior's shoulders and pulled himself up until his knees rested each side of Prasutagus's head. Then he reached for the rim of the opening with one hand. Beneath him, Prasutagus grunted with the strain of keeping himself upright, and for an instant swayed alarmingly. Cato threw his arms up and grasped the wooden frame. Slowly he heaved himself up, until he managed to throw an elbow over the rim, then quickly swayed up a foot. The rest was easy, and he lay panting on the wooden boards, staring into the heart of the fortress stretching out before him.

Nearby was a wide expanse of hastily erected animal pens, filled with sheep and pigs, quietly rooting around the slops that had been left in a pile just inside each pen. A handful of peasants were busy forking winter feed into a large enclosure containing horses. Far off to the right lay an assortment of thatched roundhouses, grouped either side of an enormous hut, eerily lit by the glow of a big fire burning in the wide open space in front. A large crowd sat in groups about the blaze, drinking and cheering on a pair of giant warriors who were wrestling in front of the flames, their efforts casting long dancing shadows on the ground. As Cato watched, one of them was thrown and a roar erupted from the spectators.

Away to the left was a separate enclosure. An interior palisade stretched across the plateau, pierced by one gate only. On each side of the gate a brazier cast bright pools of light. Four Druids, armed with long war spears, warmed themselves by the braziers. Unlike their Durotrigan allies, they were not drinking, and looked alert.

Cato ducked his head back through the opening.

'Back soon. Wait here!'

'Goodbye, Roman.'

'I'll be back,' Cato whispered angrily.

'Goodbye, Roman.'

Cautiously Cato rose to his feet and walked down the short ramp from the palisade and in among the animal pens. A few sheep looked up as he passed, eyeing him with the habitual suspicion of a species whose relationship with man was comestibly one-sided. Cato saw a wooden pitchfork lying by a pen and bent down to pick it up. His heart was pounding, and every sinew in his body urged him to turn and flee. It took all his willpower to keep on moving, slowly working his way round towards the enclosure guarded by the Druids, while keeping as far from the peasants as possible. If anyone tried to engage him in conversation he was lost. Cato stopped at each pen, as if to check on the animals, occasionally pitching in some fresh feed. If the animals were momentarily puzzled by the extra rations, they quickly got over the shock and tucked in.

The gate to the Druid enclosure was open and through it Cato could make out a number of smaller huts, and more Druids crouched around small fires, all swathed in their black cloaks. But the gateway was small, so the view was limited. Cato worked his way as close to the gate as he dared, moving along the line of the pens until he was fifty paces from the enclosure. Every so often he risked a glance towards the gate trying not to make it obvious that he was looking. At first the guards ignored him, but then one of them must have decided Cato had lingered too long. The guard lifted his spear and slowly walked over.

Cato turned to the nearest pen, as if he had not seen the man, and leaned on his pitchfork. His heart beat wildly, and he was aware of a tremor in his arms that had nothing to do with the cold. He should make a run for it, he thought, and could almost feel the cold shaft of steel at the end of the Druid's spear flying through the night to take him in the back as he fled. The thought filled his mind with terror. Yet what if the man spoke to him? The end would surely be the same.

He could hear the Druid's footfall now, then the man called out to him. Cato shut his eyes and swallowed, then turned as casually as he could. This would really test Prasutagus's disguise; never before in his life had Cato felt so Roman.

No more than ten paces away the Druid shouted something at him, and jabbed his spear towards the distant hutments of the Durotriges. Cato stood and stared, wide-eyed, and tightened his grip on the pitchfork. The Druid shouted again and paced towards Cato angrily. When Cato stood, fixed to his ground and trembling, the Druid roughly swung him round and kicked him on the backside, launching him away from the enclosure towards the peasants tending the other animals. There was a chorus of harsh laughter from the other guards at the gate as Cato scrambled away on all fours. At the sight of his buttocks, the Druid thrust his spear after the youngster, and only just missed as Cato found his feet and sprinted off. The Druid shouted something after him, provoking another roar of laughter from his comrades, and then turned and went back to his post.

Cato ran on, through the pens, until he was sure he was out of sight of the Druids. Squatting down, he struggled to get his breath, terrified yet exhilarated by his escape. He had found the Druid enclosure easily enough, but now he had to find some way into it. He rose and peered over the pens, through the steamy breath rising from the closely packed animals, towards the wall of the enclosure. Unless his eyes deceived him, it bowed out slightly, and the gate was slightly over to one side. If he could approach along the foot of the hill fort's palisade on the far side of the bulge, he might find a way over the wall, out of sight of the Druids on the gate.

Cato worked his way back through the pens towards the drain, until he was two hundred feet away from the guards. The ground around the pens was devoid of grass, and presented an expanse of churned up mud. Cato dropped to his stomach and, hugging the ground, began to inch his way around the pens to where the wall of the enclosure butted up against the palisade. The wooden stakes had been shortened so that they would end-flush against those of the palisade. There, if anywhere, would be a place he might find a way into the enclosure.

Cato forced himself to move slowly, making no swift movement that might catch the eye of the guards. If they caught him again there would be no horseplay this time. It seemed to take hours, but at last Cato was beyond the curve of the enclosure, out of sight of the guards and he could risk a quick rush over to the angle in the walls. With a last quick check towards them, he rose to his feet and ran the remaining distance to where the wall met the palisade, crouching down and pressing himself into the shadow at its base. Then another glance round. No sign he had been seen. He crept up the ramp to the palisade and looked over the top of the wall.

Inside the enclosure there were scores of Druids, not merely the handful he had been able to glimpse by their fires. Many were asleep on the ground, and Cato assumed there were yet more in the huts lining the inside of the enclosure. Several others were awake, at work on timber structures that were not unlike the frames of legionary catapults. The Druids were evidently fashioning their own crude form of artillery. His eyes searched the enclosure, but the general's wife and son might be in any of the huts. Refusing to give way to despair, Cato scanned the huts once more. He had almost given up when he saw the cage. Beside one of the bigger huts, half concealed in the shadow cast by the overlapping thatch, was a small wicker cage, with wooden bars fastened across the entrance. Behind the bars, just visible in the pale moonlight, were two faces, watching the Druids at their work. Guards stood either side with their spears grounded.

Cato's heart sank at the sight of the wretched prisoners. There was no way to get to them, no way at all. The moment he tried to pull himself up and over the wall he would be seen. Even if, by the most incredible miracle, he wasn't, then how could he alone get them out of the cage? Fate had seen fit to permit him to advance this far in his attempt, and now no further.

Cato lowered himself, knowing there was no way he could reach the hostages without getting himself killed. He had always known this was a fool's errand, but the confirmation of it was no less hard to bear. There was nothing more he could do. He had to leave at once.

He made his way back to the drain hole as carefully as he had approached the enclosure. When Cato was sure that he was unobserved, he leaned through the opening.

'Prasutagus . . .' he whispered.

A shadow rose from the slope and slid towards him. When the Iceni warrior had positioned himself beneath the hole, Cato dropped down, missed his grip and tumbled towards the gully. A powerful fist closed about his ankle and yanked him to a stop, scarcely a foot above the turds and urine trickling down the steep sides of the gully. Prasutagus swung him back onto the grass and collapsed beside him a moment later.

'Thanks,' Cato panted. 'Really thought I was in deep shit there.'

'You find them?'

'Yes,' Cato replied bitterly, 'I found them.'

Chapter Thirty-Three

The Second Legion arrived the following day, at noon. From the tree they had been using as a watchtower Cato saw a thin screen of horsemen approaching the Great Fortress from the east. Although there was no way of being sure of their identity from such a distance, the dispersal was characteristic of the scouts sent forward in advance of a Roman army. Cato grinned with delight, and joyously thumped the tree trunk. After so many miserable days skulking through the lands of the Durotriges and sleeping in the open air, always in terror of being discovered, the thought of the Second Legion being so close at hand filled him with a warm and comforting longing. It was almost like the imminent prospect of being reunited with close family, and it moved him far more than he had expected. There was a painful, emotional, tightening of his throat to overcome before he could call down to Prasutagus. The top of the tree swayed alarmingly as the Iceni warrior clambered up to join him.

'Easy, man,' Cato grunted, tightening his grasp. 'You want everyone to know we're here?'

Prasutagus stopped a few branches lower than Cato, and pointed towards the hill fort. The legion's scouts had been seen by the enemy as well, and the last of the Durotrigan patrols was marching up to the main gate. Soon, all the natives would be bottled up in their fastness, confident that they would defy the Roman attempt to seize the Great Fortress. There was no risk to Cato and Prasutagus now; the burden of concealment was lifted from them, and Cato relented.

'All right, then. But watch you don't break the trunk.'

'Eh?' Prasutagus looked up with an uncomprehending frown.

Cato pointed at the slender breadth of the trunk. 'Be careful.'

Prasutagus playfully shook the trunk to test it, nearly dislodging Cato, and then nodded.

Cato gritted his teeth in irritation. He looked east, beyond the scouts, straining his eyes for the first sign of the main body of the Second Legion.

It was nearly an hour later before the vanguard emerged from the distant haze of rolling hills and forest. A faint rippling glitter marked the first of the cohorts as the sun caught on polished helmets and weapons. Slowly, the head of the distant legion resolved itself into a long column, like a many-scaled serpent languidly slithering across the landscape. Mounted staff officers cantered up and down each side of the column, ensuring that nothing held up the regular, disciplined pace of the advance. On each flank, some distance from the legion, more scouts guarded against any surprise attack from the enemy. Towards the rear trundled the dark mass of the baggage and artillery trains, then finally the afterguard cohort. Cato was surprised by the size of the artillery train. It was far larger than the usual complement for one legion. Somehow the legate must have wangled himself some reinforcements. Good, thought Cato, as he glanced across at the hill fort. They would be sorely needed.

'It's time we had a word with Vespasian,' Cato muttered, then tapped Prasutagus on the head with his boot. 'Down, boy!'

They hurried from the crest of the hill to find Boudica, and Cato told her the news. Then, they cautiously emerged from the forest and made their way east towards the approaching legion. They passed a handful of small hovels, where in more peaceful times peasant farmers eked out a living growing crops and raising sheep and pigs, maybe even cattle. Now they were empty, all the farmers, their families, and their animals sheltering inside the Great Fortress from the terrifying invaders who marched under the wings of their gold eagles.

Cato and his companions passed the place where the Druids' wagon had been taken a few days earlier, and saw that there was still blood, dry and dark, encrusted on the wagon ruts. Once again Cato thought of Macro, and felt uneasy about the prospect of discovering the centurion's fate when they reached the legion. It seemed impossible that Macro could die. The latticework of scars the centurion bore on his skin, and his boundless confidence in his indestructability, bore testimony to a life that, while fraught with danger, was peculiarly charmed. It was easy to visualise Macro old and bent in some veterans' colony many years from now, endlessly recounting tales of his army days and yet not too old to get drunk and enjoy a geriatric punch-up. It was almost impossible to imagine him cold and dead. And yet that wound to his head, with all its appalling severity, threatened the worst. Cato would find out soon enough, and dreaded it.

The scouts appeared as they were crossing the trestle bridge. A cocky looking decurion – all fresh plumes and knee-high soft leather boots – cantered down the slope towards them, flanked by half of his squadron. The decurion drew his sword and bellowed the order to charge.

Cato pushed himself in front of Boudica and waved his arms. Beside him, Prasutagus looked puzzled and turned round to see who the cavalry could possibly be charging. A short distance from the bridge the decurion reined in and raised his sword to slow his men, clearly disappointed that the three ragged vagabonds weren't going to put up a fight.

'I'm Roman!' Cato cried out. 'Roman!'

The decurion's horse came to a halt inches from Cato's face, and the animal's breath stirred his hair.

'Roman?' The decurion frowned, looking Cato over. 'I don't believe it!'

Cato looked down and saw Prasutagus's swirling patterns through the open front of his tunic, and then touched his face, realising that it, too, must still bear the remains of the disguise he wore the previous night.

'Oh, I see. Forget this stuff, sir. I'm the optio of the Sixth Century, Fourth Cohort. On a mission for the legate. I need to speak to him at once.'

'Oh, really?' The decurion was still far from convinced but he was too junior to bear the responsibility of making a decision about this miserable looking wretch and his two companions. 'And these are Romans too, I suppose?'

'No, Iceni scouts, working with me.'

'Hmmm.'

'I need to speak to the legate urgently,' Cato reminded him.

'We'll see about that when we get back to the legion. For now, you'll mount up with my men.'

Three rather unhappy scouts were detailed for the task and grudgingly helped Cato and the others up behind them. The optio reached his arms round his rider and the man growled.

'Keep your hands on me saddle horn, if you know what's good for you.'

Cato did as he was told, and the decurion wheeled the small column and led them back up the slope at the trot. As they crested the hill, Cato smiled at the progress the legion had already made, despite having arrived here only an hour before. Ahead of them, at least a mile away,

245

he could see the usual screen of skirmishers. Behind them the main body of the legion was toiling to construct a marching camp, already piling the soil from the outer ditch inside the perimeter where it was packed down to make a defence rampart. Beyond the camp, the legion's vehicles were still trundling into position. But there were no surveyors marking the ground around the hill fort.

'No circumvallation?' Cato asked. 'Why?'

'Ask your mate, the legate, when you speak to him,' the scout grumbled.

For the rest of the short ride Cato kept his silence and, with more difficulty, his balance. The decurion halted the scout patrol just inside the area marked out for one of the legion's four main gates. The duty centurion rose from his camp desk and strode over. Cato recognised him by sight, but didn't know his name.

'What on earth have you got there, Manlius?'

'Found 'em heading for the hill fort, sir. Young lad there reckons he's Roman.'

'Oh, does he?' The duty centurion smiled.

'Speaks good Latin anyway, sir.'

'Make a valuable slave then.' The centurion grinned at Cato. 'I'm afraid it's the end of the woad for you, sunshine.'

The men of the cavalry patrol groaned.

Cato saluted 'Optio Quintus Licinius Cato reporting, sir. Returning from a mission for the legate.'

The centurion looked closely at Cato, then clicked his fingers as he made the connection. 'You serve under that nutcase, Macro, don't you?'

'Macro is my centurion, yes, sir.'

'Poor bastard.'

Cato felt a chill course through him, but before he could ask after Macro, the duty centurion ordered the decurion to report directly to headquarters and waved the patrol through. They trotted up the wide avenue between rows of tent markers set out for the legionaries to erect their goatskin tents the moment the camp's ditch and rampart were complete. In the middle of the site the legate's headquarters tent was already standing, and several horses belonging to the staff officers were tethered to a makeshift rail. The decurion halted his patrol and dismounted, signalling Cato and the others to follow suit.

'This lot want to see the legate,' he announced to the commander of Vespasian's bodyguard. 'Duty centurion passed 'em through.'

'Wait here.'

Moments later an exhausted Cato, Boudica and Prasutagus were ushered inside by Vespasian's private secretary. At first Cato blinked. It was quite hard adjusting from the hardships of the last days to the luxury of the accommodation afforded the commander of the Second Legion. Floorboard sections had been laid down, and on them, in the centre of the tent, was Vespasian's large campaign table, surrounded by padded stools. A small brazier glowed in each corner, warming the interior of the tent nicely. On a low table to one side lay a platter of cold meats and a glass jug half filled with wine. Behind his desk Vespasian finished signing a form and handed it back to a clerk with a quick dismissal. Then he looked up, smiled a greeting and waved his hand towards the stools on the other side of the table.

'I would change my appearance as soon as possible, if I were you, Optio. Don't want some fool of a recruit mistaking you for a local and poking you with his spear.'

'No, sir.'

'I expect you could do with a good meal and some other home comforts.'

'Yes, sir.' Cato gestured to Prasutagus and Boudica. '*We* could.'

'As soon as I've debriefed you,' Vespasian replied curtly. 'Boudica gave me some details a few days ago. I assume she told you what's been going on in the wider world. What has changed at your end?'

'The Druids have still got the general's wife and son up in the hill fort, sir. I saw them last night.'

'Last night? How?'

'I went in there. That's why I've got this stuff all over me, sir.'

'You went inside? Are you mad, Optio? Do you know what would have happened if you'd been caught?'

'I have a pretty good idea, sir.' Cato's brow furrowed as he recalled the fate of Diomedes. 'But I promised the Lady Pomponia that I would rescue her. I gave her my word, sir.'

'Bit rash then, weren't you?'

'Yes, sir.'

'Never mind. It's my intention to storm the hill fort as soon as possible. We'll get them back that way.'

'Excuse me, Legate,' Boudica interrupted. 'Prasutagus knows the Druids. He tells me they will not let them live. If it looked like the legion was close to taking the place, they'll have no reason to spare them.

'Maybe, but if Plautius confirms his order for the execution of our

Druid prisoners then they're dead anyway. At least we might save them in the confusion of an attack.'

'Sir?'

'Yes, Optio?'

'I've seen the layout inside the hill fort. You'll be assaulting the main gate?'

'Of course.' Vespasian smiled. 'I assume that meets with your approval?'

'Sir, the Druid's compound is at the other end of the hill fort. They'd see the game was up in plenty of time to get back to the compound and kill the hostages. We couldn't hope to beat them to it, sir. Boudica's right. The moment we take the main gate, they'll be killed.'

'I see.' Vespasian contemplated a moment. 'I don't have a choice then. I have to wait for Plautius's reply. If he's rescinded the execution order, then we might still be able to negotiate some kind of a deal with the Druids.'

'I wouldn't pin your hopes on it,' said Boudica.

Vespasian frowned at her, and then turned back to Cato.

'Not looking very good then, is it?'

'No, sir.'

'What can you tell me about conditions inside the hill fort? How many are we facing? How are they armed?'

Cato had anticipated the question and had his answers ready. 'No more than eight hundred warriors. Twice as many noncombatants, and maybe eighty Druids. They were working on something that looked like catapult frames, so we might be facing some pretty heavy fire when we go in, sir.'

'We'll match them at that game, and more,' Vespasian said with satisfaction. 'The general transferred the artillery from the Twentieth Legion to me. We'll be able to bring more than enough down on their heads to keep them back while the assault cohorts close on the gate.'

'I hope so, sir,' Cato, replied. 'The gate's the only option. The ditches are heavily staked.'

'Thought they might be.' Vespasian stood up. 'There's nothing else to be said. I'll pass the word for some hot food and baths to be prepared. I can offer you that at least as a reward for the work you've done.'

'Thank you, sir.'

'And my profound gratitude to you and your cousin.' The legate bowed his head to Boudica. 'The Iceni will not find Rome ungrateful for your assistance in this matter.'

248

'What are allies for?' Boudica smiled wearily. 'I would expect Rome to do the same for me, if ever I have any children and they are placed in danger.'

'Well, yes.' Vespasian nodded. 'Quite.'

He accompanied them to the exit of his tent and graciously held the flap open. Cato paused at the exit, a concerned expression on his face.

'Sir, one last thing, if I may?'

'Of course, your centurion.'

Cato nodded. 'Has he . . . Did he survive?'

'Alive, last I heard.'

'He's here, sir?'

'No. I sent our sick back to Calleva in a convoy two days ago. We've set up a hospital there. Your centurion will have the best possible care.'

'Oh.' The renewed uncertainty weighed heavily on the optio's heart. 'Best thing, I suppose.'

'It is. You'll have to excuse me.' Vespasian was about to turn away and walk back to his desk when he became aware of raised voices outside his headquarters tent.

'What the hell is going on out there?'

Brushing past Cato he strode out through the wide flaps and squelched across the mud outside. Cato and the others hurried after him. There was no need to ask what the reason for the commotion was; every man in the Second Legion could see it. Up on the plateau of the Great Fortress, some kind of structure was slowly rising above the palisade. The sun was low in the sky to the west, silhouetting the vast mass of the hill fort and the strange contraption in a fiery orange glow. It rose very slowly into place, manoeuvred by invisible hands heaving on a series of ropes. As he watched, the terrible realisation of what he was witnessing suddenly hit Cato like a blow and his guts turned to ice.

The construction was nearing the vertical and it became clear to everyone what it was: a vast wicker man, crude in form but unmistakable, black against the sunset except where it was pierced through by shafts of dying light.

The legate turned to Boudica and spoke quietly. 'Ask your man when he thinks they'll set fire to that thing.'

'Tomorrow night,' she translated. 'At the Feast of the First Budding. That's when your general's wife and son will die.'

Cato edged closer to the legate. 'I don't think the general's message matters any more, sir.'

'No . . . We'll attack first thing in the morning.'

249

Cato well knew that any attack would have to be preceded by a lengthy bombardment of the defences. Only then could the legionaries attempt to force a breach. What if the defenders proved resolute enough to drive the Romans back?

A desperate thought struck Cato; his mind raced, quickly sketching out a crazy plan, fraught with terrible risks, but it might give them one last chance to save Lady Pomponia and Aelius from the flames of the wicker man.

'Sir, there might still be a way to rescue them,' Cato said quietly. 'If you can spare me twenty good men, and Prasutagus.'

Chapter Thirty-Four

Long before dawn, the ground before the main gate to the hill fort was filled with the sounds of movement: the rhythmic thumping of heavy piles to compact the soil and level the ground to form artillery platforms; the endless trundling of wagon wheels as artillery carts were brought forward to unload bolt-throwers and catapults. Men strained and grunted to heave the heavy timber mechanisms into their sockets. Ammunition was unloaded and stacked by the weapons, and then their crews began a systematic check of the torsion cords and ratchet winches, and carefully lubricated the release mechanisms

The Durotriges had lined the walls of the gate defences, straining to see what was going on in the darkness below them. They tried loosing fire arrows in high shimmering arcs towards the Roman lines in the hope of glimpsing the nature of the Roman preparations. But the poor range of their bows meant that none of the arrows even cleared the outer rampart, and they were left in ignorance of the enemy's plans for them. Roman skirmishers had pushed forward under cover of darkness and fought vicious little actions with Durotrigan patrols on the approaches to the main gate, and finally the natives had tired of trying to break through and pulled everyone back inside the palisade to await the dawn.

At the first hint of the sky lightening Vespasian gave the order for the First Cohort to move up to their start line and make ready to advance. Small teams of engineers, carrying ladders and a battering ram, accompanied them. One century had been issued with composite bows to provide close fire support when the cohort was ready to force the main gate. All of them stood ready, dim ranks of silent men, heavily armoured, weapons sharpened and hearts filled with all the usual tensions and misgivings about such a dangerous assault. Fighting a setpiece battle was nothing compared to this, and even the rawest recruit among them knew it.

From the moment the bolt-throwers ceased firing on the palisade, the First Cohort would fall under a rain of arrows, slingshot and boulders. Due to the twists and turns in the approach ramps, one or other of their flanks would be exposed to enemy fire before they even reached the main entrance. Then they would have to endure more of the same while they attempted to breach the gate. Only then would they be able to close with the enemy. It was only natural that the men who had endured so much punishment would want to exact bloody retribution once the Durotriges were within swords' length. Vespasian had therefore personally briefed each officer in the cohort to look out for Cato and his party and that every effort must be made to take prisoners. He told them he needed live slaves if he was ever going to be able to afford to renovate his house on the Quirinal Hill, back in Rome. They had laughed at that, as he'd known they would, and Vespasian hoped it would be enough to prevent Cato and his men being slaughtered out of hand when the legionaries eventually burst onto the plateau.

'All ready, sir,' Tribune Plinius reported.

'Very well.' Vespasian saluted and looked over his shoulder.

The horizon away to the east was becoming noticeably lighter. He turned back and regarded the looming immenseness of the hill fort. The wicker man towered above the palisade, the auburn twists of cane and branch slowly becoming visible as dawn strengthened and banished the monochrome shades of the night. The crews on the artillery platform stood still, watching the legate, waiting for the order to open fire. Vespasian had managed to muster over a hundred serviceable bolt-throwers, and each one now sat ready for winding back the torsion arms. The iron-headed bolts were already set in each channel, their dark-flanged heads pointing up at the defences surrounding the main gate. The first rays of the sun caught the shining bronze helmets of the Durotriges lining the palisade, watched by the legionaries in the cool gloom below. Gradually the glow flowed down the slopes of the ramparts.

Vespasian nodded to Plinius.

'Artillery!' Plinius roared through cupped hands. 'Make ready!'

The dawn air was filled with the sound of clanking levers and straining men as the torsion arms were wound back and the bolt ropes locked down against the projectiles. As the last crew finished, the sound died away and a peculiar stillness fell over the scene.

'Open fire!' Plinius shouted.

The crew captains pushed the release levers forward and Vespasian's ears resounded to the sharp crack as the torsion arms sprang back. A

252

thin veil of dark lines streaked up towards the palisade. As was always the case, a number fell short and buried themselves in the slopes. Others overshot and disappeared way beyond the palisade – where they could still be a hazard. The crews would mark the fall of their shots and adjust the elevation accordingly. The vast majority, however, struck home in the first volley. Vespasian had seen the impact of such firepower a few times before, but even he marvelled at the destruction it caused. Whole timbers in the palisade were shattered by the heavy iron-headed bolts, splintered fragments whirling into the air, and the palisade soon had the appearance of a mouth filled with bad teeth.

The second volley was more ragged than the first as the more efficient crews fired earlier, and soon the disparity in loading times led to an almost continuous crashing from the released torsion arms. The palisade was brutally beaten down, and most Durotrigan warriors foolhardy enough to mount the rampart behind and shout their defiance paid the price. Vespasian idly watched as one big man waved a spear, until a bolt caught him high in the chest and simply whipped him bodily out of sight. Another was struck in the face, the blow completely shearing off the man's head. His torso remained upright for a moment, then collapsed.

Less than an hour later the defences about the main gate were in utter ruin, the stakes that had made up the palisade reduced to stumps, streaked with crimson. Vespasian motioned to his senior tribune. 'Send the cohort in, Plinius.'

The tribune turned to the trumpeter and ordered him to sound the advance. The man put his lips to the mouthpiece and blew a sharp series of rising notes. As the first call echoed back from the ramparts, the centurions of the First Cohort gave the order to advance, and in two broad columns they began marching towards the approach ramps. The sun was low in the sky, and the backs of the men's helmets threw back a thousand reflections into the eyes of their comrades watching the fight from the legion's fortified camp. A substantial reserve of men stood ready to reinforce the First Cohort should it be roughly handled by the Durotriges. More men had been sent out during the night to position themselves round the fort and stand off, ready to intercept any enemy attempting to flee the far side of the fortress should the gate fall. Nothing had been left to chance.

The First Cohort, accompanied by their engineer detachment, mounted the first approach ramp and immediately had to turn parallel to the hill fort as they climbed at an angle towards the first dogleg. Already, some of the braver souls among the defenders were popping up along the ruin of their palisade and loosing arrows or slingshot into the massed mailed ranks of the legionaries, and Roman casualties began to fall out of line. Most were wounded and tried to cover themselves with their big shields while they waited to be carried to the casualty stations. Some were killed outright and lay still, sprawled on the track leading up the ramp.

Over the heads of the First Cohort the barrage of iron bolts continued to sweep the defences clear, but soon the crews would begin to imperil their own men. Vespasian held off giving the order to cease fire, willing to risk a shot falling short rather than permit the enemy to swarm over the remains of their defences and pour down a far more damaging rain of missiles on the heads of the legionaries.

The cohort reached the first dogleg and turned the corner, doubling back on itself as it climbed towards the main gate. The bolts were whirring less than fifty feet above their heads now, and the staff officers around Vespasian were getting edgy.

'Just a little longer,' the legate muttered.

There was a splintering noise from the artillery platform, and Vespasian swung round. The arm on one of the bolt-throwers had snapped under the strain. A loud chorus of groans came from the staff officers. Up on the second rampart the bolt from the broken machine had fallen short and skewered a file of legionaries, hurling them into an untidy bundle at the side of the track. The succeeding ranks of legionaries faltered for a moment, until an angry centurion laid into them with his vine cane, and the advance continued.

'Cease fire!' Vespasian shouted over to the artillery crews. 'CEASE FIRE!'

The last few bolts cleared the heads of the First Cohort, thankfully, and then there was an eerie quiet, before the defenders realised the danger was gone. With a roar of their battle cry they ran out from cover and swarmed onto what remained of their defences above and around the main gate. At once a hail of arrows, stones and rocks pelted down on the men of the First Cohort. The commander of the cohort, the most senior and experienced centurion in the legion, gave the order to form the testudo, and in a moment a wall of shields surrounded the cohort and covered its top. Immediately the pace of the advance slowed, but the men were now protected from the missiles pelting them from above, and they rattled harmlessly off the broad curves of the their shields. The clatter of the impacts was clearly audible down where Vespasian and his staff stood.

The First Cohort rounded the corner of the final dogleg and began to pass between a bastion and the main gate. This was the most dangerous moment of the assault. The men were under fire from two sides and could not begin to deploy the ram against the gate until the bastion was taken. The senior centurion knew his job, and in calm, measured tones gave the order for the First Century of the cohort to break away from the testudo. The men turned abruptly and scrambled up the steep slope to the bastion. The Durotriges who had survived the barrage of bolts threw themselves on their attackers, making the most of their height advantage. Several legionaries fell to their weapons, tumbling and slipping back down the slope. But there were too few of the enemy to hold off the Romans for long, and the vicious thrusting swords of the legionaries made short work of them.

As soon as the bastion had been cleared, men armed with compound bows scampered up and began pouring fire onto the defenders on the main gate, ducking down to string the next arrow behind the shields of the century who had won the bastion. The Durotriges redirected their missile fire onto the new threat, taking the pressure off the testudo standing at the base of the gate. Now the engineers moved up with the battering ram, and under cover of the testudo began a slow rhythmic assault on the stout wooden beams of the main gate.

The dull thud of the ram reached Vespasian's ears and his mind turned to Cato and his small party on the other side of the hill fort. They, too, would hear the ram, and start making their move.

Below the drainage gully on the other side of the hill fort, the pile of sewage and refuse suddenly came to life. Had there been a sentry on the palisade above, he might have had difficulty believing his eyes when a small party of what appeared to be Celtic warriors emerged from the foul-smelling heap and silently swarmed up either side of the gully, making for the wooden opening set into the palisade.

While the engineers had been busy levelling the ground, a small party of legionaries, the best men of the former Sixth Century of the Fourth Cohort, had quietly made their way round the hill fort, under the command of their optio and the tall Iceni warrior they had been introduced to earlier that night. Naked, and daubed in the blue woad designs of the Celts, they were equipped with cavalry long swords, which might just pass for native weapons at a quick glance. Prasutagus had led them over the ramparts and through the staked trenches to the reeking mound of spoil. There, with silent expressions of disgust, they had hidden themselves amid the shit and slops, and waited, motionless, for the coming of dawn and the battering ram attack on the main gate.

At the first distant thump of the ram, Cato pushed aside the rotting deer carcass he had been hiding beneath and clambered on all fours up towards the wooden structure. With natural agility; Prasutagus scaled the far side of the gully, reminding Cato of an ape he had once seen at the games in Rome. Around them were the rest of the men Cato had selected, tough and mostly of Gaulish extraction, so that they stood a better chance of passing for Britons.

By the time they reached the top of the gully, the thudding from the ram had become a regular beat, sounding the death knell of the hill fort and its defenders. Cato pointed at the space under the opening and, as before, Prasutagus shifted his powerful frame into position. Cato clambered up, and cautiously looked over the rim into the hill fort's interior, by daylight this time. The plateau immediately to his front was deserted. Off to the right, beyond the giant figure of the wicker man, a dark mass of bodies was packed around the main gate, waiting to hurl themselves upon the First Cohort the moment the ram burst through the thick timbers of the gate. Among them were some black cloaks of the Druids and Cato smiled with satisfaction; the odds against him and his small party had lessened.

He pulled himself over the rim, and reached down for the hand of the next man. One by one they clambered through the opening and crawled to the side of the nearest animal pen. At last only Prasutagus remained, and Cato braced himself firmly against the timber frame of the platform before he reached his hands down to Prasutagus. The Iceni warrior grabbed Cato's forearms and heaved himself up, transferring his grip to the rim of the opening as soon as he could.

'Are all the Iceni as heavy as you?' Cato gasped.

'No. My father – bigger than me.'

'Bloody glad you're on our side then.'

They scrambled over to the other men, and then Cato led them along the pens towards the Druid enclosure. At the last pen he signalled for his men to be still, and then slowly poked his head round the wattle panel, cursing softly at the sight of two Druids still guarding the gateway into the enclosure. They were squatting down and chewing on hunks of bread, apparently unconcerned by the desperate fight at the gate. Cato pulled his head back and motioned his men to stay down. They must keep out of sight until the main gate fell, and pray that the Druids had not already executed their hostages.

* * *

'This isn't going very well,' Vespasian grumbled, watching the distant battle in front of the gate. Most of the men on the bastion were down, and the British fire was concentrated on the legionaries massed by the gate. Already the ground was littered with red shields and the grey mail armour of the Romans.

'We could call them back, sir,' suggested Plinius. 'Lay down another barrage and try again.'

'No,' Vespasian replied curtly. Plinius looked at him, waiting for an explanation, but the legate remained silent. Any relaxing of the pressure on the front gate would put Cato and his men at risk. For all the legate knew, they might already be dead, but he had to assume their part of the plan was going ahead. Only Cato could save the hostages now. He must be given a chance. That meant the First Cohort had to remain in the killing ground outside the hill fort's gate. There was another reason for keeping them there. If he ordered them back down the rampart, they would lose more men on the way. Then, while the bolt throwers renewed their barrage, the survivors of the first assault would have to wait, knowing they had to face the perils of the attack all over again. Vespasian could well imagine what that might do to their fighting spirit. What they needed up there right now was encouragement, something to strengthen their resolve.

'Get my horse, and get another for the eagle-bearer.'

'You're not going up there, sir?' Plinius was shocked.

'Get the horses.'

While the mounts were fetched, Vespasian tightened the ties under his helmet. He looked at the eagle-bearer and was reassured by the man's easy composure, one of the key qualities looked for in men picked for the honour of carrying the eagle into battle. The horses were rushed to them by running slaves and the reins handed over. Vespasian and the eagle-bearer swung themselves up.

'Sir!' Plinius called out. 'If anything happens to you, what are your orders?'

'Why, to take the hill fort of course!'

With a swift kick of his heels Vespasian urged his horse towards the foot of the ramp, pounding across the open ground with the eagle-bearer just behind him, reins in one hand, the shaft of the standard clenched in the other. Up the ramp they galloped, swerving round at the first dogleg and on to the second ramp. Here lay the first Roman casualties, pierced by arrows or crushed by stones, their blood pooling on the track amid the feathered shafts that seemed to have sprung up from the soil. The wounded, seeing the horsemen approach, painfully hauled themselves to the side of the track, some of them managing to raise a cheer for the legate as he thundered past.

They turned the second dogleg, and quickly reined in as they came up against the rearmost century of the First Cohort.

'On foot!' Vespasian shouted over his shoulder to the eagle-bearer, and swung himself from the back of his horse. At once they were spotted by the defenders above them, and an instant later Vespasian's horse screeched as an arrow whacked into its flank. It reared up, front legs flailing, before scrabbling round to tear back down the ramp. More arrows and slingshot thudded home around the legate. He looked round and snatched a shield from the ground where it had fallen beside its dead owner. The eagle-bearer found another. Both of them pushed forward into the tightly packed ranks ahead.

'Make way! Make way there!' Vespasian called.

The legionaries parted at the sound of his voice, some with looks of blank astonishment.

'What the fuck is he doing up here?' an awestruck youngster wondered.

'Didn't think you were getting the enemy all to yourself, did you, son?' Vespasian shouted as he passed by. 'Come on, lads, one last push, then we'll put paid to those bastards!'

A ragged cheer rippled out from the men as Vespasian and the eagle-bearer made their way up towards the gate, arrows and slingshot rattling off their shields. When he reached the flat ground before the fortified timber gate, Vespasian tried to hide his despair at the scene before him. Most of the engineers were dead, heaped round their ladders and to the side of the battering ram. The ram was now manned by legionaries who had had to lay down their shields to take up their position on the thick iron capped shaft of oak. Even as he watched, another man fell, shot through the gap between his helmet and his mail vest. The senior centurion thrust a replacement forward, but the legionary hesitated, looking anxiously at the savage faces screaming at him above the gate.

Vespasian ran forward. 'Out of my way, son!'

He dropped his shield and grabbed the rope handle, joining the rhythmic swing of the other men on the ram. As it smashed into the gate, with a shattering crash, Vespasian could see that the big timbers were starting to give way.

'Come on, men!' he shouted to the others along the ram. 'We're not being paid by the bloody hour!'

As soon as the Durotriges saw the legate they let out a great roar of defiance and turned their weapons on the enemy commander, and the man bearing the dreaded symbol of the eagle. The men of the First Cohort responded with a deafening cheer and renewed effort, hurling up their remaining javelins into the marred ranks of the Durotriges. Others snatched at the slingshots lying on the ground to hurl them at the defenders.

Another man fell beside the ram. This time the senior centurion threw his shield down and took the vacant position. Once again the ram slammed forward. With a crack, the central beam on the gate broke in two, and the surrounding timbers were wrenched out of alignment. Through the gaps the Romans could see the snarling faces of Durotriges and Druids massed on the other side. Through a narrow gap Vespasian spotted the locking bar.

'There!' He raised a hand to point. 'Shift the head to there!'

The line of the ram was quickly adjusted, and they swung again, forcing the gap to open wider. The locking bar shuddered in its brackets.

'Harder!' Vespasian shouted above the din. 'Harder!'

Each blow splintered more of the timbers until with a last wild swing the locking bar shattered. Immediately the gates gave way.

'Get the ram back!'

They backed up several feet and laid it down. Someone handed Vespasian a shield. He slipped his left arm into the straps and drew his sword, holding it horizontally at hip height. He breathed deeply, ready to lead his men through the gateway.

'Eagle-bearer!'

'Sir!'

'Stay close to me, lad.'

'Yes, sir!'

'First Cohort!' the legate bellowed at the top of his voice. 'Advance!'

With a deep roar from hundreds of throats, the scarlet shields charged the gates and crashed into the screaming ranks of the tribesmen beyond. Packed in with the front rank of the First Cohort Vespasian kept his shield up and thrust into the dense mass of humanity before him, sinking his blade into flesh, then twisting and wrenching it back, before striking again. All around him men screamed, shouted their warcries, grunting with the effort of each thrust and slash, crying out in agony as they were wounded. The dead and injured fell to the ground, those still living struggled to protect themselves beneath their shields and avoid being trampled to death.

At first, the dense mass of Romans and Durotriges was locked solid, neither giving an inch of ground. But as men fell, the tribesmen began to give ground, thrust back before the shield wall of the Romans. The ground beneath Vespasian's boots was slick with churned mud and warm blood. His greatest fear at that moment was that he might lose his footing and slip.

The First Cohort ground forward, hacking a path through the Durotriges. The defenders, urged on by the Druids in their ranks, fought with desperate courage. Tightly packed as they were, their long swords and war spears were almost impossible to wield effectively. Some dropped their main weapons and used their daggers instead, trying to wrench the Roman shields aside and stab at the men sheltering behind. But few of the Durotriges were armoured and their exposed flesh was easy prey for the lethal swords of the legionaries.

Slowly, the Durotriges crumbled, falling back at the rear of the press in ones and twos, the men throwing terrified glances at the relentless approach of the golden eagle. A line of Druids stood behind the defenders and scornfully attempted to drive the less courageous of their allies back into the battle. But in a short time too many tribesmen were fleeing the terrible Roman killing machine and the Druids were helpless to stop them. The mighty defences the Durotriges had placed so much faith in had failed them, as had the promises of the Druids that Cruach would protect them this day, and smite the Romans. All was lost, and the Druids knew it too.

Standing behind the line of Druids, a tall dark figure with an antlered headpiece shouted an order. The Druids turned at the sound, and saw their leader pointing back towards the enclosure on the far side of the hill fort. They closed ranks and began to run towards their last line of defence.

'That's it!' Cato called quietly to his men. 'They're breaking. Now's our time!'

He rose to his feet, beckoning to his men to follow him. Tribespeople were running across the plateau, away from the main gate and the legionaries. Many were women and children, fleeing the disaster about to befall their menfolk. They hoped to escape the hill fort by scaling the ramparts and disappearing into the surrounding countryside. The first of them had reached the pens not far from Cato when he decided to make his move.

With Prasutagus at his side and his woad-painted men grouped loosely behind him, Cato ran towards the enclosure entrance. The two guards had risen to their feet to watch the action at the main gate and spared the approaching tribesmen only a contemptuous glance. As Cato closed the distance, one of the guards jeered at him. Cato raised his cavalry sword.

'Get 'em!' he screamed to his men, and ran at the Druid. The surprise was total and before the shocked Druid could respond, Cato had smashed his spear to one side and swept his blade into the side of the man's head. Flesh split open, bone cracked and the Druid crumpled to the ground.

Prasutagus dealt with the other guard and then kicked open the gate. It was a thin affair, designed only to discourage access rather than resist a determined assault. The gate crashed inward and the handful of Druids still inside the enclosure turned at the noise, startled by the sudden invasion of their sacred soil by these painted men, their erstwhile allies. The momentary confusion had the effect Cato had hoped, and all his men were through the narrow gateway before the Druids began to respond. Snatching up spears, they made to defend themselves against the wild sword-wielding furies rushing down on them. Cato ignored the clash and clatter of weapons. He sprinted towards the cage. Ahead of him a Druid came out of a hut, spear in hand. He took one look at the mêlée and turned towards the cage, hefting his spear.

There was no mistaking his intent and Cato drove himself forward, running as fast as he could, teeth gritted with the effort. But the Druid was nearer, and Cato realised he was not going to make it. As the Druid reached the cage and drew back his spear to thrust, a shriek rose from inside.

'Hey!' Cato shouted, still twenty paces away.

The Druid glanced over his shoulder, and Cato threw his sword with all his might. As the blade spun through the air, the Druid whirled round and deflected it with the end of his spear. Cato ran on towards the cage. The Druid lowered the point, aiming it at Cato's stomach. At the last instant, almost on the point of the wickedly barbed tip of the spear, Cato threw himself down and rolled into the Druid's legs. Both men crashed against the wooden bars of the cage. The impact was worse for Cato than the Druid, and before he could catch his breath the man had jumped on his chest and clamped his hands round the optio's throat. The pain was immediate and intense. Cato snatched at the man's hands, straining to pull them away, but the Druid was big and powerfully built. He grinned through yellowed teeth as he squeezed the life out of his enemy. Black shadows smeared the edges of Cato's vision, and he lashed out with his knees, striking uselessly on the man's back.

A pair of slender hands reached out between the cage bars and clawed at the Druid's face, fingers working for the man's eyes.

Instinctively, he threw his hands up to save his sight, howling in agony, and Cato drove his fist up into the man's chin, snapping his head back. Cato struck him again, then heaved him aside. While the Druid lay stunned on the ground, Cato scrambled up, retrieved his sword and thrust it into the Druid's throat.

He turned to the cage. 'Lady Pomponia!'

Holding the bars, her face squeezed against her hands; the general's wife looked at the painted figure uncertainly.

'I'm here to rescue you. Get to the back of the cage.'

'I know you! The one from the wagon!'

'Yes. Now get back!'

She turned and crawled to the rear of the cage, placing herself protectively in front of her son. Cato lifted his sword and began to hack at the ropes binding the barred door to the rest of the structure. Wood splintered and severed strands flew up from each blow, and then one side of the door came free. Cato lowered his sword and wrenched the bars aside.

'Out! Come on, let's go!'

She crawled out, dragging her son by one hand. His other hand was heavily bandaged. Aelius's eyes were wide with terror, and a faint keening noise came from his throat. Lady Pomponia had difficulty standing; after days of crouching in the confines of the cage, her legs were stiff and sore. Cato looked round the enclosure; it was littered with bodies. Most wore the black robes of the Druids, but half a dozen of his own men lay among them. The rest were gathering round Prasutagus, many bleeding from wounds.

'This way,' Cato said to Lady Pomponia, half dragging her towards his men. 'It's safe. They're with me.'

'I never thought I'd see you again,' she said in quiet wonder.

'I gave you my word.'

She smiled faintly. 'So you did.'

They joined the other men, and turned back towards the gateway.

'Now we just have to make our way over to the First Cohort,' said Cato, heart beating wildly in his chest, partly from his efforts, partly from the sheer excitement and pride of having succeeded. 'Come on!'

He took a step towards the gateway, and then stopped. Stepping through it was a tall figure, robed in black and carrying a shining sickle in one hand. The Chief Druid took in the scene in an instant and stepped to one side, shouting an order. The rest of his men came piling into the enclosure, eyes glinting and spears lowered towards Cato and his small band. Without waiting for an order Prasutagus roared his war cry and charged the Druids, followed at once by Cato and his men. Lady Pomponia turned her son's face into her tunic and crouched down with him, unable to watch the fight.

This time the contest between the Romans and Druids was more evenly matched. The Druids had not been surprised, and their fighting blood was already up after their experiences at the main gate. There was a loose mêlée, swords striking on spear shafts or clattering to one side in a desperate parry. Unable to stab effectively with their spears in the confined struggle, the Druids used them like quarterstaffs, swiping at the Romans and blocking their sword slashes. Cato found himself fighting a tall, thin Druid, with a dark beard. The man was no fool, and neatly parried Cato's first few thrusts, then feinted to the left before ramming home the tip of his spear. Cato jumped to one side, too late to avoid having his thigh slashed. As the man recovered his spear, Cato swept the shaft to one side with his free hand and flashed forward, burying the end of his blade in the man's guts. He jerked the blade free and turned, looking for the Chief Druid. He was standing by the gate, watching the fight with cold eyes.

He saw Cato coming and crouched low, sickle held up and to the side, ready to sweep forward and behead or dismember his attacker. Cato thrust his sword forward, keeping an eye on the glinting sickle. The Chief Druid lurched back against the gatepost with a jarring thud. Cato thrust again, and this time the sickle swung at him, slashing towards his neck. Cato threw himself forward, inside the reach of the weapon, and smashed the pommel of his sword into the Chief Druid's face as hard as he could. The man's head crashed back against the gatepost and he dropped, out cold, the sickle falling to the ground at his side.

As soon as they were aware that their leader was down, the other Druids dropped their weapons and surrendered. Some were not quick enough, and died before the legionaries were aware of their surrender.

'It's over!' Cato shouted to his men. 'They're finished!'

The men calmed their battle rage and stood over the Druids, painted chests rising and falling as they struggled to recover their breath. Cato waved Prasutagus over to him, and together they stood in the gateway, swords up, discouraging any of the fleeing Durotriges from trying to enter the enclosure in their desperate flight from the Romans. Over at the main gate, too, the fight was over, and the red shields of the legionaries were fanning out across the plateau, cutting down any who still dared to resist. Above the ruin of the gate stood the standard-bearer, the golden eagle glittering in the sunlight.

A small formation of legionaries was quick-marching across the plateau towards the enclosure and Cato saw the red crest of the legate rising above the other helmets. He turned to Prasutagus. 'See to the lady and her son. I'm going to report.'

The Iceni warrior nodded and sheathed his sword, trying not to look too intimidating as he walked over towards the general's wife. Cato kept his sword in hand as he stepped out of the gateway and raised his other hand in greeting to the legate, now clearly visible and smiling happily. A warm glow of contentment washed through Cato. He had kept his word, and the wicker man rising above the hill fort would not claim its victims after all. He noticed that his body was trembling, whether from nerves or exhaustion he could not tell.

Behind him Lady Pomponia screamed.

'Cato!' Prasutagus shouted.

But before Cato could react, something slammed into his back. The breath was driven from his body in an explosive gasp and he dropped to his knees. He felt something like a fist deep inside his chest. He jerked as the object was wrenched free. A hand grabbed his hair, pulling his head back, and Cato saw the blue sky and then the triumphant sneer on the face of the Chief Druid as he raised his bloodied sickle high in the air. That was his blood, Cato realised, and he closed his eyes and waited for death to come.

He dimly heard Prasutagus scream with rage, then the Chief Druid's grip convulsed, tearing at Cato's hair. A warm rain dripped down on him. Warm rain? The Chief Druid relaxed his grip. Cato opened his eyes just as the Chief Druid's body collapsed by his side. A short distance away rolled the Druid's head, still in its antlered headpiece. Then Cato fell forward on his face. He was conscious of the hardness of the ground against his cheek and someone grasping his shoulder. Then Prasutagus dimly shouting. 'Roman! Roman, don't die!'

And the world went black.

Chapter Thirty-Five

It seemed as if he was shimmering between a deep, thoughtless dream and moments of painful, sharp, reality. There was no sense of the passage of time, none at all, just disconnected fragments of experience. The sound of plaintive cries on all sides, their source invisible in the dark. The vague outline of a man's back sitting on a bench above his head. The smell of mules. Beneath Cato, wheels rumbled, jarred and the moment faded and blackness returned. Later, he felt hands gently rolling him onto his front. Something was removed from round his chest, and a man, his voice distant, sucked in his breath.

'Messy. Mostly muscle damage. The blade struck a rib, which stayed intact, mercifully. If it had shattered . . .'

'Yes?'

'Fragments might have penetrated his right lung, there'd be infection and finally, er, death, sir.'

'But he will recover?'

'Oh yes . . . In all probability, that is. He's lost quite a lot of blood, but he seems to have a strong enough constitution, and I have had considerable experience of dealing with wounds like this, sir.'

'You've considerable experience of sickle wounds?'

'No, sir. Lacerations resulting from sharp edges. Sickle wounds are something of a rarity. Not your usual choice of battlefield armament, if I may be so bold as to generalise, sir.'

'Just look after him, and make sure he goes into quarters appropriate to his rank when you reach Calleva.'

'Yes, sir. Orderly! Drain the wound and change the dressing!'

'I'd really rather *you* changed the dressing and, er, drained the wound.'

'Yes, sir! At once, sir.'

Cato felt someone probing his back, halfway down, and then an

265

agonising prickling sensation. He tried to protest, but merely murmured and then lost consciousness.

His next awakening was as gradual as the passage of a shadow across a sundial. Cato was aware of a faint light through his eyelids. He heard sounds – the muffled hubbub of a busy street. Snatches of human voices speaking a language he did not understand. The pain in his back had subsided into a steady throb, as if some giant with fists the size of boulders was roughly kneading his flesh. As Cato thought of the wound, he remembered the Chief Druid wielding his shining sickle, and opened his eyes with a start. He tried to turn onto his back. The dull throb at once turned into a searing, stabbing agony. Cato cried out and slumped back onto his chest.

Footsteps thudded on wooden flooring and a moment later Cato sensed a presence behind him.

'Awake, I see! And earnestly trying to rip open your back. Tsk!'

Fingers gently probed the area around the wound. Then the man walked to the other side of the bed and knelt down. Cato saw the olive features and dark oiled hair of the eastern empire. The man wore the black tunic of the medical corps, trimmed with blue. A surgeon then.

'Well, Centurion. Despite your efforts the drain is still in place. You'll no doubt be delighted to hear that there's almost no pus this morning. Excellent. I'll have that closed up and bandaged in a moment. How do you feel?'

Cato moistened his lips. 'Thirsty,' he croaked.

'I imagine you are,' smiled the surgeon. 'I'll have some heated wine sent to you before we put the stitches in. Wine mixed with a few rather interesting herbs – you won't notice a thing, and you'll sleep like the dead.'

'I hope not,' Cato whispered.

'That's the spirit! Soon have you back on your feet.' The surgeon rose. 'Now if you'll excuse me I have some other patients that need my attention. Our legate seems to want to keep me fully occupied.'

Before Cato could ask any questions the surgeon had gone, his footsteps receding at a fast pace. Keeping his head still, Cato squinted at his surroundings. He seemed to be in a small cell with walls of timber and plaster. From the damp smell, the plaster must be quite fresh. In the corner sat a small chest. His armour, with its distinctive phalerae, lay on the ground beside the chest. Cato smiled at the sight of the medallions – he had been awarded those by Vespasian himself, after saving Macro's life back in Germania . . . But where was Macro

266

now? Then Cato remembered the terrible wound his centurion had suffered. Surely he must have died. But didn't someone say he had survived? Cato tried to remember, but the effort defeated him. Someone slipped a hand under his head and gently raised it. Cato smelt the sweet, spicy vapour of the heated wine and parted his lips. The wine was not too hot, and Cato slowly drained the cup held in the medical orderly's hand. The warmth spread out from his belly, through his body and he soon felt pleasantly sleepy as his head eased back onto the coarse material of the bolster. While his mind slowly drifted off, Cato, with a soldier's delight in small luxuries, smiled at the fact that he had been given an entire room to himself. Wait until Macro found out.

When he next woke up, Cato was still lying on his front. He could hear the shouts and bustle of many men. The orderly had just changed the soiled bedding, and cleaned his patient. He smiled as Cato's eyes flickered open and fixed on him.

'Morning, sir.'

Cato's tongue felt thick, and he nodded his head slightly to return the greeting.

'You look much better today,' continued the orderly. 'Thought you was a goner when they brought you in, sir. Must've been a clean wound that Druid gave you.'

'Yes,' Cato replied, trying not to remember. 'Where am I?'

The orderly frowned. 'Here, sir. Here being the new hospital block in the new fort that's been thrown up in Calleva. Quick work. Just hope it don't fall down around our ears.'

'Calleva,' repeated Cato. That was days away from the hill fort. He must have been out for the entire journey. 'What's all the fuss?'

'More casualties coming in from the legion. Seems the legate has turned over another of them hill forts. We're out of space and the surgeon's tearing his greasy hair out trying to reorganise things . . .' The orderly's voice trailed away.

'And it would make my life a lot easier if my staff got on with their work instead of gossiping with the customers.'

'Yes, sir. Excuse me, sir. I'll be on me way.' The orderly hurried from the room and the surgeon came round the bed to speak to Cato. He smiled his bedside smile.

'You're looking chipper!'

'So I've been told.'

'Well now. I've got some good news and some bad news. Good news is your wound's healing nicely. I imagine you'll be up and about in a month or so.'

'A month!' Cato groaned at the prospect.

'Yes. But not all of it will have to be spent lying on your stomach.'

Cato stared at the surgeon for a moment. 'And the good news is?'

'Ha ha!' The surgeon chuckled obsequiously. 'Well then, the thing is we're a bit pressed for space, and while I'd normally not dream of imposing on my officer patients, I'm afraid you're going to have to share.'

'Share?' Cato frowned. 'Who with?'

The surgeon leaned closer, looking over Cato's shoulder in the direction of the doorway. 'He's a bit of a sod. Grumbles all the time, but I'm sure he'll respect your privacy and pipe down a bit. Sorry, but there's nowhere else I can stick him.'

'Does he have a name?' muttered Cato.

Before the surgeon could reply, there was a commotion at the door and muttered curses.

'Watch it, you bloody fools!' growled a familiar voice. 'This isn't a bloody battering ram you're playing with.'

More muttered curses followed.

'Who's this you've landed me with? If he talks in his sleep I'll have your balls off.'

The orderlies struggled round the end of Cato's bed and set their patient down with a thump on the bed next to him.

'Oi! Careful, you hopeless wankers. I've got your number!'

Cato looked over, smiling fondly. Centurion Macro looked as white as a toga, his face pallid and gaunt beneath the tightly bound bandage. But there he was, very much alive and on form. With Macro snoring in the same room, he'd never get another decent night's sleep.

'Hello, sir.'

'Hello yourself!' Macro snapped back, then his eyes blinked wider and he propped himself up on an elbow, grinning with unrestrained pleasure at the sight of his optio. 'Well, I'll be buggered! Cato! Well, I . . . I . . . It's good to see you again, lad!'

'You too, sir. How's the head?'

'Hurts like hell! An every-hour-of-every-day hangover.'

'Nasty.'

'And you? What happened?'

'Druid stuck a sickle in my back!'

'Get away! A sickle in the back? That's bollocks, that is!'

268

'Centurion Macro,' interrupted the surgeon. 'This patient needs his rest. You mustn't excite him. Now, please settle down – and I'll see to it that you get some wine.'

At the promise of wine, Macro clamped his mouth shut. The surgeon and the orderlies left the room. Only when he was sure that they were out of earshot did he turn to Cato and continue in a whisper, 'Heard you got the general's wife and son – minus a finger, I'm told, but otherwise intact. Bloody good job! Should be a gong or two coming our way.'

'That would be nice, sir,' Cato replied wearily. He wanted more sleep, but the sheer pleasure of seeing his centurion again made him smile.

'What's up?'

'Nothing, sir. Just glad to see you still with us. I really thought you'd had it.'

'Dead? Me?' Macro sounded offended. 'Take more than some bloody Druid with an attitude to top me! Wait till I have another crack at those bastards. They'll think twice before they wave a sword in my direction again, I can tell you.'

'Glad to hear it.' Cato's eyelids suddenly felt very heavy; he knew there was one more thing that needed saying, but for the moment it eluded him. Beside him Macro was complaining about being confined to bed, and if he heard the surgeon tell him to sleep one more time he'd have the man's guts for garters. Then Cato remembered.

'Excuse me, sir.'

'Yes?'

'Can I beg a favour of you?'

'Of course you can, lad! Name it.'

'Could you make sure that I get to sleep first, before you try?'

Macro glared at him a moment, then angrily launched his bolster across the gap at his companion.

A few days later they had visitors. Cato had been shifted round and lay on his back, still bandaged, but much more comfortable. A board lay between the edge of his bed and Macro's and they were playing dice, at Macro's insistence. The run of the luck had been going Cato's way all morning, and the piles of pebbles they were using as stakes were very uneven. Macro looked ruefully at Cato's latest cast of the dice and at the few remaining pebbles before him.

'Don't suppose you could sub me a few of yours if I lose this one?'

'Yes, sir,' Cato replied, clamping his jaws together to stop a yawn escaping.

'Good of you, lad!' Macro smiled, swept the dice up into his cupped hands and shook them. 'Come on! Centurion needs new boots . . .'

He opened his hands, the dice dropped, tumbled over and came to rest.

'Six! Pay up, Cato!'

'Oh, well done, sir!' Cato smiled in relief.

The door opened and they looked round as Vespasian stepped into the room, clutching a woollen bundle to his chest. The legate waved a hand at them as both men ridiculously tried to struggle towards some equivalent of coming to attention.

'Relax.' Vespasian smiled. 'It's a private visit. Aside from being diverted from the campaign to sort out a little problem Verica is having with his subjects. I brought some people to see you before they head back home.'

He stood aside to allow Boudica and Prasutagus to enter. The Iceni warrior had to duck under the doorframe, and seemed to take up a rather larger portion of the room than was really fair. He smiled broadly at the two Romans in their beds.

'Ha! Sleepy heads!'

'No, Prasutagus old son,' replied Macro. 'We've been injured. But I suppose you wouldn't know about that. Being built like a bloody rock and all.'

When Boudica translated, Prasutagus roared with laughter. In the close confines of the room the sound was deafening, and Vespasian flinched. Prasutagus finally got control of himself and beamed down at Cato and Macro. Then he said something to Boudica, and the words came hesitantly, as if he was embarrassed.

'He wants you to know he feels a brother bond with you,' Boudica translated. 'If you ever want to join our tribe, he'll consider it an honour.'

Macro and Cato exchanged an awkward look, before Vespasian leaned over them, whispering anxiously.

'For Jupiter's sake, watch what you say. That's quite an honour he's suggesting. We don't want to offend our Iceni allies. Understand?'

The two patients nodded, then Macro replied.

'Tell him that's, er, very kind of him. If we ever quit the legions then I'm sure we'll look him up.'

Prasutagus beamed happily, and Vespasian puffed his cheeks and relaxed.

'Anyway,' Macro continued, 'when are you heading off?'

'Soon as we leave you,' replied Boudica.

'Camulodunum?'

'No. Back to our tribe.' Boudica looked down at her hands. 'We've got to prepare for our wedding.'

'Sa!' Prasutagus nodded happily, placing his paw on Boudica's shoulder.

'I see.' Macro forced a smile. 'Congratulations. I wish you both well.'

'Thank you,' said Boudica. 'That means a lot to me.'

A difficult silence thickened uncomfortably, before Vespasian stirred.

'Sorry. I meant to tell you straightaway. The general sends his greetings to all four of you. In fact, what he said was, he trusts that the mission you undertook to rescue his family will be emblematic of the relations between Rome and her Iceni allies. Plautius does not think any reward he could give you would do justice to the great deed you have done . . . Anyway, that was the gist of the message.'

Macro winked at Cato and smiled bitterly.

'I think he really meant it,' Vespasian continued. 'I really do. I dread to reflect on what might have happened if they'd been killed. The whole invasion would have degenerated into a massive effort to wreak vengeance on the Druids. Not that he'd ever admit it. And while he might not have provided you with a reward, he did authorise me to arrange a decoration, and organise a little adjustment in rank.'

Vespasian laid the bundle he was holding on the end of Macro's bed and carefully unwrapped the folds. First out came two phalerae, ebony inlaid with gold and silver, one each for Macro and Cato.

While Cato reverently handled the medallion, his legate continued unwrapping the bundle.

'One last thing, for you, Optio.' The legate suddenly drew up, smiling to himself.

'Sir?'

'Nothing. I just realised that's the last time I can call you that.'

Cato frowned, not yet understanding. Vespasian flicked back the last fold of wool to reveal a helmet, with a transverse crest, and a vine stick.

'Got them from the supplies this morning,' Vespasian explained. 'As soon as Plautius confirmed the promotion. I'll put them over in the corner with the rest of your kit, if that's all right.'

'No, sir,' replied Cato. 'Pass them to me, please, sir. I'd like to see them.'

The legate smiled as he handed them over. 'Of course you would.'

Cato raised the helmet up in both hands and stared at it, swelling

271

with pride and emotion. So much so that he had to cuff away a tear that was moistening in the corner of his eye.

'Hope it fits,' said Vespasian. 'But if it doesn't, take it back to stores and demand one that does. I doubt those officious clerks will be giving you much grief from now on, Centurion Cato.'

Author's Note

One of the most enduring symbols of pre-Roman Britain is the huge complex of earthworks at Maiden Castle in Dorset. It impresses the eye of any visitor and stirs an imaginative empathy towards those who would have had to assault such apparently daunting defences. Yet Maiden Castle, and many other hill forts, were no match for the legions and were stormed and reduced within a short space of time. One wonders why the Durotriges continued to cling to their belief in the defensive properties of hill forts even as they were being systematically destroyed by the Romans. It was not as if they lacked the example of a more effective method of defying the legions. Caratacus was enjoying far more success with his guerrilla tactics. Despite such evidence, the Durotriges remained bottled up in their hill forts when the Second Legion was unleashed upon them. Perhaps blind faith in the promise of ultimate salvation given by their spiritual leaders kept them there.

Compared to the voluminous evidence of Roman history, not much is known about the ancient Britons and their Druids. With almost nothing by way of a written heritage, knowledge of these people has passed down to us through legend, archaeological evidence and the partisan writings of more literary races. What can be surmised is that the Druids were held in great respect and not a little awe. They bestrode the Celtic kingdoms and were frequently approached for advice, and for arbitration between disputing tribes. The Druids were the guardians of the cultural heritage and memorised vast quantities of epic verse, folklore and legal precedents, which were passed down through successive generations of Druids. They formed a kind of social cement between the fractious small kingdoms that, at one time, sprawled right across Europe. Small wonder that the Druids were a prime target for Roman propaganda and were harshly repressed whenever Celtic lands were added to the burgeoning Roman empire.

Yet there may have been a darker side to the Druids, if we can believe some of the ancient sources. If human sacrifice took place, then it did so in the context of a culture that took great pride in collecting and preserving the heads of their enemies; a culture that had devised methods of torture and execution that repulsed even the Romans, whose love of the carnage of the arena is well-documented.

With their geographical spread and cultural peculiarities, the Druids were not a homogenous body, and would have had their factions, much like contemporary religions are riven by competing interpretations of dogma. The Dark Moon Druids are fictional, but they represent the extremist fringe that exists within any religious movement. They stand as a corrective to that naive and nostalgic re-invention of Druid culture that parades around Stonehenge at certain times of the year. And, as I complete this work, they stand as a timely reminder of the extremities to which religious fanaticism can be taken.

Simon Scarrow
12th September 2001